BURNT NORWAY

A Novel

JOHN VANDERSLICE

ISBN: 978-1-312-39537-4

Note from the author

The following is a work of fiction. While superficial similarities exist between my life and the life of my protagonist, and while the editorial voice of the "Real Author" (me) is a prominent aspect of the novel, the characters that appear and the events that occur in the narrative are imaginary. Any resemblance to actual persons and events is either unintentional or unimportant.

Acknowledgements

I would like to thank both my wife Stephanie and my sister Julie for the careful reading and editing they performed on this manuscript. Their concern—and expertise—are evident on every page. I would like to thank my wife even more for her daily and invaluable encouragement as I pursue this difficult, difficult art.

For my parents

BURNT NORWAY

ONE

1

I'm going to show you something I've never shown anyone before. Not even my agent. In fact, Lolly would freak if she knew I was doing this. I can hear her: "You're going to destroy it for them, Paul. You're going to turn their tongues sour. You know, the tongue of their brains? They don't need to know what you *cut*. What you cut stays in the trash." I appreciate her theatrical sense of maintaining appearances, sticking to character, not letting one see the blemish on your cheek or the cut in your heel or the gash in your soul. *Chin up. Face front. Pull curtain. Act one.* But I can't help it. Now that it's over. All of it. Besides, it's only a page. Less. 344 words. But these are the 344 words that started everything.

Lars kicks at the pitiful black and red remains in his hearth. If he doesn't do something, the blaze—which they've bribed for months—will soon extinguish. Lars has to open the bottom embers to the liquid resuscitation of air. The charred, barely glowing fag ends that have been on top roll to the side and go out. It doesn't really matter. They aren't helping anyway. They take more heat than they give out. The newly freed ember underneath glows brighter orange. Lars bends over—slowly, so as to not topple from the sudden movement and rush of head blood—and cracks fourteen pieces of kindling in half at once. He tosses the stick halves on to the would be flame. The sticks catch: smoke first, then a kind of subtle orange brimming, then yellow tongues stand up and do a full shimmy as if in a conga line. Lars waits a minute or two. Then he puts one small log on the flames and takes a rolled tobacco cigarette—the last one he owns—from his oily coat pocket. He brings the cigarette close enough to flame that it too ignites. Lars takes a drag and lets the the smoky, pine-flavored warmth travel through miles of his being. Then he blows a mottled gray stream directly at the fire, commingling mouth mist with the ropes of hot black smoke now rotating from the burgeoning blaze. He needs this fire. He needs more cigarettes. He needs hot coffee. (How would he get that?)

He needs his worn woolen jacket—rubbed through at the elbows, ripped at the right shoulder line, evidencing in every inch stains from smoke and blood and tallow and oil and dirt—even if it gives him imperfect protection. He will take any protection at all against the Norwegian February wind.

It better happen tonight, Lars thinks. He can't let her suffer anymore. It's no life for her. Or for me. Breathing out, he feels how close his ribs are to his winter skin.

Besides, I could use the meat.

Pretty atrocious, huh? First of all, I didn't know where or when in Norway this action was supposedly happening. I figured roughly three hundred years: far enough back to be pre-industrial but not so far back that no one would really remember it. Okay, three hundred years. 1703? No later. 1753? Hmm . . . 1793? And why Norway anyway? The truth is it was a spur of the moment choice. I could have said Sweden. I could have said Finland. I could have said Iceland. I could have said Germany. All I know is that I wanted north. I wanted white people. I wanted some poor starving pre-industrial northern European farmer. I didn't know a darn thing about Norway. I knew the Norwegian jokes Garrison Keillor tells every Saturday afternoon on the radio. I knew IKEA. I knew "Norwegian Wood" by the Beatles. I knew that in 1994 the Winter Olympics were held in Lillehammer. And I knew—because during those games I watched one of NBC's ubiquitous, sports suffocating, up-close-and-personal segments about him—that Norway had a king. The King of Ice. The King of the North. (I think NBC actually showed him getting pulled around on some silly sled by reindeer. Or maybe I'm making that up.) A useless, ceremonial modern king. A king who knows he's lucky to have the job at all, so he's willing to let NBC pull him around by reindeer. A king for a democracy; that blatant contradiction in terms. Actually, to tell true, when I began my novel I wasn't even sure Norway was a democracy. Don't you have to be a democracy to be in the EU? Is Norway in the EU?

Well, if you don't know, find out.

But it doesn't matter. Lars doesn't live in modern Norway.

It matters because you ought to know. What kind of philistine are you?

None at all. I'm just saying, for the sake of the book—

And IKEA isn't Norwegian; it's Swedish.

Swedish?

They serve Swedish meatballs in their cafes. At least they did.

Did?

Last time I checked.

Which was?

1991.

Do IKEAs still have cafes? And indoor playgrounds? And babysitting? All that progressive, feel-good, heralded-at-its-U.S.-opening-in-the-1980s European stuff that Americans hate, not because they are bad ideas but just because they're not American ideas.

Stop! I'm not going to let you get away with this.

Get away with what?

Who knows. I didn't. What I did know was this. It would be Norway: preindustrial, pre-democratic, pre-springtime, primordial: a white-skinned farmer kicking at a near dead hearth fire and hoping that his dear old cow, his one cherished remaining mammalian livestock and veritable kin, gives birth to a calf that night so he won't have to kill her for meat with that baby still in her stomach. But he will have to kill her for meat. The poor dear. It seems almost an act of cannibalism.

Eating one's cherished family cow may be gross, but it's hardly cannibalism.

But they've had it so long. You know? It's like a friend; it's like a baby.

It's a cow. Unless an actual person is involved it can't rank as cannibalism. Look it up, why don't you?

Hey, there's an idea.

What?

Why not make Lars so desperately starving and so out of any other options that he commits a real act of cannibalism?

Do you know if cannibalism even existed in Norway 300 years ago? Or ever?

But he's starving!

Yes, and he's also Norwegian.

It's winter. The hardest winter in fifty years. Lars's cow dies along with the baby inside her; it turns out the meat is diseased. The gangrenous brackish slime is a dead giveaway. Lars can't help it; he tries a chunk anyway but turns critically ill. While he is bed ridden vultures devour the rest. Maybe they get ill; maybe they don't. Things get worse for Lars and his wife. The three remaining chickens are mauled by a fox. Lars discovers only feathers and a couple stray beaks in the chicken house. They use up the last cup of flour, the last ounce of butter, the last of the stored potatoes, even the seed potatoes. (It had been a bare, disappointing harvest.) Melted snow provides water, but there is no food. Lars becomes gaunt and his knees ache. He begins to wheeze when he walks. Spots demonstrate like fireflies in the front of his vision. His stomach feels like its been carved out with a dull knife: bleeding hunger every minute of every day. He begins to look at his wife in a new way. Her skin is so velvety, the texture of a plucked, succulent chicken—that white and that smooth. The flesh between her fingers looks like the thin meat on a wing, what you suck on to get every bit of flavor. Her shoulders could be muscles of beef. And her ribs! They make his mouth water.

Excellent! Now I had a conflict. A man determined to eat his wife. That's an attention grabber.

Or a stomach turner.

A risk I can accept.

But this is a farming community, right? What about the neighbors? Wouldn't Lars try to get help from them first, like before he *committed murder*?

Hmmm . . . Good point.

All right, so the whole village is struck: a series of miserable events and acts of God over a period of months. First, the harvest is reduced to almost nothing by a mysterious crop disease; then in late fall lightning fires devastate a number of properties; finally, cattle begin dropping off as if poisoned, but poisoned by what no one could determine. The village is so critically hurting that most decide to get out before winter even arrives. They migrate south to wait out the worst weather; maybe try to learn to be fishermen. Other families move north, because they had heard rumors that in some lone places above the Arctic Circle temperatures become magically warm. Other families move where they know someone who can take them in. Family by family, the village leaves, until it is a village in name only. But, Lars—at least until the night when he attempts to kill his wife—scoffs at such reckless bedouinry. Things are bad, yes. But lighting out half-assed might only make matters worse. He, for one, will stay put. He will outlast the winter. This is his house. His farm. His home. He will stay.

2

It was with great good feeling, a veritable wave of calm, that I wound down my spring 2003 classes, what would be the last teaching chores for me until the fall of 2004. 2004! I was about to start my first ever sabbatical—I even wrangled a year long leave from the university's cheapskate Sabbatical Application Review Committee (must have been a skeletal group of applicants)—and there was nothing alive that could impede my elation. I gave A's to anyone even close, wrote generous comments on all my students' papers, recommended any of them who asked to the best grad schools in the country, and then, come mid-May, started tying up those won't-be-back-here-for-more-than-a-year details at the office. Never have I felt more sanguine, more approving of university bureaucracy. Sign another form? No problem! E-mail book reps? I'm on it! Write an instructional report for the new chair of the curriculum committee? That would be my pleasure! By the end of the month I was done—anything and everything to do with school. I took my eight-year-old son to Destin for a week. We survived our vacation together and on June 7, 2003 returned to our cozy little home—yes, I have custody—on the outskirts of Conway, Arkansas, a comfortable if sleepily bland berg as much Midwestern as it is southern. I told myself that now I could finally get on with writing my book while Ryan told me that he was ready for some company his own age. Namely, at the pool. I obliged him on the pool, but found it harder to oblige myself with the book writing, even with all my newly arrived supposedly care-free free time. In these early forays into the novel I felt I was coming up out of the mud: struggling to the desk every day and once there sweating over every sentence. A paragraph might take a day, a page a week. After that early burst of idea a few weeks before, I was writing scared.

(Necessary historical background [or you can call it a shamed and pissed off note]: Writing my first book—a way too serious tale with little plot and a terrible many paragraphs of gloomy rumination by my hero—was like sitting under a lead weight for five years, not an experience you'd ever want to repeat. It also cost me my marriage [more on that later]. The book lived in the world for about two minutes. For a month you could get it "wherever good books are sold." Then for a few months you could get it out of the remainder bins for a buck. A few months later even that wasn't possible. My book even failed in the remainders. So less than a year after being published the thing was extinct. Nowhere. Vacuumed from history. The publisher—who will go unnamed—didn't seem surprised or all that bothered, but did refuse to ever work with me again.)

I was worrying too much and calculating too hard, determined that even with all the dark elements licking at the edges of the narrative, this was not going to be another gloomy, 600 page exercise in monotone. This book was going to move. This book was going to sing. This book was going to have a plot! But weeks into it—my precious sabbatical underway along with the humid summer heat—I was composing in fragments, drinking too much coffee, staring out my study window, torn by worries that I might try to be a poor man's Dostoyevsky all over again. I was like a baseball pitcher who aims instead of throws. I wouldn't let myself loose. I had no groove, no velocity.

In early July I got a call from Lolly. She was on the beach in Barbados finishing a Planters Punch while attending to the summer sun slowly dipping into the other side of the ocean.

"Make any literary discoveries?" I said.

In Conway it was 7:30 and I sat in my study: notebook open, pen in hand, coffee mug filled with high test. Ryan was at my ex-wife's for nine days, so I was trying to be especially productive. At least in theory. But I'd spent the week mostly arguing with myself and watching my front lawn turn to straw.

Lolly chuckled raspily. "I'm not discovering a thing," she said.

Lolly talks—and laughs—like Kim Carnes used to sing. Remember? *Betty Davis Eyeeeessss*? Whenever I heard her voice on the line I was afraid she was going to tell me she had throat cancer. She certainly wasn't going to tell me she sold any book of mine. I hadn't given her one to sell in almost three years.

"Not a thing, except that I like sitting here, getting pissed, staring at the most gorgeous sunset this side of Mel Gibson's ass. Thousands of miles from where anybody can ever bother me. This, Paulie, is nice. That's what I've discovered."

"How many of those Planters Punches have you had?"

"Counting this one?"

"Yes."

She paused.

"Four."

"Four?"

"No—wait—five."

"Lolly, slow down."

"Hell I'm slowing down. I'm on vacation."

"I want you to come back from vacation."

She laughed. Kim Carnes again.

"I'm sure you do, buckeroo."

(Note to reader: Yes, this is how Lolly talks. Really. Suffice it to say that if she were not my agent I would not have let her call me "buckeroo." Or "Paulie." But she was the only agent I had—and probably ever would have—in the whole universe. So I let her call me whatever she pleased.)

"You know," she said, in a sudden vocal lurch, as if mentally she'd gotten up and repositioned herself in her seat. ("As if," I say now. Really she was just drunk.) "You know," she said, "it occurs to me that I could do anything here and nobody would ever know about it. None of you."

"Who?"

"You."

"Us?"

"Yes."

"Who?"

"Back there."

"Where?"

"In New York!"

"I'm not in New York."

"You know what I mean. All of you: my secretary, my ex-husband, my landlord, the garbage men, Michael Bloomberg, Ray Scarlieri—" (A spy-writing guy; one of her more difficult authors.)

"—Norman Mailer—"

"Norman Mailer?"

"He's an asshole."

"But you don't represent him."

"So what? He's still an asshole."

"So by 'us' you mean everyone in America."

"Right on, babe."

Now I got it. New York = America. Or, reversing the equation, America = New York. I was familiar with the mentality. My ex-wife's relatives were from Long Island.

"What exactly are you thinking of doing?" I said.

"Well, for instance, what if I just took off my clothes—right now?"

"Are you on a nude beach?"

"No."

"So wouldn't that be illegal?"

"I'm on vacation, Paulie. Getting arrested is part of the deal."

"Oh."

"For a hottie you can be a real sourpuss, you know."

(I include the above line of dialogue for the sake of verisimilitude, not for physical accuracy; i.e., I am not a hottie. Lolly, understand, was trashed out of her skull.)

"Besides, I'm not talking about getting up and putting on a demonstration. I'm talking about sitting here in my private beach chair drinking my private drink buck naked as I watch the buck naked sun go down over the buck naked beach. I could do that and none of you would ever know about it."

"I guess not, except you're telling me now."

Her laugh became a rollicking, throaty guffaw. I guess I made a funny. At least Lolly thought so.

"Touché, babycakes. But I'm only telling you what I could do. How would you know what I actually did?"

"I'm getting confused."

She laughed once, harder.

"Oh," she said, drawing out the word, "I can foresee all kinds of possibilities. For instance, how do you know I'm not buck naked right now?"

I should probably tell the reader that Lolly got her name from Nabakov's famous heroine. Her father consumed the book as soon as it came out. He loved it so much that when his daughter was born six years later, Lolita was the only name he would abide. (A non-practicing Jew, it never mattered to him that you couldn't find Lolita in Deuteronomy.) His wife reluctantly agreed but quickly diagnosed Lolly as an acceptable nickname. Funny thing is, her father was no Humbert Humbert. According to Lolly, the man never had sex in his life. Okay, so maybe that's an exaggeration, but the point is he was a very mild character. (Of course so was Humbert, at least on the surface) Still, Lolly liked to play up the Nabokov connection. To strangers she would tell the story about her father naming her and then, in her Kim Carnes voice, say, "I had a very interesting life when I was twelve." The ones who had read the book would snicker appreciatively—or swallow a nervous gulp. The ones who hadn't read the book just stared. For that, Lolly instantly dismissed them.

In truth, Lolly knew no Humberts growing up and herself was not Humbertized until she was almost twenty, and drunk, after a party for the Oswego Young Democrats, with a guy who was the local organizer for the Campaign to Reelect President Carter. Apparently, it was a less than overwhelming first experience, with the guy—already gray at twenty-five—acting jittery and dissatisfied. "I think all the blood scared him," Lolly said. "Or just grossed him out. He's thinking I'm a sex goddess and it turns out I'm not even an angel yet."

Lolly told me this story the first time I met her in person, just after she sold my first novel. We were doing lunch to celebrate. Yes, I actually flew to New York just for lunch. The fare wasn't bad, and how many times do you get to celebrate selling your first novel?

"What's going on with that book!" Lolly shouted. "I want to sell it!" For an instant, I had a picture of her clothes-less on a beach in Barbados trying to hawk xeroxed, spiral bound copies of a draft. "I mean the Denmark one."

"Norway," I said.

"Norway?"

"Yes."

"I thought it was Denmark."

"No."

"But it's got two Swedes in it."

"No."

"No Swedes?"

"It's not about Sweden."

"Damn!" Her expletive wasn't angry, only exclamatory, full of liquid off-center urgency. I hoped she was still sitting down. "So it must be about Danes."

"No."

"What then?"

"Norwegians."

"Oh. Right. So that would be Sweden."

"No, that would be Norway."

Long pause.

"Norway?"

"Right."

"Are you sure?"

"Definitely."

She offered an astonished grunt. "Where the hell *is* Norway?"

By this time, I could actually give her an answer to that question. The first thing I did when I got back from Destin was go to Torreyson Library at UCA with a fistful of quarters and photocopy everything I could find in Britannica about Norway.

Why photocopy when you have a computer?

Because I don't subscribe to Britannica.

There are other online encyclopedias.

What: Wikipedia?

Yes, Wikipedia.

This is a novel. I want to start with the best. Not something written by anybody.

So subscribe to Britannica.

Do I look like I have money?

Who's running to the library with a fistful of quarters?

Quarters. Listen to yourself.

So I went to the library, dragging Ryan along with me. I couldn't take the chance of leaving him at home. Not at eight.

Not with an ex-wife ready to pounce on the slightest slight she could detect in my parenting capability. Even though I know for a fact Joy has left him alone before. I've given up questioning her lapses. It's not worth having my eyes scratched out—metaphorically speaking—and, besides which, it always ends up being my fault anyway, even if I'm twenty-five miles away and not legally in charge when whatever happens happens.

"I don't want to go to the library," Ryan said. He moved his eyes from the tv for half a second. "And you don't have to shout."

Yes I did. I asked him twice in a regular voice.

"Yes, I do," I said.

No response. On the tv I could see an electric blue camel with elk horns and wings, trying to bite the leg of someone who looked like a bare-fisted cross between the Lucky Charms Irishman and Ty Cobb. Offscreen, some kids were screaming, as the strings built to a crescendo. Cut to commercial.

"You have to," I said.

"Have to what?"

"Go with me to the library."

"Why?"

"Because I can't leave you."

"Why?"

"Because you'll get eaten by a coyote."

He gave me a look.

"Or so says your mother."

"I won't leave the house."

"They'll trick their way in. Like the big bad wolf."

"Mom leaves me alone."

"I know."

"And?"

"And you're still coming."

He frowned.

"Only if you take me to the pool afterward."

"Deal."

"And—" he held up one index finger—"if you buy me a Kaiba deck."

"Why Kaiba?"

Sly shrug.

"Is that the best?" I said.

"No," he said, as if the notion was preposterous, "the Joey deck is the best."

"All right, deal."

"Hah!" he shouted. He pointed his eight year old digit right in my face. "Tricked you. The Kaiba deck *is* the best."

"How much does it cost?"

"I don't know. Ten bucks?"

"Ten bucks! For playing cards?"

"Yu-Gi-Oh cards, dad. *Kaiba.*"

Britannica Online, brother.

Shut up.

We did go, and I did find out plenty. Such as: Norway occupies the same degree of northern latitudes as Alaska. To its immediate east is Sweden, which extends further south than Norway but not as far North. To its immediate west is the Norwegian Sea, which if you traveled on it long enough would take you (well) above and past Scotland, past Iceland, clear to Greenland. North of Norway proper is Svalbard—an archipelago over which the kingdom has sovereignty—and beyond that, the absolute top of the world.

That's not all I discovered. To wit: Norway has four regions: Ostlandet, Vestlandet, Trondelag, and Nord-Norge. Western Norway (Vestlandet), has a marine climate with mild winters and 80 inches of annual precipitation. The city of Stavanger is a Vestlandet industrial center, primarily for canning and engineering. Trondelag, graced with flat fertile land, is an important agricultural region in west central Norway. Eastern Norway (Ostlandet), containing the capital city of Oslo, is the country's most populous region. Meanwhile, Northern Norway (Nord-Norge), located above the Arctic Circle, is the land of the midnight sun in the summer; but in December and January the sun never rises.

"I didn't actually want to know," Lolly said.

"Sorry."

"You think I want to listen to a geography lesson when I'm sitting on a beach with a Planter's Punch in my hand?"

"I said I'm sorry. But this stuff is relevant, actually."

"Relevant how?"

"Well, for instance, during the great Ice Age of the Quartenary Period—"

"The *what*?"

"The Quartenary Peri—"

"Coronary?"

"Quartenary. The Quartenary Period."

"What's that? No—wait—DON'T TELL ME."

She chuckled deeply. Very self-amused.

"I don't actually know, Lolly. But back then glaciers sculpted U-shaped fjords in western Norway. One is the Trondeim Fjord."

"Ford? Like Henry Ford?"

"*F-jord*," I pronounced. Before she could even respond I finished my point: "In the melting periods between ice ages, large areas were flooded because the land had been so depressed by the weight of the glaciers. Because of this flood, layers of clay, silt, and sand, were deposited on the western coast and in the Trondheim area. Because of the rich soil, a lot of agricultural activity is evidenced in these places."

"Writers," she muttered, I think affectionately. Then I heard her slurp her drink.

"Agricultural activity," I repeated. "As in farmers."

"Right, farmers."

"Forget it," I said.

"Ouch," she said, "you should see the dark-skinned god that just walked by. Talk about your skin of gold."

"Lolly."

"He's looking back! I think he heard me."

"Lolly."

"No, maybe not, there he goes. Hey, bronzed one!"

"Lolly!"

She exhaled a deep drunken amused warble.

"He must have heard that. He waved. Oooh, Paulie. I am sooo tight right now."

"I never would have guessed."

"Not just drunk, Paulie, but *drunk*. I am pissed. I am torched. I am sloshed. I want to get naked. Right this minute."

"By yourself?"

A chuckle.

"Why not by myself? Why not? If I want to. Bronzed god must be around here somewhere. Where'd he go?"

"I mean, you're traveling by yourself?"

"Of course." A liquor-misted pause; a moment of processing. I could hear her breath on the line. "Hey, don't pity me, buckeroo. If I wanted people, I could have brought people. I have plenty of people. I didn't want people. I wanted beaches. I wanted sunsets. I wanted Planters Punches. If I need to talk to NYC I have a cell."

"When are you coming back?"

"Never."

She said it so positively I almost believed her. I saw my second book fading into the Caribbean sunset.

"Actually, next Tuesday."

"Oh."

"Give me a call, Paulie."

"I will."

"We should do lunch sometime. In the city."

"We can."

"I mean *my* city."

"I know."

"I want to hear more about this Denmark thing."

"Norway."

"I thought it was Denmark."

"No."

"Or was it Sweden?"

"Norway."

"Is it like your first book?"

"No," I said.

"Good. Your first book was a piece of shit."

"Oh."

"I told you that, didn't I?"

"Well, no; actually, you didn't."

"Hmm. Sorry. It was though. I'm not surprised it bombed."

"Why did you represent it then?"

"Because of this book, stupid. The next one. I don't take clients for one book. They're my clients. I want them to stay around for a while. I want to see the next book and the next book and the—Oh, Paulie, there's the god again."

She represented my first novel to get to *Burnt Norway*? That was the pay off?

"Lolly—"

"What? Oh. Oh god."

I don't know what I meant to say. Maybe warn her off. Tell her not to pin any hopes on this yet-to-be-really-started tome. But did I want to say that to my agent?

"You should see his buns, Paulie. He has one of those Speedo things on."

"That's all right, I'll pass."

She chucked, once, like a burp.

"I'm gonna sell your Denmark book. Seriously. It's gonna be a hit."

"Thanks, Lolly."

"Hey. God disappeared again. What is he doing, teasing me? I better go, Paul. Let me strap on my ass-tracker and hunt him down."

"Don't hurt yourself."

"What? Oh." She shrieked a watery cachinnation that lasted for seconds. "Don't worry. No hurt involved. None at all."

3

[Hi. Real author here. Not Paul. (No, Paul Mullen is not my real name, and I'm not working on a book about Norwegians, even if he is—or, more correctly, was—and even though Paul's life and character bear *some*—please note and respect the italicized emphasis on that word—resemblance to my own, we are far more different than similar.) I've been biting my tongue for twenty-three pages now but I just can't any longer. Academic integrity requires that I make a confession. I more or less cribbed the above geography lesson from a single Encyclopedia Britannica entry (15th edition, Macropedia, Vol. 24: Metaphysics—Norway). Like Paul, I actually went to the trouble of going to my campus library—I'm in the academy too—sticking coins in a photocopier, and running off actual paper copies of an actual bound paper article. I'm not exactly sure of the Britannica's article's author(s) name, but at the end of the article, in parentheses, I found this: Jo. We / G. Sa. Their names abbreviated I'd hazard to guess. If so, dear reader, please tell Jo. We. and G. Sa. that I'll share appropriate royalties with them on my book. They will need to talk to Lolly, though. She knows all the legalisms. But they won't want to talk with her while she is drunk and shouting on a beach in Barbados. (Well, maybe they do actually, if they ever saw her in a bikini, but not to discuss legalisms.) She has of course, in the timeline I've established for this narrative, long ago returned from Barbados, but if Jo We. and G. Sa. press too greedily on the royalty thing I'll imagine her to some much remoter vacation spot, where they'll never catch up with her. Maybe I'll imagine her into a temporary leave from the agent biz as she goes back to her first love: let's say, arctic biology. Believe it or not, she could actually take classes in this at Oswego in the early 80s. (Okay, so I made that up too.) I'll send her on a research trip to Nord-Norge where in a drunken escapade with sled dogs and a teenaged guide named Rolf she gets lost in a snowstorm and is never heard of again. Which is sad in and of itself but especially so for Jo. We. and G. Sa., because they would need to talk to my publisher's legal division who will serve them up the most artfully and inscrutably contorted near-English language proclamation that they ever had the tortuous misfortune to decode; they will never be able to figure how much royalties they have coming, not if they study that parchment under an atomic microscope for weeks. And because they will never be able to figure what they are owed they will always grouchily assume that they are being ripped off royally—no pun intended—and thus will always regret ever having raised the issue at all.

Or, another option, I'll keep Lolly in New York but endow her with a wickedly miserly temperament, make her a person who won't lay out a nickel if she can lay out a penny, and won't give up the penny if she can give nothing. In that case, it will just be tough titties to Jo. We / G. Sa. You don't want me to have to do that to a lovely character like Lolly do you, the perfect foil to my anxious, self-deprecating, coffee slugging and not very fun author-character? But the sad final truth about royalties, dear reader, and the main thing for Jo. We. and G. Sa. to remember— what you must press upon them before they decide to take up a protest—whether to me, Lolly, or my publisher—is expressed in those famous words of Billy Preston: "Nothing from nothing leaves nothing."
Now back to Paul.]

By the time Lolly called me from Barbados I'd written exactly one scene since the end of spring semester. Here it is:

One night after Olga dies to a bitter exhausted sleep, Lars pulls himself out of their frigid bed. His aching joints crackle like thin tinder. He walks to the far corner of the room where against the wall rests an assortment of small tools, all but unused these days, which he doesn't feel like carrying back to the barn. He knows the piece he is after: his axe: a yard long and topped with a head that, unlike every other instrument in the house, he has kept sharp over the years. As if he knew he must use it some day for just this purpose. He grunts as he lifts the axe. He feels a wincing pain along his shoulder blades. He realizes more than ever the reduced condition of his body. Used to be he could swing this for an hour without feeling anything. Now he can barely carry it across the room. But he does. He must. She'll die anyway. If I don't do this, Lars thinks, she'll die anyway. And so will I. I can't last another month. I may be only a week from the grave. I may be days.

Lars trips over his feet, then the axe, and lands face first against the floor: hard as iron in this ungodly season. He can't see; there's nothing but yellow everywhere and the pulsing sting in his forehead. His lungs collapse, empty sacks in his chest. He can't breathe. He wonders if he is dead. Then he hears his wife turn on the bed, mumble. His eyes clear. He sees the gray brown floor. He pushes himself up and checks on Olga. She is on her back, her eyes closed, apparently still asleep. Whew. Lars takes hold once more of the axe. No mess ups, he thinks. I've got to do her the first time. It's only right. He takes the last step to the bed. With a jerk and a new pain swording along his arms he pulls the axe all the way over his head. He sees Olga—a collection of meat under the thin blanket, barely living. The few muscles left in his arm shudder under the weight. He tries to transfer energy from his arms to the long handle but all he feels is the weight of the axe head pulling him backward. His arms quake. He buckles. Lars collapses to the floor, the axe tolling against the wood. He begins to cry.

"What are you doing?" Olga sits up, wide awake, all eyes. She sees her husband on the floor, an axe behind him.

"Nothing," Lars says. With severe effort, he pushes himself to a sitting position. He can feel the ribs of his butt against the iron-cold floor. "I thought you were trying to sleep."

"I can't. I'm too hungry."

"Really," he says. "I'm okay."

"Rooster poop. You're as skinny as a buzzard. Skinnier. You're so skinny if I had to eat you it would be more trouble than it's worth. I'd get nothing off your bones."

Lars tries hard to frown: his best hurt face.

"I'd never think those things about you."

Olga raises an eyebrow. "Thanks, I guess."

She settles against the pillow and lays still. "Oooh," she groans. She turns on her side, showing her husband her back.

"I'm so hungry my joints hurt," she says.

Lars nods but, in truth, he doesn't hear her. He's only thinking how delicious that stretch of flesh must be: from pointy shoulder blade to pointy shoulder blade. It sticks to her skeleton just like a fitted sheet. He imagines tearing it off with his teeth and gorging on that crisp salty wattle. Then sucking on her bones to get every bit of grizzle and blood juice. He is so hungry even the idea of eating bones makes him excited.

"Yes," he says, for no apparent reason.

"Yes, what?"

Olga turns over. She sees his eyes. She sees his face: lean and needing.

"Yes, *what*?"

Lars shakes his head.

"What?" she says for a third time. "What does that mean? I never asked you anything."

Lars's eyes tread from wall to wall to floor to ceiling.

"I just meant—you know—yes, I'm listening to you. I'm affirming my husbandly interest in your thoughts and emotions."

Olga snorts. "You don't give a hen's hash brown about my thoughts and emotions. Do you think I don't know who I'm married to?"

Lars turns red. He has enough blood left for that. He shrugs.

"Yes," Olga mutters mockingly. She turns her back to him again. "And if you're thinking of killing me and eating me, you should know that I'm hiding a knife just beneath my left leg."

All the new air leaves Lars's lungs. His mouth opens. It won't shut.

"I choose weapons I can handle, husband."

Lars gulps. He falls back against the floor.

In that scene, Lar's wife used expletives. But what expletives are authentic to Norway in 1793? Certainly not "rooster poop." That one couldn't stand. Nor "hen's hash brown." But where would I go to find out how preindustrial Norwegians cursed? Could I call the Norwegian embassy in Washington, DC? (You know, I really could do that.) Or I could just Google "Norwegian expletives" and see what comes up. Google would surely work. Google knows everything.

I tried Google. It failed me. I was so cocky I actually chose "I'm Feeling Lucky" and what I got was something called The Monochrome Set, with an accompanying message that the site is "always under construction." Didn't like the sound of that. So I tried a regular search. The most intriguing possibility referred me to the YLC (Yamada Language Center) Quarterly of the University of Oregon. It's Fall 2001 issue focused on Scandinavian Studies. Here is what the hit looked like on Google: "Professor Westerleg, a **Norwegian**, boasts that the most popular of the Scandinavian . . . become mere bikies) and peppering your speech with as many **expletives** as possible . . ." I noticed of course the distance between my two search terms. Not only did they not follow each other but they were separated by ominous ellipses. Still, the site was worth exploring. I found on page seven of the *YLC Quarterly* for Fall 2001 the reference to Professor Westerleg—Grethe Westerleg, that is. The *Quarterly* reported that according to Professor Westerleg, "the most popular of the Scandinavian languages is her native tongue." It went on to quote her directly: "Of all the languages it has the simplest grammatical forms making it easier to learn, especially for someone speaking English. Norway also has the highest standard of living in Scandinavia, making it the most popular destination for study abroad."

Okay, fine. But what about the expletives?

I continued to page eight where I found an article titled "How to speak Australian." The writer of this article cheekily explained that YLC sent a reporter "to the wilds of Australia to investigate the local lingo and compile a large list of slang for a special 50 page report for your edification and enjoyment." Just what I needed. A tongue-in-cheek academic quarterly about foreign languages. Since when were university quarterlies supposed to engage in masturbatory sarcasm? The article continued:

> Unfortunately, our intrepid reporter disappeared into the desert on a camel. He was last seen heading west from the town Alice Springs, and has yet to turn up. Among his personal

possessions abandoned in a bar and later returned to us by the authorities was our investigator's copy of the *Lonely Planet guide to Australia*, with the following passage underlined: If you want to pass for a native try speaking slightly nasally, shortening any word of more than two syllables and then adding a vowel to the end of it, making anything you can into a diminutive (even the Hell's Angels become mere bikies) and peppering your speech with as many expletives as possible.

I was not amused. Worse, I still hadn't found my Norwegian expletives, only Australian ones.
Maybe I could move my scene to Australia.
C'mon, dummy. Crocodile Lars and his sheila Olga?
What difference does it make?
I think it would matter to Australians.
What am I supposed to do about the expletives?
And three hundred years ago; wasn't Australia like still a penal colony then?

"Give me the straight poop, will you? Lars? *Lars*."
Olga, sitting across the tiny broken table, leans in to her husband. "Lars. How ya goin?"
Lars, his hands glued to an empty coffee mug, can't look at his wife. Besides, his dazed mind is too filled with images of tucker, heaps and heaps of beautiful tucker. Floaters and chips. Bloody, juicy, chewy lambies, like the kind he used to get from the Kiwi up the road. Croc meat. A giant tortoise. Shrimp on the barbie. Lagers from the bottle-o stuffing his eski. Lars thinks he sees a floater on the table: round and fat, heaps of meat pushing up from underneath, making bumps on the buttery crust. But no, it isn't a floater. It's an apple. But then it isn't. A mozzie, maybe.
(Note to reader: As you may have intuited, in this passage I made sure to use every single word listed as Australian slang in the fall 2001 issue of *YLC Quarterly*.)

Yes, a mozzie. A mozzie would taste good, wouldn't it? Even a mozzie? Now? He slaps it.

"Ow!" Olga waves her hand. "Whatja go and hit me for?"

"What?"

"Whatja hit me for?"

Lars closes his eyes. He squeezes them as tight as he can. He opens them slowly. He squints, focusing on the table. The mozzie is gone. Instead, a bare white hand lays on the table, an attractive wrist with still some flesh around the bone.

"Lars? Lars?"

Lars looks into his wife's pale, skinny, once freckled but now decimated face.

"What are you looking at?" she says. "You just hit my hand, you know. Are you loony now?"

"What?" he says. Then: "No."

"Oh, I see," she says. "I see, husband. That's how bad it's gotten, is it? All I am is food to you."

Lars looks at her for a moment.

"Yes," he says.

She stands. "I reckon I married a blooming Yank, didn't I? Or a Pom. Might as well have married a fucking 18th century, imperial Pom. All that matters is what you want. All that matters is your hunger. My body is just one big eski to you, in't it? Or maybe I should say a bottle-o. Or maybe I should say a serve-o. After all, we're all just 90% water, eh?"

Lars half-nods, half shakes his head. He can't tell if maybe she is inviting him to drink her. He closes his eyes and enjoys the image.

"Lars!"

"What?" Stars and fireflies dot his vision; their dull shack seems too bright.

Olga is leaning over the table. "This can't go on. We got no tucker. We need you to get us some tucker."

His mouth moves, noises come out of his throat like "Yes."

"Get in the ute. Drive to the serve-o. Bring your rifle. Take every bit a tucker they got. Right? I don't care if it's junk."

Lars doesn't answer.

"Lars."

Lars doesn't answer. He is looking at her bright blue eyes and thinking he could pop them in his mouth like maraschino cherries. A little bigger but just as juicy. The sheet of skin over her tall forehead and long of her face he could peel with a paring knife and eat in strips. Sweet hors d'oeuvre. Then the main course: her once buxom chest, whittled by starvation, but still with meat to last him a week. Dry but not too dry, chewy but not tough, not like a croc. Lean, but so much more delicious.

Oh, that was terrible. Ridiculous. I liked Norway better. I preferred a hoary, brain-addled northern farmer starving and freezing to death. Besides, how could I go back three hundred years with "utes" and "serve-os" in my novel? So that was it. No more indecision. Lars stayed in Norway, in his bare cabin on a wintry plain.

4

I should probably explain that I did have other research sources as I started this project. Well, one actually: a book called *Summer Vacation 3rd Grade*, a workbook of exercises and a few facts covering a narrow span of elementary school subjects: Math, Spelling, Reading Comprehension, Science, Geography. Ryan's teacher, through a relentless series of notes home and sales messages broadcast into her pupils' craniums, had arm-twisted all of us parents to buy this book for our kids. The idea was to keep your child's smarts from atrophying during the warmer months. Fine. But I also assume, judging by Ms. Landry's signally committed sales job, that either she or the school received a kickback on every purchase. The book itself, of course, was innocuous enough. Divided into 13 weeks, each week featured a different country in the Geography section. Only days into my sabbatical I discovered that Norway was not only among the 13, but the star country of week one. Talk about a good omen! Talk about serendipity! I hungrily studied the book for information. I learned that Norway from top to bottom stretches 1,750 kilometers. ("About the same distance as from New York City to Orlando, Florida!"). I learned that a fjord is a "narrow waterway between steep, rocky cliffs." I learned that the Vikings who first discovered America were from Norway. And at the bottom of the page, beneath a map dotted with smiling icons of reindeer and fish, a cheery little "Factoid" told me that "Almost everyone in Norway knows how to ski. Children are taught to ski almost as soon as they can walk."

That was something, but . . . I went back to YLC Quarterly and checked that name. Grethe Westerleg. On UO's web site I found an e-mail address for her in the Department of Foreign Languages and Literature. I figured I would ask her my question about expletives. What could it hurt? Worse she could say was "Bug Off." But if she were agreeable, I'd have a readymade Norwegian Answer Man (Woman). That could prove invaluable as my book grew. First I would start small, one question. The important thing wasn't the information really but beginning the relationship. If I started small, she'd be more receptive to answering. If I threw a laundry list at her she'd delete me immediately: the electronic guillotine. A lot riding on how I worded one e-mail. Too, there was the fact that UO was on summer vacation, although I knew that many e-mail addicted academics religiously keep checking right on through the warm months. Most crucial was the factor of the personality of this Grethe Westerleg, whom I didn't yet know. If she were of a certain crotchety—or just busy—disposition it wouldn't matter how harmless I sounded. She'd never reply.

The e-mail:

From: Paul Mullen
Subject: Norwegian questions
Date: July 17, 2003, 9:58:03 AM
To: grethew@uoregon.edu

Dear Professor Westerleg,

I am a writer and academic who lives and works in Conway, Arkansas. I teach creative writing at the University of Central Arkansas, although currently—and for the coming year—I am on sabbatical. I'm working on a novel set in eighteenth century Norway, specifically a farm. Surfing the web, I discovered the YLC Quarterly, which in one issue mentions that you are a native of that country. Having no personal contacts who are authoritative on matters Norwegian, and having a rather trivial if pressing question about your country, I'm writing you today to simply ask for help. Might you have time to answer a question? Here it is: How would an eighteenth century Norwegian farmer— or his wife—curse? Are there any curses unique to your country? Specifically, curses that might have been used 300 years ago?

I certainly do understand if you are too busy to get back to me immediately. It's your summer break, after all. While I am on sabbatical this year, you probably are not, and thus you surely are trying to get the most out of your time off teaching. Maybe you're not even looking at your email. On the other hand, any information, guidance, and/or assistance you could provide would be greatly appreciated.

Sincerely,

Paul Mullen
Assistant Professor
University of Central Arkansas
Department of Writing and Speech

Despite my courteous pro forma protestations, I wanted her to write back *immediately*. I knew from writing my first novel that little, mounting questions could quickly become a pain in the neck and might even mean the wrecking of my novel if they went unanswered and I kept going. You know, those little corruptions, inch by hidden inch, until you step back and realize the whole thing is shit. Kind of like the Leaning Tower of Pisa. How long can you depict a farmer's wife cursing, if you don't know how she'd do it? I hoped that Professor Westerleg would be flattered that somebody cared enough about her homeland to write a novel about it. So flattered she'd want to write back. On the other hand, she might see through my disingenuous obsequities and delete me. In that case, I'd never hear a word, and my germ of a novel would be doomed before it ever had a chance to live.

So I held my breath, picked up my pen, and kept trudging on. In short order—the excitement of making an outside contact must have spurred my creativity—I composed two more scenes, even with Ryan back from his mom's and my afternoons mostly spent wilting in a poolside lounge chair. Here's the first scene in its entirety:

Hours pass. Day is nearly breaking. Lars lies supine on the wooden floor of his frigid farmer's cabin.

[Real author again. Sorry to interrupt, but did you know that "supine" always means one's back against the ground and "prone" always means one's face against the floor? Yes, *always*. My trusty American Heritage Dictionary (hardback, 2nd edition, copyright 1982, 1985—yeah, I know, I've had it forever) tells me this, putting the word in purposeful italics. As I read this I experience separate shivers of recognition. First, although I have known the difference between prone and supine for some years I've ignored or just forgotten that difference many times in my writing life. Maybe I even published some things with "prone" in them when I meant "supine," creating an entirely false picture for my readership. For huge spaces in my writing life, I've thought of prone as just "laid out," whether that be face up or face down. (Even now, I was about to write—or, rather, have Paul write— "Lars lies prone on the wooden floor.") "Prone" just sounds, well, more laid out than "supine." "Supine" sounds like a biology experiment word. "Prone" sounds like a human word. But, turns out, I've been dead wrong. Who knows how many stories I have misdirected? Who knows how many of my readers have incorrectly imagined my so otherwise carefully wrought scenes?

And by the way, is American Heritage still published these days? Traditional dictionaries—all of them—are facing bad enough competition from dictionary.com and the whole of the net, but I heard all the way back in the pre-www 80s that the American Heritage was a losing proposition for its publisher. As a caveat, however, I should admit that I heard this in a graduate course on Book Publishing at George Mason University, taught by a whiskey faced, big-boned, still blonde-red (it looked natural), fifty-something of a visiting prof who wasn't a prof at all but a guy who'd worked in publishing for forever and—having just retired—felt like teaching a course on the business. He clearly relished lording over a group of students. This guy had started out on the editorial side ("I wanted to be an angel," he said, with no little self-mockery) but gradually transitioned to the money side. Having served on the money side for many years he seemed to believe that the editorial side is for lightweight, mommy-pampered, self-satisfied English majors who don't really care if they have a future in the business, or if the business itself has a future. "If you care about books, you have to care about business." He projected the message as hard-earned gospel, and was convincing enough when he said it, but looking back I can see it as typical Reagan-Bush I corporate-hero bullshit that floated in the air all over America back then—at least until the 90-92 recession and the Borsky scandals. He loved to offer confidently negative opinions about companies and publishers he knew nothing about—like American Heritage—opinions rendered with what he saw as his smooth patrician charm. (Re the charm: His favorite story from all his years in publishing, which he repeated about every other class, had to do with a Beverly Sills autobiography for which he acted as editor. The first line of the book is, approximately, "I'll always remember my first public performance." The first print run of the book, however, evidenced this line: "I'll always remember my first pubic performance." Does that seem funny? Maybe I laughed the first time he told the story, but let me swear to you the Beverly Sills's pubic hair was not an image I needed publicly reiterated eight or nine more times that semester.) In our end of the course house party, I discovered that our prof had a thirty-something, curvaceous blonde wife and a brown-eyed three-year-old, accomplishments he seemed more proud of than anything he did in publishing.

Back to Paul; or Lars, rather.]

He stares at the grayed boards on the wall beside him, examining the way a knot in the center of one board acts like a rock in a stream: bending the flow of the wood so that it moves around that center, a mobile living force. How does it do that, Lars wonders. It is not water, after all. It is wood. A solid substance, a cut slab, even off, sanded down and nailed to. How can such wood still flow like water? If Lars moves, the ripping pain in his back rips even worse. It rips like actual fingers are underneath his skin, inside his lumbar, tearing the muscle one piece at a time, as the resulting blood pools inside his lower back making a rosy wet glow.

He wonders if he ought to try again his original plan, bad back and all. If he fails again she might decide to kill him rather than put up with his annoyingly incompetent attempts on her life. Olga has all sorts of knowledge and talents at her disposal: old Norwegian wives' recipes for liquid poison, old Norwegian know-how for where to make the most precisely invisible yet fatal cut, old Norwegian know-how as to where to find and how to catch the most venomous reptile in country. Olga would have so many more ways to attack him. She might be plotting already, this minute, playing out multiple scenarios or narrowing and readying only one; she might this minute be thinking to herself, trying to remember the whereabouts of the local witch, the one rumored to provide beleaguered wives with a legendary death cream.

Lars hears Olga's cavernous, drilling snore.

Then again, maybe she's not.

In any case, he's not going to try to kill her again. He couldn't live with himself if he failed. He couldn't live with her needling and belittlement. That embarrassment would be worse than any death cream.

But he must get off the floor.

"Wife?" Lars says.

Olga snores, her cranky honk rising to a summit, where she pauses, chews on her wet breaths, moves on the bed, then starts to snore again.

"Wife!"

"What?" Olga sits up. "Who is there? What do you want?"

Lars hears her maneuvering over the bed, looking left and right, muttering to herself.

"What did I hear?" Olga says loudly. "Are you a ghost?"

"It's me."

"Lars?"

Olga rolls all the way to the edge of the bed and peers over. Her pale blue eyes are sleep-muddled and grayish. "What are you doing on the floor?"

"I tried to kill you, remember?"

"Oh, that."

"And I dropped the axe. It was too heavy."

"(Unknown Norwegian expletive.) So?"

"And then I fell."

"I remember now."

"Help me up."

He hears her roll to the bed's other side.

"Get yourself up, husband," she says, her voice all the way over on the other side.

"I wish I could."

"What?" He hears her roll back.

"I am stuck here, Olga. My back."

"(Unknown Norwegian expletive.) You should see someone."

"Like who?"

"Like a doctor?"

"And with what will I pay the doctor, Olga? If I had anything to barter with I would eat it. Or sell it. I would not waste it on a doctor."

"Suit yourself," Olga says. "But you aren't going to do too much eating or selling on the floor."

Lars sighs: an endless, drowsy, disappointed noise.

"You are right, my wife. As always. Please help me up."

"Not a chance."

"Olga!"

"Consider it just punishment for attempting to murder me."

"I was just hungry, Olga."

"You think I'm not?"

Lars sighs again.

"You think I'm not starving, husband?"

"Of course, Olga. But I'm a man. I need more food than you in order to carry out my dut—"

"Duties? What duties, husband? What animals do you currently maintain? What crops, what fields are you working? What is there left for you to do now that our animals have died and our last crop is ruined? Complain? A woman can do that as well as a man, maybe better. And she'll need her sustenance for it."

"Touché."

"What?"

"Forget it."

"So just stay there a while and think about what you tried to do to me. Just think about who's hungry around here and who really needs the food."

Silence. No one breathes.

"I am thinking, I am thinking," Lars says.

"No, you're not. You're pretending to be thinking."

Darn, she's good, Lars thinks. For indeed he had not really been thinking, just remembering how much he was thinking before when he stared desultorily—he likes to think of it as melancholically—at the boards of his wall: an image of thought, not the thought itself. If he were really thinking he wouldn't be able to talk.

"Okay, now I'm thinking," he says.

"No, you're not. If you were really thinking you wouldn't be able to talk."

"Great Thor's ghost!"—[I know; that's Perry White; but I was tired of writing "Unknown Norwegian expletive."]—"Let me up, Olga."

"No!"

"If I never get up, I'll never be able to make it up to you."

Olga does not respond. He has struck home with that one. He feels her cogitations lighting the air above the bed, working inside her muscles, readying her to relent.

"Because I am very very sorry for what I did," Lars says. "And if I am able to get off this floor I will want to make it up to you in any way I can, husband to wife."

She still does not respond. Then: "How?"

"Somehow."

"*How?*"

Lars sighs a third time, worse than ever. He stares straight up now at the gray boards of his ceiling. He remembers putting on that ceiling nine years before. It was springtime; they were almost to be married; Lars was energized, almost giddy; constructing the abode that would last them the rest of their long, happy lives; he would take care of her, provide for her, better than any other man who had wooed her, better than his own father took care of his Lars's own mother, a woman still alive and still hearty at 72.

"Somehow," Lars whispers into the air above him.

"I'm sorry, husband," Olga says, "that's not good enough."

Not bad. I liked the repartee. Cutting and open. Maybe this tale had life after all. I kept going. Olga briefly falls asleep and makes more noise. Lars wakes her; reminds her he's still on the floor. She's not impressed, but does finally offer to pull him upright. Here's part of the dialogue:

"Wait. Olga. Wife. One question. A minute ago, in your sleep, you sighed. A beautiful, curative noise, like springtime. Now, with the fog of dreams drawn from your face, can you tell me why you sighed?"

Olga brings her hand back up. She narrows her eyes, scratches her head. "Yes, I can tell you. My sister Stina said I could sleep on her side of the bed. She always chose the left and gave me the right. In my dream, she let me take the left."

Lars frowns. "That's why you sighed?"

"That's it."

"But it was such a deep sigh, wife. So heartfelt."

"What can I tell you? I always wanted to sleep on the left side. She never let me."

Lars frowns again. Olga lowers her hand. Lars grabs it; Olga pulls. Lars shouts with the pain but is upright. He keeps one hand on the bed to steady himself while with the other he uselessly rubs his lower back. Olga informs him that they have to go hunting, like now. Lars protests: he's tired, hurt. Olga won't listen. Lars relents. After a series of extended moments, gingerly entering his clothes, Lars is ready. Olga takes the gun. Lars a knife and a burlap bag. Outside they go. Here's how the scene finished:

As soon as he steps out, the air hits his face, and he forgets his back. He ducks his chin under his coat and keeps it there, only his eyes showing. He reviews the flat, still, white plain, as white as if the snow came yesterday—disguising vegetation, covering foxholes and warrens, moistening potential firewood—though it had been weeks ago. If that is the only snowstorm they have all winter, it will still be months before it melts. By then I'll be dead, Lars thinks.

The crack of the gun startles him.

"Yes," Olga shouts.

"What?"

"Look!"

He looks where she points and finally sees it: a short, scrawny white hump almost invisible against the snow fifty feet off. Bones with a bit of fur. Olga runs to it. Lars moves as fast as he can. The rabbit, barely an adolescent, is just living. Its lungs move up and down erratically; its exposed heart—along with half its innards touching the frozen snow—races. Blood begins to seep from its ears. The lungs move slower. They stop moving. Its eyes glaze to gluey blue white.

Olga looks at Lars with wonder, her eyes glinting. "*Dinner,*" she says.

That last bit only brought on more questions, however: Would an eighteenth century Norwegian farmer own a gun? Which kind? What does a Norwegian farm family eat? And are there even rabbits for them to kill in Norway? I remembered an educational video that Ryan used to watch called "Animal Disguises." (This was before *Yu-Gi-Oh*. When he still cared about anything.) One scene shows a rabbit being chased by wolves, across a snow-covered stretch of woodland. The rabbit is white speckled brown, the exact color of dirty, trampled snow. Against the backdrop the rabbit stops and virtually disappears. The wolves, confused, look around, look at each other, and almost visibly shrug. Then they wander off screen in search of other prey. The rabbit survives. A victory for inherited camouflage and for Mother Nature. But where did that chase take place? I made a mental note to check the video out of the library. Then I decided to just change the scene. According to a Britannica article I'd read, as late as one hundred years ago, large mammals such as bear, wolf, and lynx were common in Norway. Those species are now mostly disappeared but fox, otters, beavers, and badgers—to name a few—still survive. If now, why not then? I pondered having Olga shoot a badger. Because of the University of Wisconsin, I couldn't help but think of a college football player stranded on the frozen ground, bleeding to death. Okay, so not a badger, I decided. I'll make it a fox:

A scrawny brown thing lies still atop the snow fifty feet off. Lars can't tell what it is. He can't see its head, which must be pointed in the opposite direction, away from them. It is bigger

41

than a rat, even bigger than a guinea pig. But not by much. It might be a rabbit, he thinks, but the hair is too stringy and too red. Olga runs, waving for him to follow. Lars moves with as much speed as he can muster and feels sicker with each step, even as his stomach demonstrates *meal meal meal* inside him. When he gets close he sees that the fox is a baby. He also sees that the head isn't pointed away but missing. Shot off. The last of coldly congealing blood leaves out the opening at the top of the neck, turning the ground clay red. Beneath a cover of emaciated skin the ribs show as clearly as if the scrag were already a skeleton; the shoulders point in two directions, winglike and exact.

Olga turns to Lars with a look of wonder. *"Dinner,"* she says. Her eyes glint like her smile: hard at the edges, determined by hunger.

5

"I love that rabbit scene," Lolly said.

It was mid-September already. Grethe Westerleg had still not written back, and my output had once again slowed, but I'd taken the trouble at least to enter my first few scenes into my computer and mail my agent the pages. Just to prove to her that I was actually working. *Eventually,* I meant to communicate, *I will have something for you to sell.*

"Which scene?"

"The dead rabbit in the snow."

"It was a fox."

"It was?" Silence. "Whatever. I loved the gore. Gore sells."

So much for the pathos of a dying animal.

"I am going to find a publisher, Paul. I'm going to do it for you."

"I'll just have to trust you on that."

"Yes, you will. Who knows the market better, me or you?"

Sometimes I wasn't sure either of us did.

"Speaking of which," she said. "I thought we were going to have lunch when I got back."

"Sure."

"How's Monday?"

"Monday?"

"Monday."

"This Monday?"

"No, in the year 2525. What do you think?"

"You do remember I live in Arkansas?"

"How could I forget? Of all my clients you have to be the one who lives among hillbillies."

"And there's my son. What should I do with him?"

"What did you do last time?"

"I was married last time."

"Right. Forgot."

"Now she's an ex."

"Right. My bad. I guess you never seemed much married."

"By that time, we weren't, no."

"I have an ex too, you know."

"I know."

"You do?"

"Yes."

"I told you?"

"Yes."

"I told you about Joe?"

"Do you have another ex-husband?"

Lolly laughed: a short, smart noise.

"No, I mean. I don't remember telling you."

"You've told me everything, Lolly."

"Six foot six? Hairy back? Red cucumber for a nose?"

"Yup, a real Prince Charming."

She chuckled bitterly. "You don't know the half of it. You don't know what it's like to wake up next to an ogre for nine years. God, that breath. "

If I was younger—and not in so much need to stay friends with my agent—I might have asked why she married him in the first place. Who in her right mind shacks up with an ogre? But having lived through it myself I know the question is useless. No one enters marriage in her—or his—right mind. That decision, critical as it is, is never determined by our right mind. Maybe because if it were no one would ever marry.

I wanted to change the subject.

"How was Barbados?"

Her voice immediately smoothed, deepened, colored. "Warm and windy and red and tropical and delicious."

"Did you get naked on the beach?"

Lolly started a laugh, not exactly a natural one.

"What?'

"That's what you said on the phone."

"When?"

"You called me that night from the beach, remember?"

"Ooh," she said. I could hear her wince. "So you were the one. I couldn't remember."

"Yes. You said—well, you said a lot of things—but mainly you said you want to strip and sit naked in your beach chair."

"I did?"

"Yes, you did."

"Jesus H.—"

"So did you?"

For Lolly there came a very unusual pause.

"I can't remember," she said. "But if I did, baby, you missed the show of the century."

I'm not so dense that I was unaware of Lolly's proclivity to flirt with me. But don't get the wrong idea. It never seemed that it was me she liked as much as the flirting. And she was the kind of woman who could pull it off: naturally extroverted and with the physical presence to back up her charm. At forty-two, her hair was still full as an ocean pool and as black as any twenty year old's. It didn't occur to me then that she probably dyed it. Her skin—naturally dark, olive-complected—was genuinely flawless. Having never had kids, and suffering the modern New Yorker's addiction to the gym, she still kept her figure nicely. And, at least based on what I can remember from our first lunch together, she suffered no modesty about showing it off. She wore a black leather skirt that went up her legs almost to her hips, and a silky, flimsy black blouse with the top three buttons permanently loosened. When she talked she leaned close, touched my hand, tapped my shoulder, laughed out loud at only mildly funny comments. I would have been flattered by her husky, seductive attention, except that I knew I was basically a curiosity. This aspiring literary writer living in Arkansas of all places, composing "interesting' if unsalable books. So, like Henry Higgins with Eliza Doolittle, she selected me and decided to cultivate me. Some days, looking back on that first lunch, I wondered if through all that flirting Lolly was just trying to embarrass me into sense.

"When can you make it to New York?" she said.

"Wednesday?"

"Too soon."

"Week from Wednesday."

"Two weeks from Wednesday?"

An audible sulk. "Fine."

"What about my son?"

"Bring him."

"He's in school."

"Don't they have babysitters in Arkansas?"

"He's not exactly a baby."

"You know what I mean."

"I'll try to get someone."

"Why doesn't he just stay with the ex-wifie?"

"I suppose that's always a possibility."

"You suppose?"

"Yes, I suppose."

"That bad, huh?"

"You know."

" Okay. Whatever. You figure that part out. Meanwhile, we plan. Meet me at Stage Deli."

"I never heard of it."

"Jeez, you are a bumpkin. This place is famous, Paulie. Sandwiches so big you can't get your eyes around 'em. To say nothing of your mouth."

"How do you eat them then?"

"Me? I can get my mouth around anything, Paulie. I said *you* couldn't."

"Right."

"Stage Deli. Seventh Avenue, in Manhattan. Let's say 11:45 am, Wednesday, October 1st."

":45?"

":45."

"Why not noon?"

"Noon's too easy. I like the challenge."

"All right. 11:45."

"I have big plans."

I started sniffing out airfares to New York almost immediately. But I waited more than a week to check with Joy to see if she could actually take Ryan when I needed her to: a risk that certainly could end up biting me on the ass.

Do you maybe not want her to take Ryan?

No, that's not it.

C'mon.

What?

So you want her to take Ryan.

No.

Ah.

I want to go to NY. I want to lunch with my agent.

So call her.

Yeah, yeah, yeah.

What?

You know Joy.

One of my habits of being was to talk with my ex-wife as little as possible. I dreaded every communication. Because I never came away from them not feeling skewered, not feeling depressed, useless, made fun of. If you've been through a less than amicable divorce—and how many, if any, are truly amicable—maybe you can understand my reluctance to reenter the world of that failure, the energy field of Joy's distaste. Or more like distaste on top of disappointment morphing to disillusionment smarting into total disrespect, a distaste more instinctive, more automatic, and wholly less forgiving than she levels toward any person or group or genus. Such is how we regard those for whom we've fallen out of love.

And, besides, I don't want her to know about the novel.

Coward.

Would *you* want her to know about your novel?

Of course not. But you gotta get to New York.

You might think, dear reader, that I'd want Joy to know about the novel, to show her I'm surviving, that I can keep on keeping on as well as she can. You might think that. But you don't know Joy, do you?

One of the reasons my wife gave for divorcing me was that I didn't care enough about what ought to matter to me. Specifically, the fact that my writing career had disintegrated. I didn't act, she said, like I had any kind of plan for getting back on my feet. I was perfectly passive in the face of failure.

Your book bombed, she said. Don't you even care?

I care a great deal, I said, but since I can't control it I don't see the point in eating myself up about it. At least the thing got into print, I said. That's an accomplishment.

That's how losers think, she said. That's how people think who never publish again.

Well, that's how I think.

Then you'll never publish again.

On one hand, of course, she was right. I shouldn't just rest on the fact that the book got published at all. I should hope for more; I should work for more. On the other hand, when my wife and I first met I was an indigent graduate student working some nights and every weekend as a $5/hr. desk clerk at a high-rise condominium complex for bitchy middle-agers in Alexandria, Virginia. I had only the wispiest of storybook hopes, and a beginner's determination, to make it as a writer. There was no proof I could. There was no evidence. I was not the worst fictionist in my graduate program but I was certainly not the best. I was middling good. Like everyone else in that program I said I hoped to write a novel someday, but—also like everyone else in the program—I had no actual story yet that I cared to novelize, nor any strategy for novelizing once I found that story. All I had was the expectation that someday I would. That—and not a penny more—is exactly what I had to offer Joy.

"I love it that you even want to try," she said on one of our early dates. "That's what makes you different. I can't even imagine trying to write a novel. I can't imagine trying to write stories." (She was a graduate student at the same university, but in a very different program—M.S. in Sociology. We met in line at the campus pizza pub, about the only space on that campus that we both inhabited.)

Given those humble beginnings—and the chanciness of my publishing ambitions—you'd think that years later she would be satisfied with just seeing my book in print. You'd think. But somewhere along the way trying and hoping wasn't good enough anymore. The three years it took for me to get a full-time teaching job, after earning not just one but a second graduate writing degree, befuddled her. The repeated rejections of my short stories by nearly every literary magazine under the sun, and the lack of financial recompense from the few that I did place, soured her even worse. Finally the thorny, interminable route to getting my agent and my first book contract cracked her patience, especially because she had severe reservations about the manuscript. Just before I landed Lolly, Joy wrote a seven page, single-spaced critique of my novel with no less than twenty-eight specific recommendations for improvement. I adopted maybe four of those recommendations, an admittedly paltry effort for which she never forgave me. Looking back, that's probably when our marriage ended. When I was walking out of the house to mail the "finished" manuscript to Lolly—actually, this was the second time I'd finished the manuscript; the first time was for a different agent (more on that later) and at that time I hadn't solicited any advice from her—she looked at me and said: You know, that is nowhere near the book it could be.

It's good enough, I said.

Good enough isn't good enough, she said.

Turns out she was right. The book failed and when it failed I didn't know what else to do but try to keep the good ship Paul Mullen sailing steadily: keep up my teaching, keep up my spirits, keep smiling to my colleagues, keep up writing something. But not novels. Not yet. Maybe never again. That's when she became furious.

You're settling for failure, she said. You're not examining yourself. You're not trying to learn from your own mistakes.

How do you know?

Because you're lazy, she said. And self-satisfied.

What are you talking about?

I told you how that book should be written. *I told you.* And look what happened. I can tell you what book to write now. Do you want to know? Will you listen? Will you try?

(This from someone who never came closer to publishing a piece of creative writing than posting a four line poem on Mrs. Bronson's bulletin board at Whitehall Elementary School in Scotch Plains, New Jersey in 1975.)

Go write the fucking book yourself, I said. Since you know so much about it.

That was the first and only time I threw the f-bomb at her. So I guess maybe that's where our marriage ended.

No, your marriage was already over.

Not over.

Over.

Not *over* over.
Over over. Show them.
I wasn't going to.
It's only fair.
I know.
Just to show you can be fair.
(Note to reader, titled *Just To Show I Can Be Fair*:
Exhibit 1, offered without rebuttal, without whining, without
comeback, and only one bracketed informational insert. An
email—obviously composed at home one evening, when the
writer had time and the desire to elaborate—to my wife from one
Lacy Carlson, a friend of hers and member of my own
department at the University of Central Arkansas. My wife, I
should explain, worked then, as she does now, across campus in
the Donald W. Reynolds Center for Sociological and
Anthropological Research. We never saw each other—and still
don't—in the course of a working day. I found this email in our
jointly held Earthlink mailbox, right after we separated. It must
have been there for weeks without my seeing it. It appears to
have been written in response to an earlier email from Joy to
Lacy.

From: lacycarl@aol.com
Subject: Him
Date: February 2, 2001 8:34 PM
To: joyandpaul@earthlink.net

Sweetie,

I know a lot about husbands not paying attention. I've told Jeff a
hundred times that if it weren't for the fact that he listens to the
radio in the car I'd assume he's deaf. I can talk to him for ten
minutes solid and he'll look up from a bowl of cereal or some
kitchen cabinet he's got his head in and say: What? Complete
blank look. I'll say, Didn't you hear anything I said? Usually he
blushes. Usually he apologizes. At least he has the grace to be
embarrassed when he's caught . And usually he tries to make it
up. I mean, I guess what I'm saying is I don't think he's

deliberately ignoring me. He's just a guy who gets fixated on something—even a stupid bowl of cereal—and blocks everything else out.

But your guy is the worst. Excuse my directness. From what you say, and from what I've observed, he's a million times more self-involved than Jeff. I've always thought that. I've never told you because, you know, you don't want to insult the husband of your best friend. But given how you say things are between you guys, I don't see why I should hold back now. My impression of Paul at work is that he's not there for anyone: not the students, not his colleagues, not the department. Only himself. He's there to do the bare minimum to get the paycheck. Beyond that it's all about whatever he wants to do for his own reasons. I mean, I've never seen him volunteer for a committee. Or volunteer for anything. He only serves on committees he's assigned to—and then he barely functions for them. He doesn't conference with students. They can hardly find him. No lie, he comes in, closes his office door, and stays locked in there for six or seven hours straight, unless he has to come out to teach. But as soon as he's done in the classroom he goes right back in and slams home the door. There are days when I know he's in there, and I know it's his scheduled office hours, and students are banging on his door calling for him, and he refuses to answer! You can get fired for that! I mean, technically. It's a violation of his contract. I'm pretty sure Rich has spoken to him about it. But I don't notice him acting any different. I'm right across the hall. I witness this all the time. Practically everyday.

I don't know what he does in there. From what you say, it doesn't sound like he's making the next great American novel. I don't see any evidence of that. Whenever I can—like if he goes to the bathroom or something—I peek in to try to find out what's going on. I can't tell. His office is a shit hole. He doesn't file anything. It's all just out all the time. How did he make it through graduate school? And usually there's a faint rotting smell. Like a dead orange. Sometimes I see a book open on his desk—some fat novel—like he's in the middle of pleasure reading. I wish I had time for pleasure reading on the job. I don't have time for pleasure reading at home! Sometimes the CNN web site is up on his computer. It can be anything: news, sports, entertainment. I can't ever predict. Once I saw him looking at the web site for some stupid action kiddie movie. White kids in oriental costumes with big hair and little lips, staring at you as if it really matters. I think they had playing cards in their hands. What was that about?

Oh, a personal pet peeve (sorry): He doesn't bring anything—nothing!—to our monthly potlucks, but then I see him in the lounge stuffing his face on Joanna's Mexican chicken and Kevin's potatoes. The gall!

So, anyway, it's no surprise to me that you say he's a mole at home. In his study all the time, head in the clouds. "All our conversations are monologues." Great line. I can only imagine. He has the luxury to claim that he's after some grand artistic goal; he has an excuse for staying in dreamland. Problem is, while he's in dreamland you and Ryan are still here. You're real. His stories aren't. And then they turn out to be flops anyway. (Sorry. I couldn't help it.) The guy acts like he's Stephen King or something and he's actually my Aunt Trudy. Trudy wrote something like twenty novels but kept them hidden in her bedroom all her life. We only discovered them when we started going through her stuff after she died. Then we read them. And we found out why she hid them. They were terrible! It's ironic that what's eating at the center of your marriage, and distancing him from you, isn't even all that great. It's not even worth his time. And then you try to help him—you try to participate in what he's doing, you try to make it better—and he doesn't even appreciate your suggestions. I'd be furious too.

I feel so sorry for you. I get on Jeff about being distant and not listening, but at least he's around. He doesn't lock himself in his study or go to sleep by 9:30. I don't have to watch hours of crappy tv by myself. Must be like living with some weird renter who keeps odd hours. Except this one is supposed to love you. Jeff will at least buy flowers once in a while. Give me a card. Call me beautiful. Jeff will stay up and watch tv with me. But your guy. He sounds totally cold, totally elusive, totally self-involved. Like I said, I'm not surprised. I watch him at work everyday.

Before you do anything drastic, though, I suggest you insist on counseling. Who knows, maybe it will help. At least you can say you did it. At least you can tell yourself and tell others that you tried. I mean I think people owe the marriage that. Maybe they don't owe their spouses that, but they owe the marriage. If he says no to counseling then that's that. If he says yes, then maybe there's actually hope. Despite everything I said in this email. But that raises the question: Do you still love this guy enough to hope that there's hope? I can't answer that for you.

I'll support you no matter what you decide, honey. Promise. :)

Later, L.

I must have looked two hundred times in our "Sent" file for Joy's reply to this email. No luck. I never did discover how she answered Lacy's last question. But I do know that the idea of us going to counseling never came up.)
(Followup note to Exhibit 1: I know I promised I wouldn't rebut but I have to explain that I only actually locked myself in my study once. That's when Ryan was going crazy with a bottle of ketchup and I didn't want him to ruin the computer.)

I can hear you say it: *But you did what she said.* You picked yourself up and got back to novel writing. Why not show off a little bit? Why not? Three reasons: 1) Half of me believed that Joy was right in everything she told Lacy about me; 2) the same half feared/suspected/assumed that if my Norway novel ever did find a publisher it would crash and burn as badly as my first; and 3) if that indeed ended up being the case, Joy would only have more ammunition in her tirades against my fucked-up-ness; she might even develop the courage for a custody battle that neither of us could afford. Her decision to let me keep Ryan had always seemed tactical more than generous, a temporary concession rendered so that she could dissolve the marriage ASAP, but a concession to which she might return once the divorce was legal. I had my proof for this suspicion in the way Ryan acted when he returned from his two weekends a month with her: bitter, impatient with me, almost mocking. As if he were fifteen, not eight. Another weekend at the headquarters of the anti-Paul Mullen coalition. It would take days back with me to reinvent my son's essential sweetness.

"You're still living in a goddamn hole, aren't you?" she said.

"Yes, Joy, I guess I am." What else is one supposed to do on a sabbatical? Isn't the hole the point?

"I really really really don't like this, Paul. It's not fair."

Turns out Joy already had plans for the first week of October: a sociology convention in Nashville. She was going in the company of her current boyfriend: the department chair.

"All you had to do was call and ask."

"Yes."

"Or do you just assume that everyone around you has no life except for how they relate to you?"

"That's not it."

(Maybe that's a little bit it.)

"Nothing's ever really real to you except what you need at the moment. Everything else is just—I don't know—the mist or something."

"No, Joy, that's not—"

"Christ, I'm sick of this treatment."

That was precisely—about word for word—what she said *before* our divorce. So what exactly did we go through all that hell and expense for?

"I'm sorry, but I had to jump on it."

"On what?"

"The fare. It was too good."

"You mother."

"But—"

"I can't talk about this right now.   I'll call you back."
She hung up.   I sat on the couch, numbed from the whipping
except for a dull tingle on the top of my skin.   I sat without
moving for twenty minutes before I realized she hadn't said she
would call back right away.   In fact, she didn't call until the next
morning.   It was a brief, and entirely one-sided, exchange, as
carefully constructed as if she'd written it out ahead of time,
which she probably did: "While of course I would like to keep
Ryan then—in fact, I am open to that at any time—I cannot take
him those particular days.   I've had long standing plans,
coordinated with Glen, to attend this important professional
gathering.   It is horribly unfair for you to ask me to give up my
plans for you when you had whole weeks from which to choose
the dates of your trip.   In fact, being on sabbatical, you have an
entire semester of days to choose from.   I, however, have no
choice.   My convention is scheduled from October 1-4.   Period.
And, no, I can't possibly watch him while I'm at the convention
anymore than you would be able to watch him on your business
trip to New York.   This situation is not fair, and I am not going to
be made to feel guilty for turning down an opportunity to share
extended time with my precious son.   Obviously, you should
have called and checked with me before you purchased tickets.
Having made the mistake you did, I think it's now up to you to
either eat those tickets and rebook for another time when I can
keep him—which I would *love* to do—or you can just pay
someone else to watch Ryan.   Those are your options.   But my
giving up this vital professional meeting for you is not."
    I mumbled something and got off the phone as soon as I
could.   I fell backward to my couch hemorrhaging self-esteem,
my heart jouncing in a St. Vitus's dance of guilt and chagrin and
devastation.   Just like our divorce.   But eventually it occurred to
me that I needed to find someone else, and quick.   The only
alternative I could think of was a former student of mine, a young
woman who was rarely free to babysit but who adored Ryan.
Recently graduated and recently married, a calm and intuitive
handler of children, and perhaps the most determined A student
I'd ever known, she was preternaturally responsible and
completely trustworthy.   About the only person in Conway I
could imagine handing over my living son to for a couple days

straight. But could she do it? She'd loved to. Except that she had to work at Movie Gallery in the afternoons, just when Ryan was getting off school. Of course, she could just take off work those days if—on top of flat fee I intended to pay her—I would make up her salary from Movie Gallery. Would I?

This was turning out to be a very expensive lunch.

6

Grethe Westerleg still had not replied. Here I was facing an important meeting with my agent about my novel and I didn't know if I should even continue with the darn thing.   Questions were stacking up.   How far could I keep going before I was perilously off course?   The hours of supposed creative time in my study devolved into hopeless internal skirmishes.

Should I email her again?

That would be bugging her, wouldn't it?

But she never replied.

Oh yes she did, she blew you off. There's your answer. She wants nothing to do with it. She might even be offended.

Why?

Why? You know nothing about her country and you're setting a novel set there?

Not nothing.

Almost nothing.

Norway occupies the same degree of northern latitudes as Alaska. The country has four regions—

Oh, shut up.

Almost everyone in Norway knows how to ski. Children—

You're only proving my point.

Well, what do you want me to do?

I don't know. But be careful.

What if she hasn't checked her email?

In two months?

Maybe she never saw it.

If she checked she would have seen it.

Then what should I do?

Find another Answer Man.

I don't have another Answer Man. There are not a glut of Norwegians in my life.

Your problem, not hers.

[Uh, sorry to interrupt—I realize things are heating up in Paul's world—this is R. A., by the way—but I can't help interjecting something that I've learned in ten plus years teaching in higher education, and which is actually relevant to Paul's current case. There are two essential types of e-mail readers: 1) those who regard received e-mails, and by extension the e-mail senders, as underlings who must serve and obey predetermined interests, and 2) those who regard every communication as a potential opportunity, not to be abandoned for risk of lasting regret. The first type regards every e-mail as a threat or a distraction to which he owes no fealty. He will delete unopened every e-mail that comes from a not certifiably known, boringly familiar source. And even among emails from familiar sources, the only ones he opens are the ones he already planned on opening. And even these he reads with an eye exclusively on what he already wants to find (e.g. the answer to a question posed to a colleague, the time of an important luncheon, the name of a book he must order) as opposed to anticipating some unexpected, day-altering discovery. And he never writes back. (Well, almost never.) His time is simply too precious to be wasted on gratuitous communication. That you would send an *uninvited* e-mail to such a person tells him all he needs to know about you, giving him every justification he needs to delete you, unseen and unread.

The second type, conversely, is enthralled by the potentiality of the new, by the fact that every e-mail contains at least the potential for a different and better life. She doesn't really care about the plans she brought to her computer desk. In fact, to be honest, she'd rather not have to follow through on those plans. Much better if she finds some unpredictable e-mail with a succulent, irresistible subject line. Who knows what could be waiting behind the curtain? At the very least, the e-mail offers her a few seconds distraction from all that she has to do. Needless to say, such a person is a) a better dinner date than the radical e-mail deleter, but b) much more likely to lose her hard drive to a ravaging computer virus.

The vital question for Paul: Which type was Grethe Westerleg?

FYI: Before you hazard a guess, let me caution that there are more of the second type in higher education than you might expect. On the other hand, don't expect that just because I use the male pronoun to draw the first type and the female pronoun to draw the second that the types break down along gender lines. Not so. Just last year, a male colleague of mine forgot to turn in final grades because he was too busy pursuing the ten million dollars waiting for him in a Kenyan bank. So, bottom line, you just won't know about the mysterious Professor Westerleg until I tell you. In fact, could be I haven't decided yet myself.]

My paralysis continued for days before finally, jacked up by dark coffee and underscored by fatalism, I shot off a second email.

From: Paul Mullen
Subject: More Norwegian questions
Date: September 24, 2003, 11:14 AM
To: grethew@uoregon.edu

Dear Professor Westerleg,

I hope you received my email from this summer in which I briefly outlined a writing project I have taken on. As I progress further into the novel, more questions have arisen and I'm afraid I must seek your assistance again. Last time, I asked you about Norwegian cursing. This time I have a different batch of concerns. Any and all assistance you could offer would be of mighty use to this Norway novice.

1. In the late 1700s would it have been normal for a Norwegian farmer to own a gun? If yes, which kind?
2. Are there foxes in Norway? How about rabbits? I'm not sure how far north you find these creatures.
3. What might be a typical dish for a Norwegian farm family? FYI, my farmers own cattle, although their small herd has been

struck with catastrophic illness, which precipitates the drama of the book.

All the best, and good luck in the new semester.

Sincerely,

Paul Mullen
Assistant Professor
University of Central Arkansas
Department of Writing and Speech

Did Grethe Westerleg ever write back? Before I answer that, I think I ought to explain exactly where I was with the novel right before I went to New York way back in September, 2003. In the last scene I showed you—the last one I sent to Lolly—Lars and Olga were left shivering not so much with cold, or not only with cold, as much with excitement at getting their first real meal in days, albeit a scrawny young fox with barely any muscle on its legs and hindquarters. I'd managed on to write one more scene. In that one, Olga commands Lars to skin the fox while she tends to the fire. Weak, exhausted, guilt riddled, he can barely carry out the duty and finally carries inside a sawed up carcass with barely any usable meat. Olga accuses Lars of leaving the best of the animal behind but even so cooks what he brings. In no time, they devour the meat; they begin sucking on the bones, squeezing out taste from the hardness with their tongues and lips. Lars tastes what the baby fox tasted in its short life: all congealed, gathered into one taste spread across the bone. It is delicious, this bit of flame-cured taste. Olga had been right to insist on the fire. Without realizing it, Lars begins to cry.

What is it?" Olga says.

Lars puts down the bone on his plate. He pushes the plate toward Olga.

"There's still some grizzle on that," she says. "And that one."

He nods. "You take it."

She eyes him. "Why?"

60

"It's delicious," he says.

She frowns at him, then her eye drops to the bone. She pushes it around the plate with her index finger. Then she picks it up and sucks on the whole thing at once.

"It's terrible," Lars says.

She takes the bone out of her mouth.

"No, it's not. Are you crazy?" She puts the bone back in.

"I tried to kill you, Olga."

She puts the bone down. She sits back, her spine still, her hands crossed.

"Yes, well. We'll have no more of that, will we?"

"No more," he says.

"I poured out the rest of the vodka."

(Side note: I had decided that I would revise the earlier scene to show Lars bucking up his courage with copious mouthfuls of the hard stuff. Not only would that seem true to life—after all, Ted Bundy said that he always primed himself with alcohol—but if done right maybe even lightly entertaining. A strange adjective, I know, to use in close proximity with Ted Bundy.)

He nods. He opens his mouth. He shuts it.

"What?" she says. He hears that the bone is once again in her mouth.

"Next time—" he starts.

"What?"

Lars shrugs.

"I don't need to live," he says.

"Oh, shut up," Olga says.

She hits him with her plate--not enough to hurt. Lars flinches. He grabs his shoulder.

"We'll abandon this place before I let you talk like that again," she says. She assures him that their fortunes, along with the weather, are bound to turn. "And if they don't turn, we'll leave," she says.

Lars rubs his cheeks with his palms, as if trying to stir up new blood in his face. His head feels a small measure clearer. He nods at her last sentence, hearing it fully for the first time. He is beginning to experience it: a tiny ingestion of strength from eating.

"I'm not going to let you get away that easy," Olga says. She leans across the table, brings her face as close as possible to Lars. "But if you ever try to kill me again I will cut your balls off and eat them for breakfast. Got it, husband?"

He nods harder, rubs his cheeks.

"Now give me a kiss," she says.

By the time I finished this scene new questions presented themselves. Did 18th century Norwegians drink vodka? Did they cook on an open fire or on top of a stove? Would they own salt? What is the Norwegian equivalent of "shut up"? Grethe Westerleg still hadn't answered either email. No sense sending a third. I boarded a plane at Little Rock National Airport convinced that the professor had exiled me to the land of deletion. Well, I thought, maybe that's just the way she is. A radical deleter. A security purist. One of those types who can't be bothered to open a message from an address she's never seen before. Oh no, she's too smart for that. Maybe my message was desiccated in the middle of some midmorning orgy, in which she clicked and clicked and clicked and clicked and clicked without even looking at what she was destroying. I imagined her in her office in Eugene, in front of her computer. She was a Ph.D., so I saw her with glasses sitting upon sharp, narrow, know-it-all face. Yet she was in charge of Norwegian Studies, not exactly the hippest field. So she must be older. At least middle-aged. More middle-aged than me. I gave her out-of-style, overly long hair. Pure late 60s. You know: long, straight, with a part in the middle? Melanie. Judy Collins. Whatever. Except not pretty. In fact, hers was starting to fall out; and every week more and more gray was bleeding through the thin, dry, brown, making it look like less like hair than congealed dishwater stuck to her head. She wore a dress, but a frumpy one, draped loosely over her sinking middle-aged figure; monochrome, of course, or at best a collection of unnoticeable earth tones. Sad to look at, sad to ponder, such clothes. Only a tenured university professor on the west coast could get away with hair and with a dress like that. Anywhere else these days she'd be fired on trumped up charges, the real reason being she was too ugly and too out of date. Yet while being frumpy and out of date, she was at the same time an aggressive, overefficient email checker, taking out her anger at the fallen post-feminist America by being ruthlessly impatient with its technology. Every email was an insult against the first wave. She deleted with righteous glee and a zealot's certainty. Pointing and clicking and cackling, taking her muffled victories in the privacy of her office, because bigger victories were denied her. Into that cauldron of jaded idealism, anti-modernism, anti-maleness, and zealous vegetarianism had I wafted my innocent request for information. Perhaps I shouldn't want to know what happened to it, after all.

No time to check in at my hotel. I took a cab straight to Stage Deli. It was almost noon when I got there. I didn't see anyone with Lolly's dark hair and trim figure inside the door. I didn't see her at the near tables on my right. Good. Not here yet. You don't want to keep your agent waiting on a lunch date. Not when you haven't given her a bestseller yet. I stopped to gawk at the array of sandwiches posted on the board above the deli counter, when I heard a familiar squawk behind me. Then I saw her: at a table at far left hand end of the room, sitting beneath black and whites of Joe DiMaggio, Marilyn Monroe, and Charlie Chaplin, a cell phone to her ear, a tank of corn beef in front of her, half a foot high with alternating slabs of meat and swiss cheese. The pickle next to it was a big as a baby's forearm. She lifted her eyes from the table and saw me. Still talking on the phone, she wiggled her fingers. With her head, she motioned for me to come over.

I snaked my way around a chunky Puerto Rican waitress, barely missing a table as I passed: elbows and knees, shoulders and round, white plates. Lolly moved the bottom of her phone away as I reached the table.

"Sorry," she mouthed. "I'm starving." Her shoulders stiffened, her eyes brightened with unhappy alertness. "Tell him I said so," she spoke into the phone. "Tell him—what?—no, tell him I said so. *Tell him I said so.* What is it this time, Alsatian dogs? Alsatian dogs! That's a joke. That's a joke, Frank. Yes. Frank, I have to go. I have a client here. An author. An author!"

She shook her head. "My favorite author, actually." She winked. "His next book is going to kick ass." She kissed the air in front of her lips. "I'm not telling. It's about Denmark. That's all I'm gonna—Like hell it's not sexy. You should read this thing." Another wink. "What? No, I gotta go." She hung up. I had the distinct feeling she cut her caller off mid-sentence.

"That man needs a hearing aid, swear to God."

"Maybe he's in a crowded deli too."

"No, he's in an elevator." She stopped, gave me a look. "Don't make excuses for him, Paulie; you don't even know him."

I shrugged. "Okay."

"He's all of thirty-nine years old and I'm screaming at him like an old man."

"Ah."

She stood up, took a step around the table, spread her arms. "Now, let me greet you for real," she said and pressed her cheek against mine. The dress she was wearing was pure Lolly: a wild, violet and white thing, so bright it could cause an autistic to start flailing. And as with most of her clothes, it was short enough to show off her form. The flaunt-it school of professional dressing, á la Barbra Streisand in *The Prince of Tides*. Lolly was actually a year older than me but looked ten years younger. I thought of that commercial I'd seen the night before, for an exercise machine. It featured a "fifty-year-old grandmother" who didn't look a day past twenty-five and was shaped like Miss February. If anything, Lolly was firmer than that woman, if less buxom. But also maybe more neurotic.

"So, you got here."

"I did."

"Your son is situated?"

I shrugged. "Well enough."

"Good." Lolly made a grand gesture with her hand, as if sweeping the subject out of the room. "First let me pee. Then I want to bite that." She focused an index finger at her sandwich. Up close it looked even scarier, daunting. You could charge admission to go inside. I couldn't believe that Lolly was actually going to sink her teeth into the thing. "Then," she said, "we can talk."

Lolly moved for the bathroom. Before I had a chance to look for her, the waitress was at my side about to slice my neck with a plastic menu.

"Here," the woman said, dropping it on the table. "Look at it. I'll be back."

I glanced at the crowd filling the foyer. Lolly wasn't kidding when she said this place was popular. Just since I arrived, the line had expanded to the door and even out it. But it wasn't just the number of people; it was their intensity. The ones in line studied the tables around them, their eyes big and urgent, needing and anticipatory, their shoulders tightened like basketball players before a jump ball, regarding each sandwich as it appeared with adulterous glances, as if not sure they had the discipline to wait a few minutes. As if they might have to attack. When the waitress came back, I ordered chicken salad. Not until she brought out the thing—which took all of three minutes—the sandwich bleeding mayonnaise and celery, sweating boulders of lathered chicken slipping from the edges of the pumpernickel—did I realize the obvious. This was too messy a meal for a business lunch. But I'd already ordered it. And it looked too good to refuse. And suddenly I was famished. By the time Lolly got back I had undertaken an exploratory nibble. "Good choice," she said. She sat down and straight away took in a mouthful of corn beef.

"How's the Denmark book?" I saw chewed rye bread and masticated meat at the back of her tongue. She swallowed.

"Norway."

"Norway?"

"Yes."

"So you've changed it?"

I sighed. "Yes," I said.

"Good. Denmark sucked. I just didn't want to tell you."

"Oh."

"So how is it?"

"The book?"

"Sure. No. Well, you know. Everything."

"Coming along. I'm on sabbatical, so I'm working every day. But I've run up against some research questions. They've slowed me."

She nodded, as if not quite listening, only waiting until I closed my mouth so she could say something else.

"It's going to be the next *Kon-Tiki*," she said.

"Isn't that about sailing?"

"Yeah, so what?"

I watched how she did the next bite. She opened what seemed like her mouth most of the way and lowered her head to the sandwich. Then she stretched her lips back—farther and farther—pulling her mouth open simultaneously until the orifice was inhumanly wide, but even so, only just wide enough to fit around one end of the sandwich. Then she moved in for the kill, pushing her head into the sandwich more than bringing it into her mouth. Long seconds passed before her teeth cut all the way through the layers of bread and meat and cheese. But finally she succeeded, creating a snowball of lunch in her cheek, which she proceeded to work on for the next five minutes. I looked at my bleeding chicken salad. I picked up my utensils and began cutting.

"Mine is about a farming couple. In 1793."

Lolly nodded to indicate she'd heard me, but she couldn't do anything right then except chew. She chewed for a minute straight. Then she waved her hand. "You know."

"Know what?"

"Same difference."

I must have looked as puzzled as I felt.

"The guy's name was Thor, for crissake. How many bestsellers you know—I mean bestsellers in America—have authors named Thor?"

"But my name isn't Thor."

She rolled her eyes. "Your characters!"

I paused. "Lars and Olga?"

"There you go." She bit again. I took the opportunity to eat more of my sandwich.

"But those aren't Thor either."

"They might as well be"—she chewed—"to your American reader. I mean"—she swallowed—"compared to Billy Bob and James Dean and Arlo Guthrie."

"Arlo Guthrie?"

"You know. What have you."

I tried to remember if Thor Heyerdahl was Norwegian. For some reason, The Netherlands stuck in my head.

"I think Heyerdahl might have been Dutch."

"Christ, Paulie. Who cares? It's all the same to the reader. Those northern places. That's what I'm telling you. Who do you know who can actually tell you a fart's bit of difference between Denmark and Dutchland?" When I didn't answer, she said "See?"

"But how—"

"Let me sell your book. Okay? You just write it. *Kon-Tiki* in the 1790s. Action, adventure, danger. Confronting the savage forces of nature in a desperate battle to survive. Two determined country folk in the fight of their lives. It's a fight they never anticipated, but one they have to win."

That's why she was the agent.

"You know," I said truthfully, "I can almost see that."

"Not almost. Not almost, Paulie. You need a line with these publishers. You need the hook. It's got to be exactly one sentence long and catchy as hell. '*Kon-Tiki* on the farm.' That's what we'll say. I read your thing about killing rabbits—"

"Foxes."

"Whatever. The pitch will work." She bore into me with her mineral dark eyes. "Have confidence. That's the first requirement."

"I know. It's just that after my first one—"

"Don't even think about it." She sliced the air with her hand. "That book was a piece of dung from day one. I gave it maybe a month before it went into remainders."

"But—" I started, then stopped. She'd heard the question before.

"Because of this book. That's why. *Kon-Tiki* in Denmark. It's gonna sell. And I knew it. That's why." She took a long chug of ice water. "So where are you staying?"

"There's a Days Inn in Long Island City."

"Long Island City? Better keep your doors locked."

I shrugged. I didn't know a darn thing about Long Island City, except that it was just over a bridge from Manhattan. That's what the desk guy said when I called.

"Why in the world are you staying in Long Island City?"

"It was cheap. I found it on the web."

"I'm sure you did. But there are cheaper places in New York, you know. Like my sofa."

I smiled carefully. I was grateful for the offer, but—

"I'm serious," she said. "What's an agent for?"

I made my smile wider.

"I've got water and everything."

I laughed. Lolly smiled, but barely, the corners of her mouth were turned down. She studied me directly with those dark eyes.

"You're my favorite client, Paulie."

She stretched her arm over, touched my hand.

"Thanks," I said. To my surprise, I was blushing. "Next time. I've already given them my credit card number."

"Yeah, yeah." She took the hand back. She took another drink of water. "I just wanted to see you in underwear."

I laughed again, maybe for real.

Lolly looked at her watch.

"Okay, so now I've got a meeting across town in fifteen minutes."

"Fifteen minutes? I don't see how you're going to make it."

"Are you kidding? I'll be early."

She stood up. She doused the bright violet with a long black overcoat.

"Keep me posted on the book. Show me pieces. And get it down." She adjusted the neck of her coat, picked her purse off the back of chair. "In fact, call me tomorrow. We'll do breakfast. Talk more. This son-of-a-bitch I'm ready to sell, Paulie. *Kon-Tiki* in Denmark."

"Norway," I said.

"Norway?"

"Yes."

She looked befuddled, even bothered.

"So you changed it?"

7

For the last hour I had been sitting on the bed, chewing delivered Chinese and—with the aid of my Powerbook—Googling everywhere. (FYI, not only was this Days Inn outfitted with what looked like furniture rescued from a teachers lounge fire sale, there was barely any of it at all. Certainly no desk. So the only place to prop my computer was the bed. On the positive side, the hotel did offer wireless internet access—albeit for a fee—so maybe I shouldn't complain.) One site I found, very helpful, was called Sons of Norway. Among other things it offered "lessons" in conversational Norwegian. For instance: God dag! (goo dagh). Translation: "Hello!" Morn! (morhn). Translation: "Hi!" (informal). Hvordan har du det? (vhor-dan harh doo deh). Translation: "How are you?" Hyggelig å treffe deg! (hee-geh-lee oh treh-feh-dai). Translation: "Nice to meet you!") I played with Sons of Norway for a while, then brought up UCA's web mail page. Guess what I found.

From: Grethe Westerleg
Subject: Re: Norwegian questions
Date: October 1, 2003 11:04 AM
To: paulm@uca.edu

Dear Paul,

Thank you for your very interesting inquiry! I apologize for the delay in responding. When you first wrote I was out of the country. Then when I returned I somehow missed your message. I did not see it until after I got your second message and started back searching. So sorry! It surely has been one of those semesters already. As an academic, you know of what I speak. Anyway, on to your questions.

A novel, you say. How challenging. I wish you the best of luck. Have you yet been to my lovely country? I encourage you to go—for your own sake as much as for your book. See wonderful

Oslo, look at our mountains, go cross-country skiing. I have lived in America for seventeen years and still am compelled to go back.

As for your questions, I think I can answer them. But I must warn you that I am a political scientist, not an historian. And as much as I love the quiet beauty of the more remote and rural stretches of my country, I am city born and bred. You must go back several generations in the Westerleg family before you find anyone on the farm.

Okay, your questions. Guns. Yes, Norway has had guns as long as any other nation. Do you really think we are as different as that? Nowadays, of course, we control our guns far better than rifle-crazy Americans. In 21st century Norway, it is almost only the police who carry weapons. Private citizens who wish to own guns must undergo a severe licensing procedure. Needless to say, as a result, few Norwegians own guns. And there is not the kind of gun violence you hear about over here. But that is another story. Please forgive the sermon. Back to the 1790s. What nation wasn't fighting with guns at that point?

Foxes. Rabbits. Of course we have both. I actually owned a rabbit growing up. Rag was its name. It survived in our apartment until it almost took off my sister's finger (thinking perhaps her digit was a white carrot). The next day, my father took Rag away. He wouldn't say where, just that he found her a better home. Curiously, I didn't question him any further about it. I probably should have. Maybe I suspected the truth wouldn't be pretty.

Even now father probably wouldn't admit to this murder. And I don't know if mother even remembers we had a rabbit. She has fairly lost her mind.

True, my country has a cold climate. But aren't rabbits built for that?

Food? Good question. We have our favorite dishes, none of which, it is safe to say, are known by you Americans. Not nearly so well, that is, as the dishes of the Italians or the Chicanos or the Chinese. Being the fishing nation that we are, many traditional Norwegian meals are seafood. Fiskeboller, for instance, is a familiar and easy everyday dish. Salmon and herring are quite popular. However, a farmer in the 1790s, living away from the coast? If he were a cattle farmer—we do have those—I imagine he would permit himself a healthy serving of beef, along with potatoes. If he were really ambitious he might cure his meat; that is, rub it with seasonings and let it sit for several days. Or he might dip into a supply of pork cured in brine. This would afford him a ready and hearty meal during the long, cold winter months. Appetizing? That is another story. But I don't know how much choice one's palate had in the 1790s.

Cursing? We pretty much stick to the basics in Norway. You needn't waste much imagination on that one. And to be honest I have no idea how a farmer in the 1793 would curse. Would they at all?

My, this is exciting: to be in at the ground floor of your creation, furthering it along. I have never worked with a novelist before. It is an actual thrill. If you have any other questions, just write. When I have time, I will reply. Promise.

Must go. Ha det, as we say.

Warm regards,

Grethe Westerleg

A substantial reply. And a friendly one. Hope! Possibility! My novel could live! I wrote her back immediately. No more questions, however. Not yet. Just a short, sincere thanks. I didn't want to scare her off. I would need her expertise. I glanced at two or three other emails and was set to exit the program. Then I saw a new message.

From: Grethe Westerleg
Subject: Re: Norwegian questions
Date: October 1, 2003 4:39 PM
To: paulm@uca.edu

Dear Paul,

So you are not furious with me for ignoring you. Good. I certainly meant no offense. And I am making it up to you, you'll notice, by writing back so quickly this time. I'm glad I decided to stick around and check my email. So how far are you on this novel? Are you almost done? May I see it when it's finished, as a professional courtesy? That sounds so cold doesn't it? I mean to say that I am very interested to read it, this new book about my home country, and I trust that you can pull it off. In the meantime, are there any other pressing questions you need answers for?

Warm regards,

Grethe

This was beyond what I could have hoped for when I sent out my straggling electronic missive all those weeks ago.

From: Paul Mullen
Subject: Re: Norwegian questions
Date: October 1, 2003, 6:40
To: grethew@uoregon.edu

Dear Grethe,

I can guarantee I'll have more questions for you--probably soon. Unfortunately, though, I have to report that I'm nowhere near finished the novel. In fact, I've only barely begun it. Even so,

I've been called to New York to discuss the manuscript with my agent. That's where I am now. She told me today that she conceives it as a Nordic survival tale. High adventure, perilous escapes, extreme solutions and all that. I suppose I see her point. And she's convinced a survival tale will sell. But I've never written an adventure book, much less a Jack London-ish, frozen north, man-against-nature thing. But I guess we'll see, won't we?

Hyggelig å treffe deg!

Paul

I waited a few moments. Sure enough, the reply came in.

From: Grethe Westerleg
Subject: Re: Norwegian questions
Date: October 1, 2003 4:40 PM
To: paulm@uca.edu

Dear Paul,

And hyggelig å treffe deg to you too! The feeling is certainly mutual.

In New York, you say, talking with your agent. Very good! I say trust her judgment. Your book will be a winner. What else does your agent report? Don't hurry along your story just for my sake, but I must that I can't wait to see how it turns out. So much more interesting than any paper I'm working on. Which at the moment happens to be none. I want a sabbatical too! (And I wouldn't mind New York either. So do, poor boy, enjoy it for both of us.)

Best,

Grethe

I would write Grethe a reply, but for the moment I went back to Google. I needed to check something that had been loitering in the back of my head since lunch. I typed "Thor Heyerdahl." Tons of hits. I examined the first.

You could have blown me away.

"Thor Heyerdahl is a world renowned explorer and archeologist. He was born in 1914, in Larvik, Norway."

Lolly was right. Somewhere in the restless recesses of her drug-dented brain, Lolly snared an improbable Norwegian connection. I skimmed ahead.

"While doing research on the origins of the island's animal life, the naturalist lived an otherwise traditional Polynesian life. During this time, he began to contemplate the existing theories of how South Pacific inhabitants reached the island."

Skim.

"Heyerdahl became convinced that human settlers had come with the ocean currents from the west just as the flora and fauna had done."

Interesting, but I skimmed ahead to a section titled **The Kon-Tiki Expedition** (1947).

"After the war, Heyerdahl continued his research, only to meet a wall of resistance to his theories amongst contemporary scholars. To add weight to his arguments, Heyerdahl decided to build a replica of the aboriginal balsa raft (named the 'Kon-tiki') to test his theories. In 1947, Heyerdahl and five companions left Callio, Peru and crossed 8000 km (4300 m) in 101 days to reach Polynesia. Despite skepticism, the seaworthiness of the aboriginal raft was thus proven and showed that the ancient Peruvians could have reached Polynesia in this manner."

Of course, this didn't have a thing to do with my story, but if Lolly could convince a publisher that Lars and Olga were half as exciting as Heyerdahl, we might net a contract. After all, *Kon-Tiki* was a major twentieth-century bestseller. It had gone through countless printings. One of my brothers read it for a class in high school. The old dog-eared paperback lived on my parents shelves for decades even as they accumulated and discarded yards of other books. On the front cover, the title—yellow letters in imitation ancient script—sat above a simple drawing of the sea, tiny black numerals in the right hand corner read 75¢; on the back, a black-and-white photo showed a furry bearded but strongly built man, bare to the waist, dressed in only a loincloth, gripping the mast of his vessel and staring magisterially at the ocean. More than just a publishing success, the book became a mid-century cultural phenomenon. It spawned hundreds of anthropological articles and arguments, a theatrical movie, documentary specials on American television, a BBC series, and rash of derring-do among amateur explorers who should have known better but, too hungry for fame, couldn't help themselves. One guy drowned trying to get from Australia to China in a canoe. If nothing else it made a celebrity of Heyerdahl, who went on to try other expeditions and write dozens more books. He reaped a treasure trove of awards by the time he died in 2002.

Finally, I went to Barnes & Noble.com. I did a site search for *Kon-Tiki*.

Result? "Will ship in 24 hours."

I did a search for my first book. "No copies available," it said. "Check our used and out of print store." At the used and out of print store, I found one listing, for a seller in New Mexico. His message? "Please get this thing off my hands. I'll take anything for it."

Kon-Tiki it was.

8

Wait a minute. Kon-Tiki. Kon-Tiki.
What?
Lolly is right.
I know. According to B & N—
No. She's right. Even more than she realizes.
Realizes what?
You've been stalled, haven't you?
I've been slow.
You've been stuck.
I wouldn't say—
You write like you're defusing a bomb.
I wouldn't say a bomb; not—
Too slow, trying not to—
the most constructive word, you know, in reference to a—
mess up. Besides—
book-in-progress. Especially one of your own.
You don't like any of those scenes, not even the fox one.
Lolly liked it.
You didn't like it. And I know why. A farm is dull.
It's not dull.
It's dull. Get your book off the farm.
? ? ?
I'm not falling for the deaf trick.
But that's my story: Two determined country folk confronting the savage—
Kon-Tiki.
? ? ?
Kon-Tiki.

I saw it: Starving, indigent, and utterly at wit's end, Lars and Olga walk thirty miles through the February cold and partial daylight to the Trondheim Fjord. On their underfed backs they carry a variety of supplies: rope, a small kettle, a hammer, nails, a piece of flint, the infamous axe, a few knives, their only gun, three blankets, a couple of cups. Along the way, they find a dead bird, they shoot a wolf and a raccoon. On the coast, they actually find edible vegetation. More important, they find a boat. Or, to be precise, they steal one. (It's all alone there, by the river, after all.) It's a fishing smack, just the right size: as long as two men laid end to end and barely half a body wide. It even comes with oars and a sail.

The next morning they drink their fill of frigid river water, then fill the few jugs they brought with them for supply. They pack their belongings on to the boat and by midmorning are water borne, headed to the mouth of the Trondeim, where they will take a southward turn and, far sooner then if they tried to manage it on foot—and with the waters around them as food supply—they will go as far as Stavanger on the southwest coast. If Stavanger proves unsuccessful, they will turn turn the corner on the southern coast and slam dead into Sweden. Which wouldn't be the worst fate in the world. Sweden, everyone knows, is fecund territory. They've heard the legends. It would be hard to find a better place to start all over again. If nothing else, they can cling to the coastline, feed off its marine life and its port cities, and, coming ashore when weather demands, last out the season on their craft.

Lars scoots them into the Trondheim, eager for the Norwegian Sea. He is convinced that the worst is over. Suffering and starvation are behind them, easier days ahead, inevitable as spring. But Lars is a farmer, not a sailor. And wind-driven water can be unpredictable. When their craft reaches the mouth of the Trondheim, it doesn't turn and hug the coast, but pushes out into open waters. Even as Lars resists with strenuous rowing, even though he lowers their tiny sail, the wind and the current nudge them north and west. Our heroes are not headed for Sweden but Iceland. 700 miles away.

Kon-Tiki, indeed.

TWO

9

I was on fire, pacing the Days Inn floor. My farm book would become an adventure book. Even a disaster book. What disaster book doesn't sell? Do you know, reader, of a disaster book that doesn't sell? I didn't. I allowed myself to imagine it: No more remainder bins. No more out-of-print book stores. No more nasty put-downs from Joy, she of one published academic tome. Maybe even—if I was exceptionally lucky—no more teaching. Did I dare think such a thing? *A permanent sabbatical?*

When I finally calmed down, I started a quick note to Grethe Westerleg. I'd only made it through the salutation when the phone rang. Who would be calling me at the hotel? Then I realized: Ryan's sitter. This could not be good. I lunged for the receiver.

"Yes?"

"Hey," a woman shouted, "guess where I am?"

My mouth was open but I wasn't speaking.

"Guess where I am!"

"Lolly?"

"Who did you think it was?"

"My babysitter."

She cackled raggedly until she was almost out of breath.

"That's really funny," she said.

"Why?"

"If you knew me."

"I do know you."

"Oh. Right. Guess where I am?"

"Norway."

"Hah! Funny." She stopped talking to laugh some more. It wasn't that funny. Clearly, Lolly had had a few. I heard conversation in the background, jazz music, a shout across a room.

"I'm at a party, stupid."

"You? I can't believe it."

She laughed more: knee-slapping, chopping guffaws. Okay, so she'd had more than a few.

"Isn't it Wednesday?" I said.

"What?"

"Why is there a party on a Wednesday?"

"I don't know. Somebody died."

"Somebody died, and there's a party?"

"Somebody took his place."

"So it's a coronation party."

"A what?"

"A *coronation*."

"Right," she said. She hadn't heard.

"How Russian of you."

"I'm not Russian."

"I don't mean you. I mean the idea—forget it."

"Yeah," she shouted.

"So it's a publishing party?"

"What?"

"It's a *publishing party*?"

"Guess who I just ran into."

"Tell me."

"What?"

"Tell me."

"*Stephen Morton*."

The name meant nothing to me.

"I said: Stephen Morton."

"Who's he?"

"Stephen Morton? The Philosopher King of Doubleday?"

"Philosopher King?" I said.

"Doubleday! And he likes your book!"

No one had seen my book yet, including me.

"I told him all about *Kon-Tiki* in Denmark, and he was floored."

Okay, so that was good news.

"So he wants to see it?"

"No, he wants to see you."

"Really."

"Yes."

"When?"

"Now."

"Now?"

"Get your butt out of Long Island City and down here."

"Where are you?"

"Oh, you know. Somewhere in the city."

"Where?"

"How should I know? We took a cab."

"Ask somebody."

"Just get down here, will you? Do me that one favor, writer-to-agent? You're not going to sell your book from Long Island City."

I thought she was supposed to sell my book.

"See you soon," she said.

"Wait!"

"What?"

"I still don't know where you are."

"I just told you," she said. She hung up.

Lolly called a half-hour later wanting to know what I was still doing at the Days Inn. Finally, she found the address. A half hour after that I was standing in a condo in Chelsea. For New York it was a pretty big place. For New York, mind you. And maintained in style: hardwood floors, Spartan yet expensive furniture, built-in book shelves, track lighting, signed limited series prints on the walls. About forty people were squeezed in: bumping elbows and nudging shoulders and touching rear ends and offering elaborate, lubricated apologies. It took me minutes to find Lolly. She was on a foggy green leather sofa pushed against the bookshelves in the back corner of the living room. She leaned far into the man sitting beside her, her right arm around his shoulders, her left dragging a glass of red wine behind her, her face half a foot from his. This guy was probably fifteen years younger than her, his face still chunky with baby fat, his hair cut short and then oiled into fashionable disarray. The severe, black glasses he wore were so out of character for the rest of his face they seemed fake. And the camel hair sweater vest he wore looked like it belonged to a sixty year old. (He did have a Mets t-shirt underneath, however; stylish in its disharmony.)

Behind those glasses his eyes studied Lolly with amusement, but also, it seemed, with half-drunken half-interest.

Lolly saw me.

"Paul," she shouted and jumped up. She pressed me against her. "You made it."

"I found it."

"Great!"

She pushed herself back to examine me fully. She weaved a moment before straightening.

"Am I interrupting?" I said.

She frowned. "No," she said torturously, as if still trying to understand my words even as she answered. "Oh. No." A short giggle. "No, no, no, no." She turned back to the man on the sofa. "Aidan, I need to speak with this guy for a moment. He's a client."

The young man held her glance for a moment, his lips curled in a bitten smile. Then he shrugged and took a swig of a yellow cocktail. His eyes skimmed the room. "I've got to find Lowenstein anyway." With that he stood and launched himself into the field of bodies.

"Sorry to interrupt," I said again.

"Don't be. He's nothing." She waved a hand at the figure of the disappearing Aidan. Her eyes didn't exactly communicate that he was a "nothing."

"Somebody important?"

"Him?" she said. "No, he's just a writer."

"Thanks, Lolly."

Her eyebrows went to the roof. She stabbed an index finger into me.

"You're a client. He's a writer. Big difference. I have no vested interest in him."

"Okay."

"His last book sold maybe 5,000 copies."

In other words, about four thousand nine hundred more than mine. But I didn't remind Lolly.

"Besides which, he doesn't have the ass you do." She slapped my rear and kissed the air. Then she drank more of her wine.

"What about this guy I'm supposed to meet."

Lolly practically spat out the mouthful.

"I almost forgot! Morton. Let's get him before he escapes."

She gripped my elbow and dragged me along behind her through the walls of people. I couldn't tell where we were going exactly. But I heard her apologizing every other second for bumping somebody new.

"Lolly—" I started.

"Morton's okay," she said over her shoulder. "A little prickly at times, but very enthusiastic when he really likes something. He'll stick to it and see it through. He won't give up. Not like some of these other punks. He's got real vis—" She stopped. She hopped halfway into the air. "There," she said.

"Where?"

"Kitchen."

Fine. Maybe I could get a beer.

Lolly leaned in and lowered her voice, but not all that much. "He is a little peculiar about his blow jobs. But that's not something you need to be concerned about."

I wanted to say "I hope not," but I'm not sure I got an answer out.

"He and I had a thing, you know, a few years back. An open secret in the biz. It was fun but, you know, c'est la vie and all. But I had to let it go. Not with a married man."

We started toward the kitchen, which I still couldn't see. We stopped.

"Of course, he's not married anymore. But I don't think I had anything to do with that. Don't make a face at me, Paulie. He had about a hundred girls at the same time. I don't mean the *same time*, you know. Nothing kinky. I mean during the same period. He could stick his johnny into a different hole every night of the week if he wanted. Which is pretty ironic, really, because it's about the size of a gummy worm. And just as squishy. Felt like I was chewing on a dead salamander. Come on."

Lolly pulled harder. A moment later we were in the kitchen. A man, fifty-five or so, with a graying crewcut hair and broad shoulders was doubled in laughter. The woman beside him—fortyish, her hair streaked with loud blonde gashes, the skin of her face so astricted she looked like a leathered skull or a campaign ad against the dangers of plastic surgery—was smiling with him, but not exactly laughing.

"Stephen?" Lolly said.

Morton stood straight; his laughter cut out. I saw that while barrel-chested and Marine-fit, the man was actually pretty short. And he wore glasses: small, severe, accusatory frames. He turned. "Hey, Lolly." A distinct pinch of disappointment showed on his face.

"This is Paul Mullen," Lolly said.

Morton examined me for a millisecond. "Good evening," he said. He turned back to the blonde-streaked woman, who offered Lolly a stiff, barbarous eye.

"Stephen," Lolly said. "This is Paul Mullen. You said you wanted to meet him."

Morton turned to me again, clearly confused.

Lolly spoke first: "I'm going to have to leave you boys alone, because if I don't pee right now there's going to be a mess. Back in a minute." As she stepped away, she rammed me in the side with her elbow. *There you go,* the elbow said. *Your big chance.*

Morton's expression evidenced abiding pain.

"What are you here for again?" He drank from a highball glass. Whatever was in it was clear.

"I'm in town to talk business with Lolly. She told me she had spoken to you about a book I'm working on."

I felt the crowded, noisy kitchen constrict, the air go cold around my throat. A ballast of wariness shifted on to Morton's face. The woman beside him rolled her eyes.

"You're a writer," he said, with unmistakable deadness.

"I am."

"Do I know your work?"

"You might. I published a book three years ago."

"With whom?"

I told him.

"What's the title?"

I told him that too. Something not good started in his eyes. He stared past me for a moment, to the end of the room—a desultory, hopeless gaze—then started to shake his head. He stopped himself mid-shake.

"I do know that book, actually. I haven't read it, but that's one a friend of mine worked on."

Against my better, warning instincts, I preened. After all, when the Philosopher King of Doubleday remembers your book.

"He said it was the biggest turkey they published in ten years. He couldn't believe they let that thing out into the market."

He said this with no inflection, with no apparent malice, as if he were relaying a score from a midseason baseball game.

"How did it do for you?" He looked me straight in the eyes.

"For a first novel, I was pretty well satisfied."

He held his stare, not letting me off the hook.

"For a first novel," he said.

"Yes."

"Because, you know, Paul Mullen, your book completely tanked. Editors with sales figures like that get fired. Publishers with sales figures like that go out of business."

I thought I should say something. But I couldn't imagine what.

"Where are you from?" he said.

"Central Arkansas."

His eyes widened. The woman openly smirked. She glanced at Morton eagerly, as if expecting him to dismantle me right there, with all the pitiless precision of a bullfighter. All by himself. No picadors required. And for nothing but the sport.

"I'm not following," he said. "Why are you standing here in front of me? Lolly told me about your book?"

At this point it was clear my agent had either misunderstood or vastly oversold whatever conversation she'd had with this man. Maybe Morton wasn't the man at all. Maybe it was someone else in this overcrowded cell of a Chelsea condo; maybe the heat and the crossed discussions and her professional desire twisted the facts around in Lolly's pickling brain. But she'd left for the bathroom, and here I was, holding the bag of her mistake, having to carry it through.

"She did," I started. "It's a novel that opens in Norway and becomes a kind of sea adventure. Lolly compares it to *Kon-Tiki*."

He glanced around the room. He shook his head.

"She did say something to me about *Kon-Tiki*. But the book we were talking about was set in Denmark."

"No, that's it. That's my novel. But it's Norway, not Denmark."

"My mother's from Denmark," he murmured. He stared at the floor.

"Really," I said. "I'm sure Denmark is a wonderful place."

His head came up.

"You've been to Denmark?"

"No, actually. But I'm aware of the reputation."

"That's not a substitute for actually going."

"Of course."

"Reputation means nothing. Reality is what counts."

"Yes, you're right."

"That's what I tell my people constantly."

He drank more of the clear liquid.

I tried one more time. "Is there anyone in your family from Norway?"

"No one. Denmark."

"Too bad. Since Norway is my subject I could have asked you a question or two."

Morton recoiled in undisguised horror. He turned his back to me, snagged the woman by the elbow and took a first step toward exiting the kitchen. That's when Lolly came back.

"How are you boys getting along?" she said, more than loud. Her eyes shone with a new yellow, her bangs—dewed with perspiration—curved around her forehead. She gripped my shoulders and squeezed, like a proud owner showing off a trophy.

Morton glared at her. He still had the other woman's elbow.

"All done talking about the book?" Lolly asked.

Morton smiled tightly.

"Paul is the star of my stable. I wouldn't trade him for a dozen Vonneguts."

Morton glanced at me, then at Lolly, a curt pity revealed behind those glasses.

"I'm sure that's the truth," he said.

"You won't want to miss his next one, Stephen. It's gonna rock your brain."

Morton studied her a second longer, the same damning expression in his eyes. "Sounds like a thriller," he said.

"*Kon-Tiki*," she said. "Remember."

He raised his glass, shifted his shoulders, and escaped, like a running back squirming through a slim hole in the line.

I turned on Lolly. For the first time in memory I was actually angry with her. "I thought you said he was excited about my book."

"He is. Didn't you see?"

"He said my first book was a turkey."

"It was!"

"And he showed no interest in this one, either. None."

"That's just Stephen," she said. "That's as excited as he gets. I was lucky to get a grunt out of him during a half-hour blow job. You know. Powers that be."

"He seemed more interested in not losing that woman."

Her eyes narrowed. "Who?'

"You know. Blondie."

"Her?" Lolly laughed, all the way up from her belly. "He's had her, Paulie. He can have her as much as he wants. She's the one who's got to work. Stephen Morton doesn't go chasing after anybody. You chase Stephen Morton. That's the world."

10

We stayed for another two hours. Lolly introduced me to a dozen more people none of whom made an impression, except they all seemed amused with how drunk she was. She drank more and ate nothing, and by the end she could barely hold herself upright when she sat on the couch.

"I think I want to go home," she said, and passed out. I had to get her a cab. Problem was, I didn't know where she lived. Somewhere in Brooklyn. She must have brought a bag or a purse or at least a wallet. But there was nothing on her, and except for her wine glass, I didn't recall her holding anything. I maneuvered my way to the bedroom and found about twenty coats dumped on the bed. I scrounged through them until I found one that looked like the coat Lolly put on when she was leaving the deli. In the armpit I found a small black change purse. It held a roll of ones, a few spare coins, a house key, and a driver's license. Hers.

"What are you doing?" she said, when I grabbed her arm and pushed it into the arm of her coat.

"You're going home."

"Oh," she said. "Good." She went back to sleep.

I pulled the coat around her back. I forced the other arm in. I didn't worry about the buttons.

It might have been funny if it hadn't been so difficult getting her to the elevator, down to the first floor, and through the lobby. Outside, I sat her on the curb. I positioned her head so it would stay on her knees. Then I started flailing my arms at every yellow car.

At Lolly's place, an ancient rowhouse in Brooklyn, long since converted to apartments (two per floor), I asked the guy to wait. I needed a ride back to Long Island City. He didn't say anything at first. Then he shrugged.

"Meter's running." He was a thick-faced white guy. Very pale. Very young. His chin was too big and his hair was trimmed too short, which only accented his acne.

"Of course," I spat. Moron.

It was enough to have to drag the passed-out Lolly from the cab, then to her building, then to keep her balanced while figuring which key worked in the bottom door. Then I'd have to get her into her own apartment. I didn't want to have to find a cabbie after all that. Securing Lolly's key in my hand, I had the sudden terrible thought that her license might not be current. This might not be her place at all. I'd look like a housebreaker.

She came out of the cab on my first yank, but carrying her to the door was like waltzing with cooked spaghetti. By the time I got to the door, my armpits were flooded; ropes of sweat stretched to my waist. My forehead felt hot. I pushed Lolly against the building and tried to pin her there with my left shoulder while I manipulated the key with my other hand. As soon as I took the necessary step toward the lock, she would fall.

"Hey," I heard from behind me. "I'll hold up the chick. You deal with the keys."

"Thanks," I said, meaning it.

"Don't worry about it. You're paying me."

Lolly's apartment, wouldn't you know, was on the third floor. Together the cabbie and I managed her up the narrow staircase. At the third floor landing, the cabbie held Lolly by the waist from behind while I found the right door.

"Pretty," he said, looking down at her. "Too bad she's stoned."

"I'm just a friend," I said.

He cracked a wiseguy smile. "Aren't we all?"

Whatever.

I worked the key in the lock and then held the apartment door open while the cabbie dragged Lolly in. Together we moved her to her sofa. I took her coat off and laid her down, pulling her legs straight. When I stood up, my lower back simmering with a low white heat, I took my first real look at the place. I breathed in sharply. This was even smaller than I thought, smaller than a grad student apartment. Technically, it had three rooms, but really they were just three spaces: a kitchen about the size of the half-bath in my house in Conway, most of which was taken up by a single small table; a slightly bigger living area adjacent to the kitchen—the sofa bed consumed about

2/3 of it—and a bathroom off the living room. From where I stood I couldn't tell if the bathroom was anything more than just a sink and toilet. For all of this she worked her tail off in the Big Apple?

The cabbie grew noticeably nervous, as soon as we put Lolly on her sofa.

"I'm going to wait in the car," he said and started backwards. "Come out when you're ready."

I nodded, not quite listening. I was too busy examining my agent's apartment. It was furnished in a sweet, functional way: some framed museum posters on the wall, a sleek black stereo system opposite the sofa, a few hanging houseplants, and one fatter one—a fruit tree—on the floor next to the stereo. A clean, cozy space but sad for how small it was, and sadder still when I realized that there were only two personal photos evident. Both sat atop a narrow square table pushed against the living room's "far" wall, underneath the only window in the apartment. One photo showed Lolly at some zoo riding a camel: her forehead balancing sunglasses, her hands gripping the animal's hump, her face offering the forced smile of someone trying out professional fun. The other photo showed Lolly at the bar in a foreign-looking pub. Her eyes were intent, her mouth open as if delivering instructions to the cameraman. I knew Lolly was no longer married, and these photos weren't that dated, but there was nothing in either picture to evidence any family at all. Or even friends. There was nothing to suggest that the photos were snapped by anyone other than obliging strangers.

I was at my gate in LaGuardia when my cell rang.

"How did I get home last night?" Her voice sounded hoarse and exhausted. No surprise.

"I took you."

"Great," she said, obviously not meaning it.

"No other option, I'm afraid."

"Someone at the party could have brought me back."

"I didn't know any of those people."

"I know. But it's embarrassing. This is my apartment, you know." She mused for a second. "Did I walk up the stairs?"

"Ah, no. You were not capable of that."

"You carried me?"

"Not quite. The cabbie helped."

"The cabbie? There was a cabbie in my apartment?"

"Yes. Nice guy."

"I bet he was some ape named Ahmed, wasn't he? All of them are named Ahmed. Or Ali. And they all stink."

"I don't know his name, actually."

She was silent a moment. Then: "Jesus."

"Next time you come back here," she said, "it will have to be under more favorable circumstances."

I tried to laugh, but I'm not sure that's the response she wanted.

"Okay," I said, "I'll remember that."

"Do," she said. The line went dead.

11

On the plane I began mapping disasters I could force onto Lars and Olga: storms, unexpected winds, boat butting monster fish, supplies gone overboard. My survival on land book would become a survival on water one as my heroes got pushed further westward into the Norwegian Sea. I began composing scenes, not in narrative order, just the ones I felt like writing. One I especially liked I finished it just as the captain's marbled voice sounded through the speaker system, telling us to raise our tray tables and prepare for the descent into Memphis International Airport. (Where I would change planes.) I inserted my last period just as a flight attendant bent her head over the shoulder of my seat. She stared with nervy blues eyes; then she wrinkled her nose. She might have been all of twenty-two. (I find the older ones—if not exactly the eye candy everyone still seems to expect from flight attendants these days—are not only more helpful and more forgiving, but far more content on the job.) The woman not only didn't approve of my still lowered tray table but looked at my notebook as if I were doing something contemptuous with it, even immoral. Ironically, with her skin pale as milk, her cheekbones thin as teacup handles, her hair—coifed into the frenzy of a carbonated ice cream drink but yellow as the Atlantic sand—she could have been a young, modern, well-fed Norwegian. A fisherman's daughter. Or a farmer's. Lars's great-great-great-great-great-great-granddaughter? *God dag*, I felt like saying. *Hvordan har du det?* Her nose would unwrinkle, her eyes go soft, the sides of her mouth curl upward in warm disbelief. She would spread her hands as if to welcome me to the New World. *Morn*, she would reply breathily. *Hyggelig å treffe deg*. I would nod meaningfully and explain: I am writing a book about your countrymen.

"Seat trays up," she said, in nasal Minnesota English.

"Just finishing."

"Up," she said, demonstrating with roof-thrusting thumb. "Now."

Those nervy blue eyes showed something else: a person at their wit's end, or just the end of a working day, ready for a fight.

"Okay," I said. I moved my notebook on to my lap and raised the table.

"And put away that thing. I don't want it flying around the cabin, clobbering someone. Probably be me."

I am going to show you the scene I finished on the plane, but first, a clarification: It was in fact my *paper* notebook open on the lowered tray table that scared this flight attendant, not my Macintosh Powerbook.

[Note from real author: Pardon this interruption of Paul's clarification but I just need to say that If I ever do make a trip to Long Island City—not just invent one for the sake of a novel— I'm going to search out if there really is a Days Inn there and if it's as underfurnished and barely comfortable as the one I described. The accomodational paucity worked for the scene of course, giving Paul an extra incentive, if he needed one, to ditch the hotel for a publishing party. But if you stay anywhere in and around Manhattan you're paying 50% more than the standard rate for your room. If I do that in rl I'm making sure there's at least a computer table. Of course, a real Days Inn wouldn't offer wireless internet access, even for a fee. Back to Paul.]

While the nervy-eyed stewardess was wrinkling her twenty-two year old nose at me, my Powerbook was safely stored under the seat in front of me, just as it was supposed to be. In fact, I hadn't used it all flight. The reasons for this were twofold: first, I don't like how laptops—even these days—call attention to themselves; i.e., it's impossible to work on them without everybody wondering what's up; second, and more crucially, as a barely reformed Luddite I compose all my first drafts with pen and paper and only then transfer them to computer.

[Real author redux: Not that it matters, but that statement is technically true only for Paul, not for me. You can bet your ass I'm not writing out department committee reports by hand.]

This despite the fact that I am all the time fighting to make sense of the chicken scratch which my handwriting becomes when I am in the white-hot throes of literary creation. Why do it this way? Especially since technology now exists where I can write longhand on an electronic notebook, which then converts the chicken scratch to immediately legible computer script? Why? Because scratching with a digital pen just ain't the same skin rush as scratching with a real pen on a real sheet of of pulp-made paper. Just say I'm an old hedonist and we'll call it even.

[Followup real author redux: Okay, I'll admit it. I actually have stayed nights in Long Island City; not in a hotel but in a Roman Catholic rectory, but that's a whole other story. Literally. Having been there, I'm almost positive there isn't a Days Inn in Long Island City. There is a Best Western, although I've never stayed there. I cannot say whether or not its rooms feature computer tables, comfortable beds or wireless internet access. I simply don't know. I'm not saying it doesn't. I'm saying I don't know. So don't sue me.]

The fourth day out from the Vestlandet coast, both Lars and Olga are supine on the bottom of their scraggly craft, adrift, keeping near a meager kettle fire.

"Husband," Olga says.

"What?" Lars forces the word out.

"I should have let you kill me. Back at the house."

"Mmmm," he says.

"Maybe you should push me over. Right now."

"Over," he says.

"The water."

"The water?"

"I am almost frozen anyway."

Lars says nothing. His mind knows what he should ask her: *Instead of pushing you over, may I stab you? At least that way I would have some meat around.*

But he says nothing. He hears Olga make a gurgling noise. Then a long sigh. He stares up at the endless gray of the sky, no blue to ever divide the clouds, no sun to pull them into private swatches. Only the gray, the gray, the gray, hour after hour. A muscular streak flies across his face at eye level, shooting sea water into his eyes.

"Hey."

Lars sits up, only to be smacked in the head by a twelve-inch flying fish. It lands squirming and slippery in his lap. Then another, directly atop the first.

"Gross," he says.

He grabs both fish by their necks the fish and holds them away from his lap.

"What?" Olga sighs dimly.

"Fish," Lars says.

Olga sits up. "Fish?" she says, a spark in her eye.

Lars stares at what he is holding. The creatures flap in his hands; they try to bend their working, living mouths, eager as bear traps. Lars looks at Olga. He smiles. "Fish," he announces.

Ten minutes later they are supine again, savoring the sweet smoke and flesh aftertaste of cooked fish, one animal apiece. The lumpish mass of that newly in their stomachs. The air is still frigid, the sky is still gray, the water stretches on for fathoms with no sign of a coast. They take what little comfort they can from their pitiful kettle fire. But neither sighs. Neither asks to be pushed overboard. Neither daydreams of murder.

As I walked through the Memphis airport to my new gate, Little Rock bound, I kept thinking of Lars and Olga out their on the Norwegian Sea in late February. I thought about exposure, cold water, winter air. *Kon-Tiki* happened in the Pacific. My book couldn't just be *Kon-Tiki* but needed to be *Stranded* as well. Does anyone remember that scandalous mid-70s nonfiction bestseller? About a group of people—a ski team?—trapped on a wintry mountain after their plane crashed. After a time, faced with starvation, they realized they were going to have to make use of the only food source available to them: the bodies of their dead comrades. Yes, eat them they did. And they survived to tell the tale. In fact, I remember seeing the book's two authors doing a tv promo gig, on *The Mike Douglas Show*. Even though I was a kid I was fascinated—in an appalled way—by their story. A similar danger must need hover over Lars and Olga for the whole of my story: not the danger of Pacific typhoons but of crying northern stomachs and aching, tired, food-starved limbs. How could I keep Lars and Olga believably alive on the water in winter? Fire, fire was the key. Hey, there's a drama, I thought. They have a small supply of kindling which must be kept dry. Pretty hard when you are out on the ocean. Maybe they should fight over when to restore the fire and when not. How long to preserve the kindling and when to spend it for immediately life's sake. The flying fish meal was cooked on the extant, low-level murmuring kettle fire. But would such a fire be sufficient to cook two flying fish? Would they even care if the fish were cooked? They are starving after all. And just how cold is it on the open water between Norway and Iceland in late February? More questions for Grethe Westerleg.

Of course, the whole point of a survival story is to stress your heroes past the point of believability, to put them in situations worse than imaginable, that are too difficult for even the reader to vicariously endure. Every true survival story strains credibility. That's because the limits of human fortitude and human ingenuity, and human stupidity, are far broader than we realize. Astonishingly broad. Survival narratives evoke those broad limits even while giving us pause, making us ask "No one could really survive that, could they?" Well, yes, apparently they can. But here's the thing. The big, sexy, cheesy, lurid, sensationalistic element in *Stranded*, what drove all of its sales, was cannibalism. And that tied directly into my story, as much as did *Kon-Tiki*. In that instant, afoot through Memphis International airport, my story clarified itself even further, and provided an even better, sexier, future sales pitch: It would be *Stranded* onboard Kon-tiki.

I thought I should eat something before I reached my gate. I had a few minutes, and they sure weren't going to feed me anything on the flight to Little Rock. The first sign I saw caught my attention. The Northern Grill. The menu board just below it brought me to a halt. Bordered by cartoon caricatures of dancing salmon, sunbathing cod, ice fishing pike, and soccer playing perch, a dozen varieties of the house favorite was listed: grilled fish. I saw on the grill mountains of sliced vegetables—

yellow squash, eggplant, zucchini, white onion—side by side with the stars of the show: slabs of red and white fish meat smoking up a marinated storm, gradually turning tender gray inside, the combined muster of scents so brilliant it nearly lifted me off my toes.

12

After I got back from New York, I wrote Grethe with the news: I wasn't writing a farm book, but a sea book. And I might need a little more help from her. I included a few examples: Could any old Norwegian farmer operate a water craft? Would a Norwegian want his fish cooked over a fire, or would he eat it raw out of the ocean? How cold is it on the Norwegian Sea in winter? Could one actually get knocked off course, all the way to Iceland? I half expected she wouldn't reply, at least not right away, now that I was becoming an information leech.

Surprise. She wrote immediately. Didn't she have courses to teach?

From: Greta Westerleg
Subject: Re: More Norwegian questions
Date: October 3, 2003 9:19 AM
To: paulm@uca.edu

Dear Paul,

A sea tale now! This gets only crazier and crazier. Yet all the more intriguing. However, I must point out that I am not a sailor any more than I am a farmer. I cannot tell you the average temperature in February on the Norwegian Sea. Are there not reference books and charts in which to discover that sort of information? It is certainly cold. I can tell you that. My family would never have found itself on the Norwegian Sea at that or any time of year. (We were shamefully city-bound people.) That said, I expect one could get blown off course to Iceland from Vestlandet. The Vikings famously went west, after all. They must have been assisted by the winds. While you are searching for information on sea temperatures make sure to search as well for "Wind Currents."

The fish? Sounds to me like your poor hero would eat the fish any way he could get it. But for what it's worth: No, I tell you,

Norwegians are not "above" eating their fish raw. Though we are hardly so celebrated at it as the Japanese, some traditional Norwegian dishes feature uncooked fish. On the other hand, if there is a comfort fire on board already . . . So you are fine either way. Let him cook it or let him eat it raw as suits you. You say he is on a stolen boat? Like a fishing boat? Our infamous Scandinavian explorers set out on much bigger boats, with many men, but this does not mean it isn't possible to head out in a smaller. Of course, no Norwegian farmer I know would want to. Most would rather die trying to keep the farm going. On the other hand, who is to say that one Norwegian farmer—in worst desperation—would not try to? That's the only relevant question, isn't it? Who wants to read about what's normal anyway?

By the way, you might find this interesting. When I was a girl in Oslo we used to tell Swedish farmer jokes. I thought they were clever until I came over here and was shocked to find that Americans told the same jokes about the Polish. (There's a question for *you* to answer: How many Poles are there in this country anyway? It does not seem to me to be a high number. So why are you persecuting them with these jokes?)

I am so interested in your crazy book. Can you tell me more about yourself? Why Norway? Are you Norwegian-American? (From your questions, and your last name, I guess not.) Have you always lived in Arkansas? From what I gather, Arkansas is to many Americans what the Poles in Polish jokes are. Correct? I mentioned to one colleague that I had received an interesting e-mail from Arkansas. She said "Arkansas? Do they have electricity now?" Sadly, I almost think she was not joking.

Write more. I want to know more about this increasingly fabulous tale. And you can click on the link below to see my picture on my UO faculty page. Since I've seen your picture it's only fair that you get to see mine.

Bye now.

Grethe

http://darkwing.uoregon.edu/~polisci/php/webpage.php?Grethe_Westerleg

She must have gone to the College of Fine Arts web site. Natural curiosity, I guess. Although it wouldn't have occurred to me to track down her's. I cringed thinking of what she saw. The picture had been taken by the dean's secretary five years earlier, in a rush between classes: my hair a mess, a scab on my nostril from a shaving mishap, a sloppy pelt of a beard I could never get to sit still on my face no matter how often I trimmed it. Worse, the dean's secretary had focused the camera to within an inch of my head and kept exhorting me to smile, so that my teeth occupied the whole center portion of the picture. I looked like a harried, graying beaver. When I finally eliminated that beard I thought about insisting on a new picture, but with only more gray in my hair and the same secretary still behind the helm, I feared the next one could be worse.

The good news was that Grethe liked my sea novel idea. I had an official endorsement from an official Norwegian. She didn't report me to the Scandinavian Cultural Police. She didn't jump me for trying to tell a story that I, as an American, didn't own. Of course, she'd been over here a while so maybe she wasn't the best representative of the Norwegian Street. How would her countrymen feel? Then I heard Lolly. *Who cares? Are we counting on them to buy this book?*

I hit the link and a second later there was Grethe: a blonde-brown woman, forty or so, with an angular face and almost severe short hair that, from a slightly left of center part, fell evenly on both sides of her face. But she wore a big toothy smile and an enthusiastic, even determined, glint in her eye. Someone you could imagine who would get up at 5 am and go jump in an icy river for stimulation, or run a marathon every month, or backpack on weekends through mountain ranges. A mind-over-matter person, a person who believed in using every one of a day's twenty-four hours. Also, a person kind enough to set aside the ordinary busyness of college teaching and research to answer two emails from a stranger in Arkansas. I hit on the page's email link.

From: Paul Mullen
Subject: Thanks
Date: October 3, 2003 11:32 AM
To: grethew@uoregon.edu

Grethe,

Thanks for your comments. I'm going to try to make my book the most thrilling Norwegian-farmer-turned-amateur-sailor-and-maybe-cannibal sea adventure I can. And thanks for caring enough to check out my picture. Truly a despicable portrait. Apparently, it didn't make you run into the woods and scream, as it does me. I looked at yours. What a nice photo. You look so happy. Good to see in a profession like ours, filled with so many crabby, disappointed, needy people. Do you mind if I write you with some other questions? I promised not to bug, but I might need to beg.

Paul

She replied instantly.

From: Grethe Westerleg
Subject: Re: Thanks
Date: October 3, 2003 9:33 AM
To: paulm@uca.edu

Paul,

Your picture is fine. I might even say adorable. Such the writer: the searching, hoping look, your thoughts on some subject two or five or ten steps ahead, not on the silly cameraman and his machine. It's perfect. Mine is fine, I guess. It shows me as I am.

Happy? I suppose. Not because my life is more pleasant than anyone else's, but because I see no point in wasting time being morose. I surely have better things to do. I do have bad days and I do miss home (I mean Norway) sometimes. But Oregon is lovely wilderness country: beautiful green timberland, not unlike home actually. It definitely makes up for the loss. And, really, after so many years, Oregon is my home. When I visit my parents and I say "home" to them I mean Eugene. When I first said that they both winced, but now they accept it. At least, they understand why I am here and stay here. They are proud that I have made a success for myself. They boast about me to friends.

Speaking of home, how often do you leave yours? For instance, to travel west? The next time you visit Oregon, ring me or email me or just knock on my office door. I'll make you some lovely ludefisk and we will discuss your project.

Ha det,

Grethe

Whoa, an invitation to Oregon. This was happening fast. I went back to her photo and looked more studiously. Her hair, browning and flattening as she moved into middle age, was nonetheless supremely straight and fine spun. As someone who struggled through the long-haired 1970s trying to tame an untamable mop—hair that grew out and around and over and back in as much as it did down—I have always regarded hair that falls downward without trouble as a cause for wonder. I looked into the eager brightness of Grethe's photographed eyes, those eyes full of information and impressions and longing for a place I didn't know except for a dated Britannica article, a few web sites, *Summer Vacation 3rd Grade*, and the 1994 Winter Olympics. For the first time since I began this unlikely tale I wondered what I was getting myself into.

13

    Olga lays supine on the floor of the boat, shivering within a muddle of thin blankets grown so damp they as likely to kill her as save her. Lars, after catching another fish the day before—two in a row—has more strength but Olga has turned suddenly ill. She could eat only a bite or two of fish before she vomited over the side. Now her face is a frightfully deep rouge color, nothing like the bright, shocking burns she gets in winter from the wind and summer from the sun. This red is deep and troubled and indwelling, speaking of some crisis within her body. She sweats with fever, shivers, lurches with heaves that bring up nothing. For the first time this winter, Lars considers the possibility that his wife will be taken first. He will be required to live on, to carry the memory of this erratic, terrifying time, the exact result he tried for when he lifted the axe above her head in their cabin. Now he can't imagine ever hoping for that. Olga might be dead soon. The thought shocks him and makes him deny it. It comes back: She might be dead soon. Lars is no doctor. Nor does he have anything in the way of medicine to give her. His only hope is her body itself, its determination, its innate ability to survive an invasion of chills, fever, nausea. Not just survive but overcome. In the freezing cold of the Norwegian Sea, this seems a supremely small hope to rest one's hopes on.

    Lars sits on the rower's bench and listlessly pushes the oars through the water. The wind picks up and slices the back of his neck, the side of his face, jutting the small craft forward again. He sees nothing but the broad gray expanse of water, cut up into triangles by the current. Lars is no navigator either but studying the stars and observing the passage of the sun through the bone cold days, he guesses that they are still on a rough course for Iceland. If their bodies can hold out, if he can catch fish every day or two, if the pitiful vessel is not overwhelmed by waves, and if the current does not change, they might eventually see the shores of that country. Another small, thin hope as hopeless—even more so—than counting on Olga's body to beat off her current torture. They might miss Iceland altogether. If they miss Iceland, he decides, he'll shoot himself. Already he does not know if he can endure this freezing cold and wet journey even to Iceland. He cannot imagine suffering even longer than that, past that, especially if his wife is no longer with him.

The boat jitters beneath him and Lars nearly falls into the sea. It jitters again. No, it shudders. Up and forward, as if being pushed from below. But by what? Again. Lars falls to the floor; he grips any piece of wood he can and holds tight. The craft is bumped again—twice—thrice—from below. *Something is down there.* The boat is lifted six inches into the air and falls down on the hard water, jostling the bones within his weathered skin, making his upper teeth collide with his lower. The impact is so sudden and so hard that Olga's near-death jellied eyes open into glutinous, half-conscious confusion; her mouth tattooed into an O. Her body has shifted to the farthest end of the craft, jammed up against the bow. Her hands wave lamely in an attempt to grab something, support herself. Lars, however, has no time to succor his wife. He reaches for the gun, which happens to be newly lodged against Olga's hip, and for the knife inside his belt. Whatever creature it is that threatens them, it will have to be vulnerable to these weapons. They are the only weapons he has.

The boat is bumped again, almost rising off the water but not quite. Rushed, Lars aims his loaded weapon at a huge, black swimming body and fires. The wad of shot scatters in frenzied futility, taking chips off the boat and whisking the top of the ocean. The chips settle lightly atop the water and bob with the beat of the wave. Lars is about to reload when he notices a new damp, bright red spot growing on Olga's blanket. He abandons the gun and maneuvers himself forward to where Olga is. He pulls back the blanket and then tugs her dress over her waist. He sees it: a coin-sized flesh wound oozing with the fresh slimy pulse of blood. A hunk of her skin has been turned back, like knifed fish flesh.

"Wife!" Lars calls to no real response, only a stunned whimpering. He cuts a swath of cloth out of the bottom of her dress, then another. He wads up one swath to make a bandage, the other he ties around her waist to hold the bandage in place. Olga begins to make more noise: sharp, pained noises. "No," she says distinctly.

"No what, darling?"

"I don't want that."

"I'm so sorry, darling. I must. I accidentally shot you."

"No!" she says with one high-pitched breath, which exhausts the rest of her energy. And then Lars understands. The bandage is hurting her. A second later, he realizes why. The sea salt on the bandage is pressing into her wound, as starkly as metal. He wonders if his shirt would be any less coated. He takes off her bandage, cuts new ones from his own clothes and applies those, but more loosely this time, so loosely it is only barely stopping the flow. He rests on his leg and waits to see the results. Olga says nothing, but she does not look as if she could if she wanted to. She is breathing shallowly: her eyes closed, her red-sickened cheeks gathered into a grimace, her body newly limp. At least she does not scream. After a minute, he tightens the dressing and settles back again. The grimace loosens on Olga's cheeks, drops to a simple, spent hopelessness. Her breathing becomes less noticeably shallow. Her head falls to the side, like a woman moving in sleep. He watches her closely for seconds to make sure she has not died. Her chest rises. It falls. This happens repeatedly. Finally, his own head drops. He sits back. He breathes out. Apparently, miraculously, she has survived. At least for now. Then he realizes something else. He turns and studies anew the sea rolling under their little craft. The attacking monster—whatever it is—is gone.

[Hey, R.A. again. You may or may not have been as enthralled by that last scene as Paul was when we wrote it. But please do realize what he's up to. He's just playing the novel-writing game: get your characters in deep and then deeper doo-doo. (Okay, if you want I can get academic—i.e., "introduce new dramatic tensions before the old ones have had a chance to be resolved"—but I think "deep and deeper doo-doo" says it way more efficiently.) Make the reader sweat, make him thrill, make him scared. As novelist/editor/agent Sol Stein is fond of saying, reading is the one state of existence in which someone *wants* to be made to feel uncomfortable. It's that feeling of discomfort, fully maximized before it is resolved, that makes one slap down a book and finally say "Wow! Great read! Okay so this advice is coming from Sol Stein, who can be hard to take, but when you think about it, isn't he speaking the truth? A book that doesn't make you feel uncomfortable is a book that goes nowhere. You can analyze such a book for flaws in characterization and/or dialogue and/or language and/or scene construction and/or scene organization and/or thematic breadth and uncover all sorts of real weaknesses; but underscoring all those weaknesses is the fact that reader is not being made to feel anything. And that may be because, quite simply, not enough is going on.

So, instead: Get your characters in hot water (or in Paul's case, cold) and then make it hotter (in Paul's case, colder). Then make it even more hotter. (In Paul's—well, you get the idea). And hotter. And hotter. And . . . so on. Don't resolve anything until the book can't go on anymore. Don't worry about making your book "important;" do not, under capital threat, include any philosophical pronouncements, either by the characters or the narrator—especially not by the narrator—and don't you dare try to dump upon the poor reader any gloomy bouts of introspective psychologizing. Nobody wants to hear it. And nobody needs to hear it. In short: the more you try to make your book "important" the more it will become a piece of derivative, self-important, self-satisfied shit. Anything "important" you have to say is all clichéd anyway, said by a million other people in a million other sources. Don't believe me? Write your own "important" ponderous novel and see for yourself. What you DO need to worry about as a fiction writer is very simple and at the same time very hard: *make stuff happen.* And then: *make more stuff happen.* In case you are one of those souls who curse genre-fiction—and let me tell you I'm usually one of them too—I don't see the realization of this lesson in any cheesily contrived, plot-heavy, character-thin cowboy tale or horror novel or the latest top-selling fantasy trilogy. I see proof of this lesson in Richard Russo, as mimetically realistic a literary writer as we have in this country. No author loves his characters as much as Russo does, and yet no other author makes his characters suffer so vigorously and unstoppingly and—ah, here it is, folks—*entertainingly.* Because, when it comes to reading, aren't we the most entertained when we just can't take the tension anymore?

Don't believe me? Read *Nobody's Fool* or *Risk Pool* or *Straight Man*. Then we can talk.]

Idiot.
What?
This is winter, in the Norwegian Sea.
So?
"In December and January the sun never rises."
But that's Nord-Norge. They took off from Trondelag.
Close enough.
I don't know.
Close enough! Can you at least check your map?
I don't have one.
Don't you think you should?
I don't feel like paying for one. I'm poor enough already.
What about online maps? Point, click, and print.
The free ones suck. They don't tell you anything.
What about Ryan's globe?
Ah! I passed by that thing so often in his bedroom I'd stopped seeing it. Now I went to look at it (and move it permanently to my study). Turned out that Trondelag was only barely removed from the boundary line of the Arctic Circle. Crud.

Except it's not December or January. It's February. I pushed the date back, remember, so that it would even be more likely that they would be at the end of their wits.

It's early February.

It's February.

It's not like the sun magically billows because you turn a page on the calendar.

All right, so I'll make it late February, almost March. There might be some tiny quotient of light sometime during the day on the Norwegian sea. Daylight to catch a fish. Or shoot a monster.

Maybe, but I doubt it.

What should I do then?

Hell, just ignore it. You can't have Lars and Olga sailing around in the dark.

Ignore it?

Not for a whole book.

Ignore it?

Ignore it and hope no one notices. Besides, as long as you have enough sun for one scene a day . . .

The sun wasn't my only problem, either. There was the issue of guns again. Exactly what kind of gun would a seventeenth century Norwegian farmer carry? I knew from I don't know where that during the American Revolution, 1775-1783, our soldiers used flintlocks. I suppose I could borrow one of those for Lars, but that brings up another issue. The flintlock, like any rifle of the age, was a single shot weapon. It required the user to reload after every discharge. That means gunpowder and paper. (The rifle itself, I recalled, provided the spark.) The flintlock had a straight, uniform, and relatively narrow barrel. But I remembered pictures of other, older, rifles, rifles in which the barrel expanded like a trumpet mouth at the end. This made for an impressive, eye-catching shape—a great gun to be holding on to for your portrait, for instance—but in terms of marksmanship all such a gun would do is scatter a large quantity of shot broadly. It couldn't invest hope in the utility of any single bullet because the gun was incapable of aiming any single bullet. Suppose this is the gun Lars brings on board with him. Maybe he inherited the outdated device from his father or a friend; it's a heritage piece and—as a committed pacifist if also a potential murderer and cannibal—the only gun he owns. Which also explains why he's lousy with it. And if this gun tends to scatter its shot wouldn't it be possible, even likely, that someone close by could get accidentally hit; even someone whom the shooter especially would not want to be hit, someone precisely like Olga? My thrilling adventure scene was becoming more plausible by the minute. But it depended on that gun being plausible. Other questions: 1) Is it humanly possible Lars or his father or his friend would ever own such a weapon? 2) Would it still fire after being on a boat for a week?

I'd have to do some quick research on guns. I could write Grethe, but she'd probably just repeat that she wasn't a gun expert. I could go to the library for a book on guns; in this state there were surely plenty of those to be found. I could go back to trusty old Britannica. Or I could Google again.

[Me again. FYI, I confronted similar research questions in grad school when I was writing a short story set in the 1660s. In one scene my solider-protagonist puts a pistol to his head and almost decides to pull the trigger. After I wrote the scene it occurred to me that I didn't know if pistols even existed in the 1660s. So I looked up "Guns" in whatever encyclopedia the school library happened to favor, probably Britannica. To my surprise, I discovered that the pistol was not only extant in the 1660s but as far back as the 1590s. I walked back to my apartment relieved and energized—armed, if you will—with historical possibility. And lest you think I was being too nitpicky toward my own story, that no one would care, I should tell you that workshop discussion about my story was not five minutes old before one young woman, at most twenty-four years of age, a short chunky fireplug of a girl—with both a babyface and a commitment to the lore of witchcraft—narrowed her eyes and scolded breathily: "Did they even *have* pistols back then?" I paused for greatest possible effect, and only barely suppressing my victorious contempt, I smiled and said: "Yes. I looked it up." You don't want to miss opportunities like that. Especially if it makes your story better.]

I had an excuse to write Grethe if I wanted one. But I went first to good old bound Britannica. (A handy excuse for not writing one afternoon.) Macropedia, of course. The only one worth reading. But, horror of horrors, it failed me! First, I tried plain old "Guns." Nothing. I tried "Rifles." Nothing. I tried "Weapons" and found a brief reference to rifles under "Weapons of War." No good. For the first time I was forced to abandon Britannica. In its defense, I should say that I also came up empty in Colliers and World Book. (But surely that must be a cold comfort for EB. No one expects Colliers and World Book to rival Britannica.) Not surprisingly, given the subject matter, I finally found information in Encyclopedia Americana under "Small Arms." But not that much really. All it told me was that for the time period in question the muzzleloading flintlock would have been the common rifle of the day—about the only rifle, really. The article included pictures of five different rifles, two of which dated from 1770: a "Brown Bess" which was the principal firearm of the British army for decades, and a Kentucky flintlock, a long, lean-barreled thing that looked exactly like what you'd expect Daniel Boone to carry. But Daniel Boone was in Kentucky, not Norway.

Back home I Googled and sure enough found a reasonably informative About.com article. Problem is, it pretty much said the same thing as Encyclopedia Americana: all rifles of the period would have been known as muskets, and almost certainly would have been a flintlock musket. Did I make up that image of a rifle with a fat, wide trumpet of a mouth? I swore I remembered—from my research on guns back in grad school—seeing a picture with a curved barrel and the big fluted mouth. But so far I'd found neither picture nor reference to such a weapon. It did tell me, though, that some flintlocks had multiple barrels. If I gave Lars a double-barreled flintlock that might allow for some extra measure of chaos. I decided to try one more site on the Google list. Wikipedia. When I used to teach Academic Writing and Research (gag) at UCA, Wikipedia was a favorite of my students, so much the favorite that a whole host of them failed for plagiarizing. But I'd never used it myself. It was rough going at first trying to wade through a sea, pardon the pun, of surprisingly technical information. I hit **Long Guns** and then a link to **Rifles** and then **Muskets**. Nothing I especially wanted to use. I went back to **Rifles** and read a little further. It discussed **Shotguns**. Hmmm. "A rifle has a rifled barrel that fires single bullets while a shotgun fires packets of shot, a single slug, or a specialty round." Eureka! That explains why I'd only been finding info on muskets under **Rifle**. A shotgun isn't a rifle. Who knew? I read on and it got better: "Rifles are often built for accuracy and long range . . . while **shotguns** are usually designed to quickly hit a moving target." Exactly! That's just what poor Lars is trying to do: *hit a moving target at close range* . A shotgun is precisely what he would want, besides the fact that the *packet of shot* would allow for the calamity of him hitting Olga. So a shotgun it was. But wait! Here came the characteristic nitpicking fear of historical-researching creative writers. Would shotguns have been available to farmers back in the late 1700s? (I didn't give a damn whether they were common or not, just that they be theoretically available.) I hit the link to **Shotguns** with as much dread as hope. Not much there. But I found a link to **History**. Okay, here goes. Right off the bat, I found the most beautiful sentence in the world. "Shot guns have also been referred to as 'scatterguns,' 'fowling pieces,' or 'two-shoot guns' historically, and were used as a replacement for the **blunderbuss**." A blunderbuss! I felt the surge of cozy synchronistic excitement at the long delayed reward now coming true. A *blunderbuss*. That's the gun I was originally imagining, and indeed here it was: not only actual, but a relative of the modern shotgun. The link to blunderbuss showed me a picture and referred to its "flared, trumpet-like barrel." Was it available in the 18th century? Hah! It was available in the 17th! The blunderbuss was a favorite, Wikipedia told me, of our pilgrim fathers, who of course came from Europe. And Europe, of course, includes Norway. So there. What's more, the actual term "shotgun" was unknown before 1776, a mere 17 years before the action of my novel happens. So it seems not only convenient but likely—likely!—that a blunderbuss, rather than a modern shotgun would have been the weapon found in Lars's hungry little hands.

Problem solved. A good day's work. I might even write Grethe to tell her.

14

One day, midday, about three weeks before Christmas, I was alone in my study. Another regular day of another regular week. I'd had lunch and reread the paper. I'd retrieved and sorted through my mail. I'd made every call I'd had to make, sent every required e-message. There seemed to be nothing else to do but actually get back to work. To that end, my notebook was open and my computer on. But I just wasn't ready to tackle the next spine-tingling Lars and Olga episode. Even as I felt the working minutes evaporate into nevermore, I did nothing but stare out my study window. The morning's fog had long since burnt off, clearing the picture of day outside. I saw the usual ring of trees—all but bare now—at the edge of our development, my neighbor's ugly brown house up the street, the gravely "pavement" that is our street, the red brick tower of my own mailbox, my winter-yellow and hopelessly underachieving lawn, presently being chewed on by a fat brown rabbit who would leave gifts of shit pellets for me to step on the next time I was out there.

The phone rang.

"What are you doing?" Lolly said.

"I'm wondering how easy it would have been to fire a blunderbuss from a fishing boat on the Norwegian Sea in 1793."

"No, I'm serious."

"So am I."

She made a windy noise through her teeth.

"I'm glad you're the writer and not me."

"So am I."

She hesitated. "I'll take that as a compliment, although I don't know if I should."

"You should," I said. "By all means."

Silence.

"Someone's in a mood today."

"A mood?"

"How is the story coming? We do have interest, you know."

"Stephen Morton?"

"Stephen Morton maybe. Look, don't write him off. I know you two weren't lovebirds at that soiree. But, understand, he's famously an asshole at parties, especially at parties where writers congregate. He likes to show off the power he has over them. He has the power to put them in print or not. He likes to remind them of that once in a while. It has nothing to do with whether he likes you or likes your work. In fact, if you haven't been insulted by him that's when you really need to worry. Because that means you're not worth his time."

I tried to remember if he had actually insulted me or not. Seemed to me he just rolled his eyes and tried to get away.

"Lolly, that's the most inventive spin I've ever heard on a completely humiliating conversation."

She issued a cynical chortle.

"I'm not an agent for nothing, babe."

"No, you're not."

"How's your story? Are you done yet?"

"Done?"

"Yes. Done. I'm here in the capital of the publishing world telling everyone I'm sitting on the next *Kon-Tiki*. I want to show them."

"We decided on *Kon-Tiki* only a couple months ago."

"A couple months is a couple months."

"A couple months is short in novel-writing time."

"A couple months is forever in agent time. A day is a long time in my world, Paulie."

"I'm not done."

"So where are they?"

"They're in the Norwegian Sea shooting guns at hostile fish."

"Guns are good."

"I'm wondering if I should make it an orca. I don't know of any other big fish you might find in cold waters."

"An orca isn't a fish, Paulie."

"You know what I mean."

"I'm just saying."

"You know what I mean."

"You don't want every first grade teacher in the country writing you saying that a writer ought to know the difference between a fish and a sea mammal."

"Lolly—"

"Teachers buy books, Paulie. They buy them and they read them and they form those cute little reading clubs out in the hinterlands."

"Fine."

"And those clubs buy a lot of books, if you don't know. Books of your type."

"My type?"

"You know. Highbrow."

"I'm just trying to tell a story, Lolly. There's nothing highbrow about it."

"Fine—whatever—but don't piss off the teachers."

"I won't!"

"We need them to buy *Kon-Tiki*. Your *Kon-Tiki*."

"We need everyone to buy it."

"Now you're talking my language. So what else is happening novel-wise?"

"His wife is about to die from sickness and an accidental shooting."

"Ooh, better! Why accidental?"

"He was aiming at the fish."

"Whale, Paulie!"

I thought back to my short stay in New York: the roiling traffic around LaGuardia, the swarm of bodies on the sidewalk outside Stage Deli, the fight to get a taxi, the toe to toe battle of cars and pedestrians for ownership of the street. And for Lolly there was so much more: getting up before dawn to paint and powder and outfit herself; the jammed morning subway rush, elbow to elbow with strangers, one of whom spills Starbuck's on her purse; in the office, hours of e-mailing and letter writing and telephoning and negotiating and cajoling and power lunching; or working through lunch to have a hope to get away before six so she can get to that stack of manuscripts piled up at home; the jammed subway again, elbow to elbow again, someone's briefcase eating into her shoulder blade; the fight to get off at her stop, the walk to her building, the three flights of stairs, finally into that sorry warren of a Brooklyn apartment. For her, a day *was* a long time.

"It'll be months before I'm done, Lolly. I'm sorry."

She emitted a sharp, groin-deep sound. For a second, I thought she might have cut herself. "You slay me with sincerity, Mr. Sweetcheeks. I swear, it's the sexiest thing. Do you know how many people ever apologize to me?"

"How many?"

"Zero. Especially not my husband. Ex-husband."

"Really. I'm sorry about that."

"Hah! Now that one was fake."

"How could you tell?"

"Are you kidding? I've got a nose like a bloodhound for disingenuous male reaction. It's a survival instinct for a single woman in this town."

"I can imagine."

"So you're saying months."

"At least."

She sighed, a long wavering unusually dreamy sound. "Okay. But pay me another visit when the manuscript is done. We can celebrate. I won't make you transport me this time."

"I'm glad."

"See you, babe."

"See you, Lolly."

Nut case though she was, I liked talking with my agent as much as anyone in the world. It almost felt like living through a 1930s movie script. Every conversation was a little chance to playact, to pretend our way through the minutes. On the other hand, there were the real facts of Lolly's divorce and her depleted personal life, her world-bitten hardness, edging around every word. But that was part of the 30s glamour too, the chiaroscuro of her noir.

The phone rang again. That never happened in the middle of the day except for salesmen. (My number is unlisted and yet the salesmen still find me. Explain that.) If I hadn't been purposefully delaying getting back to my novel, I wouldn't have answered. Even so, I answered warily.

"And a very good day to you," I heard a woman say. A chipper voice, with a touch of an accent I couldn't place. "Is this Paul?"

"This is Paul."

She chuckled, as if I'd said something funny.

"So it is," she said. "And this is Grethe Westerleg."

I sat up straight in my chair.

"Grethe. Hello. How did you get my number?"

The chuckle again.

"A person has her ways, which she need not reveal."

"Come on; how did you find it?"

"I told your department secretary I have crucial business with you."

"That's all it takes?"

"That is all, I am afraid. Thankfully."

"She's not supposed to do that. Then again, she hates me."

"Why?"

"I'm more trouble than I'm worth."

"I am sure that's not true."

"I don't know. That's pretty much what my wife came to think too."

"Your wife! My, we're getting personal and this is the first time we've ever spoken on the telephone."

"Sorry."

"Do not apologize. You are just being American. You're wife, you say. In past tense."

"Past tense, yes."

"Widowed?"

"Divorced."

"Ah."

"She is very much alive."

"Ah."

There was a clumsy pause. I would have expected Grethe to offer a clearer reaction to my personal revelation than "Ah." But since that's all I got I didn't exactly know what to do with it. Whatever "Ah" meant it didn't sound good. It was up to her to redirect this stalled conversation.

"How is your wonderful book coming along?" she said.

"That's just what my agent just asked me. Just now."

"*Kon-Tiki*, you say."

"It's looking more like the Titanic at the moment. "

"Really."

"I mean the aftermath."

"They are dead?"

"I mean the ones who escaped. Afloat on those puny life boats in the North Atlantic. Must have been cold as hell."

"I am sure."

"Right now, they are being threatened by some unnamed sea creature. Do you know which sea creatures occupy the Norwegian Sea in winter?"

She was quiet a moment. Thinking hard. I guess she really did want to help.

"I suppose one might see a whale."

"My thoughts exactly. So it's a whale then."

"I can ask someone in marine biology if you like."

Of course, I could do the same thing on my campus.

"Only if it's no trouble."

"Not much trouble. I know someone over there."

"Then there's the guns."

"Guns again."

"I have to have the right kind. You know, for Lars."

"Why?"

"He shoots his wife."

"Oh, dear."

"By accident."

"By accident?"

"Messy and all. But exciting. You know. *Kon-Tiki*."

Actually—did I say this yet?—I have never in my life read *Kon-Tiki*.

"Sounds more like Hemingway to me."

I laughed. "So you know Papa."

"A little. I took an American literature course in college. But he is readily available in Norway, translated and all. And widely liked."

"Really."

"Such the American archetype."

"Good god. The Papa myth. It goes on and on, polluting young minds everywhere."

"Don't fret. We also read the French and the Spanish and the Swedes and the Russians. And our own. And everybody. We read the whole world in Norway, Paul. That's what Europe does."

"Okay," I said. "Insult received."

"No insult intended. Well, maybe just a little."

"Grethe"—it was the first time I spoke her Christian name—"I don't understand how someone gets from Oslo to Eugene, Oregon."

"Airplane," she said. Then she giggled, proud of her joke.

"Seriously."

"Okay," she said. "Seriously."

For the next hour she told me about herself: about being twenty-two and a graduate of Oslo University with a B.A. in Political Philosophy. She loved her country but was hungry to study other democratic systems up close. She had an inherited European notion of America as a lawless, cowboy society. But too the greatest carnival of a democracy the world has ever seen, from our balloon-spattered conventions to barbecue eating candidates to a press which periodically goes into feeding frenzy over alleged sexual crimes but ignores a government teetering on the edge of bankruptcy. She wanted to see it for herself, so she applied to a half-dozen American masters programs in political science. She received both the cheeriest acceptance letter and most generous graduate assistantship from the University of Washington and for those reasons (along with a friend's gauzy recollection of a trip to British Columbia as a thirteen year old) she chose it over the University of Texas-Austin, Wayne State, LSU, Southwest Missouri, and the University of Pennsylvania. She expected to follow the normal two year plan of study, then return to Norway, with impressions, observations, and data she could resurrect and reinterpret for a lifetime. For that reason, during summers and vacations she took as many trips as she could squeeze in: Broadway, the Chicago Loop, the Gulf of Mexico, Disneyworld, the Jefferson Memorial. In her second year, her professors encouraged her to apply to the department's doctoral program. Acceptance was automatic to any Masters student in good standing. Assistance, however, was not. "I'll need money," she told her advisor, a pale, too thin, forty-two-year-old man who seemed at all times dimly dissatisfied and whom Grethe suspected was in love with her. He was married to a gossipy, nonacademic woman who laughed too loud and tried too hard. The man seemed to do anything he could to avoid going home. He put in long hours ruminating over paperwork at the office. He volunteered for departmental committees. He mentored a gaggle of grad students. But whenever Grethe appeared, he put down whatever he was doing and gave her his full attention.

"I'll need money," she said.

Her advisor nodded. "I'll get you money," he said.

So she stayed on under a graduate fellowship—much more money and no teaching duties—for an additional four years, graduating in 1992 as Dr. Westerleg. By that time she had become so thoroughly immersed in American life and culture, political, social, and economic, she couldn't imagine just packing up and leaving for good. She entered the job market and to her eternal surprise received an offer to the very first job she applied for: as an assistant professor of political science at the University of Oregon. She couldn't understand how she got a job so easily when two of her fellow Political Science graduates, native born Americans with the political culture vibrant in their blood, were left to languish without offers. One of them finally accepted part-time work at Walla Walla Community College while the other became so disheartened that a year later she gave up her professorial ambitions to become an aerobics instructor at a Seattle health club. In the coming years, as she sat on hiring committees and hosted visiting scholars, Grethe watched normally steely-eyed and sharp-minded colleagues blanch with a childish awe in the face of anyone who spoke European flavored English: an age-old, irresistible sense of inferiority rising to the surface. It was hard to accept but impossible not to conclude that the reason she had been hired in the first place was not the evident hard work she had put into her dissertation, nor her insightful responses to interview questions nor her splendidly animated teaching demonstration, but because of her thick-tongued Scandinavian accent.

"As my mother always said, it's not what gets you through the door but what keeps you there that matters."

"Well, of course," she said. "And, believe me, I do plenty to keep my place here."

A year after winning tenure she initiated the Scandinavian Studies program, which, in addition to her usual course load, she was now stuck with administering. And on top of that there were her graduate students: only a few, but needing close attention. And then there was her research which, to her own surprise, kept coming at an article or two a year.

"Sounds like full professorship is only a matter of time."

She hesitated. "Thank you. I appreciate that. Yes. Full professorship. That is the course I've set myself on, isn't it? Only problem is then I am pretty much tethered here. I mean permanently. If I'm a full professor, I can't ever leave. For anyone."

"I have news for you, Grethe. If you're tenured, you're already tethered. Haven't you ever heard the phrase 'Golden Handcuffs'?"

She chortled. "That is funny. No, I have never heard of 'Golden Handcuffs.' But that is pretty much correct, I suppose."

We had talked for so long the phone was turning oily against my ear, and my palm was wet from clutching the body. The scene I'd put aside—Lars v. the enemy whale—was so old it was beginning to stink from neglect. I only had an hour or so of working time left before I had to pick up Ryan from school and shut my book down for the day.

"Me too," she said. "I have piles of work." I could feel her nodding vigorously at the other end of the line. "I am being bad by putting it off."

"I doubt it."

"It has been so good to finally talk to you," she said. "Someday, if you are traveling the northwest you must show up at my door, novel in hand. Or maybe I should show up at yours."

"That would be great, Grethe."

"Storartet."

"What?"

She laughed, a hiccupping string of noises.

"Right," I said. "I should have guessed."

"You should have known."

"Maybe."

"Next time I call you will know."

"Next time," I said.

15

Though the days are mostly black as night, Lars stares relentlessly at the water, waiting for his attacker to return. Olga, barely alive, sleeps nonstop. Lars watches and prepares. He removes an oar from a cock and lashes his longest knife to the end, so he can dart it in and out of the creature's body like a lance. The second longest knife he keeps tucked in his belt. He loads new shot in the blunderbuss and keeps it near his leg as he waits. And waits and waits. And waits. He knows he is not waiting in vain. The monster is not through with them. After all, they are the only plaything in this whole portion of the frigid, empty sea.

As it has for the last twenty-four hours, the water remains calm. Finally, under the combined influence of the gently rocking raft, his exhaustion from keeping watch, and his permanent hunger, Lars falls into a heavy sleep: hands on his knees, head on his chest, his mouth open in a raspy, dry-mouthed snore.

A bump startles him. The same bump as before. The boat is shoved yards forward. Lars is instantly awake and even while instantly feeling the bite of the winter cold, grabs his spear and raises it above his ear. He looks right and left for any sign of the swimming bulk. He sees it coming, from behind and to his left, aiming its neck—the only word he can think of—at the human craft. Lars turns, sits up, takes aim. But before he can throw the boat is struck and he is toppled onto his back. The spear slips from his hand. It, and he, almost go overboard.

This skurk is teasing me.

He retakes the spear and stands up, for the best possible view and best possible throw. *A lance in his øye; let's see how he likes that.* When he spots the monster again, on the other side of the boat from where he's looking—it clearly has an idea of strategy—it is almost too late. There is no eye to aim at, only the surging black muscle. Seconds before the dark body will collide with the boat, Lars thrusts the spear as hard as he can at what he sees. But he doesn't throw it. The knife enters the creature, all the way. When he pulls back on the shaft, the blade comes out, still roped to the oar and covered with slippery blood.

Lars laughs giddily. A hit! Best of all the monster's forward line has been disrupted, his aim broken. For whatever reason, and Lars likes to believe that reason is his weapon, the creature goes under the boat, barely grazing the bottom as it passes. The boat rocks only slightly. Lars remains on his feet. He turns. He looks. He can't see the monster anywhere.

"I have done it!" he shouts to no one. "I have chased it off!"

For now, this is true. For now. The creature is apparently gone. But even Lars is not so foolish as not to realize it might return—and soon.

"Are you hurt, skurk? Have you had enough of the fight? Or are you busy with more of your plotting?"

A sudden instinct makes him grab the gun just as the boat is rammed from below. It rises almost a foot in the air—its wooden body creaking and stretching, almost breaking, from the hit—and slams back home. Cups fly overboard and a blanket and two knives. Lars lands on his back again. But he still holds the gun in one hand, the spear in the other.

"Just like a djevel," Lars shouts. "You can't beat me in a fair fight."

For the first time since the atrocious winter set in, Lars feels tinglingly alive with purpose, with determination. He screams words only he can understand into icy air that obliterates them. But he doesn't care. He's only thinking of the battle. "Come on then," he says.

He sees, yards off the back of the boat, a black missile approach. Lars aims his gun even as he readies for the shock of impact. He bends his knees, tenses his shoulders, feels the long coiled muscles in his legs. He has to wait for just the right moment, just the right shot, if he is to kill this skurk. If he shoots too early or too late, he'll never get another chance. He'd like to shoot it right in its eye. Wherever that is. That would surely teach it a lesson. Lars immediately adopts that as a strategy, if the monster decides to circle instead of ram. But if it rams the boat directly—head down, no eye to be found—Lars will bring up the spear and cut as much as he can out of the bastard. But then the monster surprises Lars. It changes strategy. It neither circles nor pummels. Instead, it tries to climb on top. The kjempe's behemoth black and white head, its mouth decidedly open, revealing rings of small but jagged meat-eater's teeth and a huge red tongue, lands only a foot from Lars's foot and nearly upends the boat. Lars is so astonished he can't react at first. He just tries to hold on—he drops the gun again—as he sees a furious black jellied eye staring at him directly with all its consciousness, all its contempt, all its daring. Never is he more sure that this monster knows exactly what it is doing. It is as if the monster wants to see its victim before it kills him. Even more, it wants this victim to know he will die, to feel as much terror as that knowledge can create. It wants to persecute Lars before finishing him off. It wants to extend the pain. *This skurk is killing for pleasure,* he actually has time to think. Most haunting is the unavoidable feeling that the monster read Lars's mind. He knows Lars wants to shoot him in the eye. *And he's challenging me.* Lars never expected to find such human traits, almost a full human personality, in a wild animal.

But there the speculation ends and necessity takes over. Cups and knives and blankets and Lars's wife tumble toward the creature's open mouth. Lars, somehow still on his feet, tumble-steps wildly to the creature, while trying to hold his spear level. He rams the spear deep into the monster's gullet. The agile beast jerks backward immediately, releasing its weight from the boat, which levels with a bang. Olga's body and every peripheral item bounce and scatter. Lars is on his stomach now, gripping what crease or knob of wood he can with all the strength in his fingertips.

The boat steadies. Lars sits up. He sees the monster spiraling and wriggling and thrashing under the water, trying to lose the distasteful spear. The water turns dark red as the weapon stays in place.

Good. A steady drain. Lars can't kill the evil thing in one thrust but maybe the spear can over time, if it holds. Even a gunshot would not have been as effective.

The creature begins circling the craft in its frenzy, apparently gambling that sheer speed will dislodge the spear.

Wear yourself out.

The beast pauses, jerks close to the boat, as if in a spasm, then backs away and circles again. This time, however, it moves much more slowly. In fact, it drifts off and begins indifferently treading water ten or fifteen yards away. Now Lars goes for the gun. After all, now he has a stationary target, more or less. Almost as if to make it easier for Lars, the creature pushes with one fin and moves slowly to within five yards of the boat. Now it is barely moving at all. The perfect target. Suddenly with all the time in the world—praying it's not some monster trick, some monster death act (he wouldn't put it past this bastard)—Lars aims his rifle with care. He pulls the trigger. The blast rocks him but he doesn't fall over. Meanwhile, a shower of bullets lodges into the creature's bulk. It jerks but does little except to bleed more profusely. After a couple more minutes, the creature stops moving altogether. It drifts to within two feet of the boat, nothing but a stiff carcass. Lars pulls the knife from his belt and attacks. He swung his arm wildly at every piece of the creature he can cut, at every opportunity to draw more blood. Lars wants revenge for the terror.

What am I doing, he asks himself, after a minute of this flailing. He is breathing coarsely, the knife suddenly heavy in his undernourished hand. Lars begins cutting strips of flesh and fat from the creature's body, stuffing them in his mouth: skin, lard, and muscle combine in a chewy enormous wad. That rubbery texture. It has no taste beyond fishy bitterness but he doesn't care. It isn't taste he needs. He cuts another hunk and eats that too. Then another hunk. Then another. Then another. He cuts off three more hunks and throws them onto the raft for Olga to eat, if and when she ever gets better.

Wait a minute, Lars thinks. He has been thinking desperately, not strategically. He has been thinking out of his stomach not his mind. This enormous sea creature, whatever it is, and however terrifying its attack, seems to be have been *delivered* to them in the middle of this vast, flat emptiness. *It's a floating pantry*. If he can tie the corpse to the raft they need not worry about food for days. *Days!* They can actually feast. He finds the rope they brought, miraculously still on board. But can he get it around the beast and will it stay? And how will he connect the rope to the raft? He finds his hammer almost immediately; it shifted to his side in that last attack. But he doesn't see the nails they brought. He'd bound them in a kerchief and put them near Olga their first day on board. But they are nowhere to be found. He runs his hands around her body, under her neck, under her shoulders, under her shrunken legs. *Ah hah!* There. Lodged securely beneath her kneecap. Another miracle. With rope and nails and hammer in hand he swings back to the creature just in time to see its rigid body dip under the sooty water and plummet, spinning as it goes.

I was shamelessly proud of this scene, the first true action-adventure scene I'd written since declaring years ago that my ambition was to be A WRITER. Not a journalist or sports writer or ad man or essayist or science fictionist, mind you, but A WRITER. Proud too of how I'd manage to slide in a few Norwegian words: not so weirdly spelled that you can't figure them out—in fact in some cases remarkably similar to their English counterparts—but clearly foreign nonetheless. *Øye* (eye), *djevel* (devil), *skurk* (bastard), *kjempe* (giant). (Okay, so *kjempe* is spelled nothing like giant.) After being embarrassed by Grethe in that last phone call, I ordered online a Norwegian-English dictionary published by the Berlitz people and another called *Say It in Norwegian*, composed way back in 1957 by one Samuel Abrahamsen, Ph.D. and still—believe it or not—in print. Apparently, it is regarded as a little classic in the genre. Little is right, by the way. Both books, together, fit in my palm. So far I hadn't had use for *Say It in Norwegian*, but the Berlitz book was turning out to be mighty handy, forgive the pun, as well as mighty hip, for such a slim little volume. Not only did it show me "bastard" but "fuck," "damn," "butt," "condom," "drunk," "sex," "homosexual," "idiot," and "lesbian." (Of course, these Berlitz people do pride themselves on having their ears to the ground.)

[R.A., here, momentarily. I was going to lie and, for effect, have Paul tell you that the dictionary also included "twat," "dick," "piss," "shit," "puke," "dyke," and "asshole" but I wouldn't want to get in trouble with Berlitz. And I wouldn't want you to imagine Paul as someone who spends half his writing day looking to see how many dirty words he can find in an itty bitty Norwegian-English dictionary. Who would do that?]

16

By the time I was done with the scene, Christmas was over, 2004 soundly rung in. I hadn't heard any more from Grethe and her Oregonian invitation but that's because, as she explained in a quick email before she left, she was taking her usual Christmas voyage back to the motherland.   In the meantime, Ryan, Joy, and I had done our awkward, divorced family Christmas day dance. Four hours with me . . . six hours with her . . . lunch with me . . . dinner with her . . . presents from me . . . more presents from her. It brought out the worst in Ryan, who became snappy, demanding, and accusatory. "Why can't you and mom just get it together for once," he said. "It's just *one day.*" He had a point.   Certainly his experience of Christmas was nothing like mine when I was his age.   Maybe one of these years things will be civil enough between Joy and I that we can "get it together" (where did he pick that one up?) for the holiday, but that year ain't coming soon.   For one thing, Joy would have to stop hating me first. Second, she'd need to stop telling people I was the worst husband in recorded history.

Long story short, I survived the holidays and got Ryan safely back in school before I finally finished the scene. That's about when Lolly called. No joking, the lady is prescient. And nothing if not attentive. I never knew an agent who so actively ministered to her clients. As a writer working outside the fortress walls of New York publishing, what you sense more often than anything is how damnably BUSY those people are. They have NO TIME. Query first, don't send a sample. Send a sample only if we ask you to send a sample. And when we ask you to send a sample, only send the number of pages we ask you to send. NOT A SINGLE PAGE MORE.   Overly long samples will not be read. Unsolicited manuscripts will be thrown in the trash. And don't ever ever—no matter what other sin you might commit— ever call. We are TOO BUSY to chat on the phone.

Before Lolly I actually did have another agent, briefly: a man named Leslie Knox. He came recommended by a former teacher of mine. Because my former teacher asked him to, he reviewed my novel and halfheartedly agreed to represent it. I actually signed a contract with him. I never met the man, only communicated through e-mail. To this day I have no idea what he looks like. In his e-mails he claimed to be "working the streets hard" for me, contacting a bevy of editors at a couple dozen outlets. I never saw any evidence of such activity, just the claims. After a while, he stopped answering my e-mails. So I started calling him. But all I ever got was a robotic voice mail voice commanding me to leave a message. I did. Eight times. After the eighth non-return of my phone call, I tore the contract to shreds. Legal or not, I began doing web searches for names of other agents. That's how I found, and eventually signed with, Lolly. Who always returns my calls. Who won't, in fact, stop calling me. There's a lesson in there somewhere for somebody.

"Guess what?" she said.

"What?"

"Morton is back on board."

"He is?"

"On board. Isn't that cute? I'm using a nautical metaphor."

"Right."

"So laugh."

"Lolly."

"Okay. So anyway, he's back."

"I didn't think he was ever here."

"Listen, Crabby. I told you months ago. The man is dead sold on *Kon-Tiki*. I told you before the party." The picture flashed again gravely gray and disheartening: an embittered older man, crew cut, Marine-like, drinking hard liquor and insulting my first book.

"He just had to be reminded," Lolly said.

"He had to be reminded that he was dead sold? Shouldn't he know that?"

"He had to be reminded of how thrilling it was: two luckless Danes, without preparation and almost without hope, lost on the high seas as winter winds burn them, dangerous animals circle, and food becomes scare. They are almost out of time, out of hope, and out of life. Will they make it to Iceland and safety?"

"That's pretty good, Lolly. And you haven't even read those scenes."

"I don't have to, Sweet Buns. I know what I'm doing."

"Yes, clearly."

"So when are you going to let me see this masterpiece? Morton is chomping at the bit. He wants to see these Danes. His mother is from Denmark, you know."

"He told me."

"When?"

"At the party."

"So you did have a nice conversation."

"No, we didn't. And my characters are from Norway, not Denmark."

"Norway?"

"Yes."

"Did you change that?"

"I didn't."

"Not Denmark?"

"No."

"Why Norway?"

"At this point, I can't even remember."

"Change it then."

"I'm kind of committed to Norway. I mean, that's why I have them headed for Iceland. They leave from the western shore of Norway, expecting to go just a ways south. But the sea currents—"

"Fuck the sea currents. The sea currents can take them from Denmark to Iceland, can't they?"

"They can?"

"Who knows? Who cares? Will a reader care?'

"Probably not."

"So make it Denmark. Do that and we'll have Morton in the bag. His mother is from Denmark, you know."

"Yes."

"So get cracking, mister."

"All right," I said. Then: "You know, Lolly, I'm just trying to make it good. As good as I can."

"God, you are such the little worker bee. I wish I had twenty writers like you."

"But you don't."

"No, I don't. Just get me the book. I'm sure it will be great. You're great."

"Thanks, Lolly."

"How's Dixie, by the way?"

"Dixie?"

"That's where you are, right? Isn't Arkansas in Dixie?"

"Decidedly."

"And."

"Same old Dixie."

"I want to see it sometime. I want to see what else there is in this country besides New York sidewalks. The farthest south I've ever been is Wilmington."

"You're forgetting Barbados."

"I can't even remember Barbados, Paulie. Swear to God."

"I'm not surprised."

"I was letting loose. It was vacation. I—"

"You don't have to explain. And, yes, you're welcome in Dixie."

She chuckled. I'm not sure why.

"And you are welcome here, you know. You're allowed to visit more than once a year. We're only the publishing capital of the United States."

"I know."

"Even the world even."

"I know."

"You can, you know."

"I *know*."

"So?"

"I do have a job, and then there's that darn son I'm responsible for."

"Now the loving father bit! If you were here this minute I'd have to jump your bones."

"Thanks. I guess."

"You guess?"

"Thanks, Lolly."

She began laughing in hard, short, forced chortles. Made to sound careless. I think I might actually have hurt her.

"I'm teasing you, Paulie. That's what I do. You know that."

I listened a second longer.

"I do. Thanks for the lift, Lolly. I mean, for calling me."

She went quiet for a moment. So long a moment I thought she might have hung up.

"Anytime," she said, with a voice so level and so serious I could have sworn it was someone else altogether.

17

It was Saturday morning in our living room. As Ryan watched television, I looked around for *Summer Activity 3rd grade*. I thought I'd left it in the box of kid's books near the television. Now that we'd officially canned Norway for Denmark I needed to do some fresh research. What better place to start than Ryan's workbook? But where was the damn thing? Ah, underneath the television stand. I yanked it out. I readied to explore.

"What are you doing?" Ryan said. The exact same question my wife used to ask. I looked at him: muddy brown eyes, tawny hair, turned up nose. There she was, and would forever stay, written on the face of my eight-year-old boy.

"What do you have my book for?"

"No reason."

"Dad, why do you have it?"

"I need some information."

"You do?"

I looked away, nodded: fast, ridiculous head jerking.

"From my summer workbook?"

"I was just checking," I said. "I do have other sources."

"About what?"

"Denmark."

He just looked at me.

"It's a country."

"I know."

"You know that?"

He rolled his eyes; he nodded with superior slowness. Joy again. He turned back to the tv. On the screen a boy dressed in black with golden lightning bolts for hair raised his voice importantly.

"I summon Dark Fairy Girl!" The boy pulled a playing card from a stack connected to some gimmicky plastic-looking board attached to his wrist and threw the card forward. Thunder crashed, lightning changed the sky, colors blinked on and off. A creature who looked like a cross between Brer Rabbit, Mr.

Spock, and Betty Boop appeared. Or maybe I should say Raquel Welch. Of course, I don't mean the sixty year old Raquel Welch pushing a book on Larry King. I mean *10,000 B.C.* Raquel Welch. You understand.

"What do you know about Denmark?" I said. "Ryan?"

He turned his head, as if to reply, but never made it all the way. His face was blank, stolen by the television.

"Ryan?"

"What?"

"Can you tell me anything about Denmark?"

His eyes—soulless, thoughtless—met mine for a moment and the head moved a fraction of an inch. Then he looked back at indomitable screen. Mr. Spock/Betty Boop landed a monster kick into the leg of some creature that looked like a cross between Arnold Schwarzenagger and a lobster. Lobster/Arnold danced in B-movie pain for a second. Then he stopped. He grimaced. He growled. He unleashed a muscular lobster swipe at Spock/Betty Boop—a hell of a right hook—that knocked her out cold. The boy with the golden lightening hair gasped. Friends of his nearby, none of them had golden lightning hair, gasped. Spock/Betty Boop disappeared. A voice, cackling in evil, victorious waves, filled the screen as pearls of phony, engorged sweat streamed down golden lightning-haired boy's face. Then a commercial.

"Ryan?"

"What?"

He was back, no longer possessed.

"You said you knew something about Denmark."

"I said I knew it was a country."

"What kind of country is it?"

"Scandinavian."

"What else?"

"It's in Europe."

"What else?"

"They belong to the EU."

"And?"

"They eat pig's liver."

"They do?"

"Uh huh."

"How do you know that?"

"School."

"They tell you that in school?"

"I guess."

"Do they or don't they?"

"Well, I know it's a fact."

"All right, all right." I had to hurry. They were coming back from commercial any minute. What did I really most need to know? Too late. Golden lightning-haired boy had returned, gritting his teeth, about to pull out another card. "I summon Red Eyes Blue Dragon!" he shouted. Sure enough, one second later an ocean hued dragon with incandescent eyes popped into existence, floating in a nimbus circle just above the boy.

Ryan's eyes went blank again; his consciousness gone. I might as well have been talking to a cabbage.

I would just have to wait the ten minutes it would take for this dragon to demolish Lobster/Arnold. Which it did. At the end of the episode, the villain, a guy with orange skin and goggles. packed his bag mopily and walked off, shoulders slumped, like a kid who'd just lost his bubble gum. Meanwhile, Golden-haired boy showed no evidence of having sweated out forty gallons of body water just minutes before. His friends hugged him and none of them said he stank. Thankfully, the show ended. The credits rolled. Lots of Japanese names. I walked over and turned off the television.

"Hey!" Ryan wailed. "I was watching that."

"It's the credits."

"I like the credits."

"Too bad. What else can you tell me?"

He regarded me dimly, with total suspicion. Utterly my wife.

"About what?"

"Denmark."

"Dad! Do we have to talk about this?"

He stretched his arms behind his head and leaned back against a sofa cushion. Strangled, peevish noises came out of his throat.

"Yes, we have to talk about it."

He dropped his arms: cheeks sunken, eyes glowering. "Okay, okay, okay." He took in a studied breath. "Denmark occupies a peninsula called Jutland and an archipelago of islands, the largest of which is the home for Copenhagen, Denmark's capital. Denmark is attached to continental Europe by Jutland's 42 mile border with Germany. All of its other frontiers are maritime, including the one with Britain which sits approximately 400 miles to the west, on the other side of the North Sea."

"That's pretty good," I said.

"Can I stop?"

"No. Yes." I stood up. "Let me get a pen and paper."

"Why?"

"Why do you think?"

He didn't reply, not letting himself enjoy this forced bit of recapitulation, even though I could tell he did.

"Okay," I said. "Continue."

"To the north and east of Denmark, respectively, are the kingdoms of Norway and Sweden, separated from Denmark by sea lanes which link the North Sea with the Baltic Sea. These lanes are known as the Skagerrak, the Kattegat, and Bresund. The widest of these is Kattegat which lies directly between Jutland and upper Sweden."

"Amazing."

"What?"

"What they teach you."

He shrugged.

"Mrs. Foster says this will be on the benchmark."

"It will?"

"That's what she says."

"Why does the benchmark test you on Denmark?"

He frowned, then sulked. He didn't know and didn't care. As a student in the Conway, Arkansas school system—where curiosity is forcibly extinguished like an invading virus—it wasn't his business to ask why. His only business was to stay in his seat and shut up. Oh, and to love the Lord.

"Sorry," I said. "Go ahead."

"I don't want to."

"Come on. Please. This is very helpful."

He sighed. He huffed. "But that's almost all."

"I want all. Not almost."

Another sigh, another demonstration: eyes and shoulders and cheeks.

"Come on," I said. "I'll give you a fruit snack."

He straightened instantly; he wrinkled his nose.

"Fruit snacks are for babies."

"All right. I'll make you a hamburger."

"I don't want a hamburger."

"What do you want?"

"Jelly beans."

"Jelly beans?"

"The good kind."

"Which are those?"

"You know."

"No, I don't."

"The red kind. And the bright yellow ones. And orange. And green. And blue. But *not* black. And not green speckled. And not the creamy yellow speckled."

"Buttered popcorn?"

"I think."

"We don't allow those in our house."

"Good. I hate them. Actually, I hate all the speckled."

That was heartening. Buttered popcorn, a completely inexcusable flavor for a jelly bean, was Joy's favorite.

"All right," I said, "can we get back to Denmark?"

He nodded, almost eager now. He cleared his throat.

"At its widest, Kattegat is approximately ninety miles across. Bresund, which lies between the east coast of Zealand and Sweden's southern heel, is the narrowest of the three sea lanes; for instance, Helsinger (on the Zealand side) is separated from Helsingborg (on the Swedish side) by less than five miles of water. Copenhagen, meanwhile, is separated from Sweden's west coast by only twenty miles."

He stopped. He stared at me, as if expecting something.

"What?" I said.

"That's it."

"That's it?"

"That's all I know."

He stretched out his arm, palm flat.
"Now give me my jelly beans."

[Note from real author: This conversation, of course, never happened. To Paul or anyone. My son, for one, knows nothing about Denmark. But I thought it would be funny to put encyclopedic information in an eight-year-old's mouth, especially if I set it in relief against an anime cartoon. But one craft note to which I hope you will pay attention: Sol Stein insists that any one stretch of dialogue spoken by a character must not be longer than three sentences. Any bit of dialogue that runs longer than three sentences isn't dialogue but a speech. And speeches, of course, are boring. Thus, in composing the above scene I made sure that no stretch of Denmark data went longer than three sentences without interruption. Although in that last section I maybe cheated by using a semicolon after "three sea lanes." I say maybe. According to the rules of Standard Written English it still counts.]

[Follow-up side note from real author: i.e., a brief, semi-relevant anecdote: About the time I composed the Ryan / Paul scene, I took my (real) son to the *Yu-Gi-Oh* movie, which was probably the most difficult cinematic experience I have ever had to outlast. It was actually more stupid than *Big Top Pee Wee* or *Leonard Part VI*. Really. With the *Yu-Gi-Oh* movie, however, I came prepared for stupidity, namely a flashlight and a novel (Tim O'Brien's *July July*). My armor would have held except for three critical factors: the heat generated by the overflowing kiddie crowd in that cramped theater, my stomach full of buttered popcorn, and a headache from too little sleep the night before. Midway through the movie, and in the middle of an O'Brien scene I fell asleep. (Not a commentary, by the way, on O'Brien's book.) The flashlight slipped from its downward facing position and settled in my lap with the bulb facing rightward, shooting a spidery line of light across the aisle. Next thing I knew, a voice was in my ear. "Turn that thing off, will you? It's shining right in my eyes." I apologized to a blonde-haired man crouching in the aisle: some kid's father, his face showing red, whether from the heat, his bother, or the carnival colors assaulting us from the screen, I couldn't know. I turned off the flashlight and sat in a dull daze. Eventually I couldn't stand it anymore. I tried reading again. This time I kept the light so close to the page than not an electron could escape. It proved impossible to read in this fashion, though, so I gave up and just tried to sleep. But now that I wanted to sleep I couldn't, of course. I was forced to sit in place and, like a man suffering through CIA-sponsored torture, watch the last twenty minutes of the *Yu-Gi-Oh* movie. It wasn't a total loss, I suppose, since it was then I discovered the Dark Fairy Girl which I squirreled into the Ryan/Paul scene. Today's writing lesson? Use Everything. And don't eat buttered popcorn in a crowded theater if you intend to stay awake.]

18

In the next chapter, I'll return to myself and Ryan and finish my rendition of what happened that January morning. But first I want to assure you, dear reader, that eventually, albeit days later, I actually did carry out some library research—i.e. Britannica again (15th edition, Macropedia, Vol. 17: Decorative—Edison)—and found many nuggets of data about my new featured country. To wit: Denmark, its landscape cut by a great glacial mass in the last Ice Age, is a lowland area, not more than 100 ft. above sea level. The highest elevation in the whole country is only 568 feet! In Northern Jutland exist numerous areas of sand and gravel which became bogs, bogs which are of interest to archeologists for the ritual deposits interred in them from antiquity. These bogs are also a valuable source for peat.

This is utterly boring.

No, it's not boring; it's—

Monstrously boring.

Hey!

Jump forward to some human stuff, why don't you.

Denmark supports a high standard of living, with a network of social services and one of the highest per capita GNPs in the world. Denmark's economy is based on service industries, trade, and manufacturing, with less than 10% of the population employed in agriculture, fishing, and forestry. Its farms are mostly small or medium-sized family owned businesses. Cereals are the primary crop. In western Jutland, where the soil is less fertile, oats, rye, turnips, and potatoes are grown. Milk and dairy products, pork and eggs, also amount to a significant percentage of farm production.

This is no better.

All right, I admit it's no better, but don't you think they might feel a little thrill of pride for knowing pork and eggs are a significant portion of Danish farm production?

In recent decades, Danish exports have tended toward industrial products. Denmark has also created an export market for its creatively designed modernist furniture and other household items: silverware, ceramics, textiles, clothing, toys.

Ceramics?

So Denmark is, like, IKEA to the world.

No IKEA is IKEA to the world. And I told you already: IKEA is Swedish.

Same difference. It's like Minneapolis and St. Paul. It's like the U.S. and Canada.

Ouch.

What?

Better hope a Canadian isn't around when you say that.

Denmark is a small but culturally active nation. The country supports ten symphony orchestras and the internationally acclaimed Royal Danish Ballet. They are also a sports minded people. Denmark received a wake up call in 1864 when they lost the Danish-German War. The Danes decided to get in shape. Small arms and physical training became the culturally-enforced norm. Today, soccer, swimming, cycling, canoeing, and rowing are all popular.

(Note to reader: As I pen this history of my second novel's creation—and, most pertinently, as I penned that last sentence ["Today, soccer, swimming, cycling, canoeing, and **rowing** are all popular"]—it is late summer 2004. Olympics time. I just heard a marble-voiced NBC announcer—he with the big forehead, puffy upper lip, and mattress of salt-and-pepper hair—announce that Denmark is going for its second straight gold medal. In . . . ? I missed that part. But while the announcer spoke, they showed in the lower right corner four white guys in a narrow boat yanking with exacting precision on the oars. Must be a rowing event. Synchronicity!)

[Follow-up note from the real author: Lest you think I'm writing this novel (?) in front of the tv, I should admit that I didn't, as Paul claimed to, just see the announcement about the Danish rowing team. I don't know about Paul, but I witnessed that announcement three days ago, around noon on a Saturday while I wasn't even trying to write because who can write with a loud eight-year-old banging around the house on a Saturday morning as he acts out *Yu-Gi-Oh*? I inserted that trivia about the Danish rowing team here because narratively it makes the most sense and causes the most impact, what with me just finished typing the words: "and rowing are all popular." Although, truth is, it's still a pretty cool coincidence even if it happened three days ago.]

[Real author follow-up to the follow-up by real author: To be totally honest, I heard the announcement from the man with the big forehead, puffy upper lip, and mattress of hair not three days ago, but only a day. In the above note I stretched the distance to three days because I wanted to exaggerate the nature of the lie "I" (I writing for Paul) told in his "Note to Reader."]

[Follow-up to that follow-up: It's not a lie, is it, if it's spoken by fictional Paul in fictional Paul's fictional rendition of his fictional life? It's not like *I* was claiming to be concurrently witnessing the announcement about the Danish rowing team.]

[Follow-up to follow-up to follow-up: To be even more honest, I never saw what the announcer looked like. Maybe with the "mattress of salt-and-pepper" hair I had the ubiquitous Bob Costas in mind, except his hair isn't really salt-and-pepper but a fading blondish-brown (at his age, probably touched up with Clairol for Men) and he doesn't have a big forehead, and would never be seen on Olympics coverage until the evening prime time. But he does have a puffy upper lip. In any case, I couldn't say Costas but I wanted to specify some announcer to make the scene more vivid. I pulled the old creative nonfiction writer's writerly trick of making up details in order to bring the otherwise basically truthful scene fully alive to the reader, so the reader, as creative non-fictionists like to say, can experience the "deeper truth" of the situation. (Which is, of course, just a high falutin' excuse for lying. An excuse we fiction writers never need or think to offer and, for that reason, I'd rather they [non-fictionists] spare me the disingenuous excuse and just lie to their hearts content.) I never saw any announcer at all, actually. Here's the real truth: I heard a smooth-voiced man say something about Denmark and I looked up from whatever I was doing to see in the lower right corner a miniature piece of video showing four barely dressed caucasians in a narrow ship skimming along. The video lasted maybe three seconds and then disappeared. Maybe there was even a graphic: *Coming Up Soon, Coming Up Next, Coming Up Before Dinner.* I can't remember. And I can't remember what sport I was actually supposed to be watching in the first place. Maybe basketball. Maybe sprinting. Maybe table tennis, which was the most entertaining of all the sports NBC broadcast during those games.]

[Follow-up to follow-up to . . . : Fuck it. The reader is instructed to forget the confession confessed in above "Follow-up"s and for the sake of this novel (?) assume that Paul's aforementioned "Note to Reader" represents the true facts of the case. That's my story and I'm sticking to it.]

19

The first thing I did after giving Ryan his jelly beans was to try to force him outside. Not because I wanted him to get exercise—although I have nothing against exercise—but so I could raid *Summer Vacation 3rd Grade Workbook* in peace. After Ryan's lecture, I didn't need an encyclopedic rendition of Danish trivia; I just needed a few plain facts.

"It's cold out," he said.

"You can play in the car," I said.

"Really?"

"Really."

"Want to play with me?"

"I can't."

"Why?"

"Stuff."

Ryan rolled his eyes. "The book."

"Maybe."

"Don't lie to me," he said.

"All right, the book."

"I don't have to go outside for you to write the book."

"True," I said. "But go outside."

"Why?"

"Because I said so."

"Why can't I watch *Yu-Gi-Oh*?"

"Because *Yu-Gi-Oh* isn't on."

"I don't believe you."

I huffed and made a showy show of checking the TV Guide with supreme parental exactitude.

"No, it's not on," I said. In fact, Cartoon Network was in the middle of an all-day *Yu-Gi-Oh* marathon.

"You're lying," he said.

"Look, Ryan, just go outside."

"But *why* do I need to go outside?"

"Because it's good for your brain."

"How can going outside be good for my brain?"

"I don't know. That's what they say."

"Who?"

"They."

"They who?"

"They. You know."

"They're lying," he said.

Finally, I had to pay him. He agreed to stay outside for fifteen minutes. I went back to the living room and took possession of that workbook. I went through it mechanically: page after page, week after week: *Fun With Math. How Things Work. Word Puzzle. Craft Challenge. About the Universe.* And with every chapter, a different featured country: Norway (you knew that already), Poland, Mexico, Canada, Kenya, Japan, Ireland, Brazil, Saudi Arabia, Germany, Thailand, and . . . the United States of America.

I threw the book in the trash and went on the internet. At the very least I would need different names.

Eluf moves in and out of his days like a groggy sleeper who turns over, not quite waking, and merges into a another dreamland. When he does wake the sky is usually dark; only briefly is it gray. And for a few rare minutes of the day it is actually light.

(Note to reader: After a fit of writerly conscience, and fear that some editor would be schooled in Scandinavian winters, I decided to go ahead and make the February sky over the Norwegian sea quite dark indeed. How would Eluf see what he needed to for the story to work? I'd have to figure that out as I went along. And maybe just hurry up spring.)

Always the air is freezing. He has no sense of his wife or of a calendar, only the steady funeral galumph of the ocean and a short spark of surprise that he has not died yet. He knows he is as sick as Rikke. He is exhausted from the inside out. Most of all, he is out of hope. At some anonymous midpoint of his spell, he hears movement on board. At first, Eluf imagines that the monster he hunted has returned. He thinks to grab the gun which ought to be nearby. But even the thought of moving is too painful. He cannot find and hold any weapon. Let the monster come. Let the monster end it. Eluf curls into a protective cringe, not having the energy for the full fetal position. Then he realizes the sounds he hears are not the illiterate thumpings of a beast but lighter and more purposeful. The sound of human steps. Rikke? No, Rikke is dead. He shot her leg off. He watched as she pitched into the ocean, her sick arms making a last plea atop the water, turning it from gelid blue to bubbly, mobile white. But only for a moment. Then her chin went under; her nose; her eyes. Her red-brown hair trindled above her head, like lines of yarn about to be woven; then she sunk like a dropped knife toward the bottom.

His wife is dead.

He curls an inch tighter and asks himself what are those sounds. But he is too tired to decide. And it doesn't really matter. A new sleep and a new dreamland, not a place so much as a collection of color—purple, maroon, emerald, black—comes to him and flares sudden spots behind his eyes. Just before his mind is about to disperse into the largest purple wave he has ever seen, he hears movement again: arms and hands. Equipment being shifted. A voice.

"So, we're not finished yet husband, after all?"

That's what I wrote that same Saturday while Ryan played outside. (He never did tell me how he occupied himself. Or when he came back in.) I'd only gotten that far when I was interrupted by a phone call from Grethe. We quickly caught up on our vacations: my awkward, testy, divorced-father Christmas, her trip to Norway. Norway was great, she said. Her parents looked great. She'd told them she knew an American writer setting his latest novel in their own country. They were quite interested. Quite.

"Well, Grethe, that's just it," I said.

"What?"

"Some things changed with the book over Christmas."

"What things?" she said. I actually heard fear in her voice. "You're not giving it up."

"No. Nothing like that. I'm not one of those kinds of writers." Which is true. For all my faults as an artist one fault I don't have is skipping from project to project, never completing any of them. I see something through to the bitter end, no matter how terrible it is.

"What changes are you talking about?"

I took a breath.

"I'm moving the setting to Denmark. I mean before the characters enter the sea. While they are on the farm. They're going to be Danish not Norwegian."

"Denmark? I don't understand." She sounded even more bothered than she let herself sound, which was pretty bothered.

"The publisher my agent wants to woo has a soft spot for Denmark."

"So you're changing your whole book?"

"I've already changed it, remember?"

She paused, started a huff that wouldn't come. "Yes, I remember," she said.

"This is just one more."

"I never knew this is how it works."

"What works?"

"Authors. Books. So the agent decides? And the publisher decides? What does the author decide?"

Grethe's hurt resounded clearly through her bluntness. I tried not to feel that my writerly manhood was being questioned, because essentially she was speaking up for me, but still, in the far deep center of my chest, almost where the skin of my back begins, I felt the sting.

"I guess it depends on the author," I said. "And the book."

"But don't you care?"

"I cared a lot about my first book. Look how that turned out."

"You published that book!"

"Yes, to critical dismay and sales that soared into the tens."

"Come on now, Paul."

"Okay, maybe dozens."

She made a shshsh-ing noise between her teeth.

"So it's all about the sales." In that, I heard more than just personal dismay. I heard something much broader: a base-level, bottom of the soul, European distrust for American free

147

enterprise and American wealth, a hyper-cognizance for the compromises and social trauma that the worship of wealth unleashes. I would expect to hear such bare knuckled cynicism if I traveled to the continent, but not from someone who was here by choice, who deliberately made this country her home.

"No, it's not all about sales. But to sell a single copy of this stupid book I've got to publish it first."

"So publish it! The way you want it."

"Grethe—" How to begin? I was up against it again: the myths of the book world. Myths so persistent, so more fiercely and irrationally held than almost any other myths I knew. The myth of an heroic industry, dedicated to improving the cultural life of the nation and serving the cause of individual genius. The myth of the lone outlaw writer, working in complete isolation, and near complete ignorance, in some squalid urban shack, drowning in an ocean of black coffee and jiggers of whiskey, feeding on nothing but his own heart, who somehow erupts his self-styled masterpiece, a work of art so original and so compelling and so different and so raw—and so not in need of revision—that it floors every weasely, addle-brained agent and editor who encounters it. The book is immediately rushed into publication and sells ten million copies, not only making the young genius author rich and famous but permanently altering the nation for the better, and guaranteeing that the young genius will be studied for decades in college literature courses. *Those myths.*

"Grethe, my first book was a sales disaster. It was a humiliation. My publisher took a bath. You don't get to pick and choose after that. You just don't."

I knew my voice was rising, but I let it. That old bleeding hurt was still so raw. She needed to understand. She needed to realize the myths.

"Most people can't get a contract after a flop like that. They're practically outlawed from New York. Trust me, the streets of Manhattan are littered with writers who were once on top of the world but can't get anyone to even skim their manuscripts now. They've been cast out. They're not wanted. Because their last book, and maybe it was their only book, didn't sell."

"Sales, sales, sales," she clucked.

"How many books of fiction did you buy last year?" I said.

"Buy?"

"Buy."

"Not read?'

"How many books of fiction did you *buy* ? New fiction, I mean. As in just released and therefore most likely sold in hardcover?"

"A few."

"A few. So like three?"

"Two or three. Two, I guess."

"Two. You are a college professor. You have a Ph.D. You are among the most bookish people in the country. And a woman to boot. People like you make up the audience—and it's a dwindling audience, trust me—for literary fiction in this country. There's nobody else out there to buy it. *You're it*. And you only bought two books last year. That's not enough to keep an industry afloat, much less subsidize underselling books."

"Oh come now, surely the industry does not rely—"

"Yes, it does. And they can't afford to carry someone whom they regard as a proven bust. It's not a matter of what they want to do. They simply can't ."

"What about artistic conscience?" She snapped her words off her tongue as if with a pair of kitchen scissors.

"Whose?"

"Theirs."

"Whose?"

"The publishers!"

I started laughing. Definitely not a polite thing to do, but I couldn't help it. I'd been in the game so long now that the idea of an artistic conscience in big house publishers seemed more far flung than any ideal I could imagine: World Peace. A balanced federal budget. Democracy in the Middle East.

"Grethe, if publishers had to publish every book that was worthy on artistic grounds alone, they would be out of business in a month. And then nothing would get published. They have to consider their investment. And really, they just want to recoup their investment. That's considered a success in the publishing world."

"They can recoup on your Norway story."

"Maybe. But how can they know? They recouped nothing on my first book. That's mathematical fact."

Underlying my peevishness—though I didn't know how to properly explain this to her on the phone—was that I no longer saw the failure of my first book as an issue of artistic accomplishment versus market-driven tastes. That would be a convenient and satisfying lie to tell myself, but like all self-told lies it would only damage me in the end. Truth was, my first book sunk because it stunk. Period. I couldn't even bear to look at the thing anymore. I could not believe it ever got published. Only a last second call from my mother stopped me from incinerating the final boxful of copies I'd gotten from the publisher as part of my contract. Mom told me to send the box to her. She would keep it out of my sight. Of course, I acquiesced. It was my mother, after all. But now I wished I'd burned the box instead. Incineration is exactly what the book deserved. And to not face up to that, to not admit it, was to keep myself from growing as a writer. If I really did care about the art itself, I'd have to study hard the lessons my first book taught me.

But I couldn't, or just didn't want to have to, explain all that to Grethe in the middle of that sour phone call.

"The publisher prefers Denmark to Norway," I said, almost out of energy for my rant. "Fine. Let it be Denmark. What do I care? It doesn't affect the heart of the book."

"It affects the heart of the book for me," she said.

Dial tone.

So as not to give the wrong impression of Grethe I should tell my readers that she called me not fifteen minutes later crying and apologizing. She had overreacted. She had no business telling me my business. She was just sad for her country, which she had hoped would gain a little much needed celebrity from my novel. Denmark didn't need celebrity. Everyone knew Denmark. But she believed in me and in my book still. She still wanted to read it. She was sure it would be wonderful.

"And I want to see you," she said.

She offered to fly to Little Rock from the west coast. She would buy the ticket. She would arrange her schedule, even though she was the one teaching. She would go through the trouble. We picked a weekend in February that seemed to work for us both.

"What I'll do," she said, "is that I will cancel my Friday classes. That way I can fly out Thursday and stay a long weekend."

"That would be nice," I said.

"Just nice?"

"That would be great, Grethe."

"Ah," she chuckled. "The next time I hear you say that, I will have you meaning it."

Again, that was fifteen minutes after she hung up on me. What happened the second after she hung up on me is that I screamed toward the study ceiling, a long brute inarticulate yawp warbling through the room, attacking the walls. As if I might shatter them with sonic force, like a wounded, deranged cartoon superhero.

It was my book. Not hers. *Not hers.*

I said it, out loud this time, not quite in my senses: "It's my book."

(I should probably explain that in the moment—with my particularly unpleasant, uncharitable, retaliatory, and mildly deranged state of mind—I must have seen a life pattern renewing itself, i.e. the specter of my ex-wife. Somewhere in the course of my marriage, my professional ambitions became Joy's. My career became something she felt she owned as much as I did. I didn't notice exactly when this happened. I wasn't paying close enough attention. I only noticed after it happened, when I was slapped in the face with the consequences. And we all know how that turned out, don't we?)

"What are you doing?" Ryan said.

He was standing at the door of the study, examining me with one of his excavating brown-eyed gazes, more bothered and critical than worried.

"I'm emoting," I said.

He didn't change expression.

"Why?"

"Because I'm angry."

"Why?"

"Does it matter?"

He put his hand on his chin, tilted his head, squinted.

"I guess not," he said. "But you're way too loud. Stop it."

I didn't realize until that moment that my arms were suspended above my ears; hands were balled into fists.

I smiled. I dropped my arms.

"Sorry. Did I scare you?"

"No. You're just too loud. I can't hear *Yu-Gi-Oh*."

Someday I was going to have to lay down some rules to that kid about tv. Someday.

THREE

20

Sooner or later I would have to decide if they live or die. I'd just written a scene in which Rikke catches a turtle and force feeds meat to Eluf, which only makes him vomit. He begs her to stop, and she does, but she won't leave him alone. She wants him awake; she wants him up. She's terrified he might not make it. "I do not want to die out here alone," she says, sobbing. It was supposed to be touching, breakthrough scene as Rikke shows her fears for the first time. But all it did was put my Inner Critic on high alert.

Will she or won't she? Will he? Shouldn't you know?

I suppose I could let them both live. That would ensure it becomes an "inspiring tale of survival."

Vomit.

I didn't say that's what I wanted.

You could also kill them both off. That would turn it nice and dark, literary.

And also piss off the reader who's followed these people for hundreds of pages only to find them gone.

Okay, a middle course. Kill off one. A touch of the dark while not jettisoning all hope. The reader might buy that.

In every disaster story someone has to die, right?

Sometimes a few someones. But those sacrificial victims are usually secondary characters, not the main ones.

You don't have any secondary characters.

True, so do I really want to off one my leading lights?

You know how I vote.

Not only did I not know my novel's climax, I didn't even know what would happen to my Scandinavian wayfarers before they got there. Eluf killed a whale. Rikke caught a turtle. Eluf puked. Got that. So what else can happen? And exactly where were they anyway? By now they'd be closer to Iceland. But I didn't know how close. How many days it would take them to get there? And how do I keep them alive on a freezing cold ocean so I can finally kill them off?

Other voices snapped in my head, badgering and chastising. Or rather, one other voice. Sol Stein's. I had read his *How to Grow A Novel* after I'd finished my first book and found myself in noncompliance to virtually all of his axioms, especially one about planning your novel out scene by scene. Stein advises that the writer jot down a brief explanation for every single scene in the book. Not only what happens but why. That is, what the scene contributes to the overall progress and emotional power of the novel.

The scene outline also provides a means of seeing which scenes—on a comparative basis—seem strongest. Sometimes that will suggest that the strongest scene be moved forward to help captivate the reader earlier. . . . A scene outline provides the same opportunity for examining what's most wrong in the story and fixing it before spending months of wasteful writing on chapters that were conceived badly and needed to be excised or changed.

Reading that chapter in bed one night, thirteen months after my first novel stumbled invisibly onto the market, a month after my wife left, and about fifty minutes after downing an entire bag of dried apricots and mug of decaffeinated coffee, I felt pure heartache and even a burgeoning, bottom of my body nausea that was not entirely the fault of the apricots. *No wonder* it had taken me five years with that thing. *No wonder* I'd had to cut and cut and cut and cut and cut—only with profound reluctance and after long intervals of inattention, months necessary to defang my emotional commitment to all that extraneous, gratuitous, and essentially boring material. *No wonder it took me so long.* And then all that time adding. And reorganizing. And cutting some more. But only after the manuscript was beaten up by two writer friends of mine, and rejected by scores of agents, almost always with a terse comment that went something like this: "I just don't find it that engaging." Or: "It doesn't force me to read on." Or: "This is so sluggish you should market it as a sleep aid." *No fucking wonder.* Five years, two months, and seventeen days between the first sentence scrawled into a 99¢ notebook from Walgreens and that halfhearted letter from Leslie Knox saying he would take on my manuscript and, well, do *the best he could.* No wonder. I never had a plan. I had some notions about some of my characters, and a few incidents I might like to write, but that was all. The great bulk of the novel, at least 90% of what became my first working draft, just slopped out of me in fits and starts, lurching and turning and changing and contradicting as it went. I was too much in love with the principle that writing is an act of discovery, what I preached every semester to my classes, creative or not. *We write so that we will know what it is we have to say.*

So true a statement. But dangerous for a novelist to live by.

In class, I loved to quote Flannery O'Connor's essay where she claims not to have known the ending of "Good Country People" until she was three lines from it; I loved to quote Raymond Carver's essay in which he quotes—approvingly—from O'Connor and adds with relief "I thought I was the only one who wrote that way." I would tilt my head and say artfully, in sotto voice, *We find our story by the act of writing the story.* That's the magic, the mysterious intuitive alchemy of literary creation. I'd tell "bad" secrets on myself. When I was in your shoes, I'd say to the class, what I just starting to write fiction, I'd feel like I couldn't start a story until I had the plot entirely figured out down to the last action. Only when I worked that out could I feel like I could begin. I'd say this and chortle as if it was an inconceivably stupid concept, all the while knowing that many of my students, beginning fiction writers, were probably thinking: I still write that way. (Gulp). The subtext would be obvious enough: *You are only beginners. Pay attention to a master.* I continued: "Now that I know more, I don't worry about plot. Plot will take care of itself if you just write the story. What you do have to worry about is character."

So true a statement. But dangerous for a beginner to live by.

After all, even if that statement were always true of accomplished short story writers—and it isn't—accomplished short story writers weren't my audience. Instead, I was feeding the most sloven excuse making machinery into the minds of these students who hadn't read enough to develop an intuitive grasp of plot structure and a commitment to the ideal of a story's internal integrity. Students who didn't know the power of subtlety or the first thing about how to employ it. Students who weeks after my haughty talk would write the most bizarre, uncalled-for developments into their stories offering as their excuse—always with a confident smile; after all, hadn't I the teacher handed it to them?—*I just thought it would be cool for the story to go that way.*

Dangerous for a beginner. But more dangerous for a novelist.

Which Carver wasn't.

By not planning, I ended up with a 662 page draft bloated with slow, self-indulgent scenes, ponderous descriptive interludes, and a self-involved narrator who meandered through contorted and uninteresting meditations. It's a wonder I had the gall to continue with that book. It's a wonder I cared enough about it to ever get to the cutting and reorganizing phase. And even then, even getting it "good enough" for publication, the book sucked. Because from the outset it never had a plan.

I fell back to my pillow that night and let Stein's judgment overwhelm me, stunned into lifelessness. If only I had read the man's book earlier, when I was actually composing my novel and not suffering the consequences of it. Joy had bought me the book years earlier, a new release she noticed browsing the Writer's Reference shelf at Barnes and Noble. (This was before she'd given up on me, when she still thought she could help save my book.) I thanked her tepidly, placed the book on my nightstand and proceeded to ignore it with a patronizing certainty. I was an experienced, practicing, *published* writer. I didn't need no amateur's handbook. I let other books accumulate on top of it on the stand. I didn't remove it though, because that would necessitate seeing the title again, perhaps glancing at the blurbs on the back, or even opening it to a random page. And then I might be hooked. Then I might have to read it. I'd read it all and find out exactly what I was doing wrong. See, that was the real reason I didn't want to read it. I knew what I was doing was somehow wrong and didn't want to own up to it. I didn't want to undergo the drastic re-seeing of my novel that I realized it needed. So I ignored Stein and blundered along, months later deciding that dramatic cuts and surgical additions were needed, but completing these in half-assed fashion, forming a book that still sucked but just sucked a little less than before, that was still too long, just not as long as before, but which Lolly miraculously wanted to represent and, even more miraculously, she found a publisher for.

There I was: in bed, thirteen months after my book's release, separated from my wife, an involuntary eunuch, not sure if my son would be allowed to remain in my home, watching hopelessly as my book fell from an Amazon ranking of 712, 294 to 1,139,517, finally opening up Stein and hearing him tell me what I should have known from the start.

You're a dumbass, Stein said underneath his gamey yet diplomatic instruction. *For the price of a Burger King lunch, I offer the secrets to publishing and you ignore me . For you, I make it even cheaper—it's a freebie. A gift from your wife. And you still ignore me.   You waste five years of your writing life ignoring me and what do you have to show for it?* Volcanic gas gurgled across my stomach, pressing the walls, hardening and firing my skin, and sending a searing streak of pain through my abdomen. I flipped Stein back on to the nightstand and rolled over to the half of the bed where my wife once slept. Next time, I would know. Next time I'd have a plan for my book before any character so much as breathes. I got up, went to the toilet, and relived myself. My stomach settled. I went back to bed. I lay down.

Next time, dumbass. *Next time.*

Two years later, Eluf and Rikke were somewhere in the Norwegian Sea , lost, starving and near frozen to death.

And I still didn't have a plan.

So okay, come up with a plan.

And, sure enough I did, at least for their time aboard ship. It's sketchy, I admit—it's not Stein's chapter-by-chapter outline—but hey, finally, at long last, it was something.

<u>NEW STUFF PLANNED</u>

Getting ship ready.

Getting off course.

Catching first fish.

Rikke sick.

Attacked by monster fish.

Defeating monster fish.

Rikke better—Eluf sick.

Rikke catches turtle.

False hope of land.

Signals passing ship.

Rescued from hunger/thirst(?) again.

Sees land but misses it.

Makes it to Iceland.

I was happy to discover that I was closer to the end than I thought. In a month or two I could be done with a draft of the darn thing.

21

Dewed and shivering, Eluf opens his eyes. All the world is the level gray of the cloud blocked dawn. Nearly all day, every day is cloud blocked. The hard bottom of the boat has stung his body to red. He is sore all over. He is ill. He cannot move. Or does not want to. Today he will die. The hard finality of the thought surprises him, but then in the same moment he feels reassured. What beautiful definition, after weeks of fruitless drifting: *I will die today.* So that is that. Eluf can relax. Suddenly he can move. He stretches his legs as long as they can go. Then rolling to his side, he arches his spine, splendidly working the accordion of disks in his lower back, down where the memory of that mishap with the axe still surges once in a while. He actually feels much better, even stronger, knowing what he does. A couple days ago, stretching would have been out of the question. A couple of days ago, he hadn't the energy to do anything but lie still under a consumptive blanket, a lump of shrunken muscle and wasting bone. Today, now that he knows he will die, he can begin to feel better. He raises his head to check the landscape of the sea. It is unchanged: east and west, north and south there is only metal gray flatness. He has no idea where they are. Except that they are exactly nowhere, heading nowhere. He props himself on one elbow and looks more closely. What a dismal, angry color, Eluf thinks. But then it occurs to him that the sea is almost deliberately matching the circumstances. On his death day, the water shows as little life as possible. Beneath acres of gray battle hard sky, the water is dark, turgid, iron cold and unforgiving. Truly a grave. Lying on his side, his perspective is slightly off but it occurs to Eluf that part of the sea, on the northwest horizon, seems stiffer, blacker, and more fixed than the rest. And it could almost be said to be higher than the water, more like a hump sticking barely out of the water. Weird, Eluf thinks. Your senses change toward the end. Right at the edge of existence. Your mind changes. Your eyes fool you. That lump almost looks like—

Eluf stands up. His blanket drops like a rag to his feet. "Hey!" he shouts. "That's a—" He looks again, looks harder. If it weren't late winter, if the sky just held a bit more light. Just a bit. "That's a—"

He turns to see that his wife is at the other end, huddled as close as possible to the kettle fire, which somehow still burns. Her whole figure is pinched, as she tries to fit underneath her own tenuous blanket. Her head and shoulders are covered, but her booted feet stick out the other end, a pathetic revelation of suffering. But at least she's not sick anymore.

"Rikke," he says. "Wake up."

For a moment the terrible understanding that she might be dead cuts through, skewering his mind. Then her arms jerks. The pot of her head moves under the blanket.

"Rikke! *Land*!"

She pulls the blanket off her head, her eyes already narrowing and ranging the sea's terrain, her face squeezed with a lookout's intensity. Her head is a horror of fractured hair, under a stained blouse her bosom is retarded, her cheeks are way too thin, but it doesn't matter because she's not really there, inside her body. All of her is concentrated on the water.

"Where?"

"There." He points.

Her eyes narrow even tighter. Her mouth opens a half-inch. She begins to shake her head, then stops.

"I see . . . " she begins to say but closes her mouth.

"Do you see, Rikke? Do you see it?"

She does not glance at her husband but keeps looking at the sea. Finally, she stretches out her arm: a slow, tentative process. "Is that what you mean," she says.

"Iceland," he says. "It must be."

"How do you know?"

In fact, he doesn't. At all. But he guesses out of what he does know. What other land could be out there in that water, coming from where they came, moving gradually over a period of days due west and just north? Eluf had never heard rumors, gossip, strange stories or tall tales of any other island in this part of the world. It had to be Iceland. What else could it be? Most of all, he wanted it to be Iceland. And that was that.

"It is, Rikke."

She turns her face toward him for the first time: a casual look at first, then harder and steadier.

"You are not sick," she says, mystified.

He smiles. "And I'm not going to die either."

Damn that telephone. I had given these farmers their first real ray of hope since the novel began, and I was all set now to dash it. I was eager to. No mercy on my characters. (Another Stein adage.) I was going to push them away from the mass, whatever it is. Make it not land at all, perhaps, but a whale. Or an oil slick. (In 1793?) Okay, something else then. But then the telephone rang. Just let the machine take it, I thought. But the machine never picked up. Mysteries of science. Maybe the ringing will just stop, I thought. The ringing continued. Urgent noises. It occurred to me it might be Ryan's school—an emergency. I'm not allowed to ignore calls like that. I answered.

"Cancel Denmark," Lolly said.

"What do you mean?"

"Cancel Morton. He's not your john."

"He's not."

"Never was."

If there had been a moment to spare, I would have questioned her use of a prostitution metaphor but as it was I had too many other questions elbowing for space in my mouth.

"You said he was all fired up about it. You said he was excited to see the next *Kon-Tiki*."

"Well, that's what I hoped. But when I finally cornered him—"

"I thought you cornered him already, back at that party."

"I can't remember a thing about that party, love."

"Lolly—" My voice did a singsong of whining. I was struggling very hard not to sound like a frustrated twelve-year-old, but that's precisely how I felt.

"When I finally cornered him yesterday, he told me he was totally bored with the idea. And you. Apparently, he didn't like your first book."

"You only cornered him yesterday?"

"Yeah, so what?"

"Lolly, he's the reason I went to that lousy party. You called me at the hotel and said I had to come because Morton said—"

"The party is just one big Tylenol headache to me right now, Paulie."

"Yes. That doesn't surprise me."

She paused. "What's this I hear? Snippiness from my favorite author? What's up with you these days?"

"Nothing. It's—I've got my characters in the Norwegian Sea, floating off the coast of Iceland. They've spotted land for the first time."

"Cancel *Kon-Tiki*," she said.

"Cancel?"

"*Kon-Tiki* has been done. No sense doing it again."

I wasn't doing it again. That's the thing. My northern castaway tall tale had actually very little, if any, resemblance to Heyerdahl done-on-purpose and multi-ship expedition across the south seas. In fact, I'd been worried I was making a lie of Lolly's marketing hook.

"Lolly, my castaways have just spotted Iceland."

"Sorry."

"You're telling me to start my story all over again? I was just thinking this morning I'd have it drafted in a couple months. Maybe less."

"Sorry."

"You said it was going to be the selling point. *Kon-Tiki* in Denmark."

"Cancel Denmark."

"What's wrong with Denmark?"

"He likes Finland better."

"Who?"

"Oswald."

"Oswald who?"

"Luther Herman Oswald. The great one. If you want to publish original fiction with Norton, you have to conquer Oswald."

"I've never heard of him."

Lolly laughed breezily, as if I'd told a joke on purpose.

"That's why you need me, sweetie. You're not supposed to have heard of him. It's my job to."

Lolly gave me the rundown. Luther Herman Oswald was the big man in Norton's small but prestigious Contemporary Fiction division. Literally the big man. He weighed over 300 pounds. His hands were like tranches of mutton, his forearms as wide as legs of lamb. And his ass was a load of lead. But he dressed magnificently—tailored suits, silk ties, $400 Italian shoes—way better than anyone in publishing can afford, which suggested family money in the background, like the Knopfs and the Farrars. But the Oswalds weren't a New York publishing clan. Somehow their boy just made his way into the business. And how. Not too long ago, he ran Norton's ubiquitous, and obscenely profitable, literature anthology business. Everyone who has ever taken a lit course in college knows about Norton's anthologies. There are so many of them, and they are each so gargantuan, the used copies alone could fill every landfill in the United States. Like I said, obscenely profitable. It was too easy for Oswald to do nothing but show up, let the business run as it always had, and let the profits flow in. Too easy and too boring. So under his sireship, Norton began releasing a series of deliberately edgy anthologies. Edgy for Norton, at least. Postmodern Fiction. Postmodern American Poetry. Vietnam Literature. Gay and Lesbian Literature.

Lolly claimed that Oswald was set to approve an S & M anthology—purportedly titled *The Norton Anthology of Painful Experiences*—until the higher ups blew the whistle on that one. Frustrated and still bored, Oswald got himself switched to Contemporary Fiction: a comparatively minor, but a lot more interesting (read: risky) division of the company. The higher ups were happy to oblige the shift, hoping Contemporary Fiction would be a place to hide him. But Oswald was determined to throw his weight around, which was much easier to do with such a miniscule operation. He became the division's arbiter of taste, gambler of record, and notorious hard-ass on contracts. And, she said, he was having the time of his life.

"Sounds like a tough sell," I said.

"Not really. He's a pussy cat if you treat him right. Which I do."

I didn't follow up on that one.

"We get on famously. He likes to drink and he likes to laugh. He likes to announce his presence. When he's in a room you know it. Unlike Morton. Oswald is all on the surface, which I like. No petty insecurities. No mind games. No secret compartments. He is what he is. All I have to tell him is how fine he's looking, how firm his shoulders are, ask him if he's lost weight, and he's practically nibbling on my dress and breathing in my ear."

Didn't sound like the most grounded sales plan.

"You have to know him, baby. He seems like such a bear at first but put one drink in him and his guard falls completely down. After one drink he's the easiest person in the world to read."

"And you read him?"

"I read him like a book—your book." She chuckled at the witticism.

"So why can't I use Denmark?"

That explanation took a while. We had to go through Oswald's whole family tree. Oswald's grandfather on his father's side—Luther Osvalt—along with his grandfather's wife, two oldest sons, and two daughters, died at Bergen-Belsen. And they weren't even Jews. In fact, they were one of Germany's leading steel manufacturers: famously wealthy and rumored about in Weimar gossip pages. The children went to private boarding schools; the daughters would marry impeccably when the time came. When the Nazis took over the political landscape, they courted Oswald's grandfather intensely. They wanted access to his name, his reputation, his fortune, and, most importantly, his factories. Instead of merely going along with the Nazis, as 70% of the country did, or pretending to go along, as another 25% did, the grandfather openly refused to cooperate. He could not believe a ludicrous and amateur bunch like the National Socialist Party had any real future in Germany; besides which they were hooligans. He was not going to let himself be bullied. In the mid-30s it was still possible to believe that a world war could be averted, even believe that National Socialism would pass. Osvalt was certain both time and principle was on his side. The Nazis tolerated his refusals for as long as they thought prudent but in June, 1939, with war looming and about the whole German population under their thumb, the family was summarily rounded up, arrested, and put on a train, never to be heard from again. Osvalt's factories became government property and every employee a worker for the National Socialist cause.

One son, however, managed to escape the family's fate: sixteen-year-old Frederick Osvalt, who at the time his family's home was raided, was camping in the Black Forest with friends. On his way home, he took a detour to Bonn to visit an aunt. There, he caught word of the arrests. At her urging, he took the aunt's car and drove without stopping to France. There he remained for the remainder of the war years. He volunteered for the French resistance, setting off countless furtive bombs at strategic German depots, carrying messages to the Allies, inventing codes, even acting once in a while as a sniper. He claimed to have sniped a half-dozen German soldiers in his years of service. He claimed to know Samuel Beckett. After the war, Osvalt talked his way into a job as a hand on merchant marine ship bound for New York. He brought with him the clothes on his back, a measly cache of devalued francs, and a determination to leave the Old World behind. In New York, he anglicized his name, found a job as car salesman—his lifelong career—never returned to Europe, and forever cursed the Nazis for the life and family they had taken from him. It took him almost six years to marry. Two years after that, in 1954, a daughter was born. He named her Edda, after his mother. Then in November, 1958, his only son arrived, named of course after Frederick's father. When the boy came of age, Frederick tutored him relentlessly on the heroic stubbornness of his grandfather in the face of Hitler's pressure, and on the devastation wrought upon Europe by the Nazis and any citizen of any country who passively lay down before them.

"Luther says, and I quote, 'The Danes were nothing but stinking Nazi symps.' He can't and won't have anything to do with them. He says if you have to use Northern Europe make it Finland. The Finns remained independent."

"But my book is set in 1793."

"Doesn't matter. He can't stand the Danes. He won't forgive them. Or abide them. Another direct quote."

"So I have to change my novel about an 18th century Danish family because his family was murdered in Germany sixty years ago?"

"Yes."

"Lolly."

"Play the game, baby. Just play the game."

Wait a minute.

"How about Norway?"

"What about Norway?"

"Would Norway work for him?"

"I don't know. He didn't say anything about Norway. Just Finland."

"Maybe Norway would work."

I hoped to be able to tell Grethe that Norway was back in the picture. I also dreaded another Britannica excursion, this time into Finland. I already knew the country was absent from *Summer Activity 3rd Grade*.

"Why Norway all of a sudden?" Lolly said. "You were sold on Sweden."

"It's never been Sweden."

"It's never been Norway."

"It's always been Norway. Until it became Denmark."

"I thought for sure it was Sweden."

"It's not Sweden. And it's not Norway either. It's Denmark now. Or was."

"Well, it can't be Denmark. That we know."

"So I understand."

"And no *Kon-Tiki*. He says it's been done. Make them farmers again. He likes that."

"But they are farmers. Lost at sea."

"Cut the sea. No *Kon-tiki*."

"But it's not *Kon-Tiki*. And they're almost to Iceland, Lolly. I can't just take them back now; I can't just totally reconceive—"

"Yes, you *can*. Because you have to. And because you're a genius, Paulie. You are my sweet, cute, baby-assed baby genius. You are the best writer I know."

The air went out of me. My head hurt. The kitchen felt too warm and slightly rotten, this side of overripe, but at the same time distinctly and palpably sweet. Damn her flattery.

"Oh, Lolly."

"Call you this time tomorrow," she said.

She did, and I was prepared. As soon as I'd hung up the day before, I reread everything I had on Denmark. Then I got hot under the collar. Maybe I would and maybe I wouldn't be able to lure Lolly back to Norway. But I wasn't taking on Finland; at least not on account of the Nazis. I leaped to answer the phone.

"They weren't symps," I said immediately. "They might have had to roll over in 1940 but they weren't symps. Did you know that in 1943 the Danes engaged in a series of labor strikes aimed to directly hurt the Germans?"

"No."

"Did you know that the Danish government refused to take action against the strikers, that it refused to introduce the death penalty against saboteurs, and it refused to allow the persecution of the Jews?"

"No."

"Did you know that because the Danish government refused to cooperate, the Nazis had to install their own Reichskommissioner?"

"Their what?"

"Their own puppet."

"Are you done?"

"They weren't symps, Lolly. The Austrians were symps."

"Hey, baby, watch it. My grandma was Austrian.'

"Sorry. I didn't mean—"

She started laughing: full throttle delight.

"I'm joking! My grandmother was a retarded Basque who claimed she was Jewish but never offered any proof. We used to tell her: Your maiden name was Escobal, not Escobalstein. She didn't think it was a very funny. But then she became a Jehovah's Witness, and it didn't matter anymore."

"Why did you—"

"Because you were ranting, babycakes. You've become a spontaneously spouting history book."

"Encyclopedia, actually. Britannica."

"Look. I don't know anything about Denmark. Maybe you're right about all that. But Luther thinks you should use Finland. He says they were always independent during the war."

I had absolutely nothing on Finland. I couldn't tell one way or the other.

"Norway?" I asked, helplessly.

"Norway is a nonstarter. He says Finland. Sorry."

So, another trip to the Torreyson library was in order, my face fat and awkward and sabbatical-passive, my hands full of stupid silver change. I'd have to make a wide berth of the Writing and Speech building and hope I didn't meet any of my colleagues in the stacks. I didn't want anyone asking me how my novel was going.

"All right," I said slowly. "Finland it is."

"Thanks, Paulie. You're a wonder."

(Note to reader: In the interest of historical accuracy and in the spirit of fairness, I should point out that by 1943, consumer shortages and steep inflation had made the Danish public less comfortable than ever with the German occupation. More to the point, with the war clearly going worse, Germany had begun to look vulnerable. A cynical revisionist, or even a not so cynical one, could easily argue that it was merely stymied self-interest and opportunism, not democratic principles or human fellowship, that made the Danish workers strike that year. After all, a revisionist could say, where were the strikes in 1940? 1941? The Nazis were no less a threat then to world peace or Danish self-government. To that argument I say: a) Don't ask me; I only read the Britannica article, and b.) Don't underestimate the enervating effect of having a boot heel in your face.)

22

Ismo and Inka row furiously against a bitter headwind which, even as they work, pushes them further from the looming island. What they have waited for, struggled for, survived for, is slipping away with each hopeless thrust of stick. Ismo shoulder's are burning from the effort, the interior fabric of his muscles on fire and ruined from strain. He coughs up whatever air he takes in between pulls. Inka, however, just rows harder: head lowered, shoulders hunched like a game animal's, arms stabbing down and back, down and back, fighting the power of wind and friction of water. She does not cough, but that is because she is not breathing, only struggling as hard as she can for the green-brown shore more than a mile away.

Five minutes later, Ismo falls sobbing and breathing, gasping and coughing to the floor of the boat. He grabs at his shoulders as if to tear away intruders there. Inka shouts as the boat takes a sudden surge backward, then sideward. The wind is shoving them at its will.

"Get up, you lousy farm boy," she says and begins to cry even as she keeps rowing.

But Ismo can not. He is inert except for the crying and gasping, except for gripping his pained shoulders and wagging his head.

Meanwhile, the craft loses more territory. The island is a mile and a quarter away. Soon, it is a mile and a half. Inka stops. She lowers her chin to her chest, shakes her head, only able to mouth her curses because she had no air left to push over her tongue and across her teeth.

That's where I was one morning when the doorbell rang. I grunted an expletive. Probably UPS. Or the post lady. Only when I'm involved with something, or half-naked, does she ever come to the door. Some box that I don't want needs my signature. Screw it. I wasn't expecting anything in the mail anyway. I pushed on, started the next sentence. It was a Friday, after all. I needed to get a lot done. The next day would be consumed by the single parent docket. You know: soccer game, Wal*Mart, a third grade birthday party, a late afternoon grudgingly promised *Yu-Gi-Oh* duel with Ryan. (He claimed to have no one else to duel with. Turned out his best friend Daniel was forbidden by his mother to duel. Her reasons were Baptist and crazy—the game "promoted witchcraft"—but I can't argue with the result: no more *Yu-Gi-Oh* cards in your life. Ryan's other friends, meanwhile, were "clueless." [His word, not mine.] They didn't know a Blue Eyes White Dragon from a Mystical Tomato.)

The doorbell rang again: more precise, more insistent. Angry? Do doorbells have attitudes? What's with this post lady all of a sudden?

I trudged to the front door. At first I only cracked it, hoping I might see someone I could shut it on: e.g., a gray-haired pollster with a clipboard and long suffering, civic-minded patience; a young woman with dizzy eyes, frumpled clothing, and a homemade pamphlet in her hands for yet another local church; a toothy, mock-friendly teenager selling magazine subscriptions. Shut it and go back to work. If they kept ringing, I would call the police.

Instead I saw a composed blondish woman with straight hair and a hearty, sun-brushed complexion. Only a few entrenched lines at the side of her eyes verified her age. Her face was square, no nonsense, her nose short and blunt: almost pugilistic. She was focusing lucid blue eyes on potted caladiums hanging near the door. Dead caladiums, I should add. Joy had hung the pot before she left and forgot to take it with her. I had neither watered the flowers nor gotten rid of them, so all that was left in the pot was dried dirt and brown stems. In the same instant I saw this woman she turned to face the door squarely, her back straight, her shoulders set. She looked—and understand this was all a second's initial impression—like she could scale a rock wall if I said *Go*. I knew exactly who it was. My mouth dropped. I pulled open the door.

"Hello!" she called. "Here I am!"

I couldn't speak. My mind was scrambling across itself like a hamster on a wheel. Then the answer dropped out. I remembered: Friday.

"Grethe?"

She frowned.

"You didn't recognize me. I recognized you. Even without the beard."

"No. No. I recognized you. I did. It's just—it's just—" I could not even stumble to an end of the sentence.

"Didn't you get my message?" she said.

Damn. I could have predicted it. I have a string of not immediately obvious but very real bad habits that one day will be the ruin of me. I drink too much coffee. I don't clean my house. I haven't learned yet what exactly makes my car move. I listen to talk radio as entertainment. And I don't check my answering machine. Not much. I'm always afraid it's going to be bad news, so I'm content to wait as long as possible. Besides, I don't feel any particular obligation to anyone who calls me when I'm not ready to answer.

"I'm sorry, Grethe. When I was working yesterday I turned the ringer off. I forgot to turn it back on. I must not have realized the machine picked up."

A patient smile started slowly across her lips. A few seconds later it was complete.

"That at least explains why you did not call me back."

"When did you call? What happened?"

She moved her hand pertly, a flick of the wrist.

"It was nothing. Airline nonsense. I was stuck in Dallas last night."

"Why?"

"You know. Some delay somewhere in the system. We left two hours late from Eugene, so I missed the last flight out of Dallas. I called around eleven, I think."

At that point I was asleep on my couch, the tv flickering late evening dross. I woke up at 1:30 half-blind and my mind a puddle. I never even glanced at the answering machine when I went to bed. Her message must still have been there waiting for me, that tiny circle screaming *red red red*. I couldn't remember if I saw it when I woke up.

"Really. I'm so sorry. Come on in." I motioned her through the door, aware all of a sudden that it was almost noon and I was still wearing pajama pants and the t-shirt I'd slept in. Worse was the state of my house. The window above my sink and the three by my kitchen table were so fogged from dust and cobwebs and fossilized hand prints you could barely tell it was daylight outside. Spread across the table was the leftover detritus from breakfast: cereal bowls and spoons, juice glasses, a coffee mug, plastic place mats sawdusted with toast crumbs and oiled with drops of white milk, a jar of strawberry jam with the lid off, the lid itself two feet away and turned on its back like rock showing it mossy underside, two jam smeared knives, the almost empty orange juice jug, a few crumpled but not effectively used white paper napkins. And that's not to mention three day's accumulation of mail, last Sunday's *Democrat Gazette*, the *TV Guide*, a *Yu-Gi-Oh* collector's magazine, about a dollar's worth of loose change, a pair of scissors, a used kleenex (Ryan's), a sock, a near empty Country Crock tub, two crayons, and a week old bag of groceries (nonperishable) I hadn't put away yet. The vinyl flooring beneath the table was decorated with Kellogg's Corn Pop kernels, an Air Heads wrapper, a dried cranberry juice spill, and the encrusted remains of various recent dinners: mac and cheese, spaghetti with meatballs, tuna salad. My plastic trash can by the dishwasher was so full I couldn't get the top to close right. Greta was immediately greeted by the bowels of my life.

If you can believe it, and you should, my living room was worse. First, there was Ryan's mess: competing armies of *Yu-Gi-Oh* cards, spread out in lines as if the game was just interrupted, unstored Spiderman and Hulk and Rescue Heroes action figures, an open container of Chili Cheese Cheezits, a banana peel, a math workbook with its paper cover half-detached, Hardy Boys and Magic Tree House and Harry Potter books, sheets of stray notebook paper covered with drawings of his latest imagined inventions, and—unsightliest of all—a tipped over junk box, which had left a mound of Matchbox cars and plastic Happy Meal Toys and broken watches and magnifying glasses and Shrek figures and checkers and dice and Monopoly pieces (the top hat and dog) and miniature stuffed creatures and dozens of other assorted crap that I don't know how we ever accumulated. Then there was my mess: another juice glass, a wine glass, an apple core, two blankets scattered every which way, an open hardcover *American Heritage* dictionary, a hammer (a hammer?) a *Runner's World*, a pillow I'd brought out from my bedroom, my address book, a AAA map of the Southeastern states, a barbell—don't ask—*Saul and Patsy* by Charles Baxter, my dress shoes, a stack of utility bills, opened but unpaid, an empty root beer bottle, and a five dollar bill.

Grethe stepped cheerily across the doorway, but then took in the house at once.

"You weren't expecting me were you?" she said.

I started to deny it, but then I figured that would only double the insult. "No."

Grethe, bless her, only grinned.

"I was worried when I never heard back from you yesterday. I called your cell too."

My cell phone is never on because I don't like having to worry about charging it. And, besides, I always forget to take it when I step out the door. The only reason I own one is because everyone else does.

"Sorry," I said, "it was off."

She nodded as if she expected as much.

"And I e-mailed you twice last week."

"My e-mail's been down." That, in fact, was true.

Grethe started laughing, hard. "Why, this is like a television sitcom!"

"You don't know the half of it."

Her laughter cut off instantly. She looked at me with real concern.

"What do you mean?"

I cleared the kitchen table as best I could in a minute and made some coffee. I found a couple of bagels, only a week past the Sell By date, in a cloudy plastic bag in the back of the refrigerator. I put the lid back on the strawberry jam but left it out, and I left out the Country Crock. I added a jar of peanut butter and a hardened yellow wedge of cream cheese not quite at the molding stage. As we ate, I regurgitated all the commands and pronouncements out of New York, my attempts to navigate them. A few days before I had tried moving Ismo and Inka to a farm along the southeastern coast of Finland, just north of present day Turku. I put them back in the farmhouse, shivering and at each other's throats, eyeing the succulent if meager skin on the other's neck, knees, eyelids. I even had them attack each other, an 18th century Finnish version of a Jackie Chan fist fight. They did each other no real damage, since they were both so weak and not good fighters anyway. A silly scene, mildly fun to write, but when it was over I wasn't sure what else I could do with these two on a farm. Seems to me they faced the same decision Lars and Olga did: leave or starve. I wondered if I could talk Lolly into letting me get them into water. Maybe the Gulf of Bothnia or the Baltic Sea. In the end, in a bitchy mood, I gave up and put them back in the Norwegian Sea. These would be Finns, I decided, who as babies were kidnapped off a farm by a pack of touring gypsy actors. They were the love and pride of the pack as it worked its way across the northern countries. The gypsies kissed them, slept with them, played with them, even nursed them. But when taking care of babies seemed not romantic anymore—in fact, a pain in the ass—the gypsies stranded the babies at a farm in western Norway. The farmer, named Knute, adopted them both, but goodheartedly offered one of them to a neighbor farmer Rolf whose wife Ragnhild was barren. For

Ragnhild, owning and mothering babies was nothing less than a pure bodily desire, so long frustrated that it flared uncontrollably when she saw Knute enter their home with two infants. She scooped the babies out of his arms and retreated to a corner of the room like a wolf mother ready to fight to the death. Good hearted Knute knew exactly what he must do. So Inka and Ismo were raised by Rolf and Ragnhild in western Norway. And when the terrible winter of 1793 came they were forced to leave their own ice-desert farm for the perils of the water.

"That sounds very complicated," Grethe said, her teeth working hard on the half-stale bagel.

"It was the only thing I could think of to get them to Norway, so I could get them into the Norwegian Sea."

"Couldn't they enter the Baltic Sea and then go around?"

"That's a long way to go in a fishing boat."

She thought for a moment, shrugged.

"And what about the two of them? I don't understand. They sound like brother and sister now. But they are married too?"

I rested my cheeks in my hands. I rubbed my eyes with the thick ends of my fingers.

"That's another complication I have yet to work out. I'll think of something."

"I still don't see what was wrong with your original plan."

"Which one?"

"The Norwegians."

"This guy at Norton insists on Finland."

"But you have two Finns raised from infancy in Norway. It's the same thing."

"Not for him."

She released a sigh.

"So anyway," she said, "you are still keeping them at sea?"

"For now, yes."

She gently slapped the table top. "Good for you. It is your book. You are the author. Fie on your publisher."

"Well, we'll see."

I guess my attitude seemed particularly defeatist that morning.

"You know," she said, "you really should feel empowered to question this publisher. After all, he says he does not want *Kon-Tiki*, but your book is not like *Kon-Tiki*. Growing up in Norway, we all read *Kon-Tiki*. Heyerdahl is a hero to us, one of the few modern Norwegians who has become famous for something other than skiing. I must have read *Kon-Tiki* five times in school. Your novel is not *Kon-Tiki*. The only similarity is water."

"I know."

"*Kon-Tiki* is about heroic derring-do. Improbable theories being tested, and coming true. A man conquering time and history and nature. Your book is more like, more like—"

"The Titanic," I said.

She laughed—that sharp, direct, squeezing sound. Her blue eyes became more clear, more blue.

"Something like that," she said. She took a swig of coffee, her eyes still showing above the rim. "But in the end what is most important is that it is your book, no one else's. And if you stick to your guns about where the characters go why can't you stick to who they are?"

"You mean Norwegian?"

"Yes, I mean Norwegian."

Her laughter was gone now; the look of expectation heavy on her face. I thought carefully how to answer. I knew what it was I meant to say but I could not be too delicate with the words. "I've got to pick my battles, Grethe. If they say they want Y and Z, I can negotiate—maybe—on Y. Maybe they accept that as author's right. But if I refuse both Y and Z I look like the obstinate bastard who's too much trouble to work with. Because after all, his first book tanked anyway."

She held her face still. Then her eyes softened. Her cheeks relaxed by careful degrees. She was determined that we not get in another argument. "It must be hard working with these people."

"It seems closer to the heart of the adventure," I continued, "that my nomads be stranded on the sea between Scandinavia and Iceland. That's crucial. It seems less crucial that they come, you know, from any particular country." She winced. She tried to suppress it, and when she couldn't she tried to cover it by rubbing her eyelid, but it was too insistent a reaction, a pure and purely honest bodily response. Her voice grew small, heartbreakingly contrite. It wasn't fair of me to expect her not to be hurt.

"I guess I can understand that," she said. "Just do the best you can."

I nodded slowly. "Thanks. You're a lot kinder than the publishers."

Her eyes brightened. They were clear again. Then she yawned. She hurried a fist to cover her mouth. "My. I am dragging this morning. I got to the hotel late, and then I was up early in order to catch my plane in Dallas."

"Take a nap," I said. "I'll clean up. You might as well use my bed." I didn't want her going near the embarrassment of my living room. Not yet. Fortunately, she took to my suggestion.

"I always have been a napper," she said. "I believe it is essential to one's mental health. Sometimes, if I'm tired enough, I lock my office door and just lie on the floor."

I laughed. It was a funny, unexpected image.

A line of worry crossed her face. "Understand," she said, "that my floor is carpeted."

"You're a wonder, Grethe."

Her smile went as wide as I'd seen it all morning: a long warm winking expression.

"Yes I am," she said and went promptly to her nap. The bedroom itself was messy enough, but nothing like out here. I scanned my living room and sighed. One positive thing: she'd already seen it at its worst. And she hadn't walked out.

23

[Note from real author: Since it appears that our hero and his visiting friend might be warming up to the inevitable, ahem, it might seem an inopportune time to interrupt the scene for some encyclopedic information on Finland. But I'm going to. Why? Two reasons: a) consistency demands that Paul—or I, if Paul is otherwise occupied—treat Finland with the same respect he (really "he" through me) did Norway and Denmark. I wouldn't want anyone thinking Paul or I had an inherent grudge against the Finns just because Luther Oswald is so uninformed (more on that shortly), and   b) as I suggested earlier—in my discussion of reader discomfort—maybe it's my writerly job to make you wait on the "ahem" for a while.   That's what Sol Stein says.   No mercy on the characters and no mercy on the reader. Stress him, strain him, raise his blood pressure, delay his gratification. It's what he *wants*, after all. He'd actually rather you tease him then give in to him, like the frat boy who will dump the one he slept with only to keep hounding the one who said "No."

And so, some facts on Finns:

1) One-third of the territory of Finland lies north of the Arctic Circle. In this forbidding region, with its prolonged winters, temperatures drop as low as -22°F, and the snow never melts.

2) In addition to the arctic territory, there are two other regions of Finland: a coastal plain in the south and an interior lake district.

3) Most of the urban centers of Finland are found in the more temperate coastal region, while the north and northwest areas may still be called colonial. That is, they are areas still expanding and developing, and as a result they demonstrate conflicting social interests.

4) The continental glacier that cut Finland is still retreating. As the weight of the ice sheets lessens, the land continues to rise. Put another way, Finland is still emerging from the sea.

5) Finland is dominated by conifers, but in the south exists a zone of deciduous trees: birch, hazel, aspen, maple, elm, linden, and elder.

6) Finland has two official languages: Finnish and Swedish. The Swedish speaking population is located mostly in the coastal region while the rest of the country speaks Finnish.

7) When World War Two started, Finland was only semi-industrialized. Since the end of that war, however, it has rapidly gained ground with its economy turning from agriculture, forestry, and mining to industrial production, services, and information. It suffered a recession in the early 1990s with the collapse of the Soviet Union, its chief trading partner. Since that time, the country's economy has recovered by refocusing its trade toward western Europe.

8) Finland has a static and even declining population. Also an aging population. Each year it loses more people to emigration—Sweden being the most popular destination—than it gains through immigration. Since the émigrés tend to be younger people in search of rewarding careers, the remaining population skews older.

9) In World War Two, due to its history—then—of antagonism toward the Soviet Union, Finland was sympathetic toward the German cause, even while remaining officially neutral. German armies were in Finnish territory when the Third Reich launched its first strike into Russia. In the early years of the war, *the Finns themselves* (emphasis mine) launched attacks on the Soviet Union, in one expedition actually capturing large sections of East Karelia, which a few years earlier it had been forced to cede to the Soviets. Only in 1942, when the war in Russia began to go badly for Germany, did widespread support for peace talks take hold in the Finland.

Back to Paul and "ahem."]

I'd put away the last action toy and was beginning the final living room task—tidying up the toppled junk box—and drifting mindward toward the Norwegian Sea (where Ismo and Inka had exhausted themselves against the power of wind and water) when I heard a small, crisp voice from the bedroom.

"Paul?"

I stood up. I hesitated.

"Paul?"

I took a couple steps in the direction of the bedroom. I heard the door open. Grethe leaned out. Her face had visibly deepened and relaxed; her eyes showed the grog of someone just wakened.

"Can I take a shower?"

"A shower? Of course."

Before I could think of, or assume, anything else she said: "It's just that being stuck in that plane and then the rental car and just now waking up. I do not feel comfortable in my own skin. Plus, I smell."

I laughed. I knew better than to utter my first thought: *I thought Europeans didn't care about smells.* I guess she'd been over here long enough.

"I'm still cleaning up out here anyway."

She cringed with real feeling. "I did not mean to make you have to straighten your whole house."

"It's my fault. I didn't look at the calendar. I didn't answer my phone. Being on sabbatical, you become hermetic."

"I envy you."

I shrugged. "And not being married. It—you know— distances you."

Her eyes sharpened in the moment. They glinted white with interest, then purposefully relented. She nodded: evenly and slowly, as if stringed by a resisting line of thought. I realized that she couldn't possibly know what I was talking about.

"Don't mind me," I said. "I'm just rambling."

"I understand. I was married once."

"You were?"

"Just once."

"That's all it takes."

She smiled. "Only for a month."

"One month?"

A firm nod. "That's all the time we needed."

"How long was—I mean when—"

"A couple years after I came. I was still new, still awed by America. I don't think I loved him as much as I loved the idea of marrying your country. But he did seem all right."

"He wasn't?"

"Oh, you know." She looked at me sideways then stretched her shoulders uncomfortably. "In his own way, he was all right. He was not bad; he did not hurt me. For another woman he might have been a fine husband. Not for me."

I nodded. I knew too well from my own life that divorce didn't come with black and white hats.

"It was more of an embarrassment, really. I've not ever been more ashamed for acting stupidly. My parents were angry: marrying someone I barely knew, and American no less. They almost did not come over for the ceremony. Almost. And they weren't surprised that we divorced. They were relieved actually. But they also enjoyed too well the satisfaction of being right, let me tell you."

"Ah."

"I tried to cover up when we separated. Except for my parents, I did not tell. I was just too embarrassed."

"Must have been a hell of a month."

She stirred the air with her fingers as if clearing smog; then with purpose she shook her head.

"I don't care to talk about it. Because I don't want to think about it. And I never do. Except I cannot say I have ever forgotten—in my heart I mean—what a disaster it was."

She looked long at me: that clear direct northern gaze.

"I need to get you a towel," I said.

She followed as I went into the master bath and found a clean towel in the closet. I handed it to her, not quite meeting her stare.

"This should not take long," she said. I felt her looking for my eyes, trying to catch and hold them. "I'll just undress and jump in."

I nodded and started for the bedroom door, my head about to pop like a squeezed blueberry. I opened my mouth, ready to speak. It felt dry and sweet at the same time. When I spoke the words came out sluggishly, like molasses over boulders.

"I'll show you the book when you're done. You can see it." I could not have really known what I was saying. The book at that point was still only pages of cramped, hurried handwriting in a notebook, to say nothing of all the passages that were crossed out, of all the stars and arrows in the margins, of the curt coded commands to myself: "Move to after fish," "Her talk about dad," "Insert C here." I opened the bedroom door.

"I'd love that, Paul," she said. "That's what I've been waiting for."

Something in her tone made me look back. The smile in her eyes was timid now. She held the top of the towel against her chest with both hands and let the rest of it spill to the floor, as if to cover her exposed front, though she was fully clothed.

"Yes," I said. "Okay." I stepped out and gently pulled shut the door.

What am I doing, I thought. I stood in my kitchen in front of the sink. A newly emboldened sun, just free of morning cloud cover, attacked the dirty window. The yellow-white brightness fractaled against the glass and moved over my face in every direction, slicing my eyes, generating red pebbly spots and black flares. I turned on the faucet. I put something underneath the argent column of noise and a second later came up with a glass of drinking water. I gulped it in one draft. I had not slept with a woman since the separation. I hadn't even been on a date since the separation. Not even when the divorce was legalized did I take action that would lead to my sleeping with a woman. My wife—and here's a damning confession—was the only woman I had actually ever slept with.

(Quick clarification: In college, I had slept—literally, I mean—with a couple of others but not, you know, to my profound disappointment . . .)

I took another drink of water. The phone rang.

I didn't hesitate. Even having just been thinking about what I'd been thinking about, it was such an automatic behavior. I went straight into my bedroom and picked up the receiver from its cradle.

"You have got to move to New York, baby. I need you here."

"Why? What's going on?"

"What am I supposed to do when I'm talking your book up to an editor and he says 'Sounds terrific. I'd like to do lunch with him someday.' Then I have to say 'Sorry. Can't. He's in Arkansas.'"

"I can fly up if it's pressing."

"That takes too long. And what if it's not pressing? What if it's a spur of the moment thing? What if it won't work the next day? What if I have to strike while the iron is hot?"

"Does someone really want to do lunch with me?"

"No. But I've got all sorts of interest in your farmer thing. There's Luther, of course. And I was just talking to a guy from FSG. I swear, one lunch with you—I mean us—and that twerp would be in the bag. He was that interested."

"So Luther Oswald isn't necessarily the only audience for this novel?"

A pause. "Of course he's not the only audience."

"So I don't have to make it Finland?"

"You mean Denmark."

"No, Finland. That's what you said. Before."

"I said Sweden before."

"Lolly, Sweden was never in the picture. You said Luther wanted Finland."

"Oh." Silence. "All right, maybe I did. For Luther's sake you *have* to make it Finland."

"But what if this other guy wants Norway?"

She erupted: a sarcastic, searing sound midway between a cough and a sneer.

"This 'other guy' is a thirty-two year old momma's brat from Omaha. He's got his head so far up his ass I don't know how he found his way to New York. He doesn't know Norway from Hoboken. He probably thinks Norway is populated with buffalo. He won't care."

"But if he won't care—"

"I haven't stopped counting on Luther, Paul. Luther is still in my back pocket. I'm working him all the time. So don't do anything to piss off Luther, okay? He, right now, is still the prime candidate. I'm just saying—I'm just trying to encourage you—we could have—we hope to have—a bidding war on this thing if we get some people to bite. And that might be easier if you were here."

"But the book's not even done yet."

"Who cares? You think Norman Mailer doesn't write books on contract? You don't think he gets paid well in advance, and then writes the book he's been paid for? You weren't born yesterday, Paulie."

"No, and I'm not Norman Mailer."

Lolly let out one hideous sigh: languorous and supremely peeved.

"You're a published author," she said. "You have a history. You're not some blue balled MFA kid."

I heard a noise behind me. I turned, and through the open door of the bathroom I saw Grethe. She stepped to the shower stall, without clothes on, the towel still held against her front except now of course it offered no protection against inspecting eyes. She dropped the towel at the foot of the bathtub. She leaned into the stall and turned the handle. I couldn't not see what she was allowing me: the pale skin of her back; the wrinkles at the bottom of her neck and around her armpits; the birthmark on her right shoulder, triangle shaped and the color of weak hot chocolate; the lines of her shoulder blades, once probably sharp and clear as swords but more hidden now behind the flesh of middle age; the straight line of her spine, disc after disc after disc, down to the cup in her lower back, just above her waist; her waist tucking squarely into her hips; her hips; the soft down on her behind; her thighs and her calves, fit-looking, almost muscular, for a forty-something woman. For that second, as she adjusted the faucet, I stared. Then she stood upright, looked wistfully over her shoulder, and smiled.

"Lolly," I said, "I have to go now."

24

"I don't get it," I said, stroking Grethe's thigh. "The guy has a problem with Denmark, but then he wants me to use Finland, which cooperated with Germany."

She nodded once, a vague, long movement, and stretched her arm across my chest. The hairs on her forearm made a subtle friction against my bare skin.

"He has an idea he believes in," she said dismally. "He wants it to be your idea."

"But his idea is wrong, that's the thing. It's wrong for him, for what he believes. It doesn't fit what he cares about."

She made a noise in her throat: small but contemptuous. She turned her palm flat against my chest and kept it there, as if measuring the heartbeat beneath.

"It is stupid," she muttered. "No denying. But I am hardly surprised."

"It's not just stupid. It's stupid for him."

"Like I said, I am hardly surprised."

Her voice was flat as a gutter as she said it, her head unmoved on the pillow.

"Tell me about your husband," I said.

"Ah"—she lifted her hand momentarily and moved it, as if scattering a simulacrum that had formed in the air—"There is not much to tell." Her hand roamed carelessly then over my chest to my hip skimming and testing the surface of my skin. It landed, as if haphazardly, on my penis, spent from the recent excitement. She gave it an affectionate squeeze.

"You met him at the university?"

The hand let go. Her head jerked up, as if to study me.

"He was in one of my classes."

"Which?"

"Geography."

"They made you take geography in grad school?"

Her head dropped again. She returned her hand to the starting point: the center of my chest.

"I was not taking the class. I was teaching it."

"Oh, I see." I dragged out the last word, saying it mock-scandalously. But in fact I was a little surprised.

"He was not a teenager, Paul. He was thirty-five, a logger trying to come back for a college degree one course at a time. He was rough around the edges. Not used to the culture of the university, you know. But he wanted to come anyway."

"That's admirable." I meant it.

"It is admirable, and I admired him. His determination. I was shocked, though, when he asked me on a date."

"He asked you?"

I felt her glance.

"When the semester was over. I could never have done such a thing myself. I was too young to the country. Besides, I knew the rules. They were drilled into us as GAs. You don't approach students that way."

I nodded, familiar with the injunction. Not everyone obeys it.

"In the old days, plenty of relationships started that way. I mean lasting relationships."

"Yes," she said, "and not lasting ones as well."

"Touché."

"You're not romanticizing the 'old days' are you? Many of those 'relationships' were harassment. Intimidation even."

"Tell me more about your husband."

She looked at me as if uncertain she should leave the current subject behind. "Him," she said, and sighed. I needed to remember, the sigh said, that this marriage only lasted a month. One month out of her whole life. But she told me anyway. He was rougher around the edges than she expected. For someone trying to raise his station, to make a whole new life for himself, he remained disturbingly committed to old friends, old haunts, old habits. Watchful in class, and refreshingly reserved, even formal, during their dates, once he had her at home he took on the ugly bravado of a bad winner. He began criticizing her, badgering her—only weeks into the marriage.

"The spell wore off fast. I saw where the marriage was headed. If I didn't get out, I wasn't going to be able to do what I came to America for. He was not going to support me in that work. It didn't finally matter to him."

"Sounds like an asshole."

The hand startled. "I don't know. I think he was intimidated, actually, and afraid to say so. He liked the idea, he liked the bragging rights, you know, of sleeping with his 'college professor'—but it scared him at the same time. While we were dating he acted so impressed with my background, but then as soon as we were married the same background seemed to be a threat. Maybe he was afraid I would extinguish him."

"So he tried to extinguish you."

She shrugged. "I guess. He remarried before I left Seattle. I saw him once with his wife. They looked happy enough."

"Everybody wins."

"Correct. Now, no more talk of my ex-husband. I did not visit you to talk about him."

Her hand found my penis again. After the respite it showed a little more life. She put her lips to my bare shoulder and started gnawing. I rolled in her direction, finally settled myself above her: the pale face, transparent blue eyes, the hummocks of her breasts as they relaxed against her torso. She smiled and put her hands around my neck.

"No more about him," I said. I lowered my hips so that the new erection fit snugly against the triangle at the center of her thighs.

"After all," she breathed, "now there's you."

The phone rang.

"Shoot," I said.

"Can't we let it ring?"

"We could," I said, pushing away. "But I have a feeling I don't want to."

She frowned: openly. I caught the receiver just before the answering machine went off.

"Can we talk now?"

"I guess."

"You guess? Why don't you want to talk to your own agent?"

"I've got company."

"In the middle of the day? It is the middle right, for you? What time is it there?"

I checked the clock radio next to the bed. "3:05."

"You have company at 3:05 in the afternoon?"

"Well, one. One visitor."

"A visitor? Are you *sleeping* with someone?"

The second she gave me was certainly not enough time to formulate an answer.

"Are you in bed with someone right now? As I talk to you? *Right now?*"

Grethe moved off the mattress. She stepped into her underwear, picked up her bra.

"No, I'm not in bed."

The erection dissipated, my cock flaccid as a rubber band. I felt ridiculous: standing there naked, a receiver in my hand. Grethe buttoned up her blouse.

"Is this visitor a woman?"

"Yes."

"Is she a colleague?"

"Sort of."

"Oh, shit."

"She's helping me with my book."

Grethe glanced at me darkly. She hiked up her pants and walked out into the kitchen. A second later I heard the water running in the sink.

"I'll bet she's helping you," Lolly said, a paring knife running along the tip of her voice.

"What's going on?" I said.

"I told you before. I want you available when I need you. As in New York. I've got people jumping on this Norwegian thing like it's the catch of the day. And I don't just mean Luther. We might be able to pull off a real deal on this one."

"Finnish," I said.

"I'm not done talking."

"You said Norwegian. You meant Finnish."

"No, I think I meant Danish.'

"Finnish. Luther wants it set in Finland."

"He does?"

"Yes."

"I don't think so. I think he said Denmark."

"Lolly."

"Let me check my notes."

"I think that was Morton."

"No, he wanted Sweden."

"He wanted Denmark."

"Denmark?"

"His mother is Danish, remember?"

"Morton's mother is a Brooklyn Jew. I've met her. I've eaten her latkas. If she's Danish, I'm a negro."

"I'm confused."

"Let me check my notes."

"I'm totally confused."

"*Let me check my notes.* Crap. Where are they? Hold on." She put the phone down. For seconds on end, I heard no more from her. From the kitchen I heard the water still running, the titter of plates and glasses. Grethe was cleaning up from lunch.

"No, it's Norway," Lolly said. "With Luther, I mean."

"Jesus."

"What?"

"Are you sure?"

"Yes, I'm sure, Smarty Pants. It's right here. 'L. suggests Norway. Finns were Nazi collab.' That means 'collaborators.'"

"I know. That's just what I said."

"What?"

"That they collaborated with the Germans."

"So what's the problem?"

"You told me Luther wanted Finland, and now I have this whole Finnish scenario in my head. I worked it all out. Finnish twins, stolen by gypsies, left in—"

"Finnish twins?"

"It's not as ridiculous as it sounds."

"But Luther didn't ask for Finland."

"You told me Luther wanted Finland. Because of the Nazi thing."

"No, that was Oscar."

"Who's Oscar?"

"Oscar Espanoza. He's with Vintage. Now, his mother *is* from Finland. And his father is from Puerto Rico. There is one scrumptiously handsome man. But I never slept with him, so I can't tell you anything."

"But—I thought—I mean, I swear, you told me Luther said Finland."

"Luther hates Finland. Why are you so fixated on Finland?"

"I'm not fixated on Finland. Finland is a problem, actually. I was fixed on Denmark because that's what you said Morton wants. But really I'm fixed on Norway."

"Luther wants Norway."

"He can have Norway!"

"Of course we may not ending up selling the book to Luther."

"Jesus—"

"We're gonna try, yes. But realize, Paulie, I'm going to sell the son of a bitch to the highest bidder. The thing we want and need is the bidding. And to get the bidding we've got to snag one of these big boys first. If I snag one, then I've got my hook to snag the others."

"You know the business, Lolly."

"Of course, baby, that's why you need me."

"Yes," I said, "I guess I do."

"So are we clear now? Are we happy?"

"Yes. Actually, I'm very happy, Lolly. You've solved a problem."

"God, I love a joyous man. If I were there I'd kiss you. But I'm not, thankfully. I'm in the civilized world."

"Yes," I said.

"So when are you coming?"

"Coming?"

"To New York. Do lunch again."

"Sure. When?"

"How about Monday?"

"Monday? *This* Monday?"

"This Monday," Lolly said.

"That's impossible. I won't be ready. Can you wait a couple weeks? Can you wait a month?"

"A month? Are you trying to kill this deal?"

"Lolly, the first draft isn't even done."

"Well, finish it. Soon. And then call me. I want you in New York as soon as possible."

"All right, chief."

"You're very sexy when you're submissive. Did you know that?"

"No, I didn't."

"Well, you are. See you later. You can go back to your girlfriend now."

"Lolly—"

"Don't, Paulie. I'm a woman. I know everything."

"Okay."

"I knew that you wouldn't come on Monday because of this chick. I just wanted to hear you squirm."

I opened my mouth. My tongue sat still.

"See," she said. "I am right."

"I think I'll have the book ready in a few months. Thanks for working so hard."

"It's all for you, sweetness."

When I put the receiver down I practically ran to the kitchen.

"Norway is back!"

Grethe jumped. Then her cheeks forced out a smile.

"How did that happen?"

"My agent. She says Norway is what the guy wanted all along."

Her brown blonde eyebrows slanted hard like boards on her high forehead.

"What about Finland?"

"That was a misunderstanding. Finland won't fly. Thank God for the Nazis."

She frowned again. I hugged her lightly, my hands joining at the small of her back. She leaned her head back, brought up the broken boards of her eyebrows to equanimity, and kissed me full on the lips. She ran her sink damp hands along my sides, over my still naked skin.

"Now," she said, "is that woman going to call again?"

"Oh my God," I said. I pulled away. "Ryan. I was supposed to pick him up fifteen minutes ago."

25

Ryan stood outside the front door of his school, his arms crossed, overloaded purple backpack pinching his shoulders, his face a pit of accusation. He was alone except for the one teacher remaining, who looked just as cross. Even after I pulled to a stop and waved to him, Ryan waited before starting to the car. He was going to play this for all he could get. As he came close he scowled at Grethe in the front passenger seat. I hit the unlock button by my left hand. A mechanical clunk sounded along the body of the car, inside and out. Ryan opened his door. He took off his backpack. He tossed it into the middle of the back seat. He climbed in. He seat belted himself.

"Sorry I'm late," I said.

He looked at me. He looked at Grethe.

"Who is she?"

Grethe turned as far around in her seat as she could.

"I'm Grethe Westerleg, Ryan. I am a friend of your father's, and I am happy to meet you." She jutted her hand back, practically into Ryan's face. I winced. This was probably the worst thing she could have done. Ryan always turned shy, even stony, in the face of a stranger. And forcing him to "Be a big boy and shake" only ever made matters worse. Presently, he looked away from the hand. He didn't touch it. Grethe glanced at me, worried. I waved it off. *It's okay.* She turned back around.

"Sorry, bud," I said. "Time got away from us."

"What were you doing?" he asked, just as suspicious as that. Grethe and I peeked at each other.

"Grethe came to visit, and we were catching up."

"Catching up to what?"

Grethe chuckled, a very public kind of noise.

"I live in Oregon, Ryan. Do you know where that is? I flew out here to talk to your father about the book he is working on. Do you know about your dad's great book?"

Ryan didn't answer her. His eyes narrowed.

"How come you didn't tell me she was coming?"

Grethe laughed louder: an exclamation. She was putting up a truly noble effort.

"Because your father forgot. And because he didn't check his answering machine to get my message that I was on my way. I'm afraid when I got to your house today, your father was quite unprepared."

At this point, I had pulled away from the school. I glanced back. Ryan scowled at me. I tried to smile. I tried to shrug. *You know how it is, Bud. You know me.*

Grethe resumed her forays, repeatedly trying to draw him out. All unsuccessfully. I should have warned her. But still, after a while, she seemed too determined, too cheery. Clearly she was making Ryan uncomfortable. Before she could ask again what subject he liked in school or who his best friend was, I asked her about her classes. "Oh," she said, surprised. Then she settled into her answer, grateful to speak about what she knew.

"Is she staying with us?" Ryan said, the line of nervousness apparent in his voice.

"I'm staying the whole weekend, Ryan," Grethe said, as if this news ought to make his day.

I watched in the rearview mirror for a reaction. His eyes met mine, held them for a second. Then he looked away.

When Ryan went to bed I brought out the novel and showed it to Grethe, including the passage I was working on when she rang the doorbell. She settled in with a glass of wine and started. Somehow she was able to translate my chicken scratch.

"Oh, this is crazy, wonderful," she said periodically, chortling the whole while. She was an effusive, active reader, which made me nervous. I thought about running to the store for milk or eggs, just for an excuse to get out, but in the end I couldn't help but stay. "Of course, your people seem almost slapstick. Not quite Norwegian. But that is okay."

Not quite Norwegian.

I spoke slowly: "I guess that bothers you."

She looked up, surprised, eyes abuzz with nervous blue. "Not really. Why would you say that?"

"I guess I'm sensitive about how well I'm handling the people and the period."

She studied me for a moment. She glanced at the manuscript. She tapped the cover.

"Since you're not Norwegian I can hardly expect your characters to act like true Norwegians. Not yet, at least." She smiled.

I nodded. "Yes," I said. "Thanks." She was trying to be generous. I knew she was. But I couldn't help but be disappointed. *People aren't Norwegians,* I wanted to say. *People are people. If I make them true people they will be accepted as true Norwegians . So what you're really saying is that I didn't make them true people.* "Thanks," I said again. I took back my notebook and went to get her more wine.

The weekend passed as awkwardly as it started. Grethe kept trying to draw Ryan out, but he refused to be drawn. When she wasn't looking, he stared at her as if not convinced she was real. Then he stared at me. *What is she doing in our house?* We did get out on Saturday morning for his soccer game and Grethe insisted we take Ryan to McDonald's to lunch—her treat. I let her do it, but I could tell that it wouldn't make a difference. My son had shut down. He'd become a stone. In part, it was Grethe's foreign accent putting him on alert; in part, it was her eagerness to capture and celebrate any word that escaped his mouth; but mostly it was the fact that he hadn't been prepared. I never told him. My fault.

Grethe and I slept in the same bed both Friday and Saturday nights. But with my son and his knotty reluctance occupying the other bedroom, the place didn't feel like the sloppy bachelor's pad it had on Friday morning. On Friday night we made a short, dutiful, rubbery act of love as I listened at the back of my ears, scared of any sound from the far side of the house. On Saturday night, neither of us particularly wanted to do anything, even though Grethe was leaving the next day. The urgency was gone, replaced by awkwardness and a pervasive sense of the weekend failing. As Grethe moved into bed she rolled toward me, even put her arms around my neck. We were both naked, but all we did was lie still in the darkness.

"Your son does not trust me," she said.

"He's a kid."

"Usually children trust me."

"He doesn't know you."

"Usually that doesn't matter."

"Really."

"Yes."

She indifferently rubbed a spot on my neck then stopped. No more. Her thoughts had taken over: patrolling the bed, pressing on the quilt, slipping beneath the covers, gathering and breeding gloomily at the pillow.

She let loose a resigned, fatalistic noise, as if something were happening that she was all too familiar with. Something she had lived through too many times.

"But he is a good boy," she said.

What else could she possibly say? Her first time in our household. It was not her place to criticize him. It was, however, my place to apologize for him, to try to set her at ease.

"He is a good boy," I said.

She brought her hand off my back, let it glance my thigh. For seconds, she did not speak.

"Tomorrow I will do better," she said at last. She rolled away to the far side of the mattress and within a half hour her sighs had turned to light snoring. I closed my eyes and almost instantly went under, grateful for the chance of some uninterrupted rest.

26

For days they do nothing but drift atop the heavy water, letting the current take them backward and away. Iceland—if that's what it was—is no longer even visible; the horizon is as pale and hopeless as ever. Fighting the drift is impossible. Their thin savaged muscles don't have the energy to resist anymore. They are lucky to still be alive. They lay as close as they can to the barely acting fire and sleep.

Lars stirs. He groans, as he does whenever he moves now, but he is able to pull himself upright. Olga is still asleep, her shrunken mouth sawing a snore, sharp and high-pitched like water forced out of a crack in the earth. She can still do that, Lars thinks, grateful. Inside, a permanent companion, is the buzzing of need, the debilitating call for sustenance, which because he has not satisfied it in scores of hours, has turned his body against itself. Lars reaches for a spear. As he does so, he feels the wince of pain in his shoulder: yesterday's wasted effort lingering in his body.

With his other hand, he shakes his wife, astonished at how small and fragile her bones feel, no wider than kindling.

"Get up, Olga. If we don't catch something to eat, we will die."

She issues a low, brutal noise and turns over. A wave tumbles underneath them. Her body rises and falls as if on a shelf.

"Come on, Olga."

He hears her utter one more sleep noise. But she doesn't wake.

Soon enough.

Lars sits up fully on his knees to get the widest possible, and still stable, view of the water. At the moment—spring still not come—there seems nothing with them out here, nothing alive. No movement at all save the slow turgid gray-black roll of the sea itself, beneath a sky nearly as dark as that. It seems impossible this water can contain animal life. But it must. Lars knows that if he were just able to examine a section of water from bottom to top he'd find a scene more lively than any human city. Long ago, he'd heard his father pass on rumors about a miraculous new instrument, what it revealed in a single drop of water. And then once, at nineteen, when he'd had a chance to travel with his father to Oslo, he'd seen the instrument up close. A street corner barker sold looks at the "mysterious worlds in a single drop of water" for half a krone. Lars paid up and put his eye against the instrument's narrow tube. His head went light, his heart moved audibly inside him. He couldn't quite believe he was being afforded this chance. Nor could he quite believe he would see anything. But he did. That single drop contained multitudes of storming, swimming, colliding living creatures, all behaving as if they belonged there. He yanked his head back, startled, squinting into the rearranged daylight. "What's wrong?" the salesman said, his voice close and smelling of rotten teeth and boiled leeks. "Didn't you see?" Lars did not respond, neither did he turn to the voice. "Well, try again, young man," the salesman said quickly. "You've earned a minute." Lars shook his head and walked off. He'd seen enough. He didn't know what it meant to have that much invisible life swarming all around him, in the water he washed his hands with, in the water he drank. Plagues of invisible creatures entering his mouth, falling down his throat to his stomach, to live and breed there. He didn't know what to think about it.

But now he remembers that day and tries to squeeze from it hope. He thinks: What if I were to look at a whole league of the ocean under a microscope? Imagine how much life there is to see. And to eat.

Lars raises his spear to the ready.

He has to act immediately if he acts at all.

He has to wait with spear raised, if he waits at all. The fish will not pause and, in the nature of fair competition, will not linger long enough for him to retrieve his weapon. To kill them, he has to kill them immediately.

He brings his spear higher, ear level, and pulls it back. He remembers the sea monster he killed. Maybe they will be visited again. One just as large. Except this time he will not be left standing while a month's worth of meals spins unclaimed toward the sea bottom. This time he will be ready. He focuses intently on the water. Not the water close by, but yards further out, from which a monster might approach. He stares for nearly a minute at the same gray-black stretch, then raises his eyes a little more: further out. A little further. He sees, just barely in the dim afternoon, three sound masts, curtains of white sails, a scooped out body of a hull that from this distance seems a gleaming, too perfect unearthly black.

"Hey!" Lars shouts. He stands. He jumps. "Hey!"

Olga stirs. With one eye, she eyes her husband. She stands. She looks where he looks.

"Hello!" she calls. "Hei! Stop right now. Nå! Stop! Turn you! Turn! Svinge! Svinge!" She whistles. She waves her palms. But the ship continues: on a straight unchecked line toward the northwest. Within a minute it shrinks to the size of a drinking cup; then to a coin. Lars still hopes someone with a spyglass will happen to look back, happen to notice. He jumps higher, he makes semaphore motions with his arms. He pumps the spear up and down, as high as he can make it go. "Look, damn you," he says. "Here we are. We are here." The ship is the size of a ladybug on the water far to the northwest. "You're going the wrong way," he says, and in that moment feels not only the words on his tongue but the salty influx of tears.

"Faen!" Olga cries. "Idiot!" She grabs Lars's spear and hurls it at the all but invisible vessel. The spear heads in a mean, exact line, then dies quickly, plunking against the water. "You are bliiiinddd!" Olga screams, then falls into herself. Her knees buckle. Her body hits the body of the boat. She is bawling incomprehensibly. She pounds her thighs with her fists, her face like a twisted bed sheet. Soaked through from sorrow.

Lars turns and watches as the spear with which he intended to get their saving meal is slowly absorbed by the black-blue water. A wave moves over it. Then another. Another. It no longer floats on top, but inches below. Visible still, but sinking. Then he cannot see it. He drops his head; he hears squeaking noises escape gassily from his chest.

"You!" Olga shouts. "This is because of you!" Only when he hears her feet begin to move does he turn, just in time to see his wife's broad white palms pushing at him, with all the power her shoulders can provide. The palms hit his chest and he careens backwards. In a moment he tastes salt water: astonishingly cold; he is floundering for his life.

"This is because of your stupid ideas!" Olga shouts at him. "If I'm going to die, I want to die in my own home. Now, I will die out here." She signaled to the world around them. "I should have killed you. If I killed you at home I could have roasted you. It would have been a pleasure. Not for the meat but for the revenge. I should have killed just to rid the earth of such a stupid man!"

"Help," Lars tries to say while he does mad strokes with his arm and kicks downward with his legs, which are stinging wildly from the cold. The sting is so bad he can barely breathe. His word only comes out as "Ha." His mouth, then his nose, go under water. He drinks the ice cold saltiness. He fights his way back. "Please," he says now, but it only comes out as "Plee." He thinks he should be able to propel himself three feet forward to the boat. He doesn't know why it's not getting closer, why his body seems stuck in place

"I'm not going to rescue you," Olga says. "You can die now. Die now. Dø!"

She actually raises both hands, balls them into fists, and shakes them madly in the air so he can see.

That is just what I'll do, Lars thinks.

He has no more energy for this battle with water, with the cold. He is about out of energy. He gathers one more mouthful of air. He keeps moving his arms and legs, but can no longer feel them. Or rather, he only feels the blazing red fire of extreme muscle fatigue, not the muscles themselves. He feels that they are giving out. His chin is fully under water. Then his mouth again. A second later, his whole head is under. He tries to move his arms, but he is pushing against the body of the sea now: too much resistance, too powerful an enemy. He is sinking like his spear. *Just like my spear.* He realizes that that thought may be the very last thought of his life.

Something wooden bumps his hand. Reflexively he grabs it. He holds, even under water. Then he feels himself being pulled. But his head is still under water. He still can't breathe. He brings the other hand around and holds on with both. He is being pulled upward. He lifts his head and tastes a tiny breath of air along with seawater. He hears his wife crying above him. A hand grabs the collar of his shirt.

"Help me," Olga says. "Help me!"

He understands. He lets go the wooden instrument and grabs the side of the boat. His head is above water. Olga is crying. She is bawling, wheezing. Lars hangs there, too tired to pull himself up.

"Get back on, you fool!" she swears, and then returns to her bawling.

Somehow he does it, though it takes the last of him. He lies in a ball, breathing, the same as dead. That's what he thinks. It is just the same as being dead. Which he will be soon if he doesn't dry out his clothes. His teeth begin to chatter. His skin, the outer shell of him, begins to turn numb .

Olga shrieks. But a different sound this time, underscored by joy.

"Husband," she says. "Look."

But Lars cannot. All he can do is stay fixed to the bottom of the boat, hearing his teeth move, feeling all feeling evacuate his body. But he does hear: a quick shuffling noise, a thin scraping, again and again. Like the flapping of a wing against paper.

He manages to turn his head in time to see a flying fish beside his shoulder. Its mouth opens and closes, its fins move, its gills expand deeply, starved for a breath of water. It flops onto its other side.

"F-f-f-ire," Lars says but it comes out as "Faahhh."

Then Olga is next to him, on her knees. In her hand is a cup. She brings it down on the fish's body. Hard. She pounds it repeatedly. When it can't flop anymore, she holds it in place and pounds more. Fish blood and brain and innards spread in small explosions. Some fly onto Lars's eyelid, onto his cheek. A second later, the fish is dead. Olga pounds one time more. She falls back onto her calves and take a deep breath.

"Husband," she says. "The ship has brought us lunch!"

"F-f-f-f-ire," he says. He points.

"No way," Olga says. "Too hungry. I'm just going to eat the son of a bitch raw."

"Ryan informs me that you're bringing home strange women and sleeping with them. Is that true?"

It was the Monday afternoon after Grethe left. I was in the throes of showing Lars almost freezing to death, only to get interrupted by my ex-wife. Ryan was at her place. We'd agreed some weeks ago that she would pick him up from school that day and keep him overnight, because she couldn't be home the next Saturday, the 28th, the next scheduled Ryan visit.

"It's not like that," I said.

"He says she was foreign."

"She's not foreign. She's American."

"He says she was foreign."

"She's Norwegian, originally."

"Ah ha!"

"She's lived here for years, Joy. She's a citizen. And what difference does it make anyway?"

"I don't like that you bring strange women home to bother my son. What kind of fathering is that? I never—I repeat never—have Glenn come over when Ryan visits. Never."

"She was visiting from out of town. Excuse me if I'm wrong, but I think Glenn has his own house to live in."

"Don't get technical on me."

Technical.

"And why did she have to visit last weekend? Why not wait until Ryan's with me?"

An excellent question. I didn't feel like saying, *Because I completely forgot she was coming.*

"It was the only weekend she could come."

"Then call me and tell me and I'll take my son for that weekend. Why are you exposing him to this person when you don't have to?"

I hesitated a fatal second.

"I don't like what you're doing with Ryan," Joy said. "I think I should get more time with him."

"What do you mean, 'What I'm doing with him'?"

Olga is halfway through a mouthful of flying fish sushi when she realizes Lars is turning blue.

"Wow," she says to him. "You look like the fish I just caught."

Lars makes a noise in his throat. "F-f-f-f-aahhhhh."

"Yeah, I know. Grilled is best. But in a pinch . . . " She finishes the mouthful.

Lars's leg jerk out, an involuntary movement. His whole body erupts into violent spasms--the last throes of life.

Olga stands up.

"Lars. Stop it. Lars! Oh, my god. *Why didn't you say anything?*"

She drops the fish and immediately strips off her husband's clothes. She gives him every blanket they still own, including the one across her shoulders, and carries the dimly active kettle fire to his side of the boat. She throws in one of their last sticks, reenergizing the blaze. She pushes on Lars's body so that he surrounds the kettle, like an infant across a mother's open breast. The entire time, she talks aloud, chastising him.

"Fool. You're freezing to death and you waste your breath telling me how to eat my fish? Why didn't you say something? Just say 'I need the fire or I'm going to die.' A little communication would help."

She grunts.

"And now we have to use up all of what wood we have. Live today, so we can die tomorrow. Great. It's not like you had to fall into the water. I didn't push you that hard."

Lars lies still and shivers. The feeling all but gone from his limbs begins to return in icy needles stabbing his toes and fingertips, his elbows and shoulder blades. Stabbing him from within.

"Here," Olga says. "Let me rub you some."

She keeps the blankets atop him but pushes down on the outermost layer. Pressing the wool against his skin, moving her hands in circles. More needles. He can barely lie still it hurts bad. But then the stabbing dissipates, replace by another sensation: touch. He can feel the blanket. He can feel Olga's hands. He can the felt heat coming off the kettle. He rests his head against the bottom of the boat and begins to cry.

"What? What?" Olga says. "I'm working as hard as I can."

Lars nods, forehead against the wood.

"Stop the crying," she says. "Stop the crying!"

Lars nods. He is able to talk. "I was almost dead, Olga."

She snorts. "Yeah, well. I should have just let you die too. I bring you back just to have you die again later. You wait and see."

Lars shrugs. His forehead is still against the wood. He keeps it there enjoying knowing what wood feels like. Cold wood against a cold human forehead. He keeps it there, knowing how that feels.

27

A couple days later, I called Lolly. At first she wouldn't come to the phone though I heard her unmistakable voice in the background.

"She's out," her secretary said. "She'll be back soon."

"How soon?"

"I don't know. Soon."

"What does that mean?"

"She left a while ago."

"I just heard her."

"Who?"

"I just heard her speaking with you—or somebody."

The secretary shut down, flummoxed into silence. Where was Lolly getting her help? The girl wasn't creative enough to keep even the most simple misdirection going.

"All right," she said glumly. "I'll look for her."

I heard her put the phone down. I heard her leave the desk. I heard, dimly, conversation between her and Lolly, yards away.

Apparently the girl also didn't know about hold.

"What is it?" Lolly said.

"Your secretary doesn't lie very well."

"I know. I am not happy."

"Or stonewall. She can't be a secretary if she can't stonewall."

"My problem, Paul. Not yours."

"It is if she's telling me you're out."

"I meant to be. I do have business."

"What business?"

I'd never heard Lolly sound so taut, so cold. If I didn't know better, I'd suspect my agent was about to drop me.

I kept talking: "I just wanted to report in on the project. I'm actually nearing the end. I think. I mean of my first draft. I thought you'd want to know."

Lolly made a noise, something in her throat. Perhaps it was involuntary. Perhaps it was just ordinary biology: leftover phlegm. But when she spoke again after that noise her voice sounded decidedly more like herself.

"So you've finished this farm tale?"

"Actually, it's still more like *Kon-Tiki*."

"'More like'?"

"I've still got them stranded in the Norwegian Sea."

"Don't they ever get anywhere?"

"Like?"

"Like home?"

"Iceland is where they're headed; more or less."

"Don't you ever show them getting to Iceland?"

"Not yet."

I hadn't actually decided about that. In fact, I'd started to question my outline. I was thinking again of killing them both, viz., having them die heartachingly in the open water just before they reached shore. Maybe their little boat overturns? Maybe the orca comes back? The angry wife of the other monster, full of red-eyed vengeance?

To speak true, I was dawdling. So close to the end but not able to see it through. Because I didn't want to have to choose. But I did have to choose. Which is probably the real reason I called Lolly.

"Don't you plan on showing them getting to Iceland?" Lolly said.

"I'm not sure they actually do make it to Iceland."

"What do you mean?"

"I'm not sure they survive."

"If they don't survive, it's not *Kon-Tiki*."

"Yes, but—"

"This is *Kon-Tiki*, Paul. This is danger on the high seas. This is disaster movie novel. In disaster movies, the heroes survive. Kill off whoever else you want but Lem and Matilda have to make it to Iceland alive. No one's buying this book if they don't survive."

"Are you saying this will be made into a movie?"

"You better pray your scrotum off this gets made into a movie. If you want your book to make any money, that is."

I guess I had my ending.

"I suppose money is a good thing."

"You suppose?"

"Yes. It is."

"So when are you finally coming?"

"I can't say yet. I need to finish it. And then I need to type it."

"Christ, I forgot. You know you're the Grizzly Adams of my stable, don't you? All my other writers have made it at least into the 20th century. Some even into the 21st."

"You're just going to have to put up with me, Lolly."

She gave out a long, suitable moan.

"Yes, I guess I will."

"I'll tell you when I'm done the draft."

"Do. And please hurry up please. We need to schedule a date for you to come."

"We will."

"We better. And what about your girlfriend?"

"My what?"

"What's she going to do while you're here tied up with me?"

I really couldn't answer. Or I could, but in any one of a dozen different ways. I couldn't decide which reply came closest to the truth.

"If you're talking about the woman who was here last week, she lives in Oregon."

"Your girlfriend lives in Oregon?"

"The woman who was here last week lives in Oregon, yes."

"Oh."

A silence stayed between us, but it was about twenty degrees warmer than before. More like a comforter than a frosted blanket.

"Then it won't matter," Lolly said.

"Probably not."

"Okay. Right then," Lolly said, crisply. "Finish the damn thing, Paul. Get those Swedes to Iceland."

Required Icelandic data (a.k.a. I'm nothing if not consistent): Iceland is the second-largest island in Europe, roughly oval in shape but indented by fjords and bays. The country is covered by the world's largest ice field outside the polar regions, but "Iceland" is still a misnomer. The mean temperature for January is about the same as New York. The only native land mammal is the arctic fox. Other extant mammals—reindeer, rats, mice, minks—were purposefully introduced or accidentally imported. Birds, however, are plentiful, especially waterfowl, for which Iceland is a major breeding ground. And, of course, with the numerous waterways, fish are abundant in the country, especially trout, char, and salmon.

(Btw, I couldn't use dear old Britannica for Iceland. Not because Britannica provides no information but because Vol. 20 (what comes right after Excretion—Geometry and right before India—Ireland) was only an empty space on the shelf. (Grrr.) It was nowhere to be found anywhere in the reference section. Believe me, I checked every book cart within half a block. I even checked the copy room. Giving up, I turned once more to Americana. The entry there was written by one Hallberg Hallmundsson. If you know him and see him, tell him I appreciate the jocular tone of his entry. Jocular? An encyclopedia? Well, more so than stodgy Britannica.)

Iceland was settled some 1100 years ago, a period documented in a unique literary tome titled Landnámabók or Book of Settlements. According to Landnámabók, most of the settlers came from southwestern Norway, but there was also a considerable infusion of Celts who arrived from Viking outposts in Scotland and Ireland.

(Southwestern Norway. As in the home territory of my two heroes! So, Lars and Olga are actually retracing an ancient emigration route! And doesn't that make their implausible journey—picked out of the sky by me for the sake of narrative convenience—*suddenly entirely plausible*? Actually I don't really care how you answer that one. I had my answer as soon as I saw those words.)

Its culture and language places Iceland squarely among the Nordic peoples. Icelandic, a close kin to other Scandinavian tongues, has actually changed little since the original settlement of the country. Whereas the Danish, Norwegian, and Swedish developed into their modern forms, Icelandic stood nearly still. In other important ways, however, the country has evolved. Whereas in earlier centuries the country was thoroughly rural, today 80% of the population live in cities. These contemporary Icelanders are a hospitable and generous if permissive people. (One quarter of all children are born out of wedlock.) Extreme poverty, however, is almost unknown and violent crime is rare. In fact, the country enjoys one of the highest standards of living in all of Europe, and its population leads the world in fondness for travel. Up to 20% of all Icelanders visit another country each year.

(All that was interesting enough, I guess, but, hold on to your hats, I was about to uncover information that directly affected my narrative.)

Prior to the late 19th century, the economy and infrastructure of the country was entirely undeveloped. Subsistence farming and fishing in small, open boats were the only occupations. There were no roads and few bridges. There were *no harbors* (emphasis mine) except for natural ones. The only town of any size was Reykjavik.

(No harbors? None? For my novel, at least as I conceived it then, there had to be a harbor in Iceland in 1793. I didn't care if it was only the mobile home version of a harbor; I didn't care if it was nothing but a plank. I didn't care if it was some guy's private beach. It just had to be there. And a town too. There had to be a town for the last few of my Lars-Olga scenes. And I don't mean Reykjavik either. I didn't want Lars and Olga going all the way to Reykjavik. Look at a map. Or a globe, rather. Rejkjavik isn't where they're going to land—even by mistake—coming from Norway. Besides, even Reykjavik would have been tiny in 1793. In the late 19th century, a hundred years later, it only had 1000 people, according to Americana.)

For a country almost wholly undeveloped before the 20th century, Iceland evidences a surprisingly vibrant cultural life. Almost all education is public and free. Illiteracy is unknown. Iceland has even produced a Nobel Prize laureate in literature—novelist Halldor Laxness (1955)—as well as other writers of international renown, such as Gunnar Gunnarsson. An interest in art, meanwhile, is prevalent among Icelanders. Paintings decorate most private homes and offices. The National Gallery is one of many art museums in Reykjavik which feature permanent exhibitions. Reykjavik also features a music conservatory, a symphony orchestra, and several smaller musical ensembles.

(Now, with a wider appreciation of the place, I can show you how I brought our heroes literally to shore, using only natural harbors. Grrr.)

28

The following day as they huddle by the kettle, and use up the very last of their wood, another fish lands on board. They tell themselves this is a sign from God that He means to keep them alive. He means for them to be saved. Why else drag it out like this? As if to offer further proof, the wind, idle for days, picks up and scoots them in a northwesterly path. Back the way they came. They'll take the chill if it means they're moving toward safety. Finally. Just as their wood runs out. For the next twenty-four hours they sail with partially filled stomachs and hungry eyes. Hungry for a sign of that lost black hump of land. The sun offers them only those few hours of light of course, during which they see nothing. Lars begins to paddle.

"Save your strength, husband," Olga says. "Sleep, why don't you?"

"But what if we miss it?"

Olga snorts.

"It's nowhere in sight. How in a few hours could we pass it?"

Lars nods wearily, defeated by unapproachable logic.

"You sleep; I'll watch," she says. "When you wake up, relieve me."

"What if I don't wake up?"

"Then I will wake you up. Now go. Stop arguing with me. This might be your last chance to rest, and if you're not careful I'll take it away."

"All right, all right, all right." Lars settles in by the kettle. The fire there is only embers now. But it's better than nothing. Far better. If only for the idea of warmth. He doubts he will sleep. He is too excited. The idea that perhaps in hours they will be within shouting distance of land, that they might almost be off the freezing water, fills him with a sticky glee that turns his mind in circles. There is no way he will sleep. But to please his wife he lies down. He closes his eyes. In a second, he is out.

He wakes sometime later to almost worshipful silence. There is no sound, except an occasional floop of water as it tucks against itself. The sky is lighter than usual: a blue almost weaned of gray, brighter than cobalt. Is spring on the way at last? Then he realizes: It should be time for his shift, shouldn't it? Olga never woke him. He sits up. He feels the sting of cold against his ears. The wind has lulled but the air is as chilly as ever. He sees two things: first, the fire has gone out. Completely. Whoever watches is supposed to maintain the fire. Why didn't she? But then he remembers. They used up all the wood. At the same moment, he sees Olga keeping watch, her back to him, legs against her chest, arms stiff around her knees. Completely still. The blanket has fallen off her shoulders.

"Olga, your blanket. Put it back on."

She prefers to keep watching. She makes no movement at all.

"Put it on. Come on now. And why didn't you wake me?"

She acts as if she never heard him speak. She must be asleep.

He crawls over and grabs for her shoulder. As soon as his hand meets her body, he feels it: the cold inertia, the lack of animating presence, as if his wife was no more than a piece of fallen timber, a milk tank, an ox cart.

"Olga!"

He pulls her toward him and sees telltale blue lips, white skin hardened to ice, eyes staring sightlessly ahead.

He shoves her hard. She topples to the floor of the boat, arms still fixed around her knees. "No!" Lars shouts. "Tosk! Fool!" He is not sure if he curses Olga or himself. But pushing her has pushed his own blood. He feels the stir of that essential center liquid. He pulls an oar out of the oarlock and begins beating on the stiff carcass. "No! No! No! No!" In five minutes he has actually created sweat on his forehead; he feels his feet fully; he knows his hands again. He beats on her more. Without a fire, he will have to beat on her all day long.

He hears a shout behind him, or what sounds like a shout. In future days he will question his memory, question even his sanity in those moments after discovering his wife had died, because he would have been too far away still to hear anything as precise as a human shout. And never in the middle of an ocean wind. But, in fact, that is what the noise sounds like. Perhaps it is a seagull. But seagulls do not sound like human shouts. A sea lion would be a constructive guess, except sea lions do not linger in this part of the world. Landlubber Lars has in fact never seen one, only been told by those who have that sea lions are the humans of the ocean. In the coming months he will ask everyone he meets: Have sea lions ever been spotted here, where lands meets water? Those he asks will stare as if he is insane. Of course, they will think to themselves, he is a foreigner.

Lars hears the shout and turns around. He sees, fully apparent now, the jagged outline of a shore. And not just a shore. He sees boats. Tiny, fishing boats idling on the sand. Men, small from this distance, stand beside them, huddled in coats, smoking. One boat is being pushed off shore by a man who, in one practiced yet urgent and shockingly graceful movement, gives a final shove outward and pulls himself up, his barely booted feet just missing getting soaked by the frigid body of water. In a moment he is on board, looking completely dry, and moving to the oars. Lars screams. He returns the oar to its lock, turns the boat in the direction of the shore, and begins rowing with all his life. Almost simultaneous with his efforts, the wind picks up. At his back. Within fifteen minutes, the land is actually close. It is actually big. It is not going away. Nor is the wind. Lars stops rowing. He falls to a lump, his shoulders on fire, and begins to weep.

[Note from real author: I know, it's been a while. Just want to say that my original conception of Paul's original conception of this crucial scene was certainly different. Lars was to see not just a shore but a harbor. Not just shitty little fishing boats but schooners docked there. (Assuming of course that "schooners" fit the time period, which I didn't know for sure.) In fact, the scene ended not on the picture of Lars weeping but of a large boat with sailors passing near him as he cruises into the harbor. Here, I'll just let you look.

ORIGINAL (REAL AUTHOR'S) ENDING FOR ABOVE SCENE: "At some point in his breakdown he becomes aware of a large schooner bearing down on the same shore. It is following an almost parallel line to Lars, about a quarter mile away but getting closer. He sees men on board signaling and calling to him, but he cannot make out what they are saying. He sees their small, pinched, sun-darkened faces squinting with interest—or disgust. He can't tell. Now he sees that they are pointing: to the shore. He looks at the port looming before him and can see more clearly the dozens of ships moored there, the men moving on board. One—a large, brown, weather-beaten beauty of a boat— is currently being loaded with crates almost as large as Lars's craft. One down from this boat is a smaller, squatter vessel, pure black on its bottom but a starkly contrasting white on its upper half. Men and women dressed in civilian clothes—heavy coats, hats, and shawls—and carrying too much luggage slowly step onboard. Their faces seem uniformly grim, or perhaps it is just tiredness. A passenger ship. Lars wonders what long journey these people are embarking on, just as his finishes. He notices a few children among the group. He can even see streets directly behind the dock now, streets busy with midmorning activity; and behind those streets rows of assorted homes. A town, an actual human place, where after all these weeks he has arrived and will need to find help. He glances over at the schooner. It is past him now but the men are still pointing, still signaling. He thinks he understands. *Keep going*, their motions seem to say. *Strike for home*."

I kind of liked it. The re-immersion into swirling human activity after weeks of solitude. The suddenness of it, the difference.

And the implication of those last couple sentences that Lars has finally reached a place of security. A shelter, if not a permanent one. But after reading about Iceland—"no harbors except natural ones"—Paul and I had to jettison the whole passage. As well as come up with another explanation for Lars hearing a shout, a detail I wanted to keep. Thus the sea lion. Or whatever it was. Paul apparently liked the way his scene turned out. Still, when all is said and done it's still my book, and Paul is my character. So I think—as the director of his crummy, domestic drama—I'm entitled to take an interlude to show you a deleted scene.

Enough said. Back to Paul.]

     After finishing that last segment, I called Lolly again. This was less than a week after our previous conversation. I didn't need to talk to her but I was excited to be able to tell her that I'd gotten Lars to Iceland safely. I'd killed off Olga, yes. There didn't seem a way to avoid eliminating one of them. But at least Lars had made it. I'd write maybe one more scene, a kind of epilogue in which the reader learns in brief about his months in country and then follows him as he returns to Norway. (Exactly how I didn't yet know, what with no large commercial ships coming in and out of the country and no transocean travelers, except for Lars, who isn't about to head out into the water all by his lonesome on that tiny boat.) That epilogue would be the technical conclusion of the book, but the scene I'd just finished was its emotional climax. Lars, after all he'd been through, being restored to civilization, to human company, even if for the moment that company was only a straggling collection of godawful poor fishermen. I was proud of the scene, proud of my not-too-pie-in-the-sky-yet-at-the-same-time-redemptive climax. A happy ending edged all around with darkness. I was proud. I wanted to tell someone. Lolly's phone was ringing but no one was picking up. Strange.

     In the week-plus since she'd left, Grethe had sent me a string of conversational emails: asking after Ryan, asking after the book, suggesting that I come visit her sometime when Joy had

Ryan for the weekend. Sounds good, I wrote back. Let's think about that. And/or: How is Oregon? Actually, I couldn't keep up with her relentless stream of communication—two, sometimes three emails a day—especially since it's never been my habit, even at work, to check my email every day. Sorry, I can't say more right now, I might respond. I have to finish this book. Most of the time I didn't respond at all.

Lolly's phone rang ten times before someone picked up.

"Lolly?"

I heard a groan in the form of nasal exhalation. "Ms. Lolly's not here. This is Kristen."

"I don't know you, Kristen."

"I don't know you either."

"Sorry. I'm Paul Mullen. One of her authors."

Silence.

"Well, she's not here."

"Did I speak to you, maybe, about a week ago?"

"No, I'm a temp."

"You don't know the other girl?"

"What other girl?"

"Forget it. Do you know—"

"I'm just here to tell people Ms. Lolly's not here. That's what she said for me to do."

"You're doing a fine job."

"Thanks."

"You actually sound a little like her."

"Ouch. Rock and roll."

"Why do you say 'ouch'?"

"I don't know. I guess I like thinking I sound like Ms. Lolly. What's wrong with 'ouch'?"

"Nothing. Can you tell me where she went to?"

"Ms. Lolly?"

"Yes."

"A funeral."

The answer was so specific I believed her.

"A funeral for whom?"

"Somebody."

"You don't know who?"

"Somebody upstate."

"Upstate?"

"Yeah."

"Why upstate?"

"Cause that's where she is."

"Oh."

"But don't worry. She's okay. She didn't die or anything."

"Oh. Good."

"Somebody else did."

"Who?"

"I don't know. Somebody upstate."

"She'll be back?"

"Tomorrow."

"Good."

"Call back tomorrow and you can get the real deal."

"I'll do that, Kristen. I think I'd rather have the real deal."

She paused. I could hear her going over my words, one by one. I actually didn't mean to insult her. It just came out that way.

"Yeah," Kristen said.

Rock and roll.

* * *

The next day I was standing in front of the refrigerator, phone in hand, about to try Lolly again, looking for a leftover Mrs. Smith's lemon meringue pie Ryan and I shared fours days earlier. Last I knew, three quarters of it were left, and now the whole thing was gone. I imagined Ryan, four nights running, tiptoeing pieces of pie to his bed, eating them under the covers, getting dried meringue and sticky yellow food product all over his sheets. How could he do that without me seeing? Answer: I wasn't looking. More bad parenting for Joy to criticize. Last time we spoke she opined that maybe Ryan should stay more nights with her. As in 50/50. "So stuff like that foreign woman doesn't happen," she said. I reminded her that I had legal custody, which by definition repudiates 50/50.

"Well, then," she snapped, "maybe we should see about changing that."

She hung up, leaving me to stew for minutes on end. If it came to Joy making a formal challenge, I'd have to find a way to pay a lawyer. No way I was letting her take Ryan. After all, she'd gotten everything else she wanted. She left the marriage She'd taken our friends. She had her new pad and her new boyfriend and her lousy, satisfactory academic publications. And, only recently, a promotion to associate professor. She was not getting Ryan too. The only thought that calmed me was that Joy always talked a better show about Ryan than she delivered. Certainly when we were married, but even now, she talked more about wanting to be with Ryan more than she actually tried to be with him. If anything got in the way—the internet, a lunch date, phone calls to her mother, clothes shopping, American Movie Classics, that book she needed to read for an article, the Academy Awards show—then, well, it just got in the way.

I took a step to Ryan's bedroom to look for pie evidence. I stopped myself. No. I dialed Lolly who actually, astonishingly, picked up.

"You're back," I said.

"For better or worse."

I was truly glad I'd gotten hold of her, for many reasons, not the least of which was that I was stuck dead in the middle of the last chapter of my novel. I needed a distraction. Which is why I went in search of pie.

"Who died?"

"My ex-husband."

"You went to his funeral?"

"You know. What the hell."

"That's good of you, Lolly. I don't think too many people would attend an ex's funeral."

"You don't?"

"No."

"I do."

"You do?"

"Lots of people."

"They would?"

"Why not?"

"I don't know."

"Wouldn't you?"

"I don't know. Maybe I haven't been in the Ex World long enough."

"Probably."

"I'd think you, I mean anyone, wouldn't care to see the person again."

"Are you kidding? I get to watch them lower the creep into the cold dead ground. I get to say to him, 'Looks like I outlasted you, fucker, didn't I?'"

"So that's why you went."

"Not really. I'm just saying."

"You're a good soul, Lolly."

"Yeah, but that's my problem. Because I'm a good soul, I've got nothing but dickheads in my life. As if God sent them expressly to me, because otherwise they'd be left out of the party. Which they should be."

"Yes, they should."

"But they're not. God looks out over the transepts, or whatever, and says to the man, 'Okay, so you are the slimeball of the bunch. You're going to lie and cheat and fornicate and smell bad and refuse to wash your socks. Go to Lolly.'"

"Come on. All of them?"

"All."

"All of them?"

"All."

"Come on."

"How come I can't snare a nice catch like you?"

I swallowed. I mumbled something about "a lot of nice catches."

"Pretty hard, anyway, with you in Arkansas."

"Yes," I said.

"How is the land of cotton anyway?"

"Cotton?"

"Arkansas."

"Rice, actually."

"How is the land of rice anyway?"

"All the same. But that's not why I called yesterday."

"I figured."

I told her where I was with the book.

"Outrageous!" she said. "So when are you coming to New York?"

"Give me a month or two to enter the thing in my computer. And fix it of course."

"Okay, two months. At most. We'll rustle up some business for this son-of-a-bitch. You just see."

"I was kind of counting on that. I think you'll like how it turned out. It's *Kon-Tiki* but, still, you know, it's a farmer. It's kind of both. It's kind of *Moby Dick* meets *The Good Earth*. Except newer, fresher, faster. *Kon-Tiki* for the net gen."

Total lies.

"Listen to yourself, Paulie. You sound just like an agent."

"I'm learning from you."

"That's a scary thought."

"No, it's not. Really."

She didn't say anything, as if listening to my words over again on a stereo, adding more bass, adjusting the volume, pushing in on the sound equalizer button. Checking for tone as much as anything. Tone as much as substance.

"How's your girlfriend?" she said.

"My girlfriend?"

"Don't. Stop. Don't even try calling her 'The woman who lives in Oregon.' I'm not stupid. I never bought that crap about 'a friend' helping you with the book."

"She is."

"But you're sleeping with her too, correct?"

Boy, Lolly was good.

"It's not exactly news if you say yes, Paulie. I figured it out from like the moment you mentioned her."

I guess I waited too long to reply

"I'll take that stupefied silence as a yes."

"It's complicated, Lolly."

"Oh, yes, it always is. So how is she doing?"

"How's she doing?"

"Yes, Paul. I'm one human being asking about the status of another." She altered her voice to put quotation marks around her next words: "'How is your girlfriend, Mr. Mullen? She's doing fine, I hope.'"

"She's okay."

"Just okay? Am I hearing ambivalence?"

"I don't know about that."

"I'm hearing ambivalence."

"You're hearing, I don't know, distraction. I can't find my damn lemon meringue pie. Ryan must have taken it when I wasn't looking and swallowed the thing whole."

"Don't try to change the subject."

"And now my wife is talking about wanting him back. 50/50."

"Ouch. Sorry, baby. But don't try to change the subject."

"I'm serious. That's what she said."

"I guess she did."

"That's pretty distracting stuff, Lolly. Especially while I am trying to finish—and *am almost finishing*—a novel."

"So this woman lives in Oregon," Lolly said. "Is she Oregonian?"

"No. Norwegian, actually."

"Oh, great."

"She really is helping me with the book."

"So she's like a blonde bombshell."

"Not exactly."

"What is she doing in Oregon?"

"Teaching. At a university."

"Like you."

"Yes. Like me."

"Great. How old?"

"Her?"

"Yes."

"My age. Almost. A couple years younger."

"A younger woman. Typical."

"Come on, Lolly." I wasn't just embarrassed but nauseous. My belly felt caught between pincers and there was taste like stale limes on my tongue. My brain felt pumped with air: trapped air. Air pushing on the inside of my forehead, against my inner ear.

"Hey, I'm not judging," Lolly said. "If I could hump a younger man, I'd take one in a heartbeat."

"Lolly."

"All right, enough of persecuting you. It's just too much fun. I'm sorry about your wife. Really."

"So am I."

"Why don't you Fed Ex me your manuscript? The whole bear. Like as in soon as possible. Then we'll schedule a day for you to catch the first plane out of Arkansas for civilization."

FOUR

29

[I don't know if anyone out there reading this—if anyone *is* reading this—is familiar with Wayne Booth's *The Rhetoric of Fiction*. I read it in grad school while I was working on my dissertation. (Don't ask.) Oh, sorry. Forgot to say that this is real author again, not the author-character whose woman-bedevilled and publisher-driven antics I hope you're enjoying. As I explained all the way back in Part One, Paul Mullen's not my name and that's not my situation (i.e., "woman-bedevilled and publisher-driven"). Well, mostly not. But even assuming there actually exists somewhere a Paul Mullen in the flesh, and not just as an imagined actuary in my novel, there still isn't a real Paul Mullen, according to prevailing postmodern theory of the fractured and multivalent human psyche. But that too is not precisely relevant because that's not precisely what I mean when I say that there's no Paul Mullen. What I mean is both more subtle and more interesting. (Here's where it helps to have read *The Rhetoric of Fiction*.) What I mean is that the author composing these particular words ("these particular words," etc.) is not only not the author-character who lives and acts in the novel *Burnt Norway* (that is, "my" rendering of the imaginary author-character's account of the creation of his second novel titled *Burnt Norway*, not the imaginary second novel creation *Burnt Norway* referred to by the author-character in the author-character's account of the creation of such); he is not even the real author's-real person-person known to inhabit the corridors of Thompson Hall at the University of Central Arkansas in Conway, filling his coffee pot with more water from the tap in the faculty/staff lounge, chatting up latest College of Fine Arts gossip in the men's room, checking out the latest flyers posted by student groups on bulletin boards, working doggedly in his office through another set of "Talking Points" responses to textbook readings, taking a phone call from another frazzled student with another suspicious excuse as to why she cannot possibly have her composition ready on time. Nor is it the author-real person-person known by his neighbors on Kayla Lane: the guy proudly riding his new Sears Craftsman "Panther" mower, awed by how close a shave it gives his lawn, the guy out playing H-O-R-S-E with his son on a pathetic, dilapidated red and yellow plastic basketball set that's designed for a two year old but he's too lazy to get rid of, the guy who brings in his *Arkansas Democrat Gazette* from the newspaper box at 6:30 every Sunday morning because his son won't let him sleep any later than that, the guy who's spotted unloading groceries from his Saturn sedan (2000 LS, blackberry with charcoal cloth seats) every Friday afternoon after his customary Friday afternoon Wal*Mart grocery run, the guy who is chagrinned to buy all his foodstuffs from a Cooperate Megalopolis not so quietly intent on running off every single small business competitor (through predatory and sometimes illegal business practices, while at the same time its other giant retail face—Sam's Club—advertises itself as "the friend of small business"), but who on a professor's salary is too poor to shop anywhere else.

No, that's not the author person I mean. The author composing these words ("these words" etc.) is, according to Booth's construction, the *ideal author*, or that segment of the author's consciousness that acts and is expressed when the author concentrates specifically on literary creation not life. The widest, shrewdest, most intuitive, and most sublime aspect of the author, if you will. That part of him smarter, purer, and more talented than he really is. Meanwhile, the real-person author has not one son (actual name Jackson, not Ryan) but two. The younger son's name is Wilson, as yet unintroduced to readers of the real-author's (or, rather, the real person's ideal author self's) comic novel *Burnt Norway* (as opposed to the imaginary *Burnt Norway* novel supposedly composed by the imaginary author-character in the author-characters' fictional account of the composing of such imaginary novel); a physically adorable and rollicking four-year-old, at least on the day this sentence is being constructed ("this sentence is being constructed").

Person-author notified ideal author to keep Will, as he is known, out of the narrative for a couple of reasons: 1) That's just one more character for the ideal author to have to coordinate into his imagined   divorced-failed-novelist-as-harried-single-father scenario; 2) Little one is more timid than his older brother and might flinch under the narrative limelight. (Of course, that last reason only strictly applies to character Will not real-person Will—a dubious psychological construction, as I've noted, but an unavoidable semantic one. Real-person Will, who can't yet read, would be entirely unaware of what character Will was doing in the novel. Real-person Will would be too busy turning over an overloaded junk box in the living room, creating an unsorted mountain of plastic toys and gadgets that subsequently gets kicked and played and thrown and accidentally pushed so thoroughly that a layer of small brightly colored plastic junk spreads evenly across the floor, like concrete goo spread upon barren ground for the sake of a sidewalk, or throwing the entire contents of his pajama drawer onto the floor of his bedroom as he searches for just the pair he wants, or working with immovable persistence on cutting, drawing upon, and stapling together his own homemade *Yu-Gi-Oh* cards so that he can take them to bed with him, study them, approve of them, make plans for displaying them to preschool classmates the next day because by God the very last thing he will let himself do in bed is go to sleep. Which is a phenomenon that the real author, even after fathering two children, simply cannot comprehend, since most people—at least adult people—at least himself—most certainly himself—when they are tired GO TO SLEEP.   Isn't that like THE NATURAL THING TO DO?   Shouldn't that be a biological imperative for THE SURVIVAL OF THE RACE?   What else is sleep for except to engage in when you are tired?)

But, dear readers, to finally speak true, although it's not like I've been speaking false up to now, the real reason real-person author notified ideal author to leave little Will out of the novel was to avoid complicating the author-character's life anymore than seems productive, credible, and sustainable, given that he (author-character) is a single father after all and that he is about to leave home (i.e. offspring), go off to NY, quite possibly get a second book published, and who knows what all else and for what length of time he will needs be away. Okay, perhaps Paul's ex-wife would be available and happy to watch both kids. *Perhaps.* But given what Paul has to say about her (i.e., she only pretends to want to spend time with their one extant son), it's not likely she will watch both "happily" if at all, assuming she's even available. And maybe she's not. What if she has yet another academic conference to attend? (She is, after all, a dedicated conference-goer / industry networker supreme.) Try finding a babysitter willing and able to watch two kids for a period of days. (For the uninitiated, 2 kids equals 5 times the work.) And if that alone weren't hard enough, think of poor Paul trying to come up with enough money, on a professor's salary, to fairly pay such a sitter, and buy a plane ticket to New York, and pay for a hotel in that city. One does not want to set too many narrative traps for oneself.

The bottom line truth is that these lines ("these lines" etc.) are being composed not by the author-character and, I growingly suspect, not even by the real author's ideal author self, but by a man alone in his study at 5:26 am, whose skull resonates with a fuzzy red headache because he has been up since 2:09 because real person Will got up about then, left his own bed, crossed the house, entered real author's bedroom, purportedly to snuggle with real author and real author's wife. (No, I'm not divorced. My wife is not Joy, neither in name nor personality.) The clambering of little Will over the quilt disturbed real author, who immediately felt that his forty-something bowels needed release, which made him stumble half-blind to the bathroom, hitting as he went his big toe on the hard wooden corner of the hard wooden sweater chest at the end of the bed, thoroughly waking him. Not that real author didn't try to go back to sleep. After relieving himself and rubbing his toe, he lay back down, closed his eyes, and even turned onto his "good" sleeping side. Little Will proceeded to rotate clockwise and kick real author in the back. Then he did it again, even after real author straightened his little body—i.e., restored him to a six o'clock position: feet at six, head at twelve.   Finally, real author was forced to leave his own bed for the living room couch.   There, real author's now wide awake mind began fretting over the once-seeming-doable-but-now-less-so drafting plans for his comic novel *Burnt Norway*, which he had hoped to finish by the end of the academic year and get to an interested agent in NY before the man completely forgot about being interested in him.   But real author cannot possibly be finished the novel by the end of the year because too much else, not the least of which his job, stands in the way.   (Real author is *not* on sabbatical.)   And suddenly fretting about his job, and now even more awake, real author began—at roughly 3:00—fretting specifically about a specific writing class which was not going well and had not gone well all semester in part because, and this is something real author had fretted about many times over before this particular early morning on the couch, he had done nothing to reinvent the course.   While he promised himself every summer and   every   Christmas   break   that   he   would change/refresh/reinvigorate this course, he had again not done so and was using the same texts and same assignments as ever, which were not working and had not worked all semester.   But maybe, he fretted, if book orders were not demanded in early October (for spring semester classes) and mid-February (for fall classes) at which time real author is always too focused on the teaching of the present semester's classes, which have really just gotten underway, the real author would not be so prone to falling back on the same texts over and over again and thus the same teaching methods, which leads . . .   And of course, dear reader, you see how it went.   After a joyless, sleepless near hour on the couch the real author gave up, switched from sleep mode to wake up mode.   He fixed a pot of caffeinated brew, located his notebooks, found a workable pen, and now, with a fuzzy red headache still ambient in his skull, he attempts to reference his previously undocumented son, his heretofore unmentioned wife, the *Rhetoric of Fiction*, and the real nature of the imaginary author-character's looming imaginary trip to the Big Apple in the real author's comic novel *Burnt Norway*.   And after two hours of summoning, there's not an ideal author to be found anywhere: not at this time of day, not in this state of mind.]

30

Three months later, Lars stands on the deck of a quick, ocean cutting schooner. It left Hofn two days before with a cargo deck full of whale oil. In little more than an hour it will arrive in Stavanger. Blown off course in its journey from England to Holland to Norway, the ship landed in Lars's lap, like a sign from heaven. *Time to go home.* As soon as he heard about the unexpected landing, he rushed to the beach and found the captain, who understood enough Norwegian to understand that Lars was trying to talk his way on board. The captain relented. He was, in fact, short handed after losing two men to a back room murder in Amsterdam. In exchange for the ride, Lars agreed to carry out any menial tasks the captain asked, but now—when surely there is something around that might keep him busy—he grips a sail line, his face to the air, his eyes searching for land.

It has been a hard, lonely three months. When Lars and his battered craft reached the beach at Hofn, fishermen helped him off and even managed to remove Olga. They quickly covered the corpse with the ratty remains of Lars's blankets. Fortunately, among that gang there was a Norwegian, a man with a jaw so sharp and thin it might have been a block of stone honed with a chisel, and beneath his cap ratty brownish hair that must have been originally blonde, before aging and work wore out that brightness. His black pants were as tattered as Lars's; his boots were scuffed and dotted with the remainders of candle tallow. The morning fatigue in his blue eyes was accented by the crow's feet deeply carved into his flesh. He might have been thirty or sixty.

Where is the nearest church, Lars asked, where I can bury this woman properly?

There's a church not two miles from here, the man said. He gestured over his shoulder with his thumb. But I don't know nothing about it.

You don't know if they'll take her?

The man didn't reply. He turned to the group of seamen and spoke in another language, thick, tonguey, as heavy on the teeth as Norwegian except it was not Norwegian. Icelandic, Lars supposed.

The group nodded immediately, but with cunning smiles all the same. They knew something.

Yes, they will take her, the first one said to Lars dully.

A tall man with dirt-darkened skin and black hair knotted into a pony tail spoke. At the same time he rubbed his right hand thumb against his first two fingers. The others laughed. The dark one looked at the Norwegian. The Norwegian turned to Lars with a new smile.

Yes, the Norwegian said, as long as you pay.

The dark one spoke again.

Pay him well, the Norwegian said.

A few titters.

What does that mean? Lars said.

The Norwegian translated for the group. They all laughed again. A bony haggard looking one in the back shouted an answer. The Norwegian translated.

Everything you have.

Lars dropped his eyes. He had no money. But neither did he have a choice. He was not going to throw Olga into foreign waters, surrounded by strangers. He bent to the body of his wife, tucked the blankets more tightly around her. Then he set his feet, took hold of her waist and pulled her up, almost falling under the dead weight. The moment before he lost balance and would topple, he secured her weight over his right shoulder. He felt in control of his legs again. This church, he thought, better be as close as they say. Or I'm going to die trying to get her there. Another of the fisherman spoke: sympathetically, it seemed. But he couldn't be sure. Straining under the load, Lars didn't even notice which of the men it was. Another man added the last word. A few chuckled miserably. Lars started walking, his whole frame focused beyond this group, beyond this dingy strip of sand, to a dirt path leading through the trees. An hour later, lathered with sweat despite the cold, he dropped Olga's body beside the door of a small but tidy wooden house. Lars bent over, hands on his knees, just trying to breathe. In the moment, he wouldn't have minded joining his wife. *Maybe that was the point of finally making it here. To die in a respectable place.* After minutes of breathing he stood straight again. Beside the wooden house stood a small but adequate church: built from gray stone with a series of glass windows dotting its chest. One of the windows was stained. Lars knew enough to guess the church was Catholic and the wooden house a rectory. He knocked politely at first. But when no one came he knocked as loud as he could, as long as he could, until he could not be ignored. The priest himself, a tiny, clean man with a bald head and fierce narrow spectacles, opened the door. It took a few moments before Lars could make this priest understand that he only could speak Norwegian. The priest knew the language passably well, well enough for Lars to explain the need for a burial. The priest looked alarmed.

I cannot just do that, first thing in the morning.

Lars fell to his knees. I'll dig the hole myself. Please! Lars grabbed the priest's shoe. Please, reverend father! Holy Reverend father, holy priest of God.

Stop it, the priest said. You sound like a madman.

Try living at sea for four weeks, Lars said.

I have.

Not in a fishing boat, I bet.

True. The priest thought about it. Okay, but how are you going to pay for this?

Until that moment, Lars did not know what he would say to the question.

I can work for you, holy father! I can do almost anything.

More silence, hopeful silence, from the priest. Lars held the man's pants' leg.

Can you cook? My woman has been ill for some time.

Cook. The only thing Lars could not do.

Of course, Lars said.

Good. Go dig your hole. We'll bury your wife; then you can make me lunch.

Thus it was decided that Olga could be buried in the graveyard of St. Thorlak's church provided Lars could a) promise she'd been baptized Catholic, and b) agree to work in the rectory without pay for an indefinite period. The priest even tossed in an offer to let Lars sleep in the back bedroom. Lars proceeded to lie about Olga's baptism (she was Church of Norway of course) and then the two men shook on the deal.

It took the priest less than a day to realize Lars could not cook. But the man did not want to just summarily release Lars from his debt. He owed St. Thorlak's hard labor. The priest decided he could stomach undercooked eggs, overcooked beef, hard potatoes, and fish burnt black   In the meantime, as compensation for his patience, he gave Lars other chores to do: scrubbing floors, washing clothes, scouring pots, repairing doors, fixing the outhouse, starting hearth fires, disposing garbage, planting flowers, building fences, washing windows, sweeping the church, dusting the pews, answering the rectory door, buying meats from the butcher and bread from the baker, delivering messages to parishioners' houses, polishing the priest's shoes, digging graves, building a new horse cart, untangling fishing pole lines, sing the priest's favorite Icelandic lullabies, and many many more. Two months into his indenture, Lars wondered if being hungry and lost at sea were any more terrible, more consuming than this work. At the end of every day he found himself just as exhausted and just as poor. He considered running away but feared the priest would be located within hours, so well known in the tiny village had Lars become. The Bony Norwegian, they called him. Man servant of the priest. The priest, he came to understand, knew everyone and influenced everyone, whether they were Roman Catholic or not. It would take no great effort for the priest to have Lars jailed if he attempted to evade the stipulations of his contract. Of course, there was no written document; it was only a contract by handshake. But who would the jailer believe: The Bony Norwegian or an Icelandic-speaking man of the cloth?

As an experiment, when the priest was gone once for near a week, Lars went out with a blanket about his head for disguise. He sat at the side of the one dirt road that ran through the village and set a bowl by his knee. In his hand he held a piece of parchment upon which he'd written some of the few Icelandic words he'd learned so far: HELP ME PLEASE. He wondered if by begging he might soon earn enough to satisfy the priest that his debt was completed. But all Lars earned for two hours' trouble was getting thrashed by the baker. His disguise knocked off by a strong right to his nose, Lars now familiar mug was exposed to gawking passersby. The half-dozen spectators started giggling. "Priest's boy, priest's boy," a young voice taunted in Icelandic. "Doesn't he feed you enough, Bony Boy?" Mortified, Lars ran back to the rectory and hid the rest of the day in his bedroom like a cat just out of a bath.

On the morning of the day when nearly three months had passed in servitude, he approached the priest at the breakfast table. The man was fingering bread just cut and buttered by Lars, drinking coffee just brewed by Lars, and eating eggs just cooked by Lars.

Holy Father, has it been long enough?

The priest looked up from his breviary. His thin eyebrows bent downward toward his nose. He opened his mouth a crack, a signal of new thinking.

Long enough for what? the priest said.

What I owed you.

The priest went white, then red. He turned his face from Lars, then back, strictly composed.

I have not yet decided.

But it has been almost three months. Isn't that long enough for one funeral?

The priest closed his mouth.

Lars, he said, you have become a strangely excellent cook. How about—

I have to get home, Lars said.

The priest smirked.

And how do you intend to do that?

Lars stared at the man without an answer. He blushed. He didn't rightly know. He was so focused on getting out from under this priest's yoke, he hadn't quite figured what to do once he was unyoked.

We'll talk about it later, the priest said, with confidence. We will work out something. I'm not sure you really want to go.

The priest stood up. I need to say Mass, he said. He turned to go. He stopped. He turned back. Here, he said. From the back of the breviary he removed a palmful of Icelandic kroner. Lars noticed that wads more kroner remained stuck inside the book. It's not a salary, the priest said. Consider it a personal gift. He kept his hand out until Lars, after considerable hesitation, took the money. We'll work out something, the priest repeated. He squeezed the breviary then and held it tight against his chest.

Lars watched the priest cross the hallway to the front door. He watched the priest open the door, then shut it. He counted off the twenty seconds it would take for the man to get to the church, pull the heavy wooden door, slip inside. Lars covered himself with a blanket and went out the back door, whereupon he was greeted with the news, from the brat-nosed fisherman's son Fridjón Sveinsson, that a strange vessel had landed down at the beach.

He stares now at the gray land mass growing larger and less gray with each passing second. More expansive than he remembers and far more beautiful. I almost died, he thinks. He draws tight his fist around the rope and lets himself sway under the oppressive feeling of blessing. When he finally opens his eyes, he sees through waterlogged vision something else—some movement on shore. A gray drifting bodiless body, twirling upward. He sees smoke rising from behind a line of conifers that span the shore line. The ship continues on and the smoke continues, as the conifers dwindle and the signs of a harbor appear. Stavanger. Stavanger is on fire. His country is burning up. The thick smoke coughs and haws and harrumphs to the sky. I've come home, Lars thinks, to a burnt Norway. But then he hears music—he thinks it's music. Some cheery line of sound. He lowers his head, turns it, so the wind occupies less of his ear. The last few conifers blocking his view of the harbor disappear, and at the same moment he truly hears he sees and understands. It's a bonfire. A celebration. Fiddles. Harps. Bells. Women dressed in yellow dresses, men dressed in black Sunday best, minus their coats. They have kicked off their shoes and raised their hands skyward; and now they move their legs on the grass in time with the music: a frenzied, fiddle-driven dance. Two, three dozen people. Children too. They are shouting. They are clapping. They are singing words to the fiddler's tune. A moment later, Lars understands them: his native tongue. And Lars remembers this custom, this day of celebration. He'd almost forgotten it, like he'd forgotten so much about his country in his time away. But now he knows exactly what these too happy people are doing. They are hailing the passing of winter and the resurrection of warm time. Giddy and reeling, they welcome the returned sun.

[Real author again. (Don't worry, only one or two more interruptions.) As you might have guessed, the above section from Paul's novel-in-progress, *Burnt Norway*, is the concluding one. My character is done! First draft, that is. When we pick up with Paul again, we and he will be much further down our narrative road. Specifically, early May 2004. Two months (and maybe a few days) since he spoke with Lolly while searching for the mysteriously disappeared lemon meringue. (Note to self: what's the story with that pie?) He is almost ready to make the dreaded/fateful meet-the-editors trip to NY that Lolly's been nagging him about. What's he been doing for two months? He already told you: entering his draft on computer and "fixing it up." He can't bring hand-scrawled notebooks to New York and expect anyone to take him seriously. Who do you think he is, Thomas Wolfe?

Whatever you may think of Paul, dear reader, give him his due as a professional: he understands the drafting process. And it is a process. Whatever you may choose to believe as you sit book in hand by the poolside or in bed or on the couch or on the toilet, marveling over what seems like a miraculous synchronicity of form, style, and subject, there ain't no miracles in the writing biz. That form, that subject, that style gets realized through lots of early morning / late night / mid-afternoon *work*. Just go ask your favorite author. If you can find her. Most of us prefer to be mistaken for someone else. And—here's the really hard one—if you can get her to talk about how she constructed the book. Writers regard the struggles of creation like a woman does the pains of childbirth: once the thing is out, she doesn't care to remember anymore. In fact, the new mother's mind actively encourages her to forget so she will not walk around listless, despairing, and traumatized when she has other things to do: like take care of her new baby. And also so when it's baby-making time again she'll take care of business and not, for instance, attack her husband with a curling iron. Writers have other things to do too: like write the next book. You don't want to look too closely or remember too well what it took to get the last one right, because then you'd live in perennial horror of sitting in front of a computer. And then too there's the fact that even if a writer does recall details of the drafting process, he often prefers not to share these. He prefers to have readers believe the miraculous creation myth so they might bestow upon him all their well-meaning if deliciously ignorant adoration. If I sweated like a pig to get this thing done, he says to himself, the least I deserve is a little undeserved hero worship.

Anyway: Revision is just that: re-vision. (Cute, hey?) It means completely re-seeing what you've just constructed. And if that re-seeing is conducted honestly and well, the writer may very well need to make drastic changes in characterization, situation, motivation, location, and all the other "tions." Whatever it takes to make the book groove more consistently or dramatically as a whole. And as you're probably beginning to figure out, that all takes *time*. Lots o' time. (You don't think the five years Paul Mullen spent on his first novel were all spent just getting a first draft down on paper, do you?) Because the writer has to first overcome inertia—the attachment to what he's already created— then realize what needs to be done, and then do it. And not just do it, but do it *better*. And there's no guarantee, by the way, that in the redoing the writer won't make a whole new batch of "seeing" errors. And then he'll have to work on those and then there might be new seeing errors and he'll have to work on those and . . . You get the picture. It's not always as messy and bloody as that, but usually it is. And when the re-seeing is finally done, the writer might look up to discover that three years, seven years, fifteen years have passed. Maybe a whole lifetime!

And I haven't even mentioned line editing, the last bit. You know: sentence chopping, comma moving, period inserting, adjective changing. Not the re-seeing work but that kind. In case you didn't know, these days your average publishing house, with thinner profits, less staff, and less patience, does almost no editing work on any book it publishes. That work is expected to have been completed *in toto* by the author prior to the book even being submitted for consideration. Some authors contract with so-called "Book Doctors" to heal their drafts line by line, a not inexpensive burden, by the way. (A friend of mine was told by one prospective agent that while the agent was very interested in the novel and might eventually accept my friend as a client, she must first submit her book to a book doctor—one specific book doctor, that is—and pay for the service herself, hundreds of dollars, before the agent would give a final yes or no answer. Talk about a leap of faith! And in that unfortunate case, my friend's faith was abused, her pocket picked. Turns out the agent and the book doctor were in cahoots. The agent never intended to represent the book. Sleazeballs in the publishing biz: maybe that's my next book. Or, wait, maybe that's this book!)

So, like, *typically*, how many years must pass before both the re-seeing and reworking and reorganizing and line fixing are done? Errr. I'm not sure you want to know. Especially if you have an inkling that you might want to write a novel yourself someday. I don't want to be the one who gives you such a downer that you never have the experience of trying, and yet you never get rid of the desire to try, so you spend out the rest of your three score and ten bitter and accusatory, not even sure why, depressed at night, staring at the tiles in your bathroom as you sit there at two a.m., constipated in more ways than one, wishing you had made other choices. Let's just say that for Paul to enter his first draft on to the computer *and* bring it up to publishable standards in just two months is, well, impossibly torrid. So, really, it's unpardonable for me, to show Paul pulling off this combined revision / editing in a relative blink of an eye. But I'm going to, and so I must needs ask for your forbearance, to say nothing of a mighty tall "willing suspension of disbelief." But too I have an explanation, or should I say defense, for my behavior. To wit: Since the real novel being created by the present novel—i.e. the one you are reading—is not the author-character's *Burnt Norway Kon-Tiki* rip off non-rip off but the real author's comic *Burnt Norway* novel describing the wacky life and publishing struggles of said author-character, it's less important that the author-character's novel be made to jump through all the normal editing/drafting than it is for my comic novel be allowed to follow the dramatic arc that best heightens and actualizes, and finally resolves, the tensions building within it.

Said another way: I need Paul Mullen to be done, so I can move my plot forward. Said another way: the drafting process of a novel does not make for high drama. Said another way: I don't want my novel to cover ten years but more like ten months. Said still another (and final) way: since Paul Mullen's fictional fiction is not the "real" fiction of this comic *Burnt Norway* novel project, the making of his fictional fiction can be thoroughly fictionalized by me, the real author, for my own fictional reasons, whereas the making of my "real" fiction (comic *Burnt Norway* novel)—the

248

seeing and re-seeing, editing and reediting—must not be hurried along, excused away, trampled underfoot, forced asunder, given a perfunctory kiss or lazily ignored, else the fictional health of this "real" fiction will suffer. And I won't be able to publish it. Capiche?]

31

It was with no little trepidation that I opened Grethe's email. For weeks she had kept up the steady stream even though after her first few I'd stopped responding altogether. Not sure how I felt about our weekend together, about a supposedly budding Relationship, and finally just too intent on bulling through the last chapters of my novel, I stopped communicating. I took to only reading the subject headings of her messages, which by themselves told a story: Thousands of kisses. Then: Lots more kisses. Then: How are you, sweet? Then: Really want to see you. Then: Really missing you. Then: Missing you. Then: Hi, Paul. Then: Hi there. Then: Hello. Then: Knock, knock. Then: Quick question. Then: Just a quick question. Then: Hello?

(Side note: Grethe did try to call me as well but, as you already know, I'm partial to turning the ringer off when I'm working. As I hunkered down to finish drafting my novel and then enter it into my computer, I turned my partiality into non-negotiable policy. Problem was, I forgot to turn the ringer back on again when I was done working.)

The subject line of her last e-mail, dated May 4, read "Missing you?"—that question mark an unmistakable barb. I wouldn't have opened anyone else's message with a subject line like that. But Grethe was not a spiteful person. She had not been raised in a culture of payback, cheap talk, relationship envy, and North American cattiness. The barb I felt in the question mark was probably a manifestation of my own guilt, not of her personality. The question was likely just that: a question. Fairly stated and with full expectation of a reply.

Paul,

Where have you been? Are you all right? Have you been injured? I write emails but don't hear back. I call and no one answers. I want you to know that I would not have slept with you if I did not trust and appreciate you as a person, as a professional, as a man. I did not sleep with you as a gesture, or for passing entertainment. (Don't get me wrong: I did enjoy it.)

When I returned home, I realized how much I learned about you. Your house is comfy if also a mess; your son is a smart, quick boy if far more suspicious of me than he needs to be. I assume he still loves and misses his mother. He is made shy by the discomfort of his parents' separation. He has his father's reticence as well as his father's eyes. You are a caring if distracted papa. You are a worried author. You are under too much agent pressure. You care about what you write. You want it to be not just sellable but good. Yet, finally, you are a devastated realist, stung by your first failure—can a book ever really be called a failure if it makes it into print?—and now you are too willing to listen to what the market tells you, as if the market were gifted with a writing wisdom which you don't, even after all your years of practice. As if the market were more than what it is: a market. (Do you take writing lessons from your Conway Wal*Mart?) I am digressing but not really. These are the things I knew about you on returning from my weekend visit. But more and more these days I realize that all the else I do *not* know about you is considerably wider. Who are you behind the polite, deferential, and flexible exterior? Beyond writing worries and worries about your son, what occupies your heart? What moves you? What makes you despair? What do you despise? What did you hate most about your mother? What did you love most about your father? What early ambition of yours has yet to be realized and probably never will? What do you have nightmares about? Who was your closest friend when you were twelve years old? What do you finally believe about the state of the world? Honest, I am shocked to think how little I knew about you before we shared a bed.

While I treasure the memory of our first time together, my first with a man in almost two years, I now wonder if you found me too easy a conquest. Too willing a participant in physical love before the personal was fully established, before our spirits were soldered into a comfortable couple.

But finally I do not know what to think because I have heard so little from you. A few curt emailed replies over a month ago. Was the weekend a mistake? I do not know. Have you been getting the rest of my messages? I do not know. Do you think of our weekend and miss me? Are you simply assuming we will share another one, or are you hoping we will not? Do you think if you visit, Ryan should come so he can get to know me better and me him? I do not know.

So I work. I teach. It is almost the end of the semester. There is much to keep me busy: papers and exams coming in from every class, mandatory end-of-the-year university luncheons, the article I must revise because an editor wants it back. You know the life. I keep busy but unfortunately I begin to forget our time together, exactly what it looked like, and this becomes a stomach worry that I do not enjoy.

Grethe

Needless to say, that was the most eloquent pissed-off letter I'd ever received. And from a non-native speaker, no less. I immediately started writing. I started apologizing. I tried to explain how busy I was too: the novel, the novel. Trying to finish. Last charge. Writer's duties. But as I saw the words of my shit-faced message appearing on the screen, I stopped. That was no way to respond. She could smell the excrement of a half-sincere excuse as well as anyone. And besides there never is a good excuse for ignoring someone, even if the excuse is sincere. There is no way it will ever sound so to the one ignored. So what was the point of trying? It might only make things worse. I looked at my watch. On the coast it was 11:08. I might catch her in her office. I called before I had a chance to change my mind. I got her voice mail: "This is Grethe Westerleg at UO. Thank you for calling me or the Scandinavian Studies program. Leave a message after the tone." The message went by faster than I expected, leaving me with no words formed when it was my turn to talk. I stood there, dumb, with the receiver in my hand. The tone had long since toned. I only had seconds for this window of possibility closed. "This is Paul, Grethe," I said, my voice feeling more rushed than penitent when penitent was what I was going for. "I'm calling—" The fierce final beep beeped over my voice. I put the receiver down.

An hour later I tried again. It was now or never. In sixty-five minutes I had to pick up Ryan at school. Now or never; but, truthfully, I never expected her to answer.

"Hello?" she said flatly.

"Oh."

"Who is this?"

"Me," I said. "I called you."

There followed a silence so long I began to feel my toes inside my socks.

"Yes, Paul. How are you?"

"I'm good. Working like a dog on the novel."

"Good news then."

"Yes, my agent wants me to come to New York. Again. She wants me to do the rounds."

A pause.

"When will that be, Paul?"

"A week or two. Probably two."

Another pause; not one for effect—I sensed no malice this time—but to consider precisely what she wanted to say.

"So, there's a chance you could come out soon?"

"How soon?" I said.

"Soon," she said.

"You mean as in next week?"

"Sure."

Now I paused.

"I don't know. I really do need to get the book ready for this New York trip. But after that—"

"I understand."

"Seriously, though, after that. . . " I didn't finish the thought.

"I understand," she said.

"Thanks."

"Have you been getting my emails?"

"Sort of."

"What does that mean?"

"Well, I just read your last one. I started to write back, but then I thought I should call."

"Yes, you should. What about the other messages?"

"Which of the others?" My voice sounded as lame as the words themselves.

She hesitated; then she said solemnly "There were many others."

"Grethe, I'm sorry for being out of touch. I've shut down my whole life to get this book done. I know you can't understand that. But it's enough for me to just drop off and pick up Ryan everyday."

This might have been a half-truth, but it was a truth of sorts.

"Oh, no," she hurried to correct, "I do understand. Do you have to do that often?"

"Pick up Ryan?"

"No. Shut down."

"Not usually. Normally I wouldn't even be allowed to. Teaching and all. But, you know, I'm on sabbatical, and that won't last forever, and now I've got my agent breathing down my neck, saying she's got New York publishers interested . . . "

I stopped, listened, hoped.

"You're right," she said, at least, a palpable measure of relaxation in her voice. "You're right." Up to this point, she had been polite but strained. The strain disappeared.

"My first novel took me five years start to finish. Then another whole year to get an agent. By the time Lolly came along, I'd almost forgotten what my book was about. This one, I'm fairly zipping through. I want to zip through. Have to, really."

"Is that good?"

"Zipping through?"

"Having to. Don't you resent the pressure?"

"Not really. It's a nice pressure."

I felt her pause at that.

"What I mean," I said, "is that with my first book, while I was writing it I couldn't have any idea what would happen to it when I was done writing it. Maybe that's why I dawdled. I couldn't believe anyone would actually want to read the darn thing. This time, though, I know someone wants to read it. If only my agent. That gives me more energy."

"Oh," she said.

"Even while at the same time a kind of distraction."

"What distraction?"

"I mean from the doing. Changes in course. The ground shifting under the novel because of New York expectations. What we talked about when you were here."

She hesitated. Then: "Yes." Then: "Paul, I want to say that I am sorry if I sounded accusatory in my emails. I just had no idea what was happening with you. I could not tell if you were even still alive."

"I know, I—"

"And I am glad you called today." She said this as if that particular reaction to my calling might have been in question; which if you think about it makes perfect sense, but surprised me at the time. Even stung.

"I have to go now to pick up Ryan," I said. (I didn't.)

"Now?"

"Well, yes. See, I didn't actually know if you'd be in. I figured if you weren't I'd leave a message, then get him."

"I'd rather you call when you can talk."

"Yes, I know. I'm sorry. I'll email you a reply tonight or tomorrow."

"I'd rather you call. Call me at home."

"Okay, sure. I will. See you."

"I hope so."

I waited not quite so close to the last minute this time to contact Joy about watching Ryan. Thankfully, she'd backed off her insinuations about making a legal play for him. No threat in that direction for months. As I expected, in the cool light of day she must have decided that her freedom was more important than sticking another hurt on me. Good thing too, because otherwise I couldn't and wouldn't have asked her for this favor. As it was, I contacted her twice—first by e-mail to say that I would be calling; then by phone call. I wanted to avoid the humiliating exchange I tripped into last time. My email was simple: "I would appreciate if you could take Ryan from Tuesday the 18th to Thursday the 20th. It's another New York trip, about my book. Sorry for the late notice. If you can't do it—if you have other commitments—I understand I will call tonight."

The phone call turned out to be, by Joy standards, short and sweet. She guessed she could do it. No, she wasn't planning on being out of town. In fact, Glenn was off to Birmingham to check on his ailing father.

"So you're actually finishing the book?" Joy asked.

"It looks that way."

"How many years was it this time?"

"Less than one."

No answer I've rendered ever felt more delicious coming out. I prepared to hear stunned and humbled silence. I prepared to hear in that very silence a specific recalculation of everything she thought she knew about me. I prepared to hear a squeak, just a squeak, mind you, of awe. But I forgot how quick Joy could be.

"That's too fast," she said. "Can it possibly be any good?"

If I'd had more of my wits about me I would have told her that Hawthorne wrote *The Scarlet Letter* in six months. (Which is true, believe it or not.) I would have said: I labored ten times as long on my first book. Are you saying that book is ten times as good as *The Scarlet Letter*? Instead I squeezed the receiver and told myself to just be glad she agreed to take Ryan.

"I guess I'll find out when I go to New York."

"Just don't show them hack work, Paul. That won't get you a contract."

I should have said: Tell me something I don't know. Instead, I laughed. Then: "I have to go, Joy. I have a little more to touch up before I'm done."

"Just a little?"

"Just a little."

"Make it a good little then."

"I always do," I said and hung up. So, I still had some wits after all.

[Real author again. Last intrusion, I swear. But I am simply compelled to make the same chagrined admission that Paul did not too long ago in these pages. Recall that having not strategized the nature and sequence of scenes in his burgeoning Lars-Olga lost-at-sea / *Kon-Tiki* rip off non-rip off drama, Paul did not really know where to go with his drama. Similarly, I do not know what will come of my author-character's upcoming trip to New York. I have some ideas, yes; but I have set none of them in stone, so to speak. I haven't really thought it through. I haven't strategized, organized, calculated in any remotely systematic way. I haven't plotted yet, in the literal sense of the word. So, what will it be? Will his plane crash? (A quick end!) Will he get a million dollar deal from the first publisher who sees his sad, heart rending adventure tale? (The Poor Professor? He'd do flips over 1/20th of that.) Does his wife call him on his cell to announce that she's had it with her department chair boyfriend and now she wants a reconciliation? (A thoroughly unbelievable, if workably Lifetime Movie Event, choice.) Or does the woman use the only strings she has in the publishing world—her one book-length treatise carried the less than sexy title *The Restructuring of the Farm Family in Arkansas, 1950-1990*—to stop a deal in progress? (She doesn't seem quite that venomous—or that powerful. Her book wasn't published in New York anyway, I've decided, but by the U. of A. Press.) Will Grethe call to say that she is standing on the ledge outside her office window in the Humanities building on the campus of the University of Oregon ready to jump if Mullen doesn't return from New York with a commitment to commit? (She doesn't seem that desperate or that manipulative. Nor is it likely that she could get out on that ledge since her window, in the (I've just decided) newish building at UO, doesn't even open. And, in any case, there isn't a ledge to be found. Have you ever seen ledges on college buildings? And even if there were a ledge, and she could somehow get to it, she's probably only on the second floor—third at most—given that college buildings are not sky scrapers. Okay, I'll make it official: she's on the third floor. She'd only sprain an ankle. Not much of a threat.)

I don't know yet, dagnabit. But I do know that what happens in New York needs to be the climax of the book, the grand finale after which my character's life will be altered one way or another, will be set on some fundamentally new—and by that I do not necessarily mean better—course. As I tell my creative writing classes, resolution does not mean a happy ending. I offer them the example of Greek tragedy and, at a production's end, the catharsis it brings: the satisfying and even necessary release of all the steadily worsening tension, anxiety, misgiving, and despair the audience feels as it watches the hero become more and more a figure of ruin (e.g. Oedipus learns that he has killed his father and married his mother; Antigone is sentenced to be sealed in a cave while Haemon predicts that his beloved's death will lead to another). "The catharsis occurs," I say, my voice rising with bullshit teacherly importance, "not because the ending is happy, but because it is tragic. Things have become so entangled that only devastation, some fatal and pathetic annihilation can cleanse the world of the play, restore it to some new and palpable, even if emotionally shell-shocked, order." That's certainly a resolution, I conclude, but *no one would dare call it happy.*

So it is with our own stories. In order for a story to have resolution, the audience need not feel that all the loose strings in a story have been neatly and cheerily tied; the audience need not believe that "everything will be okay from now on" for the hero. If there's even a remotely realistic quality to the story, chances are everything won't be okay and shouldn't be okay. In fact, the ending may suggest that nothing whatsoever will be okay, that the hero has just made the worst mistake of his life. That's a resolution! Not a happy one, no, but it certainly resolves the rising action of a narrative. Besides, since no one believes in fairy tale endings anymore, an all-loose-strings-tied ending *can't* be a resolution because no audience will accept it. It will plainly appear to be exactly what it is: a delusion not an ending, a copout instead of a solution. The audience will spit and trample on it. Those are not good feelings, not catharsis.

"All that really is required," I say to the group of bored, huddled apprentices, "is for the audience to feel that an emotional cycle has been completed." This is not to say that the protagonist, a much more apt word than hero, will have no other emotional cycles to complete; this is not to say those other, future cycles won't be tragic. But we just won't be there to see them. More to the point, *we don't need to see them.* The story has given us enough that we know in our bowels how this protagonist's life will wend: that divorce is on the way, that child will run away at sixteen, that administration will ooze scandal, that gardener is going to kill somebody. A great analogy I've come across compares the ending of a story to sitting in a theater and watching the curtain come down while the actors are still performing. We know they are back there. We hear them speaking and moving, fighting and crying. We just can't see them do it. But the key point to remember here—and this is what I emphasize in class— is that *we don't need to see them anymore.* Because we've already seen enough. Not everything, just enough.

Of course, not all stories are tragedies. In fact, arguably, most are not. Every story must have complication, but not every story contains tragic complication. So the future we intuit from a story might not necessarily be as heavy as divorce, running away, scandal, or murder. We may intuit that eventually this poor dumb protagonist will graduate from high school, or he will successfully kick an addiction, or he will simply forget finding his wife in bed with a stranger. He hasn't yet accomplished those things—remember, not all the strings have been tied— AND THEY MUST NOT ALL BE TIED—but perhaps conditions are now such that those accomplishments are at least possible. And, yes, I'll admit to you gentle reader, if not to my bored UCA classes, that some stories do deserve, and successfully earn, a positive—even sunny—conclusion to the emotional cycle. In some literary categories that conclusion might even be required. Comedies, for instance, have traditionally always ended in marriage. Nowadays, I don't think audiences insist that the rule be followed strictly. Nowadays, there might be a marriage in spirit more than letter, but that's a marriage all the same.

All that said, I'm back to where I began this windy digression, with my essential problem not yet resolved, not even started to be resolved because I've been avoiding doing that work. (Why do you think I digressed so long?) All I know, which I already knew two pages ago (go check!), is that my book must essentially, if not technically, end with the New York trip. Or to use the appropriately quasi-scientific, high falutin', narratological literary language: New York must represent the climax of the novel's narrative arc, even if the falling action and denouement occur in some other location. The story of my story has got to be finished in New York if only so I can stop adding more illegible left-handed chicken scratch to this spiral bound, black covered, 200 sheet, Wal*Mart special of a notebook and start transferring the son-of-a-bitch to my computer. I have my own New York agents I'd like to send my novel to someday, you know?]

32

"Cool," Lolly said. "Oh, Paul, that's perfect. It feels perfect to me. I would never have expected it, but sitting here reading it, it feels perfect."

When I Fed Ex-ed Lolly the manuscript, I didn't include the ending because I was still tinkering with it. I told her I'd have to provide that in New York. Which I did, along with various other "improvements" hurriedly inserted in the last two days before flying out. I had to print the entire thing off again—at the cost of another printer cartridge—but at least I could feel reasonably certain about this version. The last thing I did before I left for the airport was to email her and tell her to discard the other manuscript as soon as she read it. The "real one" was coming on the plane with me. Now we were sitting in Stage Deli again. For convenience sake more than anything. We both knew where it was. No directions or descriptions to provide. But, ever the plotting novelist, I liked the idea of a staged return: revisiting the scene of our earlier lunch—when my book was still very much in embryonic form—but now with the fully realized item. The same place but a different, heightened atmosphere. It felt narratologically correct, resourcefully strategic, healthily conducive to closure, if also slightly forced as a plot element. Too forced? As always, that's in the eye of the reader.

Lolly took off her reading glasses and laid them decisively on the table, next to her iced tea. No way she would put them on again. She claimed not to like how she looked in them, although I always thought she looked great.

"So," she said, "they really do this celebration thing?"

"I have no idea."

She frowned.

"Actually, the real answer, I'm sure, is no. I made it up. I needed a way to end the book and for my title's sake I needed something in Norway to be burning. So that's what I came up with. There's no basis for that scene in research. I'm actually kind of worried about it."

Actually, I was. For months I'd been waiting for some burn scene to come up, so I could keep my title, but it just didn't. I decided I couldn't wait any longer. I forced the issue, inventing a folk ritual out of whole cloth.

Lolly offered a careless wave.

"Don't worry," she said. "Who's going to know, and who the hell is going to care?"

"A Norwegian."

"How many Norwegians are going to read this book, Paulie? The publishers aren't exactly going to be selling it hard to Oslo, population 24,000."

"Actually, it's 500,000."

"Whatever. They're selling it to New York. They're selling it to San Francisco and to Washington and to Boston and to Denver and to Minneapolis and to LA and to Seattle and to Austin and to Santa Fe. They're selling it here: the USA. Americans don't know Norway from Wichita."

"I know one who does."

"Oh." Her face stopped. "She didn't want to come along?"

"She's in Oregon."

Lolly stared at me, her eyes alive with thinking.

"Has she always been in Oregon?"

"For the last eight years."

"Did you tell me she was in Oregon?"

"Yes."

"I don't remember that."

"Someday we'll have to talk about your memory, Lolly."

"My memory?"

"Your lack of one."

She smiled, almost proudly, but mostly I saw sweetness. "Years on acid will do that, you know."

"So I hear. But you're not exactly a child of the sixties. Neither of us."

"The sixties never died at Oswego. In fact, the sixties are still going on. Walk into any dorm room and I bet you see a black light, a Hendrix poster, a bong on the desk, and a crate full of paperbacks about life on the road."

I chuckled.

"That's really good, swift characterization, Lolly. Very specific. Maybe you should give this writing thing a try."

She frowned. She picked up her napkin, wiped her mouth, then inside her palm she crushed the napkin into ruined paper pulp.

"No, I'm not a writer. I just like to be around them. Which is why I'm an agent. It's like being Gertrude Stein without being Gertrude Stein. I get to hang out with all these amazing people—like you. Even though I'm not one of them."

That's what I loved about Lolly. Most agents saw writers, especially aspiring ones, as so much roadkill.

"I'm tinkling," she said. "You want anything?"

"Thanks," I said. "I'm good."

[Real author again. I had no intention of interrupting but I have to tell you something, about that made up folk ritual. Just recently, three years after composing that fictional final scene of Paul's fictional fiction, I heard someone on the radio (NPR) reference a longstanding ritual among Minnesota Norwegians called May Day, a spring rite, inherited from the Old World which involves, among other things, *dressing up and dancing in a group around a fire.* I am not kidding you. When I heard that, you could have, as they say, knocked me over with a feather. Because I (not Paul, you realize) really did "invent that out of whole cloth." Somebody call Dr. Jung.]

While Lolly was gone, I watched a woman at the next table drink her Coke. She took the thinnest, tiniest sips through a long straw: quickly, repeatedly, leaving herself no space to do anything but continue, like a suffocating person gasping for every little bite of air. She couldn't eat her sandwich. She couldn't stare out the window. She couldn't read a magazine. All she could do was the lightning, repeated, pathetic sips: a flurry of weird athleticism. I actually saw the woman's lungs go up and down as she sipped. It was too disturbing to watch her, so I looked away. I thought of Grethe, out in Oregon. I hadn't spoken to her since that last phone conversation. She didn't know I finished the book. She didn't know what I'd come up with. But I was pretty sure she'd hate it. I brought the novel back to her home country only to falsify it in the end. If the book ever got published, could I just not tell her?

"Hey," Lolly said at my elbow. I jumped.

"The great writer," she said. "Lost in thought."

I shook my head. "Or something like that."

She was holding a new plate with a fat bagel, cut to make a sandwich. In between the two halves was a mound of cream cheese flecked with pink salmon bits.

"Where—"

She chuckled. "I summoned it, Paulie. Out of the air. Like you." She downsized to a pitying smile. "Actually I saw the waitress in the toilie. I asked her if she could rustle one up." She set her plate on the table, then sat. "That roast beef didn't fill me. I don't know why." Her roast beef could have filled a mammoth. I was still in recovery myself from a pastrami and swiss. She caught me doubtfully eyeing her plate. "I know; that's like a cruise ship worth of calories. But I'll never be a size 4 again, no matter what I do."

"You look fine, Lolly. Don't worry."

Gratitude expanded the orbits of her eyes. "My, don't stop the flattery."

I shrugged. "It's true."

Her expression changed: a new thought.

"You said your son is with mom?"

"His mom."

"His mom as in your ex-wife?"

"Yes," I said, "my ex-wife."

She bit into the bagel. She chewed. She swallowed.

"I thought you were afraid she wanted to steal him."

"She's backed off. Fortunately. For all three of us."

She nodded vaguely.

"How is the slave driver?"

"Oh, you know. Same old Joy. She's practically engaged to her department chair."

"Ooh la la. University scandal."

"Hardly. They're consenting adults. Nobody really gives a damn, I don't think. But I'm not on campus these days."

"You know, in some places you can get canned for dating a fellow employee."

She took another bite: smaller.

"Well, the university is not one of those places. Academic freedom and all."

"Penis freedom, you mean."

I nodded slowly then looked at the women at the next table. She'd stopped with the straw but was now eating her grilled cheese in little rabbit bites.

"Hey," Lolly said, bringing me back. "I'm not seeing any jealousy here, am I? I'm not seeing loneliness?"

"No." It was the truth. But also not. Even after everything, I admired Joy's gumption, her ability to take her life into her own hands.

"Good. Any bitch that dumped you deserves no jealousy. You know that."

"I know."

"This is not high school anymore."

"I know. I was just wondering about Ryan, how he's doing." This too was sort of true. And not.

"Well, I'm afraid she's got you by the nuts there. She is his mom. Even I can't deny that."

"I know."

She touched my hand for a second then pulled hers away. She took her penultimate bite of bagel. "If he's with his mom, he's okay. Just let it be."

"I know." My voice hardly sounded positive.

"Or so says some guy named McCartney."

"What?"

"A joke, Mopey Face. 'Let it Be'?"

"Oh."

"Where are you staying, by the way? Not Long Island City?"

"I didn't check in yet. But, yeah, later."

Lolly shook her head.

"You're staying with me, as we agreed. Remember?"

"We did?"

"Okay, who's got the bad memory now? Yes, we did. Months ago. The next time you come to the city you would stay in my apartment, not some B-grade motel."

"It's not that bad, really."

"An apartment is always better than a hotel. A hotel can never be home."

I couldn't argue with that. "All right. Thanks. That'll help save me some cash too."

She finished the sandwich, took a last swig of iced tea. "With any luck, you'll have plenty of that soon. Once we conquer the world with this tome of yours."

"Always the optimist," I said.

"You gotta be in this business, Paulie. Or the motherfuckers will eat you alive."

Lolly had set up a meeting with Luther Oswald—his office was only a few blocks away—for right after lunch. She wasn't promising anything, she said that twice, but she was hopeful. After Oswald, we might get some face time with that Oscar Espinoza at Vintage. She had a call in.

"Anyone else?" I said. I had just phoned Days Inn to cancel.

"Not yet," she said, "but there will be. I can feel it. Trust me."

Sad to say, I couldn't trust anything. Not after the sorry collapse of my first novel; not after that publishing party and my conversation with Morton. I just didn't want to be walking unwittingly into a trap.

"Traps," Lolly said, "are for beavers."

Oswald's office occupied a whole suite on the twelfth floor of a high rise on Fifth Avenue. Safe to say, he intended the office to project power, and a rather non-corporate, or supra-corporate, taste. The floor in the office was hardwood, or some new-fashioned perfect wood replica, covered with a few enormous Persian rugs. A sequence of oil paintings—good, provocative paintings, many of them abstracts—lined the walls. Sculptures, one from dark gray stone, two in wood, and two in metal, all abstract, were set in strategic distances from each other, and from a few potted trees, across the floor. The leather seats on which Lolly and I sat were so comfortable they felt like an insult against my old life. Old? My current life, I reminded myself. My current, decent life waiting for me back in Arkansas once I was finished with this ritual of rejection.

On the table before us in the waiting area was another and very different sculpture, crafted from black tin: a devil, who with his left hand was stuffing books down his throat and with his right prodding a fire with an poker. The only part of the sculpture not black were the eyes: the pupils dead white, made perhaps from soapstone or lime and glued in place. At the same time, this devil's open mouth revealed lines of sharp, needle thin teeth. Even as he swallowed, his mouth stayed set in a clear, sarcastic smile. The sculpture was only about foot high, but it kept my attention unlike anything else in that room. I supposed this was some sick warning to authors.

When we entered the office Lolly didn't so much as glance at the devil, or anything else. She made a straight line to the secretary. When she stopped, she leaned into the desk, pressing her thighs against a stack of mail and her head, neck, and shoulders into the woman's professional space.

"We've got an appointment with Luther," Lolly said.

The secretary's face crinkled with disgust. She looked about Lolly's age, but with a decidedly un-Lolly chunky Irish-white face, fat eyelids, permed brown-red hair, and conservative corporate blue blazer. On her lapel was an American flag pin. She rolled her chair back: the exact number of inches Lolly had leaned forward.

"What's your name," she said, in a tone as even as it was cutting.

"Lolly Furman. I'm here with my client, the author Paul Mullen." The secretary smiled: a tight, hard, thin line. "Luther has taken a great interest in Mr. Mullen's book."

The secretary didn't react at first. She stared at Lolly stonily, as if waiting for a response from her personal bullshit monitor before proceeding.

"Wait here," the woman said. She got out of her chair, crossed in front of the desk and took three steps toward Oswald's door. Lolly, who relented perhaps half a foot to let the woman by, started to follow her. The secretary stopped.

"Wait—here," she repeated. She jabbed the air with an index finger.

"Oh," Lolly said, lightly. "Sure."

The secretary entered Oswald's domain and closed the door behind her. We heard nothing. For too long, it seemed to me. I began bouncing my right leg.

"Relax, baby," she said. "We're almost in."

The secretary came out, an uncompromising look on her face. I readied for bad news. She looked at me, not Lolly.

"Give him one minute," she said and waved lamely at the door behind her. Then she returned to her post at her desk and sorting through the mail, refused to look at us.

"I guess that's a yes," Lolly said, getting up. She stopped at the desk. "Thank you," she called in a girl-sunny voice. She offered a bad curtsy, like an American tennis player before the royal box at Wimbledon. The secretary's pale brown eyes flipped up like clip-on sunglasses; she struggled against a sneer.

"Lolly," Oswald said, glancing at us but not getting up. His desk was bigger than my car and a lot less cluttered. In fact, only three items sat atop its cherry wood surface: a pencil cup, a coffee mug, and a manuscript box. He held half the manuscript in his thick hands, gripping the pages as if wrestling with them. Glasses sat atop his balding forehead; his trim black and gray beard evidenced sandwich crumbs; his suit coat was off and his tie so loose it was practically at his knees. The man was massive, that was apparent even when he was sitting: not from muscle just ordinary weight. Shoulders, neck, forearms, chest—they barely fit into his shirt, and when we caught him he was clearly starting to come out of his clothes. He seemed not the least embarrassed, nor was Lolly. So this then was no rare moment. This was how he was. He was the owner of this space; he dressed and did as he liked.

I glanced about further, trying to chart this man who was supposedly so interested in my story. On a second, more narrow desk behind him were the usual computers. Three, in fact: Mac, PC, laptop. Also a couple squat plants and a row of thick reference manuals. No more. The rest of the office evidenced personal or historical memorabilia: a poster from the Weimar Republic advertising a variety show in Berlin; a black and white photo of a tall Germanic looking man—white skin, full lips, recessed hair, heavy jowls—dressed in a tuxedo, shaking hands with a thin, equally well-dressed man (Luther's grandfather?); a collection of evidently ancient black-and-white photographs: sad-eyed, stiff-faced Hasids in their black cloaks and curling side locks standing in front of a brutal expanse of anonymous farmland; a photo of FDR aboard a steamship staring lean-faced at the ocean, some legal documents, also framed: signed and stamped papers showing the name Frederick Osvalt; a framed diploma, earned by Luther in 1978, from NYU. Prominent too was a squat dark-toned hutch that contained an assortment of hardbacks. First editions. From where I stood I could make out only a few of the names: Thomas Mann, Saul Bellow, Gunter Grass, Audre Lorde, Michael Chabon.

"What's up, mi mujer bonita?" He kept reading the manuscript, never once raising his eyes.

"Sorry to bother, Luther. You sure it's all right?"

He set the manuscript down. "It's more than all right." He looked at us for the first time. "I'm actually happy for the bother. This thing is a mess. I don't know why my editor gave it to me." He grabbed a red pen out of the cup. Across the title page of the manuscript he wrote in enormous capital letters. LEARN TO WRITE FIRST. He stabbed the pen back into the cup.

"What's up?"

"This is Paul Mullen, Luther. He's visiting the city, so I thought you should meet him. Since you're so interested in his book, you know."

Oswald brought his glasses down and looked me over for five unblinking seconds. Here it was. The party all over again.

In my mind I started returning to the airport; I started considering other careers.

"I'm not making any books about Finland," he said. "Finland helped Hitler invade Russia."

"I know," I said. "They were terrible sympathizers."

"They actually sent forces *into battle* while at the same time claiming to be 'neutral.'" He made the quotation marks with his hands. "Not only were they hypocritical; they were completely spineless. If you're going to fight beside the Nazis, declare yourself a Nazi and get on with it. Don't fucking fuck around trying to manipulate people."

I nodded vigorously. "Of course."

"So if you agree with me so much why are you writing about Finns?"

"I'm not."

"That's what she told me."

"No," Lolly said, "I told you he was writing about Danes."

"Because I was," I said, "briefly."

Oswald narrowed his eyes.

"I don't like the Danes either."

"Nor do I. So instead I wrote about Norwegians."

Oswald's eyes un-narrowed. His face relaxed. He leaned back in his tall leather seat. He looked at Lolly. "Talk to me," he said.

"Paul has written the next huge adventure novel. This one has got movie rights written on every page. It's called *Burnt Norway*. It's a sea tale, a tale of love and loss, exhaustion and renewal. A husband and wife flounder for weeks on the dark ocean in the freezing middle of a northern winter. They are lost and desperately hungry. They move between starvation and sustenance, between illness and health. They fight off enemy sea creatures; they are almost rescued; they argue; they despair. Only a meager kettle fire and thin blankets to warm them, they stay alive long enough to reach Iceland. But on the night before they reach that island the woman dies. Her husband Lars must navigate their little craft into Icelandic shores while absorbing the tragedy. Then, on this strange foreign land, he must find a way to give her a proper burial and get back home. Months later, Lars returns to Norway a changed man. Never again will he venture out to sea; never again will he take his own country for granted. He knows what he is: a man of the land—his own land—and he will live with the land or die upon it."

Oswald looked at me. "Don't fire her. She's good."

"I know."

Lolly kept pressing.

"This will be the must read adventure story of the 00s. Do you remember *Airport*? Do you remember *Towering Inferno*? Do you remember *Moby Dick*? All of them were must-reads. This will be even bigger. It's so gripping you won't let yourself piss until you've finished a chapter. You'll pee in your pants rather than miss that next scene."

Oswald frowned. "*Moby Dick* had no sales when it came out, Lolly. It was considered an embarrassment."

"Like I said, Paul's book will be bigger. This will be *Kon-Tiki* for our age."

"*Kon-Tiki*'s been done."

I was ready for that one.

"What Lolly means by *Kon-Tiki* is the fact of adventure, daring, near disaster. In many ways my book is not like *Kon-Tiki* at all. The *Kon-Tiki* mission was a planned expedition. In my novel, the protagonists find themselves unwittingly at sea—"

"'Unwittingly'? Did you say 'unwittingly'? How, pray tell, does one find oneself at sea 'unwittingly'? Are these Norwegian retards?"

Lolly took back the reins.

"You know what I mean by *Kon-Tiki*. It's a thrill-a-minute book; Paul's I mean. The excitement—the uncertainty—

the danger—of keeping a small craft going across the open sea. Just like *Kon-tiki*, there is a surprise on every page. You remember *Kon-Tiki*?"

"I loved *Kon-Tiki*," he replied somberly. "I read it four times."

"I read it five. And Paul's book is better. I swear."

Oswald paused before answering, his mouth drawn, forehead newly awrinkle, rubberbanded by uncertainty. Maybe we'd just had our breakthrough.

"I loved *Kon-Tiki*," he said again. "But *Kon-tiki's* been done. I'm not in the business of making retreads. I leave that to the networks—and to Harlequin—and to whole rest of this goddamn industry. I don't do it."

For the first time ever, I saw Lolly's shoulders drop. The first time I saw her look less than totally confident, even if misguidedly confident, in a professional situation. Oswald was offering more resistance than she expected. He was not simply refusing to publish my book—Lolly was always prepared for that eventuality--but he seemed determined not to look at one word before making that decision. You could hear it beneath everything he said: *If I have to read one more lousy manuscript . . .* We could not have come at a worse time, him having just discarded another author's book as atrocious, all too ready to believe the same of mine or anyone's. It might prove possible to move him off that belief but he was going to work Lolly to death first.

"If I may," I started.

"Paul—" Lolly said.

"No, it's okay. I just want to clarify one thing for Mr. Oswald. My novel is not set in the present day, as *Kon-Tiki* was when it appeared in the 50s. My book is set in the 1790s. So it is both an historical and an adventure book. It also begins not on the sea but on a farm. A struggling, starving farm family has to abandon its land. They want to go south but don't have the strength to manage the journey. They head east instead—to the closer coast—and find a fishing boat, which they steal. It occurs to the husband, Lars, that they could easily sail southward around the coast to reach the port city of Stavanger. So they launch the boat into a river which carries them into the Norwegian Sea, but as soon as they do, bad winds and Lars's inexperience sends them out into open water. They lose the coast and eventually start drifting to the northwest. They have to deal with cold, with waves, with monsters—"

"Monsters?" Oswald's cheeks twisted around the word: vivid bodily disgust.

"Real life monsters," Lolly said. "You know. Fish."

"Orcas," I said.

"In the Norwegian Sea?"

"Yes," Lolly said, "of course." The old hutzpah had returned just in time. She sat up straight and pursed her lips, as if to release the full effect of those words into the air. It wouldn't have surprised me if she rolled her eyes.

"Why are they starving?"

"A drought," she said.

"Drought? In Norway? In winter?"

"A summer/fall drought. By the time winter comes they've got no food."

"A plight really," I said. Lolly looked at me sharply.

Oswald almost laughed. "What plight?"

All right, it was stupid, once again, to have spoken. But having gotten started I had to answer him.

"Crop disease."

"What crop disease?"

I swallowed. "Lukea Thermopylae."

I must have had leukemia in mind. On the plane out of Little Rock, I read about one of the governor's assistants, just diagnosed. And Thermopylae? Isn't that where Athens lost all those people?

Lolly was so angry she wouldn't even look at me.

"Never heard of it," Oswald said.

"And it's already been a very bad season: poor production and bad luck. Their chicken house gets raided. Their cow and goat die—"

"You can eat a cow and a goat, can't you?"

"No. The meat is infected."

"With what?"

"Leukea Thermopylae."

Oswald smiled.

"Lolly, I think your man is bullshitting me."

"It's a sea tale, Luther. What's the difference how he gets them into the water? It's the water that matters."

Oswald thought about that for a moment. He scratched his beard. "Okay, point taken." Then he looked at me. Hard. "I think you should understand something, though. This might be the contemporary fiction division, but we are still W.W. Norton & Co. We don't just publish any old crap. My mission here is to ensure that. We don't put out garbage."

"This is not garbage," I said, staring him in the eyes. "This is my whole professional life."

"Paul—" Lolly said.

Oswald might as well have rolled his eyes; the look he gave me was that dismissive.

"That might be true, pal," he said. "But that doesn't tell me anything about your book."

You could just read the thing.

"Paul is a great author, Luther. Very perceptive, very unique. Nothing he writes is remotely like garbage. I mean his first book—"

No!

"He's got a book?"

"Of course."

He looked at me. "You've got a book out?"

All I could do was nod, as in my mind's eye I saw every chance of a deal incinerate.

"What's the title?"

Lolly told him: head up, chin straight, voice strong. Meanwhile my stomach tightened, readying for the blow.

"Never heard of it," Oswald said.

"Oh, Luther," Lolly said, leaning forward. "You must read it. It is sooo good." She stretched her arm forward, almost to the point of touching his desk. "It totally floored me."

Damn, Lolly was good. She had gambled that Oswald, like 99.99 percent of the public, hadn't read my first book and, being right, just opened a whole new wedge into the discussion. I could see it in his eyes. He liked that pretty hand of hers stretching out, almost touching his desk. He believed.

"If it's so good how come I've never heard of it? Did it sell?"

Lolly didn't hesitate. "It did very well in a niche market. It reached everyone it was supposed to."

I closed my eyes at that, just waiting for Oswald's inevitable follow-up: And who, pray tell, was "everyone"? But Lolly didn't let him.

"The thing is, Luther, this is Paul's breakout book. You know? Every great author has one of those. Sometimes it's the first book, sometimes it's the fifth, sometimes it's the tenth. This is Paul's. This is his time. This is his *Kon-Tiki*. It's going to be huge! And we want Norton to be in on it. That's all I'm saying. I'm bringing it to you, first, because you and I, you know, we have a"—she paused expertly—"relationship. I want you to have the first crack."

She sat back in her chair, satisfied. Oswald didn't say anything. He looked at his desk; he looked at his wall; he looked at his window. He looked at me, momentarily; but not really at me. Rather, the space I occupied in his office. A place for his eyes to go that was not Lolly's pleading, pushing, exhorting aspect. Clearly, he didn't like me in the room anymore than I liked being there. I expected him to stand, motion toward the door, and say *May I talk freely with your agent?*

"Leave it with me," he said, in a defeated voice. "I'll read it."

Lolly brought her hands together in front of her face, like a fourteen-year-old at a Jesse McCartney concert. "Oh, Luther, you'll be so glad you did."

"Leave it and I'll read it," he repeated. He picked up the manuscript he'd been examining when we entered the room. He looked at the red-penned note curiously, as if he couldn't remember writing it. He crushed the title page into a ball, slipped it under his desk into a hidden wastebasket, and started reading again in the middle of the manuscript. "Now go," he said, not raising his head, "and let me get back to work."

33

Lolly was all smiles when we hit the sidewalk.

"I told you. I told you. *I told you.* We snagged him. He's ours now."

"I hope so."

"Oh, we snagged him, baby. No question. I knew we would. The thing you have to understand about Luther is that he just likes the game. He'll fight you and he'll fight you and he'll fight you, just because he likes the fight. It makes him feel important. He doesn't have to win every time. In fact, sometimes he likes it when you win. And I'll bet he respects you for sticking up for yourself."

"I don't know about respect."

"Trust me on that one. If he didn't, he wouldn't have agreed to take the manuscript."

I shrugged.

"Besides, it doesn't matter. Once he's reading, he's all about the manuscript. Nothing else affects his decision. Luther doesn't fuck around with books. It's the one thing he's completely selfless about."

"So, it's all up to my book now." She must have heard the fear in my voice.

"Hey," she said, "don't start doubting yourself now." She squeezed my elbow.

"I don't know. Hard for me to believe. After what happened with the first one."

She shrugged ceremoniously. "Don't worry about it." Lolly stepped closer to the street and began semaphoring at passing cabs.

"By the way," I said, stepping next to her, "I didn't know my first book had reached 'everyone it was supposed to.' What's that about?"

Lolly smiled, as if proud of a secret. A cab braked, crossed three lanes, and stopped in front of us. "Paul, that book was such a godawful clunker no one should have to read it. And no one did." She turned to me, drew near, kissed me brusquely on the cheek. She whispered: "But this one's different."

Lolly gave the driver an address. He shot from the curb as abruptly as he cut to it, his black eyes narrowing, his jaws chewing on an active grimace, like a soldier mentally gearing for war. He was a hirsute man, perhaps Hispanic, perhaps Arabic, with caramel skin and a couple rolls of sweaty flesh evident on the back of his neck. He didn't speak, not at first, but he obviously understood English. Or at least he knew the city. He pursued Lolly's address without hesitation.

"That might have done it," Lolly said. "Luther might just be the taker. But we can't know yet; and, besides, what we really want is two of them fighting over your book. Get your copies ready."

I blushed. "Copies?"

"Your extra copies. In case any of the others want to read it."

I opened my mouth but suddenly it felt like a forest had grown over my tongue.

"Baby, you didn't bring just one copy of your manuscript on this trip, did you?"

"I'm afraid so."

"We just gave the only hard copy in existence to Luther Oswald?"

I nodded slowly, unable to look her in the eye. Lolly moaned and gripped her abdomen: a picture of a woman in labor.

"I thought I told you," she said.

"I don't know. I don't remember."

"What's the point of making the rounds if we don't have any copies of your book?"

I shrugged, speechless before the picture of my own thickheadedness. I guess I envisioned this trip as just another pow-wow about the book. I didn't quite believe that Lolly had generated all the publisher interest she claimed.

"I think have the disk," I said.

She glanced at me hard, her eyes newly acquisitive, the Lolly energy back.

"You do?"

"I threw it in my bag just before I left. At least I meant to."

"Did you or didn't you?"

I thought hard. I saw myself moving around the bag as it sat on my bed. I loaded socks, I loaded underwear. I loaded toiletries. A blurry picture of me holding a disk figured somewhere in the sequence, but it was just that—holding the disk, not putting it in the bag—nor could I be sure exactly where in the sequence it fell, because I couldn't know if it was a picture out of reality or only intended reality.

"I can't remember," I said.

"Well, open the damn bag, Paulie."

I looked over at her in shock. "My bag."

"What?"

"I left it at Oswald's."

Lolly's head collapsed against the seat. Her mouth opened in a vivid, real pain, worse than before.

"Turn the cab around," I said to the driver.

He glanced back but kept driving.

"What's with her?" he said, in perfect if accented English.

"I'm about to have a cow," Lolly said.

He glanced back again, a bare second, frowning.

"You are serious, ma'am?"

"*Turn the cab around*," I said.

"Why?"

"Because I'm telling you to, and because we're paying you. And please."

He looked at Lolly a third time, needing her permission.

She stayed against her seat, arms across her stomach.

"You okay, ma'am? Please tell me you're okay."

"Lolly?" I said.

"Yes," she said softly, her eyes closed. "Do what he says."

The driver wheeled immediately into the right lane. We made a hard turn at 40th, then another right onto Fifth Avenue. A few blocks later we were back at Oswald's.

"I don't know, baby," Lolly said. "I just don't know."

"We might as well get the disk. If it's there."

She nodded, her eyes shut tight. I really thought she might vomit--or pass out.

"Wait here for me," I told the driver. He shrugged, palms skyward.

"It is all the same to me."

"No way," Lolly said.

"What?"

"Just keep your buns here, Paulie. I'm going up."

"I can get it."

"I'm not having one of my clients go fishing around the office of a major publishing figure, looking for a piece of luggage. Talk about the wrong message."

"Well, someone's got to get the thing."

"Yes," she said, sitting up, "someone does."

She got out and walked a hard, straight line to the front door. She yanked it open with a single pull and disappeared inside. You'd never know that a minute before she looked near death.

"The lady is quite disturbed," the cabbie said.

"You haven't seen anything," I said.

He eyed me and smiled.

"She's just anxious," I said. "She wants this to go right."

"What is 'this'?"

"A business deal."

"Ah," he said and nodded. We both fell into silence. A minute later, he lay his head against the headrest and breathed a sigh. I kept my eyes eagerly on the building door. Already it felt like this was taking too long. My bag must be missing. Lolly would appear empty-handed. The trip would be effectively over.

Then I saw her, blossoming against the other side of the door. She pushed it open, struggling with something blue in her other hand.

"Thank God," I said, to no one.

"Mmm?" the cabbie said drowsily.

Lolly opened the cab door; she slid in.

"Excellent work, Sarge," I said.

She turn on me a hard, bothered face. "Let me just say two things: 1) That woman is an historic bitch, and 2) There is no disk in this bag, and I have no idea what to do."

Every muscle of my inner person dropped about two inches closer to the floor. I opened my mouth but nothing came out. Lolly pushed the bag into the floor space between us. My hands and arms went for it: an automatic, thoughtless motion; the rest of me was stunned into stupidity.

"Go on and look," she said. "It can't hurt."

I opened the bag and fingered my way around pants, pajamas, a clean shirt, a dopp kit.

"Oh, and 3) Why at age 40 are you wearing Fruit of the Loom briefs?"

The cabbie chuckled.

"You might as well have brought Spongebob Squarepants boxers."

My hand felt something hard: hard and soft at the same time: plastic against cloth. The blurry picture went clear. "Hey," I said. "Guess what?"

I pulled out a single white athletic sock, its mouth engorged into a square shape, like some cartoon snake that has swallowed an object too big for its throat. "I put it there for safekeeping." From the top of the sock I extracted the square black Sony disk.

"A sock is safekeeping?"

"Why not?"

"That's the only extra copy you bring of your book and you stuff it into a sock? Have you ever heard of dust?"

"This sock is clean, Lolly."

"It's a sock!"

"Excuse me," the driver sang, "but where to now, please?"

"Good question," Lolly said. "I guess my off—oh no!"

"What?" I said.

"Jesus Fucking Fucking *Fuck*."

"What?"

"My printer is broken. I just called the guy this morning. He can't come out until tomorrow."

"We can go to Kinkos, can't we? One of those places?"

Lolly pressed her palms against her face, then pulled them away. "Of course we can, but it won't be ready for this afternoon."

"Why not?"

"Paul, this is New York. You don't go to Kinkos and say do this for me right now. The guy probably has about a hundred orders in line in front of you who all want it today. We'll be lucky to get it by Wednesday."

"It's only a few copies.'

"To you it's only a few copies. It's another thousand pages for him."

"We can use self-service."

"For a two hundred and eighty-five page manuscript? Do you have that many dimes? Anyway, self-service takes too much time."

"Do you have a printer at home?"

"Home?" Her face darkened; her forehead knotted. "I have one at work that I can write off my taxes."

"When it works."

"Don't get bitchy with me, Paul. Not after I rescued your underwear."

The cabbie chuckled.

"I'm just saying," I said.

"And do you want to pay this guy five thousand dollars to take us all the way to Brooklyn and back?"

"Excuse me," the cabbie said, "what is the problem?"

We were still stalled outside Oswald's building. The man needed instructions.

"What?" Lolly said, as if astonished by his capacity for language.

"Tell me what is the problem."

Lolly paused only a second. "My client is supposed to have hard copies of a manuscript, but he doesn't. He only has a copy on disk. And we need hard copies, like immediately, or we can't keep some very important appointments."

"That is not a problem," the cabbie said and floored it.

"Where the hell are we going?" Lolly said.

"My lover, Marius, owns a copy shop on West 47th."

Lolly jumped in her seat, her arms gripping the headrest in front of her. "*He does?*"

"You want that I should take you?"

"Please. Yes. But, like I said, we'll need these copies right away."

"How many?"

"Four."

"How many pages in each copy?"

"Two hundred eighty-five."

"That is not a problem." We took one right, then another, began hurtling up the Avenue of the Americas. "If I tell Marius, he will make you the copies right away." He snapped his fingers.

"Jesus Fucking Fuck Fuck, what luck!" Lolly said. "Thank you!"

"Is not a problem."

"We owe you, kind sir. Majorly."

The driver shrugged and went silent. He seemed to be newly intent on the road, but then he said, "Tell me what this is a document of."

"It's a novel," Lolly said, before I could answer. "My client is a novelist."

The driver smiled, even as she was speaking, his eyes alight. He looked at me in the mirror with changed appreciation.

"This is your newest book?"

"Yes, it is."

"And," Lolly said, "the future of the son-of-a-bitch being sold depends on these copies. If you really want to know."

He nodded once, still smiling.

At 47th, we took the hardest left I've ever felt. We proceeded two more blocks, then slowed. The cabbie started eyeing the curb; suddenly he yanked the wheel to the right and accelerated. Just as quickly, he braked: hard enough to rattle my skull. We were stopped, and in a parking space.

"Here we are," he said.

I looked around gingerly, like a man coming out of a coma. I blinked; I rubbed my neck. Out the window to my right I saw the sign: *Kraken's Copies*.

"Wonderful," Lolly said. "How much do we owe you, seriously?"

"Just the ride."

"Oh, come on."

"And do not worry about the copies, please." He made the firmest gesture he could while remaining impeccably polite.

"Come on," Lolly said. "Nobody runs off a thousand pages for free."

"Marius will, if I ask him."

"Well, in that case we still owe *you*."

The cabbie's eyes narrowed as they did when we first pulled away from Oswald's building. I saw thoughts tested and rejected, clicking on and off in his eyes.

"I tell you what," he said. "You just pay me for the cab ride. But I want you to leave one copy of the novel for me."

"Deal," Lolly said. She shoved open the door.

I wasn't moving. "What do you want it for?"

The driver smiled timidly, almost embarrassed. "I am kind of a book guy. A buff. If your book becomes big, then I would be very excited to own a draft copy. Very cool."

Lolly clucked with appreciation.

"I wouldn't hold your breath," I said, "on the 'becoming big' thing."

"Shush," Lolly said. Then to the cabbie: "Don't listen to him."

"So—what—" I said, fitfully, thinking this through "—if it became big, you'd sell it on eBay or something?"

The cabbie looked crushed, a pocketknife of pain deflating his happy expression. He shook his head slowly, bewildered.

"No. I would not sell it. I told you: I am a book man. I just want to have it. Don't you understand?" His voice disappeared. He looked at the street. "I thought an author would understand."

"Sorry," I said. "No offense intended. Sure, you can have the copy."

"Of course he can." Lolly looked at me sharply.

"It's just that books are what I love. And Marius too. We met at a collector's discussion, at a little store in the Village."

"How sweet," Lolly said.

The cabbie smiled, a little of himself returning. "Browser's Books. You have heard of it?"

"No," Lolly said.

"And I'm from out of town," I said.

"Where?"

"Arkansas."

"Arkansas?" His eyes went argent with new expectations. "Damn, man. A book from Arkansas. That could be very, very wonderful."

34

The cabbie's lover did indeed own the store, which not only was a copying service but offered an array of office supplies. It wasn't Office Depot, but it got the job done. We had five copies of *Burnt Norway* made, and gave one to the cabbie, per our agreement. Marius was a tall, languid white guy, he could not have been thirty-five, dressed as you might expect for the owner and manager of such a business: dark slacks, pale yellow dress shirt, conservative blue tie. His thin blonde hair was neatly clipped in the front but he sported an evident rat's tail in the back, as if he played in rock band on weekends. Maybe he did. He smiled at his friend, patiently amused at the agreement the cabbie had doctored up on the spot. While the machine ran off page after page of my manuscript, they snuck warm fond looks at each other. Honestly, if we weren't around they might have held hands. I thought: Must be early in the relationship. I chastised myself for being cynical, but it turned out I was right.

"We have only been dating for a month," the cabbie said, when we were back in the car. "I'm just holding my breath. I'm so happy I'm almost scared."

"Oh my god, that is so adorable," Lolly said. "I don't think my husband ever said that about me, not from Day One."

The cabbie shrugged, too embarrassed to respond. Instead, he started the engine and put the car in gear.

"Did you ever say that about your wife?" Lolly asked.

"You know, I can't even remember." Which was the truth, actually. I knew, as sort of an abstract mentally-located notion, that there was a time when Joy and I were young, happy, and loving with each other: patient and forgiving: excited to have the other in our lives. But in my heart those times seemed so far off—and those behaviors so unlike who we were—as to be impossible. In my heart, they seemed like a shadow reality, as amorphous as a dissipated dream. In truth, I didn't think they ever really happened.

"How about your girlfriend?" Lolly's eyes bore into me now with all the insistence of an attack.

That one I could answer without qualification. "Never," I said.

Espinoza was out, so his secretary said, even though Lolly had an appointment. Lolly told the secretary we would come back later. "He won't be back for like all day," the girl said. Lolly offered to wait all day. I moved to take a seat, but as soon my buns hit the cushion, the girl stood up and threatened me with a painted black fingernail, like an old time nun brandishing a yardstick.

"Look," she said, her dry face showing a bloom of quick anger. "You can't just sit down when I tell you he's not coming back. You can't do that."

I stood up.

"Tell *me*," Lolly said, "exactly when he is coming back."

"I don't know."

"Come on, honey, you're his secretary."

"That doesn't mean I know everything."

"Point taken, but I suspect you do know when he is coming back."

The secretary stopped, opened her mouth, closed it, stared blankly at Lolly for a second; then she slowly shook her head.

"Tell him I was here," Lolly snapped. "And tell him I'm going to call him later—at home if necessary. And tell him I told you you're a bad liar." Lolly took two steps toward the door, but stopped. She turned around. "You're a bad liar," she said.

The girl bled red into her cheeks, as her face shrimped to a scowl. She started to write something on a legal pad, then made a show of ripping out the sheet and crushing it to anonymous pulp. She tossed it over her shoulder to the floor.

At FSG the editor Lolly wanted was there, but he said he couldn't fit us in.

"Rod," Lolly said, "I made an appointment."

He looked at his secretary. "Did she?"

"It's not on my calendar," the woman said. This secretary was tall, thin, and more reserved: a woman well past fifty, with graying blonde hair, scarlet lipstick, plucked eyebrows, and a well of dignity that at any moment could be offended.

Lolly sighed. "When can you see us?"

"Not now."

"Why?"

"I'm on a call. John Grisham's agent."

"Grisham is a hack, Rod."

"Yes, but he's a hack who sells millions."

"Paul Mullen, on the other hand, is a writer."

The man's brows twisted liked wet laundry.

"Who's Paul Mullen?"

In the end, all he promised to do was take Lolly's call the next week. He wouldn't even let us leave the manuscript.

"That's what you call a pretend friend," Lolly said when we were in the elevator.

"We've seen a lot of those today."

She gave me a quick look, then concentrated on the elevator door.

"Only in publishing, baby. Amazing how many assholes choose the angelic profession."

At Little, Brown, as at FSG, the editor came out of his office to greet Lolly but said he couldn't see her. He would only take the manuscript if we expected no answer for six months.

Lolly's patience, meager at best, was about shot.

"But Ed you said this was a killer book idea. 'Killer book idea': that's a direct quote. You said you would jump at the chance to look at it."

The editor, Ed Hurley, was a small, pasty but earnest looking guy with big jowls and a bad haircut. He looked at least five years too young for the job he had. "I said that?"

"Yes."

"When."

"Ten days ago."

Lolly stuck a manuscript in his hand. He looked at the title page.

"I've never heard of this book in my life."

"It's the Swedish-Danish *Kon-Tiki* thing, remember? Starvation. Misery. Escape. Peril on the high seas. Near drowning. You said it sounded so much like money you would hold your breath until I let you read it."

He frowned, stricken and guilty. "Lolly, I swear I didn't say that."

"You said you were so excited by the premise you'd have to beat off to keep yourself calm."

Hurley blushed, so badly he didn't turn red but white. His mouth tried to form a smile but couldn't move those last millimeters. All he came up with was a strained, thin-lipped slit.

"Who else would say that, Ed?"

"I never heard of this book," he said, in a dark whisper. "Now please leave."

He held out the manuscript.

"Keep it," Lolly said. She swept out of the office before he could respond.

"Another pretend friend?" I said in the elevator.

"That one doesn't even try to pretend."

I felt as if I ought to console her, as if it were her book being rejected. As if it were her defeat. Because, in fact, it was. She was trying as hard as she could but kept coming up empty. It was the first time I'd ever seen my agent in action; seen what it is she does and how much it takes.

"Did he really ask to see my book?"

Lolly stared at the door. "Probably not. But I happen to know he beats off like crazy."

There was only time left for one more editor, a man named James Holt at Simon & Schuster. Through his secretary, Holt told us to wait. The girl looked like she was still in high school: her face so pale it might have been yellow, her eyes a faun's brown and about as unworldly, her upper body so thin and angular she was either sixteen or starving herself.

"You can take a seat," she told Lolly uncertainly.

"Finally," Lolly said.

When Lolly moved, the girl saw me for the first time. She regarded me with an almost scared pity: this man holding manuscripts under his arm, his shirt untucked, his suit coat awry, his face admitting exhaustion. Decidedly out of place.

Slowly she turned back to Lolly. "Who is he?"

Lolly rolled her eyes: a deliberate, calculated expression. "The author."

The girl winced. "Why is he here?"

A good question. As much as these visits only increased my respect for Lolly, they also showed me that in the day-to-day parrying between editors and agents, authors are not expected and not needed. We had nothing to do with any of it. The girl was either too bold or too rude or too new, but Lolly had to know her question was a good one. Maybe the only question.

Lolly didn't answer, only fumed in her seat for a second or two; then she let it go. I saw the moment of decision. I saw the annoyance visibly disappear as if she scraped it off her face and threw it down some like so much gray-black sink silt. She turned to the girl. "Because he's fun to look at," she said.

The girl chuckled hoarsely. For the first time she didn't look half-dead.

"If you want an honest answer," Lolly said. "Don't you think he's a doll?"

The girl smiled faintly.

"You don't have to answer that," I said.

"And," Lolly said, "to get him away from his slutty girlfriend in Oregon."

"You're from Oregon? My aunt's out there now."

"I'm from Arkansas," I said and watched as the confusion careened from one side of her brain to the other, jouncing off the bumpers in erratic bursts. I wondered if I should really make it fun and launch into my place of residency list: Conway, Arkansas by way of Lafayette, Louisiana by way of Accokeek, Maryland by way of Vienna, Virginia by way of Falls Church, Virginia by way of Washington, DC by way of Durham, North Carolina, by way of Charlottesville, Virginia by way of Accokeek, Maryland by way of Silver Spring, Maryland by way of Washington, DC. No, that would be mean.

"So if he's from Arkansas," the girl asked Lolly, "why is his girlfriend in Oregon?"

Lolly glanced at me hard. "You'll have to ask him," she said. Her cell phone rang. She sent me a startled/half-worried/half-hopeful/half-terrified look. She hit the answer button.

"Yes? Luther! Hi! You did? Great." Silence. More silence. Too much silence. The big social smile hung there suspended as her eyes moved back and forth, like she was reading Oswald's words instead of listening to them. "Oh," she said. Just like that. Her mouth gathered into a tight purse. She stared at the floor. After the next "Oh" I stopped listening. I leaned my head against the wall behind me. I needed to get home. I needed to rethink everything I'd ever done or thought I stood for. I needed to consider if I had the right to stand in front of an audience of college freshman and say anything but, *Don't look at me for answers, because I don't have any. I'm a failure at my craft.* Maybe I should give up the teaching racket and renew my once upon a time dream of being an acoustic musician. Couldn't be harder than trying to get a novel published in New York. Probably not any easier either. So maybe I should just get a revolver and put a bullet in my head.

At some point the call ended. I looked over and saw Lolly staring at me grimly.

"He's not taking your book."

"I know."

"Do you want to know why?"

"Not really."

Lolly stared a second longer. "Okay," she said.

"I'm sorry," the girl said.

"Thanks," I muttered.

"You know," Lolly said, "Ed Hurley really did say the masturbation thing. But I'm not sure it was about your book."

I burped a grim chuckle.

"It might have been Grisham's."

"Somebody might as well get the benefit of his masturbation."

Lolly's face stretched into a smile. "What did you just say?"

"Forget it."

The girl pretended to busy herself in paperwork.

Lolly took my hand and squeezed it. "Well, baby, we're back to ground zero. But that's what I'm here for, after all. I mean that's what we're here for." She gestured around Holt's office.

At that instant, the editor himself appeared: business suited, briefcase in hand. The picture of an executive leaving his office at the end of the day. He was a big-shouldered man with thinning red-brown hair, a sturdy face, and a gentlemanly way about him. I took him for a Yalie; a former crew or lacrosse athlete, much heavier—almost pot-bellied—in middle age, but still handsome. He stopped in his tracks when he saw us.

"Oh," he said.

"Jim!" Lolly stood, grinning as if he were a long lost friend.

"I forgot you were here," Holt said.

Lolly's grin was gone. Evaporated. Scorched.

"We're here," she said, in the voice of someone leveling a threat. "We've been waiting."

"I can't see you," Holt said. "I have to leave right now. My wife is making lamb."

"Your wife is making lamb," Lolly repeated.

"Yes. I'm sorry. Can we do this tomorrow? No, not tomorrow. Not Thursday either. Can we do this Friday? Friday is better."

Lolly looked at me. I shrugged.

"Friday sucks," she said into Holt's face. "But Friday it is." She gave me an apologetic grimace. By Friday, of course, I would be gone. I nodded. *It's all right.*

"Good," Holt said. "That's taken care of. I really do have to run."

"You'll need his manuscript," Lolly said.

"Whose?"

"His. It's the book we're here about."

Holt looked me over, saw the stack of manuscripts in my paws. A faint but real flare of alarm showed in his gray-green eyes. He moved his head: a single, curt act of recognition.

"You can leave that with my secretary," he said.

"I will," I said.

"So long," he called to no one in particular. Then he left, stranding us in his office with the starving young girl.

35

We drowned ourselves at the nearest watering hole, which turned out to be a TGI Friday's style bar and grill but with a phony Irish appellation to give it some color: Phenians. The menu sported a map of the Emerald Isle on its cover. The servers all wore green polo shirts and orange cotton pants. Tributes to the men of 1916 were scattered about, including framed, black and white photographs, the size of traditional portraits: James Connolly, Patrick Pearse, Eamon de Valera, Michael Collins. Whereas other bars might have hockey jerseys or college pennants on the walls, Phenians had outfits from the Republican Army of the early 20s, framed newspaper accounts of the Easter Rising and the War for Independence as well as a variety of soldierly paraphernalia: playing cards, cigarette packs, maps, code books, letters, magazines; even some period pistols. If I were in a better mood, I might have looked more carefully at these curiosities, but as it was I just wanted to drink. Lolly, however, kept cocking her head and squinting her eyes as if under repeated inspection the soldier costumes might metamorphose into New York Ranger uniforms.

"They're from the war against England," I said.

She looked at me, her brows so knotted a Boy Scout couldn't get them loose.

"Ireland fought a war against England?"

"I'm afraid so."

"You lie."

"I don't."

"When?"

I gave her the dates.

"How come no ever told me that?"

She took a swig of her beer: Beck's Dark. I had a Corona. I don't know why, because I can't stand Corona.

"Well, you know. From the perspective of greater world events it was probably more like a skirmish. Britain certainly had other things on its mind, with its empire falling apart and all."

"So nothing happened?"

"Depends on your perspective. Ireland became a Free State. Then it immediately plunged into a nasty civil war."

Lolly wagged her head and stared at the table, stunned dumb by astonishment.

"How come no one ever told me this? I did go to college, you know. I even went to class. Once in a while." She drank. Her disappointment bled away to a ordinary grumbling look. "I guess that's why you're the writer."

"Not today."

She sat up straight, squeezed my hand. The grumbling look changed.

"Just bear up, baby. I know it's tough. I can't believe Holt just walked out on us like that. After telling us to wait. I hoped he chokes on his goddamn lamb. Well, not really. I do have a meeting with him Friday." She sighed in a very un-Lolly like way. "If he's dead, he won't likely read your book."

I nodded indifferently. I didn't know how outraged I should be at what happened back there. I didn't know if Holt's thoughtlessness was that at all or just the normal east coast corporate model.

Lolly was staring at her bottle now. She began to pick at the label with her plum-colored fingernail.

"The scary thing is that I thought Holt was our best shot. After Luther, that is. Luther was always our best shot." She picked some more. She drank off the last of the bottle.

I nodded again. Then I shrugged. Not because I was truly indifferent but because I didn't want Lolly to feel the burden too heavily. She was doing all she could, the best she could. The best anyone could. Truth is, after that party months before, I never had high hopes for selling my book. I wanted to write it. I enjoyed writing it, despite the erratic morphing from northern country to northern country. That alone, the enjoyment, counted for a lot. Plenty of authors can't stand composing the books they create. For them the process is nothing but torture. I couldn't claim that as the case for me. Not this time.

But selling my book was turning out to be a whole other matter. Crazy if it turned out my first novel—that slow plotless bore of "important" sincerity—got published but not this one. And if not this one, would there by any others? When I first decided I wanted to write, I pictured myself as writing novels. It never occurred to me to write anything else. But maybe the nasty, secret truth was I wasn't very good at writing novels. Or at least not good enough. I could appreciate them better than I could write them. Meanwhile, I published plenty of stories in little magazines. Maybe I should stick with that: bullet flashes of self-esteem appearing every four or five months. Instead of going for the knockout blow.

"There *is* the Friday meeting," Lolly repeated flatly. "All is not lost."

"Of course not."

Actually, all was lost. When my pathologically optimistic agent begins peeling labels off beer bottles and speaking in morose vagaries, it's over.

"Your book is dynamite, baby," she said sadly. "And that's the fact. I wouldn't lie."

I looked at her with a gently raised eyebrow.

"I mean," she said, "I don't lie to you."

"I know. Thanks, Lolly."

She brought her hand forward. She touched the tips of my fingers with hers. Then her cell phone rang.

"God. What now?" She hit the green button as if trying to knock the power out of the thing.

"Yes," she spat into the air beneath the tiny mechanism. "What is it?"

Her sour look became confusion, then moments later opened.

"You're fucking kidding me. No way." She listened. More listening. "Okay. . . *Okay*. Call me then. Yes. Right. Bye!"

Lolly squeezed the phone, lifted her arms over her head, closed her eyes and shrieked to the ceiling. All movement around her stopped. But she didn't. She stood up, and began jitterbugging, more or less in place. "I think I might have to go back to church," she said. Then she made a grand movement sideways and knocked her bottle off the table.

The concussive noise of glass against linoleum halted her dance. "Whoops. Sorry."

"It's all right. Let me call the server over." I looked around for help but didn't see a single green shirt.

"Stop it!" Lolly shouted. "Would you listen to me? We just sold your book!"

36

Well, almost. But, still, I couldn't blame Lolly for dancing. The man on the phone was our cabbie from earlier in the day. After dropping us at Vintage he quit for the day to go read my book. Apparently, he couldn't help himself. Just too curious. He was so thrilled by what he read he called an editor he knew, an old friend of Marius's. The editor was a man named Reynolds McClinton at Random House. Lolly knew of him vaguely; pretty much only the name. And even then, she said, she wasn't sure she wasn't mixing him up with another McClinton who might be dead. Apparently, this Reynolds McClinton trusted the cabbie; perhaps because a) he was a cabbie, not a literary agent, or b) he was the lover of a friend, or c) he was known in their circles as a tasteful bibliophile, or d) he was, as always, charmingly enthusiastic, or, more likely, e) all of the above. In any case, he agreed to look at the manuscript, which he did—the first 100 pages or so—that very afternoon, while Lolly and I were tramping all over lower Manhattan just trying to get ourselves heard. The cabbie sat on the other side of McClinton's desk, sipping his Starbuck's slowly, refusing to leave until the man examined enough. After an hour, McClinton stopped and pronounced himself satisfied. He told the cabbie to tell us he would meet us in the morning. Contracts were possible. And that, you see, is why Lolly was dancing.

[Hey. Real author again. I know I said I was gone for good, but I just can't resist one more interruption. I see some readers out there cringing at my "ingenious" solution to Mullen's publishing dilemma. Too contrived? Too impossible? Just too damn cute? Well, before you put me on the rack, let me speak in my own defense. If you've taught beginning creative writing for a while, one thing that begins to truly get on your nerves is the beginning student's inclination toward miraculous, unexpected, and utterly unprepared finales. The Big Surprise Twist at the End. Such twists may offer a kind of candy store thrill, but candy, for grown-ups, loses its appeal, at least compared to, boiled lobster in a lemon butter sauce, roasted herb-stuffed leg of lamb, and jambalaya with shrimp and andouille. From the narratological standpoint these endings contain two specific and glaring problems: 1) the story has laid no groundwork for them, and 2) by opting for an ending that comes out of nowhere the author manifestly avoids taking on the real complications embedded in his story. He does a sidewise step—an end run really—around, preferring a flashy ending to a satisfying one; mostly because it's easier to do. You know the endings I mean. A man who in the beginning of the story comes home to find his wife murdered, his home ransacked, and his baby daughter stolen, wakes up at story's end to find that It Was All A Dream. (I call this the *Dallas* ending after the ridiculous stunt its producers pulled in the 80s just to get Patrick Duffy back on the show.) Or a man who is being chased by hoodlums watches as an angelic force appears above him, stuns the gangsters unconscious, then announces itself as the spirit of long lost uncle Bob who for the last ten years has been guarding him. (That one is not a hypothetical example, by the way. It was actually used by a former student of mine.) These are modern updates, of course, on the infamous *deus ex machina,* that trope from ancient Greek drama in which a god figure—i.e., an actor dressed as a god (*deus*)--descends out of the clouds—i.e., on a machine (*machin*a) constructed just for this purpose—and with his godly force instantly resolves whatever unsolvable dilemma has been gradually and entanglingly developed over the course of the play: saving the hero, restoring order, giving the playwright an escape. *Deus ex machina* surely seemed a thrilling, different, original, ingenious concept when used long ago before an audience of drunken Greeks. Certainly it did. *For the first time!* After that first time, even drunken Greeks must have realized what a lazy solution it was. And nowadays, more than two thousands years of storytelling later? Don't even think about it. You'll get laughed off the stage. Or, rather, off your own book. There's a reason why Stephen Schoen, in his refreshingly pragmatic (and short) book *The Truth About Fiction* lists these as among the Forbidden Endings. (*Dallas,* by the way, received nothing but rebuke for its ludicrous rendition of It Was All a Dream, and if I remember correctly, the show died shortly thereafter.)

This is what I say in my hectoring professor's voice to my beginning creative writing students, who sit silently peeved, probably thinking I should get over it; these poor physical therapy, accounting, and art majors, who are only taking the class because they thought it would be fun. Instead they've got a crazy, zealous professor man intoning upon them about their endings--which they happened to like, damn it! That angel thing was *cool*. And, besides, they don't know or care anything about the Greeks. Like, when was that?

So am I guilty then of not following my own best advice? Am I the worst possible sinner: the one who knows the evil nature of his own planned actions but proceeds anyway? Here I plead innocent. As Paul's (and my) new guru Sol Stein points out, it's not that coincidence can't happen in fiction but that it's the writer's job to "diminish the appearance of coincidence" by "planting" or "preparing the ground for something that comes later." And, excuse me, but didn't I do exactly that? First of all, my cabbie character (btw, perhaps my personal favorite) did not drop either literally or metaphorically out of the rafters of Phenians on a machine. He's a cabbie. If you're a person visiting New York on business you take cabs. So a cab driver has every reason and every right to appear in my narrative. More to the point, I composed a rather long scene some pages ago between he, Mullen, and Lolly, giving the reader ample time to get to know him, including the (crucial) facts that he is a bibliophile and that his lover owns a copy shop. By the time Phenians enters the picture, the cabbie is an established, if momentarily forgotten, character in world of the novel and, more importantly, in the New York world of the novel. He's a known quantity, not a suddenly reifying deity.

Of course, you could say that making the cabbie a bibliophile in itself pushes the coincidence button too hard, but, pardon me, that's in the eye of the beholder. Maybe to your eyes—or should I say nose—it stinks of too convenient and self-serving development, the "story conspiring with itself." But there are far more glaring coincidences both in fiction and in life. Need I tell you the (true) story of the girl who searched for years for her long lost, long adopted half-brother, a man she'd never met? She only knew that her young, unmarried, and frightened-out-of-her-wits mother bore him in a secretive "birthing center" in the early-60s in Massachusetts and immediately gave him up, as was fully expected of her. The daughter, heart sore after encountering years of dead ends, wrong names, and false clues, finally abandoned her self-styled mission. She was out of energy and out of hope. She even left the east coast. In the early 90s she moved all the way across the country, to San Francisco, where she knew no one, just because she felt it was the right time for her and the right place. There was no job she was moving for, nor any boyfriend. She just felt like going. She didn't care that it might make the search for her half-brother next to impossible. At that point, she was too brokenhearted from frustration. And from guilt, because she had promised her mother she would find this man. She promised. But she had gotten nowhere.

After she lived in San Francisco a few months she'd found a job and created a circle of new friends for herself. Nothing special there, the ordinary stuff of life. But one night she went out to dinner with two of these friends only to find that the friends brought another person along: a man she didn't know but who seemed approachable enough. Midway through the evening's table discussion, she began reciting the trials of trying to locate her half-brother. The friends' friend (who was adopted) chimed in about his own troubles trying to locate his birth mother. As the discussion progressed wouldn't you know that it became clear that this friend of her friends, this man sitting *right next to her* in a restaurant on the *other side of the country*, a restaurant that she hadn't even heard of a few months earlier, with people she didn't even know a few months earlier, was her *very own half-brother* for whom she'd been searching for years?

If that were to happen in a novel wouldn't you say, tell true, that it is an impossible coincidence? Of course you would. *That could never happen.* And you would be wrong. Obviously, it can happen because it did. (It did! I saw these people interviewed on tv!) Now, I know what you're thinking. You're thinking that I am about to say that if a coincidence like that can happen in life, I can put a not quite so big coincidence in my novel. Wrong! The girl and her long lost half-brother example hits upon a real and rather complicated problem for fiction writers: the factual versus the believable. Just because something is factual doesn't mean it will seem credible in a fiction. And if it ain't finally believable then it ain't finally believable. And that defeats a book, real world truth be damned. So as the fiction writer you've got to anticipate the reader's incredulity and grease the wheels of her "willing suspension of disbelief." The reader will accept a big incredible plot twist—even something as seemingly impossible as the half-brother in the restaurant— provided that it seems to arise organically out of the established circumstances of your narrative. And mine does. At least that's the line I'm sticking with.

I don't think my bibliophile cabbie is anywhere near as hard a coincidence to swallow as the long lost brother miracle. In fact, it's not that hard to swallow at all. Because in a town as full of bibliophiles, and everything else, as New York, it strikes me at least as plausible. And if you've ever known a cabbie or an ex-cabbie—I have—you know what independent and even kookily intelligent people they can be. There's a reason why someone chooses to drive around all day instead of being stuck in an office. One more true (and relevant) story: I remember hearing on the radio a few years back a pop music producer talking about an experiment he tried: putting together a band exclusively from those musicians who advertised their services on a specific day in a specific newspaper: the *Chicago Sun-Times*. The producer assembled just such a band, and the group even cut a record. But that's not what's important to our discussion. What sticks in my head is an anecdote the producer told about his trip to the recording studio. The cab he happened into was driven by an especially loquacious fellow. This cabbie asked the producer where he was going and why. When the producer explained, the cabbie immediately pulled the vehicle over and said "Guess what? I'm a musician too." The man reached under his seat and extracted a flute upon which he proceeded to play an Irish air. The moral which the producer drew from this episode is that there are musicians, even talented ones, hidden everywhere. But the moral I take from it is: If a cabbie can be a flutist, he can also be a gay bibliophile.

And once you establish that the cabbie is a bibliophile, once you establish his lover too is a bibliophile and, moreover, works an archetypal white collar, clean fingernail job like running a copy shop, it seems no great stretch to think that these two gents could be friends with a publishing industry editor. Especially if that editor travels in the same social circuit as they, i.e. Manhattan's gay community. (An admittedly large group, but still much smaller a number than Manhattanites in toto.) Of course, I haven't yet established that Reynolds McClinton—cool name, huh?—is part of Manhattan's gay community, and maybe I won't even get around to doing so, but it is strongly implied. So there. And I haven't explained how the cab driver knows Lolly's cell phone number, but that should be easy enough to take care of. Maybe McClinton gives it to him. Okay, let's just go with that.

And thusly, your honor (my reader), concludes my defense. Wait, no, it doesn't. One more thing. You might care to know that when I first conceived of the cabbie and that extended cab ride sequence I had no idea that the man would return as savior later in the book. In other words, I did not compose that earlier scene just to make the latter possible. The latter scene came about on its own, organically, based on the "facts" I'd established already. So there.   No *deus ex machina*.   At least in this beholder's eyes. The defense rests.

You still don't accept it? You still think it's too cheesy? Tough. I'm not changing it.   Or as my beginning creative writing students like to say: *It's my story*.]

37

"We're going to have to give that cabbie a cut," Lolly said. We were in Brooklyn, finally, in Lolly's kitchen, after so long a subway ride / sidewalk walk that my buzz from Phenian's had worn off. Even so, Lolly was making coffee.

"After all," she said, "he's the one that got it done. In fact, you should give him everything. I didn't do anything except make embarrassing scenes." She poured one cup, the next, her face closed and plain tired. "I drink mine black," she muttered. She looked over. "You want anything in yours?"

I never drink coffee without milk and sugar, but I shook my head. "Black is fine," I said.

She brought the mugs over. She sat.

"If it weren't for you," I said, "we would not have even been in that cab. If it weren't for you, I wouldn't be in New York. If it weren't for you, I would be back home with my book cold and dead in my computer, and I would be so sick of it I wouldn't want a soul to see a word. I would be a writer without a project and without direction, doing nothing but doubting himself and feeling miserable. You saved me from all that, Lolly. You've done plenty."

When we'd gotten to her apartment she was a wreck: her hair a net of dark brown tangles, her face sagging with a quarry of strains—from hope, from loss, from sudden redemption. She'd thrown off her blazer and I saw that her shirt was untucked and her skirt askew; beer spots and even flecks of salsa stained her collar. She looked, even at forty-one, like an orphan. An orphan who, like orphans must, is exceptionally good at playing the tough, but who is an orphan all the same. Now she blushed, a natural, humble color, and looked at me anew. Directly, clearly: her dark eyes released from guilt; the strain and the exhausted instantly leavened into energy. I don't know who moved first; I know we both moved. It was amazing that I ever met Lolly in the first place; more amazing—inexplicable—that she stayed on with me after the disaster of my first book. Now, as we reached for each other, as our heads bowed and our arms came round, as we stood in order to bring our hips and our shoulders and our elbows in full combination, the relationship was about to become even more inexplicable. But even so: amazing.

"Hey," someone shouted.

I jerked. The room was black; the coils of the bed I lay in were sagging, useless; the mattress too thin. My clothes were off. The odor of my own sweat came back at me from both my sheets and my skin. A car was tearing up a street outside. I was caught in a moment of pure senility, not recognizing any of the huddled dark shapes in this room accented by the spaghetti string sheen of one streetlight's light slipping around the edges of a window shade. Then Lolly spoke again.

"Hey," she said. "You're snoring."

"Oh." My temporary amnesia broke. I lay back on the bed, fully grateful. "Sorry," I said.

"So, you're a snorer."

"In my genes. My dad did it bad."

"So do you. Is that why your wife left?"

"I don't think so."

"Are you sure?"

"Yes. She had too much else to complain about."

"Well, if it were me, I'd only complain about the snoring."

"I'll try not to."

She chuckled. "As if you can stop yourself."

"I guess I can't."

"How about I just whack you whenever it gets too bad?"

Another car moved outside, faster than the other. The room seemed less dark, now that my eyes adjusted. I could make out individual items—dresser, tv, chair—nothing threatening or inexplicable anymore, just what they were.

"Hey," Lolly whispered. "Guess what?" She reached her arm about my chest and pressed closer. I felt her smooth skin against my side, then her head against my left breast, as if she were listening for my heartbeat. Her warm hair brushed the cup of my shoulder.

"What?" I whispered back.

"On the same day I sold a book and fell in love."

"You did?"

"Hmm-mm," she sounded. Her hair moved in the cup of my shoulder.

Aristotle in *Poetics* said something about coincidence. The reality of coincidence in the living world. But the necessity of it in art. Something like that. I thought it was Aristotle. Or maybe Sol Stein. I tried to remember now, because I wanted to issue the quote for Lolly. I wanted to show off; in that beautiful moment I wanted to utter something truly profound. But I couldn't remember, so I just said, "So did I."

I heard my cell, programmed as it was to play Bob Marley's "Wait In Vain." Problem was I couldn't remember where I put the damn thing. Wait. My pants. Where were my pants? The kitchen. That's where they had come off the night before. The next thing I heard was water running in the bathroom sink. I saw the apartment angled with new daylight. Morning.

The tune still played. I pushed myself off the sofa bed, my knees creaking like a 60 year old's as I moved bare-assed to my phone.

"Hello?"

"Paul."

Joy.

"What's wrong?"

"How do you know something is wrong?"

"Because you're calling me."

Pause.

"Is that you?" she said. "It doesn't sound like you."

"I don't know why it wouldn't sound like me."

"I don't know either. But it doesn't."

"What's wrong, Joy?"

Silence. Too long.

"I wasn't sure I should call you," she said.

"What?"

"In fact, I didn't want to, but then I thought I should. So I am. Ryan will tell you anyway."

"*What happened?*"

"He's okay, all right? Don't have a fit. They're watching him real close at the hospital."

"What hospital?"

I felt lips just touch my right shoulder. I felt a small soft hand pat my rear.

"You wouldn't think a *Yu-Gi-Oh* card would do that, you know."

"Do what?"

The patting stopped. Lolly appeared at my side, her face crossed in sympathetic worry. Her eyebrows made a fretting line. She raised her hands in a question as her mouth formed a word: "What?"

"I was just giving him some frozen pizza. He had three pieces. Maybe four. He seemed starving, by the way. Are you feeding him enough?"

"He's a growing boy. What happened?"

"He told me it was time for *Yu-gi-Oh* on Cartoon Network. I told him he could watch while I cleaned up, but only while I cleaned up. I wasn't releasing him wholesale to the television, like you do."

"Whatever."

"So I did that: I cleaned up while he watched. I had to clean up a lot, realize. Not just dishes and glasses and such but that big wooden pizza board. It was actually quite a lot, Paul."

Lolly made the face again. I showed back the most exasperated expression I could muster. She would understand.

"Next thing I know he was chewing on the cards."

"Chewing on them?"

"Yes. Chewing on them. Is this a habit you've let him cultivate? He's never done it before. Not with me."

"No, it's not a habit, Joy." Which was basically a lie. Ryan's been orally fixated since birth. At some point, probably when he started elementary school, I gave up yelling about his incessant gnawing. Otherwise, I'd lose my voice. "Please get on with the story."

"All right. I was just asking. I mean I don't understand why the child is chewing on *Yu-Gi-Oh* cards."

"I don't know either. Get on with the story."

"An hour later he starts saying 'My stomach really hurts. My stomach really hurts.' He couldn't lay still. And he didn't need to go to the bathroom. We tried that. But his stomach hurt even worse, so I took him to the ER. I thought it might be an appendix, actually. You know."

"Yes," I said. "That was probably the right thing to do."

"At the ER they x-rayed him and did the blood test. Turns out his appendix is fine but he's a got a huge chunk of *Yu-Gi-Oh* card in his body. The doctors say it poisoned him."

"Poisoned him?"

"The dye."

"Jesus Christ."

"They made him throw up. They gave him this terrible drink and he threw up."

"So he's at the hospital now?"

"Yes, but they're sure he's okay."

"Where are you calling from?"

"The hospital. Where do you think I would be calling from?"

"I don't know."

"What do you mean, you don't know? Where else would I be? I'm his mother."

"All right. All right."

"You don't think I care that my own son is in the hospital? You think I would leave him?"

I shivered with the phone in hand. Not because I was cold, though. It just came over me.

"Should I come back? Do you want me to come back?"

Pause.

"You can. It's up to you. It's not like I can't handle it."

"I know. When is he getting out?"

"Soon. Today."

"I'll come back."

"I certainly don't want to take you away from your important publishing business."

I glanced at Lolly. She was looking around the kitchen counter for something. She found it: a pen.

"Actually, I think we got the business pretty well underway already. Yesterday was surprisingly successful."

"Really."

Lolly reached into her bag for a sheet of paper. She started writing a note.

"I'll try to get a flight out this morning. Get to Little Rock midday maybe."

"Whatever. It's your choice. I'm not telling you to do that."

"I know."

"Oh, and some person called for you last night. On *my* phone."

"Your phone? Why?"

"I have no idea, Paul. That's what I wanted to ask you. Have you been giving out my phone number?"

"Of course not."

"Then how did she get it?"

"She?"

"A woman. Why is she calling my house?"

"When did she call?"

"Just before the whole stomach thing. She said she's in Oregon. Is this the foreigner? Your new girlfriend?"

Lolly held the note for me to see. I'LL TAKE CARE OF THE MEETING AT RANDOM HOUSE. HOPE YOUR BABY IS OKAY. I'LL CALL YOU LATER. I LOVE YOU.

I brought my hand to my lips and kissed my fingertips. Then I reached over and pressed my fingers against Lolly's red lipsticked mouth. She closed her eyes, then opened them slowly. She smiled, all of her teeth showing. She lifted her satchel, put it over her shoulder. Then she waved: a cup-like opening and shutting of her palm. "Bye," she mouthed. She went to the door and out.

"No," I said into the phone. "She's not my girlfriend."

38

In the cab to the airport, I called the hospital and asked for Ryan's room. I was hoping I could talk to him directly, without needing Joy as the bridge. But it did nothing but ring. If he was sleeping, I should let him. I moved my thumb to push the disconnect key when I heard a tiny voice.

"Ryan?"

"Hey, dad."

"Where's mom?"

"She's out."

"Where?"

"I don't know. I think maybe she said she had to go to her office."

"When was that?"

"I don't know."

"How are you feeling?"

"Better." He sounded hoarse and tired. And maybe even embarrassed.

"Sounds like you had a real ordeal yesterday."

"Yeah."

"I'm glad the ER could take care of you."

"Yeah. They did."

"Was it scary?"

At this, he paused. I could feel him weighing the consequences of his answer. It was not just information that would be established but conditions.

"No," he said.

"No? Sounds pretty scary to me."

"I'm still watching *Yu-Gi-Oh*, dad."

"What?"

"I'm still going to watch *Yu-Gi-Oh*, but I'm just not going to swallow any more cards."

I laughed. "That's a good plan, bud."

"I think so."

"What are you doing now?"

"I'm watching *Yu-Gi-Oh*. It's the one where Joey almost throws the game."

"Oh."

"On purpose."

"Oooh."

"And Yugi has to talk him into not doing it."

"He does?"

"Yeah, but it hasn't happened yet. Actually it's coming soon. Can I hang up now?"

Glad to see my boy was still my boy.

"When is mom getting back?"

"I don't know."

"She didn't say?"

"Maybe. I don't know. I was watching tv."

I nodded. I don't know why. It wasn't like he could see me. "Okay, bud. I'll see you later. I'm flying out of New York this morning. I'll be at the hospital early this afternoon to take you home."

"Yeah, mom told me."

"Good. Love you, Ryan."

No response.

"Ryan?"

"Dad, I have to hang up. It's about to happen."

Luckily, there was no problem switching my ticket from Thursday morning to Wednesday, although it did change my route a bit: New York to Cincinnati; Cincinnati to Little Rock. On the first flight, I kept wondering how the meeting at Random House was going. I hoped of course that this meant the battles to get my book seen were over, those rounds of fruitless, even humiliating courtesy calls Lolly had to endure. And I only saw one day of it. Maybe, at least for this day for this book, she would be finished. And I could cast off the gloomy doubts from yesterday. I could start another novel if I wanted and not feel as if I were just kidding myself. But I didn't trust these budding hopes. In my heart, this last second intervention by our former cab driver seemed too lucky to be true. I remembered the publishing party, Morton's disgust when he heard the title of my first book, his polite if apparent desperation to get to anyplace in the room where I was not. I froze my hope in utero and prepared to be disappointed. Hope for the best; expect the worst. A cute mental trick, if you could pull it off. I would try.

I pictured Lolly in this editor's office, he behind a gargantuan he-man's desk, she in some tiny faux-leather slave's station on the other side of the throne. Might as well be the other side of the country. He leans back in his chair, taps his fingers together in front of his face. His middle aged white forehead is creased, his blubbery lips are drooping, his jowls are almost as big his shoulders. He speaks with evident traces of the upper south he left thirty years earlier, meaty drawn out vocables that have softened during his northeast stay but not disappeared. Presently, his voice is low and chagrined, but also firm.

—I read the rest of the book last night. All of it. It's an interesting idea. I always treasure a good rescue story. Who doesn't? (Deliberate, stagy pause.) And no doubt your boy can write.

His hand motions to punctuate what he perceives as an amazingly generous comment on his part. Lolly, however, begins to sink lower in her already low chair. She frowns in her eyes, her cheeks go flat. She understands the way this line is going. She listens for the inevitable *but*. —But, he says, the bottom line is that there are a lot of books out there that cover this territory—lost at sea—and a lot more engagingly. The Norway thing is kind of a unique angle, but finally, no, the book didn't sell itself to me.

In the face of these absolute pronouncements, even the cheerily pugilistic Lolly is not able to speak in my defense.

—Sorry to get your hopes up and call you in here, he says. Sorry to spoil your morning. But the second half really let me down.

Lolly regains her tongue. She leans forward, opens her mouth, is about to give her best effort to keep from being kicked out. But Reynolds McClinton raises up both of his two huge hands, broad as stop signs, palms out.

—Sorry, he says loudly. No.

I shook my head to cast out this dangerous, hectoring vision.

What do you know about Reynolds McClinton anyway? I mean except for his name?

Nothing.

And what's the point picturing him as some slightly evolved good old boy, policing his publishing house against your efforts? How does that help matters?

Not much.

Not much at all. All you're doing is generating bad juju. Instead, you should be imagining yourself signing some fat publishing contract, Lolly at your shoulder, bestowing a proud smile.

You're right.

Damn it Paul; of course I'm right. You're right on the edge now, can't you see? You're right there.

Sure, maybe the contract wouldn't happen; maybe I would get crushed again. But maybe there was no better help I could offer Lolly than positive thoughts, and no worse drag than my habitual gloom. I plucked the in-flight magazine out of its pocket in the seat in front of me and began flipping pages, trying to cast that poisonous scene from my head. But before I could work up any positive thoughts I found myself arguing with a man I didn't know about reservations he might not even have. Norway, I said to McClinton's fat, sweaty, waxen face. Think about it. How many books do you know that depict an eighteenth century Norwegian farmer trapped on the Norwegian Sea in a hopelessly small craft in midwinter? How many books show the same farmer returning home to see his country aflame and his fellow Norwegians dancing with ritualistic glee? That's been done? That "territory has been covered"? By who exactly? Or do you just like to toss out charges for the sound of them even if they aren't true? Do you just need some sure sounding line— even if it's a lie—in order to justify not publishing fiction at all, because basically, in these ruined economic times, you've given up on that market?

McClinton wasn't exactly cowering beneath my counterattack. In fact, he was ringing his secretary to call security and get me chucked out of the building.

—You're just an author, he says. What do you know about anything? You live your whole life acting out fantasies, like some six-year-old. If you're going to write, at least write something real why don't you? That's what sells, after all.

He picks up my manuscript.

—And don't waste my time with any more of this drivel.

What was wrong with me? I couldn't even think positive on command. It's not real, I had to remind myself. It's only fear. It's not real.

My mind moved to Grethe, waiting in Oregon, expecting me to return her call. How did she get Joy's number, and why did she even call her? If it were anyone else, I'd suspect some implicit threat. If you don't contact me, I'll track you down— everywhere. I'll hound you. But this was Grethe. There was no threat, only the desire to communicate, to find again what she thought she had. I should call her, and I would call her. Just one more time. She certainly deserved that much.

The plane conducted a subtle rotation; within minutes, the country outside my window changed. We'd been traveling due south from New York, but now instead of flat sections of green interrupted frequently by urban development, I saw gray-black, scarred and even exploded earth of the mining industry; past these, I saw vaster stretches of unoccupied, unharvested woodland; I saw farms and no cities, just rural outposts of isolated human development.

I pulled down the window cover and closed my eyes. Ryan was in a hospital bed in Conway, his rail-thin frame supine in a metallic, institutional bed: stiff white sheets and a ribbed rust-red bed spread. They told him he should try to nap but he can't because he knows he will leave today. Instead of napping he's watching Cartoon Network. He is not fully appreciative of the hit he took, the severity of what it means to poison yourself; all he feels are the results: his body empty, drained, and dazed, as if coming back from a fall. But his dad is returning early. Because of what happened. That's what his mother told him first thing this morning, before she stepped out. His dad would land in Little Rock and drive straight to the hospital. Then take him home. Ryan nodded vaguely at the words coming out of her mouth. Then, he was too tired to hear. Now, he tries to watch but can't because he doesn't like what's on. It's not *Yu-Gi-Oh*. It's not any show he watches. And, actually, he is feeling pretty tired. Maybe he should nap, after all. He leans his head back, closes his eyes, and tries to relax into the pillow. Alone. Waiting for his father's plane to land.

I opened my eyes. This could keep happening. This will keep happening. It's not like I wouldn't ever go to New York again. I'd have to go to New York again. If only for business. But not just for business; not now. No matter what transpired at that meeting with Reynolds McClinton I would be heading back to New York. Soon. *And this will keep on happening.* More calls to Joy for help, more incidents, more disputes, more questions about Ryan's habits, more blame for things that happen when I am a thousand miles away and not able to stop them. Joy would say that I am gone too often for Ryan's good. She would say that I love New York more than my own son. Since I'm there so much. She would claim to friends, and perhaps even her lawyer, that I was in New York more than I am home. Which wouldn't be true, of course, but would be truer than before. Because I would be heading to New York again soon. And frequently. At least I hoped.

Then I had a sudden idea: a radical, jarring notion, but a perfect one all the same. The kind that puts a smile on your face and lets you finally relax into your seat. The kind that lets you sleep.

39

"I've got a new ending for the book," I said as soon as Lolly answered her phone. I was at my gate in Cincinnati/Northern Kentucky International. The flight to Little Rock was boarding in ten minutes.

"A new ending. Why? He loved your ending."

"He did?"

"He loved the whole book."

"Seriously."

"No shit, baby. We started talking contracts. He wants it out in summer—next summer obviously. It's too late for this one. He likes summer for the adventure stuff. "

"I don't want to wait that long."

She chuckled.

"You want the best thing for your book, Paulie. That's what matters."

"I know."

"It's the adventure thing. He kept saying 'This would be a killer summer book.'"

"He did?"

"He loved the book, Paul."

"I can't believe it. I mean, I really can't."

"I can believe it."

"I know. Thanks."

"So, you've got another novel under your belt. Just one more of many, I'm sure. If you were next to me right now I'd take your hand. And something else too."

I laughed lamely, my hand suddenly growing warm on the phone. I looked to see if anyone noticed the strained tone of my voice.

"So what's this about a new ending?" she said.

"I don't want to say more, because it's not actually done." I switched the phone to my other hand, but it was just as warm. "It's something that occurred to me on the plane down here. I'm going to flesh it out on the way to Little Rock. But I think it's going to work."

"Okay," Lolly said slowly. I heard the announcement over the gate PA. I stood up, put the long leather strap of my satchel over my shoulder.

"I'll e-mail it to you and then you can tell me what you think. How's that?"

"That's great. Or, you know, you could deliver it in person."

"I could." I moved to join the herd of other boarders. "But I think I want to get it to you as soon as possible."

Lars lingers overnight in Stavanger, looking for a ride home. In the torg the next morning he discovers a chicken breeder who, having sold his supply, faces a lighter load on his return trip. He agrees to take Lars, but only as far as Hermansverk, about half the distance home. At Hermansverk, Lars begins to walk north, only to get picked up by a family in a wagon. They are migrating to Trøndelag in search of more fertile land to farm. They've heard that Trøndelag possesses the richest soil in the country. It has to be better than Bergen, they say. Anything's better than Bergen. Lars winces a smile but says nothing. Let them find out for themselves. And maybe they'll do better, anyway. Hard to do worse. Why are you coming up?, they ask. I'm going back home, he says. Really, where did you go? Far, Lars says. Why? they ask. Lars winces again. Oh, he says, you know. They look at him blankly. The family takes him within fifteen miles of his farm. Then they leave him in order to wend to the west. Lars has no choice but to walk the remaining miles.

When he finally reaches home that evening, Lars finds the house and the farm not that much different from when he left, except no longer surrounded by snow—and so much quieter. His cupboard is still empty, except for some supplies he purchased in Stavanger with the last of his Icelandic krona. His fields lay dark and brown, unhoed, unsown, and uncultivated; no vegetable life coming forthwith. His axe is still in the house; his plow and harness are in an otherwise empty, musty barn, which to his imagination smells like dead cattle, although it has been many months since he saw his animals droop. There's nothing here to come home to, he realizes, except more of what drove him away. All the while he was at sea he just wanted to get home. When he left Iceland he knew no other purpose, allowed himself no other. Getting home became as single-minded and thoughtless a mission as leaving home had been. But now, with his mission completed, it doesn't feel like home anymore. Nothing is here— and his wife is dead. The thought hits him like Thor's hammer: *You made it back. But you're not required to stay.*

For supper he eats some of the supplies he brought: dried jerky and a roll. He sleeps in the sagging, moldy, bug covered bed he used to share with Olga. He sleeps like a dead man, not dreaming. The next morning he sets out to find if there is any community left in this part of Norway. He walks eleven miles before he finds another occupied farm. The others who left have not returned. For all he knows, they may be dead as Olga. The farmer he finds, a man whom Lars has seen before but does not know, says his name is Jens Anderste. He offers Lars lunch and a place to rest his feet. The meal is not much: bits of boiled, spot-darkened potatoes, a quarter of a loaf of bread. Anderste is embarrassed. He apologizes for the meager board. He is a red-faced, sun and wind burned sixty-year-old with evident dignity but who, nearly as defeated by the year as Lars, has clearly not recovered. Most of our cattle caught the infection, Anderste says guardedly. The others I had to kill to feed us and our man. Right now, I've got a bull and one milker. No goats. No poultry. I've managed to sow me some crops but nothing's ready to pull yet. We are eating, you and I, the last of what I stored.

Lars stops mid-forkful. He puts the fork back on the plate.

I don't want to take your last, he says.

The farmer shakes his head, painfully. Don't worry about it. It's the last whether you eat it or not. I'm going kill my bull tomorrow.

Where's your man? Lars asks.

The farmer narrows his eyes, as if trying to keep out the picture of that person. Then his eyes widen. He stares for a second over Lars's shoulder. I don't actually know, he says. He left a month and a half ago, without telling me. I guess he was just waiting for winter to be gone. As soon as the winter was gone, he disappeared.

The farmer looks away, embarrassed again.

Lars looks at the farmer's wife. She does not eat with them but sits in a rocking chair near the table sewing a torn pair of pants. Her face is thinner than her husband's, near skeletal. Her whole body seems wracked; but at the same time hard. A woman with an excellent constitution but who has been through trials. He can't tell if she is listening to this conversation, she focuses so intently on the sewing, as if her hand would slip if she didn't commit every ounce of herself to watching her own movements. Her lined face is a study of fatigue. Her gaze shows nothing; barely life at all.

I'm thinking of leaving myself, Lars says suddenly.

The farmer shrugs. Some do, he says. Some can. I can't. This is all I know.

Lars understands. But if there is any good to have come from his recent misfortunes, it's that his farm is no longer all he knows. Norway is no longer all he knows. If nothing else, he now knows that oceans can be crossed.

Next winter might be different, says the farmer in his hoarse voice, his pebbly blue eyes showing none of the hope he speaks. In fact, I'm counting on it. That is the nature of the work, isn't it? Good years. Bad years. Middling years. Last year was the worst year in the whole of my lifetime. The next has got to be better.

Lars nods vaguely, but doesn't answer. Yes, true. Conditions might be better next winter. But they could also be worse. Lars is no longer so stupid as to not realize that. And in the meantime he has nothing at all. And no one to borrow from.

I should go, Lars says, standing.

You sure? the farmers says. You're not even finished.

You finish it, Lars says. I need to start back. I've tons to do.

The man nods slowly. He can certainly understand having work, but he expected that after the long morning walk the younger man would want to rest more than an hour. Then again, the young man looks especially lean, especially determined. Captivated by an idea. All right, he says. Best of luck to you.

The farmer's wife says nothing; she stays where she is. As Lars is moving out the door he looks back to see her collapsed into sleep, needle and thread in hand. The pants have fallen to the floor.

As he walks the eleven miles back home, Lars reconsiders; Lars plans. He remembers a conversation he had three years before with the royal mail carrier. His daughter and new husband had emigrated to America. The husband knew someone in New York who promised plenty of available work and astonishingly good wages. The husband, a cocksure type, was up for the challenge. But on that fetid, filthy, overcrowded, understocked ship the husband took ill with fever and dysentery. He died one week before the ship arrived in New York. At least a quarter of the passengers did not survive the crossing. To the mail carrier's daughter it seemed that everyone around her was dying or about to. Her husband was by necessity buried at sea, along with a dozen other bodies. The mail carrier's daughter landed in New York harbor sick with grief, horrified by the crossing, completely exhausted and utterly alone. She knew no one in the city; she knew no English. Her instinct was to turn around and go right back to Norway, but she did not have sufficient kroner for the passage, and even if she did she couldn't have faced the prospect of further weeks on a coffin ship. She followed one family off the boat, onto the dock, and through the cramped streets of this strange new city. After thirty minutes of walking to what seemed the end of human habitation, the mail carrier's daughter was far from the harbor and almost out of energy. The family stopped in front of a tenement house. They looked at the house number. They looked at the building. They examined the windows. They looked at the number again.

Hallo! they called. God dag, Rolf Mikkelsen. Dette er oss.

A window opened on the top floor; a woman's head poked out. The woman shrieked. A minute later she was on the street hugging and kissing the group of tawdry travelers. A gray-eyed, small faced, thin- shouldered matron, who was either past fifty or worn out by life, she did nothing but cry and rejoice. The mail carrier's daughter stood still, jealously witnessing this reunion. But finally knew what she had to do. She ran forward to the woman, who stepped back with wide-eyed surprise. In rambling, breathless Norwegian she explained her history, her homelessness, her widowhood. Her loss. She spoke of their common love of their native land and requested that the woman honor that love. The woman seemed confused at first. But the mail carrier's daughter won her over. She offered the girl what they had: a place to sleep on the floor and a small space at a crowded dinner table. The mail carrier's daughter accepted at once. She would pay them what she could, she said. As soon as she had income.

After a month, she found a job as a governess to the children of Norwegians who had emigrated a decade earlier. They were lovely people and they helped her learn English, but they could pay her very little, not nearly enough to save for the passage home. Fourteen months later, able to speak English passably, she secured a job as a New York city school teacher, which paid better, if only slightly, than a governess.

She's been doing that a year, the mail carrier said to Lars. She has almost enough for the passage back. But now she is not sure she wants to come.

Really, Lars said.

Yes. The mail carrier spoke with a hoarse combination of sadness, wonder, and pride. Even after everything she has suffered, she says going to America might have been the right thing to do.

Really? Lars said, more energetically this time, for that attitude was truly incomprehensible to him. He imagined the poor young widow trying to beat learning into scruffy, ill-mannered, arrogant New Worlders. In his imagination, he saw her in front of a handheld chalk board, in a tiny room with no light, perspiring, tired of yelling, close to tears, strands of her once beautiful blonde hair falling erratically down out of her bun and laying limply across her cheeks.

The mail carrier spoke with new resignation. They say New York city is a wonder. A palled half-smile bit midway into his face. I guess that's true, in fact. But I suspect what this really means is that she has found a new man for a husband.

Lars chuckled.

Some Englishman, the mail carrier said. But—he raised his shoulders in a pointed shrug—there are worse outcomes in life.

I guess, Lars said, but what he thought was that he didn't see how the outcome could be any worse.

Probably so, the mail carrier said, as if hearing and answering Lars's thought. Then he mumbled something. Then, too involved with his own musings to utter a further word, the carrier rode off.

As he remembers this conversation, Lars scoffs at his earlier self's incomprehension, his earlier self's surprise. He remembers thinking, *Why would anyone leave Norway to travel halfway around the world?* To his earlier self, Oslo would have been too far to move. And as far as Sweden would have been unthinkable. Now even New York seems not so incredible. Why shouldn't that man's daughter decide she would rather live there?

Lars stops. New York, he thinks. *New York*. Could he just erase everything he has been up to then—erase even the history of his marriage—and start all over again in a new world? In that busy city he might find, like the mail carrier's daughter, a new life, a new purpose, a new occupation. And a new person to love. A person to marry. Perhaps they will even bring forth a child. His first. A boy, he hopes. A Norwegian boy, blonde and blue-eyed—but also a New Yorker. A well-fed, wisecracking, surefooted city boy, capable of existing simultaneously in two cultures: the one Lars brought with him, but also the one of the streets and shops and schools and homes of his son's native-born, English speaking friends. New York. New York?

New York, Lars thinks at last. New York will be my future, and my son's.

He will have to find that chicken farmer. He needs a ride back to Stavanger as soon as possible. Lars surprises himself. He's not afraid. Not even a little. It's not just that having survived the sea he feels he is living on charmed, God-given time. It's not just that. It's not just that now he thinks he can survive anything. What matters most is that this time he knows exactly what he is doing. And why. For perhaps the first time, he sees his life all at once and all apiece. He knows what he must and must not do. This he positively must.

And that, dear reader, was—and is—my actual ending.

Lolly loved it.